FLEET ELEMENTS

ALSO BY WALTER JON WILLIAMS

**THE SECOND BOOKS OF
THE PRAXIS**

The Accidental War

**THE FIRST BOOKS OF THE
PRAXIS: DREAD EMPIRE'S FALL**

The Praxis
The Sundering
Conventions of War
Investments
Impersonations

NOVELS

Hardwired
Knight Moves
Voice of the Whirlwind
Days of Atonement
Aristoi
Metropolitan
City on Fire
Ambassador of Progress
Angel Station
The Rift
Implied Spaces

QUILLIFER

Quillifer
Quillifer the Knight

MAIJSTRAL

The Crown Jewels
House of Shards
Rock of Ages

DAGMAR SHAW THRILLERS

This Is Not a Game
Deep State
The Fourth Wall
Diamonds from Tequila

HISTORICAL FICTION

To Glory Arise
Brig of War
The Macedonian
The Tern Schooner
Cat Island

COLLECTIONS

Facets
Frankensteins and Foreign Devils
*The Green Leopard Plague and
Other Stories*
The Best of Walter Jon Williams

FLEET ELEMENTS

WALTER JON WILLIAMS

HARPER Voyager
An Imprint of HarperCollins*Publishers*

FLEET ELEMENTS. Copyright © 2020 by Walter Jon Williams. All rights reserved. Printed in the United States of America. No part of this book may be used or reproduced in any manner whatsoever without written permission except in the case of brief quotations embodied in critical articles and reviews. For information, address HarperCollins Publishers, 195 Broadway, New York, NY 10007.

HarperCollins books may be purchased for educational, business, or sales promotional use. For information, please email the Special Markets Department at SPsales@harpercollins.com.

Harper Voyager and design are trademarks of HarperCollins Publishers LLC.

FIRST EDITION

Designed by Paula Russell Szafranski

Library of Congress Cataloging-in-Publication Data has been applied for.

ISBN 978-0-06-246704-1

20 21 22 23 24   LSC   10 9 8 7 6 5 4 3 2 1

For KATHY HEDGES

With thanks to Dr. Michael Wester for his tour of

fractal dimensions, and to Oz Drummond for

her astute critical reading of this work

DRAMATIS PERSONAE

MARTINEZ FAMILY AND DEPENDENTS

MARCUS, LORD MARTINEZ: Terran, patriarch of Clan Martinez, patron to Laredo, Chee, and Parkhurst.

LADY MARTINEZ: Terran, wife to Lord Martinez.

LORD ROLAND MARTINEZ: Terran, Lord Martinez's eldest son and heir. Convocate.

GIRASOLE MARTINEZ: Terran, Roland's daughter.

SENIOR CAPTAIN LORD GARETH MARTINEZ: Terran, second son of Lord Martinez, awarded the Golden Orb for conduct during the Naxid War.

LADY TERZA CHEN: Terran, daughter and heir of Lord Chen, wife of Gareth Martinez.

GARETH THE YOUNGER ("CHAI-CHAI"): Terran, son of Gareth Martinez and Terza Chen.

YALING ("MEI-MEI"): Terran, daughter of Gareth Martinez and Terza Chen.

LADY VIPSANIA MARTINEZ: Terran, daughter of Lord and Lady Martinez, married to Lord Convocate Oda Yoshitoshi and head of Imperial Broadcasting.

LADY WALPURGA MARTINEZ: Terran, daughter of Lord and Lady Martinez, widow of PJ Ngeni.

LADY SEMPRONIA MARTINEZ: Terran, daughter of Lord and Lady Martinez, estranged from her family. Married to Nikkul Shankaracharya.

KHALID ALIKHAN: Terran, weaponer first class (retired). Orderly to Gareth Martinez.

LIEUTENANT LALITA BANERJEE: Terran female, signals officer on *Los Angeles*.

AITOR SANTANA: Terran male, signals officer on *Los Angeles*.

LADY SULA, HER DEPENDENTS AND ASSOCIATES

SENIOR CAPTAIN CAROLINE, LADY SULA: Terran, head of Clan Sula, Fleet officer and former head of the Secret Army. Former leader of Action Team 491.

CONSTABLE FIRST CLASS GAVIN MACNAMARA: Terran, detailed as servant to Lady Sula, former member of the Secret Army and Action Team 491.

ENGINEER FIRST CLASS SHAWNA SPENCE: Terran, detailed as servant to Lady Sula, former member of the Secret Army and Action Team 491.

MING LIN: Terran, veteran of the Secret Army, graduate student in economics, and Sula's economic adviser.

THE FLEET

LORD TORK: Daimong male, Supreme Commander of the Fleet.

FLEET COMMANDER LORD PA DO-FAQ: Lai-own male, commander of the Third Fleet at Felarus, Gareth Martinez's former commander.

FLEET COMMANDER PEZZINI: Terran male, member of the Fleet Control Board.

JUNIOR FLEET COMMANDER LADY MICHI CHEN: Terran female, commanding Fourth Fleet at Harzapid. Sister of Lord Chen, aunt to Terza Chen, and Gareth Martinez's former commander.

LIEUTENANT LORD PRINCE HUANG: Terran male, cousin to Michi Chen

SANDRA YUEN: Terran female, one of Michi Chen's aides.

JUNIOR FLEET COMMANDER LORD ALTASZ: Torminel, commander of Altasz Force during the Naxid War.

SENIOR SQUADRON COMMANDER CARMODY: Terran male, Naxid war veteran, commands Heavy Squadron Eight in the Fourth Fleet.

SENIOR SQUADRON COMMANDER NGUYEN: Terran, commanding a squadron under Do-faq at Felarus.

JUNIOR CAPTAIN LORD JEREMY FOOTE: Terran, commanding light cruiser *Vigilant* and Light Squadron Eight. Veteran of the Naxid War, the First and Second Battles of Magaria, and racing pilot for the Apogee Club.

LIEUTENANT-CAPTAIN LORD NAAZ VIJANA: Terran, hero of the Yormak rebellion and commanding frigate stationed at Harzapid.

LIEUTENANT-CAPTAIN LADY ELISSA DALKEITH: Terran, commanding cruiser *Bombardment of Los Angeles*.

LIEUTENANT-CAPTAIN ARI ABACHA: Terran, a friend of Gareth Martinez, and a sporting enthusiast.

SENIOR CAPTAIN LORD HARVEY CONYNGHAM: Terran male, former prisoner of the Naxids during the Naxid Rebellion.

LIEUTENANT-CAPTAIN LADY ALANA HAZ: Terran, former premiere lieutenant on Sula's frigate *Confidence*.

LIEUTENANT LADY REBECCA GIOVE: Terran, former second lieutenant on Sula's frigate *Confidence*.

LORD PAVEL IKUHARA: Terran, former third officer on Sula's frigate *Confidence*.

LIEUTENANT LADY CHANDRA PRASAD: Terran, formerly of Martinez's command *Illustrious*.

LIEUTENANT LORD SABIR MERSENNE: Terran, formerly of Martinez's command *Illustrious*.

LORD NISHKAD: Naxid male, senior squadron commander (retired), now businessman on Harzapid.

SENIOR FLEET COMMANDER SURANG: Daimong male, former commander of the Fourth Fleet, now deposed.

CAPTAIN HUI: Terran female, captain of *Staunch*.

JUNIOR SQUADRON LEADER KHALI: Terran male, commands Heavy Squadron Twenty in the Fourth Fleet.

SENIOR SQUADRON COMMANDER WEI JIAN: Terran female, commanding defectors from the Second Fleet.

PAIVO AND RANSSU KANGAS: Terran males, twin sons of the late Fleet Commander Eino Kangas.

LIEUTENANT LORD AHMAD HUSAYN: Terran male, formerly of Martinez's command *Illustrious*.

LIEUTENANT VONDERHEYDTE: Terran male, formerly of Martinez's command *Corona*.

LIEUTENANT GARCIA: Terran female, former prisoner of the Naxids.

SQUADRON COMMANDER RUKMIN: Torminel female, commanding two heavy cruiser squadrons out of Zarafan.

SENIOR SQUADRON COMMANDER KUNG: Terran male, commanding defecting Terran squadrons from the Home Fleet.

RICCI (MALE) AND VISWAN (FEMALE): Sula's signals lieutenants.

MARIVIC MANGAHAS: Terran female, Martinez's chef.

LADY XIA GAO: Terran female, second officer on cruiser *Defense*.

SENIOR SQUADRON LEADER RIVVEN: Daimong male, commands a squadron of heavy cruisers in the Home Fleet.

SQUADRON LEADER AN-DAR: Lai-own male, commands a squadron of heavy cruisers in the Home Fleet.

EXPLORATION SERVICE

CAPTAIN SHUSHANIK SEVERIN ("NIKKI"): Terran, captain of *Expedition* and puppeteer.

LIEUTENANT LORD CHUNGSUN CLEGHORNE: Terran, premiere lieutenant of *Expedition*.

LIEUTENANT CRESSIDA TOUPAL: Terran, second lieutenant of *Expedition*.

PILOT FIRST CLASS LIU: Terran, crew on *Expedition*.

WARRANT OFFICER FALYAZ: Terran, crew on *Expedition*.

LIHUA, LADY STARKEY: Terran female, captain of cruiser *Explorer*.

LIEUTENANT MORENO: Terran male, premiere lieutenant on *Explorer*.

PEERS

MAURICE, LORD CHEN: Terran. A convocate, member of the Fleet Control Board, and father-in-law of Gareth Martinez.

LORD SAÏD: Terran male, head of Clan Saïd and former Lord Senior of the Convocation.

LORD MEHRANG: Terran, patron to Esley, home planet of the Yormaks.

LADY KORIDUN: Torminel, the young head of the Koridun clan.

LADY DISTCHIN: Torminel, absentee patron to Spannan.

LADY GRUUM: Daimong, former patron to the newly settled world Rol-mar, now Lady Senior of the Convocation.

LADY TU-HON: Lai-own, presiding judge of the Court of Honor in the Convocation and member of the Zanshaa government.

LORD MINNO: Cree, a banker, heading the Treasury.

LORD ODA YOSHITOSHI: Terran, heir to Yoshitoshi clan and husband of Vipsania Martinez.

LORD DURWARD LI: Terran, former client of the Sulas, now client of the Chens.

LADY AMITA: Terran, Lord Durward's first wife.

LADY MARIETTA: Terran, Lord Durward's second wife, a runaway.

LORD NGENI: Terran, member of the Convocation, former patron to the Martinez clan.

LORD PIERRE NGENI: Terran, Lord Ngeni's son, member of the Convocation.

LADY CASSILDA ZYKOV: Terran, former wife of Roland Martinez and mother of Girasole.

LORD ZYKOV: Terran, Lady Cassilda's father.

LORD ELDEY: Torminel, a convocate and former governor of Zanshaa.

LEGION OF DILIGENCE
CAPTAIN VODAY: Torminel officer in Legion of Diligence.

COLONEL DAI-POR: Lai-own officer in Legion of Diligence, commanding in Harzapid system at outset of Accidental War.

LINKMEN

HECTOR BRAGA ("LAMEY"): Terran, sometime gangster from Spannan, now lobbyist.

GREDEL ("EARTHGIRL"): Terran, a street girl from Spannan.

OTHERS

CHESKO: Daimong, clothes designer in Petty Mount.

FLEET
ELEMENTS

CHAPTER 1

His nerves seemed scorched by fire. His ribs had tightened their grip on his lungs, and his heart lurched in his chest. Martinez paused for a moment in the boarding tube, took several breaths, and then opened the top buttons on his uniform tunic.

Caroline, Lady Sula had just marched back into his life.

She and her crew had come off their captured ship, *Striver*, taken after killing over forty black-clad Legion fanatics in pitched battle. Sula and her companions had been beaten to hell by weeks of hard deceleration, and the exhaustion clearly showed, but still there was a swagger in their walk, the strut of victors on parade. Sula had carried a homebuilt machine pistol over her shoulder on its strap, and the rest were armed with pistols, rifles, and shotguns. Most were officers in the Fleet but only one wore uniform, for the rest had boarded *Striver* disguised as travelers and immigrants.

All but one were human, and that other was a young Torminel female who wore an exquisite Chesko gown shining with mirrors and silver thread, accessorized with a Legion sidearm and gun belt.

Martinez remembered that it was with this sort of army that Sula had stormed the High City of Zanshaa. And now it looked as if they were ready to storm the High City all over again.

Even though his relationship with Sula had blown up years ago, he still dreamed about her, conjured old memories of the warm white-gold hair brushing his shoulder, the eyes that burned with jade-green fire as they gazed into his, the pale skin that flushed at his touch. When he woke lying next to his wife, it was with Sula's Sandama Twilight perfume singing in his senses.

The Sula who appeared in his dreams was a synthesis of his own tangled desires, and now these fantasies were torn to shreds by the appearance of the real thing. Sula was exhausted from days of high gee, pain lined her face, she wore an old gray jumpsuit, and she had chopped her pale blond hair short so that she could hide it under a wig while traveling in disguise. But still she was the most beautiful thing Martinez had ever seen, and the sight of her buried itself like an arrow in his heart. The pale, bone-tired woman in the worn jumpsuit set a fire running in his blood, and now, panting for breath in the boarding tube, he had no idea how he could survive the next few meetings.

When Sula's gang of pirates came swaggering from the *Striver*, Martinez had been one of a party waiting to welcome them. Fortunately he hadn't been expected to do or say anything: the honor of welcoming Sula's party went to Michi Chen, who commanded the Fourth Fleet here at Harzapid.

Sula marched up to Michi and braced at the salute. "Lady Fleetcom," she said. "Here I am."

"You are very welcome," Michi said. "I've scheduled a meeting with you and some of the others for tomorrow, but I know you all must be exhausted, so I'll show you to your new assigned quarters, and then I'll leave you alone. If you want food or other refreshment, please send for it, and if any of you need medical attention, that's available too."

"What I most want," Sula said, "is the strongest massage therapist on the station."

Michi nodded. "I can find that for you. But please introduce me to your . . . your crew."

Martinez stood in silence while the introductions went on. Sula had brought eighteen officers, cadets, and enlisted, along with a few civilians. The Torminel in the Chesko gown turned out to be none other than Lady Koridun, the young head of a family lately notorious for the number of its clan leaders who had died in implausible accidents. Michi introduced her own party, and when she mentioned Martinez's name, he gave a brisk nod and made his eyes go unfocused, so that he wouldn't see Sula's expression.

Michi led her guests to the line of open-topped cars, identical boxy vehicles made by Sun Ray and painted in the viridian green of the Fleet. Sula joined Michi in the lead car. Martinez took the second car along with Lieutenant-Captain Naaz Vijana, who had made his name suppressing the Yormak

Rebellion on Esley. They made polite conversation as the party sped with a whir of electric motors through the busy Fleet dockyard, past the warships of the Fourth Fleet moored nose-in to the planet's antimatter ring, past the work crews hustling supplies and equipment through the cargo airlocks, past wary guards in the red belts and armbands of the Military Constabulary.

Busy though the dockyard was, it also glittered with ornament. Harzapid's antimatter-generation ring had circled the planet for thousands of years, and during that time there was little public space that had not been embellished with a fresco, a slogan, a bas-relief, or an allegory. Walls were covered with artwork of the Shaa conquerors directing their subject species in developing science and industry, in placing the antimatter ring in the sky, in sending fleets out to populate new systems. The other species bustled to follow the Great Masters' instructions or gaped in awe as the Shaa proclaimed the Praxis in all its majesty. The antimatter generated on the ring was shown powering merchant vessels, lighting cities, providing energy for heavy industry. Slogans urged the ring's staff to Labor for the Benefit of All, to Work Cheerfully, and Let the Praxis Guide Your Life.

The ring's deck was divided by seventeen avenues that stretched the full length of the inhabited areas—seventeen to reflect the Great Masters' preference for prime numbers. Cross streets intersected the avenues at regular intervals. There were trees, green spaces, statues, and fountains. The buildings looked much the same as buildings on the surface, if perhaps a little more bland and uniform, and none rose above eight stories because there was a ceiling above, a ceiling nearly invisible behind regularly spaced lighting strips. Suspended monorail transport raced in efficient silence between the arrays of lights.

The civilian areas were filled with a thriving middle class. If you were rich, you lived on the planet below, and the Shaa had been wary about allowing the urban poor to inhabit such a vulnerable installation. Families of the middling sort were lured to the ring by the promise of affordable housing, good public schools, available universities, employment opportunities, and material comfort.

Necessarily the Fleet dockyard was arranged differently, with docking ports and sprawling warehouses and workshops, but the areas where Fleet personnel and contractors lived looked much like its civilian equivalent.

The convoy left the dockyard and entered the Fleet's residential section, where they stopped at an officers' hostel covered with gold-on-brown abstract designs and brass medallions embellished with reliefs of celebrated fleet commanders of the past. The cars stopped, and one of Michi's aides stepped out with a list of those to be quartered here. Sula's name headed the list, and she turned to thank Michi for her hospitality, left the car with some care, as if wary of an injury, and then walked straight-backed to the hostel entrance.

Watching Sula stride to the door, Martinez remembered her walking away from him in Zanshaa's Lower Town, her heels rapping on the pavement next to the canal.

The echo of those heels had seemed to pursue him into *Corona*'s docking tube. He took another breath.

He had not realized he was so vulnerable. He had seen Sula on only a very few occasions since the end of the Naxid War, and over time he thought he'd manage a meeting well enough as long as he wasn't caught by surprise. And here he *wasn't* surprised—everyone on the station had known she was coming for weeks—and he still felt as if an expert street fighter had just walloped him in the solar plexus.

The echo of the heels grew louder, and then were accompanied by a tinkling laugh. Martinez turned in surprise to see a handsome couple, a young blond woman in a canary-yellow dress, with freckles spread across her snub nose, accompanied by a small uniformed man with pale hair and delicate features. Vonderheydte, who Martinez had promoted lieutenant in his first command, and Lady Marietta Li, the stowaway who had left her husband and twin daughters to fly into exile with her lover. Martinez suppressed a sneeze as he was engulfed by Marietta's floral perfume.

"My lord," Vonderheydte said. "Are you all right?"

"Yes, of course," said Martinez. He patted the pockets of his tunic. "For a moment I had the impression that I'd forgotten something, but apparently I haven't."

"Didn't Lady Sula look dreadful?" said Marietta. "I'd always thought she was so beautiful, but now I see her in person, and ... well."

Suddenly Martinez found himself wanting to defend her. "She's been in battle," he pointed out. "She hasn't had a lot of time to attend to personal grooming."

"Yet Lady Koridun looked wonderful," Marietta said, "and someone told me she killed the enemy commander."

Vonderheydte laughed. "She might be all wrinkled and hideous under that fur," he said. "How would we know?"

Martinez fell into step with Marietta and Vonderheydte. As always, he thought, Vonderheydte made him feel just a little bit old.

They passed through *Corona*'s main passenger airlock and the cool, moist air of the yacht carrier wafted over him. The floors were polished, brass fixtures gleamed against a background of dark wood paneling, and the furniture was comfortable and stylish. A display cabinet showed the softly glowing racing trophies that the Corona Club had won in its few years of existence.

Right in the middle of the atrium was an ornamental waterfall that fell sparkling into a deep pool. There were fountains and ponds that carried exotic fish, and the room echoed to the laughter of water. There was a certain amount of bravado installing open water features on a ship that could find itself floating in zero gee, but *Corona*'s architects had included ways in which the ship could swallow all the water on short notice, and then—just in case—had waterproofed everything.

The small party's footfalls echoed in the atrium. With the exception of Vonderheydte, apparently, all the officers he'd brought from Zanshaa were fully employed on the station, so at this hour *Corona* was nearly deserted.

"Join us for a drink, Lord Captain?" Vonderheydte asked.

"No, but thank you."

Vonderheydte and Marietta strolled off arm in arm. Martinez paused to contemplate the waterfall, and he tried to let the chiming of the water soothe away the memory of Sula that still spiked along his nerves. Exotic fish flashed spines, scales, and feathery tails in the water.

"Hail, ancestor!"

Gareth the Younger came trotting up with his sketch pad in his hand. He was nine years old, an engaging child whose appearance combined his mother's celestial beauty and his father's olive skin and solid physical presence. Martinez looked at his son and felt his anxiety fade.

"Hail, progeny," he said. "Have you been drawing?"

"I've been doing graphic taxonomy," said Gareth the Younger and showed a drawing of a golden tiger-striped fish. "This is a juvenile spotted harelip."

Taxonomy was a new word. Martinez had been trying to expand his son's vocabulary.

"I spotted the spots at once," he said.

Gareth paged through the sketchbook's display to show one sketch after another. One of the officers had given him drawing lessons on the three-month journey from Zanshaa, and the images were now recognizable as discrete and distinguishable fish, as opposed to colorful torpedo-shaped objects that might be birds, aircraft, or clouds. Martinez took the time to praise each sketch as he looked at them.

He hadn't really paid attention to *Corona*'s fish, so the sketches might be perfectly accurate so far as he knew.

"There's ochoba-bean dumplings for lunch," Young Gareth said, apropos of nothing, and then ran off to find something called a "whiskered Frenella eel."

Martinez walked toward one of *Corona*'s lounge areas for

a cup of coffee before settling down to his task designing a new exercise for crew to train on. Most of the Fourth Fleet warships, having been designed for other species, were as yet unsuitable for human occupation, and everyone from commanding officers to fresh recruits were training on simulators.

On the way to the lounge he caught a whiff of Terza's vetiver perfume, and he followed the scent to a cabin filled with communications gear and dull-eyed cameras, intended as a staging room for his sister Vipsania's video reporters broadcasting the yacht races.

Terza Chen sat at a console, her mouth set in a little frown of concern as she contemplated the display. With her head bent gracefully toward the display, her long black hair drawing a comma on her shoulder, and her body in an attitude of contemplation, she might have been the subject of a pensive little painting by Rhy-to the Elder. She wore the brown uniform of the civil service and had spent the years since the war working for the Ministry of Right and Dominion, the government department that served the Fleet. She looked up as Martinez entered, and he found himself lost for a moment in the sublime perfection of her face, the result of thousands of years of breeding, assurance, and privilege. That breeding showed in the unearthly serenity that surrounded her, so unlike the impatient fury in which Sula charged through life.

Martinez felt his heart lurch at the steadiness of her gaze. "I, ah, was going to get some coffee," he said. "Would you like some?"

"I have tea, thank you." There was a slight shift in her dark eyes. "Did the reception for Lady Sula go well?"

"They were all beat to pieces by the long deceleration, so Michi gave them the day off." He thought it best to shift the subject from Sula. "Do you know anything about Lady Koridun?"

"Not much other than she's quite young and that there have been a lot of deaths in her family."

"Starting, apparently, with a volcanic explosion on Terra." Martinez had once joked about the deaths with Lord Durward Li, the husband that Marietta had abandoned on Zanshaa, saying that he was tempted to start a sports book on how long the current Lady Koridun would survive.

"Lady Koridun seems to be avoiding mortality so far," he said. "Marietta told me that she'd killed the Legion commander on the trip out."

Terza's eyes widened. "That's unexpected," she said. "But then, the Koriduns have a reputation for violence and mental instability, don't they?"

"Do they? I didn't know." Martinez, his heart still throbbing erratically inside his rib cage, felt a sudden, deep compulsion to linger for a while in Terza's aura of serenity, and he sat in the chair next to her. Strange, he thought, how he needed his wife to settle him down after an encounter with a woman he'd never forgotten. She reached out to take his hand, her slim fingers enfolding his big, clumsy paw, and then turned her attention to the console.

"What are you working on?" he asked.

"Estimates of missile production. We're ramping up, of course."

"Of course."

"But with missiles we have to make sure that only Terrans are involved in the actual production." Because, Martinez knew, other species might be tempted by the idea of sabotage.

"Isn't it mostly automated anyway?"

"Some is, some isn't. But there's conventional explosive used to trigger the antimatter chips, so that's a separate production line that has to be rendered safe."

"Everything's been quiet so far," Martinez said hopefully. Humans were outnumbered five to one on Harzapid, but Michi's coup had put humanity, for the moment, in charge. He had to hope that the other species would be willing to accept Michi's assurances that things would return to normal after the emergency ended.

Terza's free hand gestured at the interface, and production figures scrolled by. Martinez could see the numbers reflected in her long dark eyes.

She was a member of the highest caste of Peers, Clan Chen's heir, and would normally have been far beyond Martinez's reach. But the Naxid War had upset everything and had made Terza's father financially vulnerable. Martinez's older brother, Roland, had used family money to lever Terza out of Lord Chen's grip, and Martinez and Terza had been married after only a few hours' acquaintance, and mere days after Martinez's relationship with Sula had exploded.

Terza might have had every reason to resent her fate, but to his surprise she had approached marriage and motherhood with the same unruffled competence with which she seemed to approach everything else. Her air of tranquil perfection had made him uneasy—if she hated him, how would he know?—but all doubts had eventually been put to rest. After her father's finances recovered, she'd had every opportunity to leave Martinez, and she hadn't. Terza had accompanied him into exile on *Corona*, and she had been willing to share his fate when it looked as if the cruiser *Conformance* would obliterate them all with an antimatter missile. She had encouraged Martinez's plan to destroy *Conformance* with an improvised weapon and awaited her fate with a calm resilience that had earned his admiration.

For his own part Martinez had taken advantage of the perquisites that came with marrying the Chen heir. He'd accepted Lord Chen's patronage, and Chen's sister, Michi, had employed Martinez at a time when few commanders would. If he was now a senior captain instead of an obscure elcap commanding a training school somewhere, it was the work of his in-laws, and when Terza became Lady Chen, he would have the option of becoming Lord Chen at her side.

The stowaway passenger Marietta Li, Martinez knew, had fled her own arranged marriage to a much older man. Lord Durward Li had lost his heir at the First Battle of Magaria, and needing a new one, he first needed a fertile wife and found one among his clients. At least she'd given him a pair of children before running off with Vonderheydte.

Martinez had managed, at least so far, to keep his own life from becoming a tale so entirely ridiculous.

He had also told himself that he wouldn't dishonor Terza by failing to be a proper consort. She had lowered herself to marry him, and he would not disgrace her. If she was not quite the object of his deepest passion, he would act as if she were. It might have been a marriage hastily arranged at the last minute, but he would make it a real marriage if he could. And so far as he could tell, he'd succeeded.

All might have been well, if only Martinez hadn't kept dreaming of Lady Sula.

CHAPTER 2

The battleship *Perfection of the Praxis* was far from perfect. It was unfinished, for one thing, and gangs of workers were moving material both on and off the ship—*on* went equipment to make *Perfection of the Praxis* an effective fighting machine, and *off* went items intended to transform the ship into a gleaming showcase of opulence for whatever lucky fleet commander got to install herself in its deluxe quarters. So *off* went uninstalled luxuries: the rare wood paneling, the parquetry, the hand-painted tiles, the gleaming bar fixtures, the crystal chandeliers, two unassembled marble steam baths, the backdrops and scenery for the ship's theater, and the instruments intended for the ship's orchestra.

The woman called Caroline Sula walked through a vast empty space, the ceiling all girders and spray foam, the walls cheap gray resin slabs awaiting the installation of glossy wood paneling, the blazing LED floods mounted on brackets built to resist high gees. Her heels clacked on temporary flooring and echoed in the vast cavern. "What *is* this place?" she asked.

Her guide, a staff lieutenant named Sandra Yuen, glanced up at the dim, empty ceiling. "The ballroom, my lady."

"Good grief."

Eight years before, Sula had watched an entire squadron of Praxis-class battleships annihilated in a storm of antimatter fire at the First Battle of Magaria. The huge ships had carried a massive battery of weapons, but in the face of antimatter missiles they were destroyed as easily as an unarmed pinnace.

The lesson was clear: the big ships were too vulnerable, and the resources to build one of them was better spent on a squadron of smaller, more flexible vessels that couldn't all be blasted out of existence by a single missile. But a half-dozen years after the end of the Naxid War, with no more fighting expected, the Fleet's leaders had found themselves unable to resist building themselves new flying palaces, complete— apparently—with ballrooms.

And now, ballrooms or not, *Perfection of the Praxis* was bound for combat. Sula tried to console herself with the thought that the enemy would have more battleships than her own side.

Sula's body ached from days of deceleration, and as she walked she twisted her trunk to unkink her spine. She followed Yuen out of the ballroom, down a corridor hung with scaffolding and reeking of solvents, and then through a hatch into a very different world. Luxuries had actually been installed in this room: yellow chesz-wood paneling, indirect lighting, video screens tuned to a shifting array of abstract colors, soft carpets. Sula could only hope it had all been fireproofed, as per regulations.

Soft music burbled from hidden speakers. Aides passed with trays of drinks and snacks. Prominent in the room stood a half-dozen Terrans in the viridian-green dress uniforms of the Fleet. Sula had escaped to Harzapid in civilian disguise, leaving her uniforms behind, and wore a nondescript jumpsuit of dark gray, rumpled and creased from days of hard deceleration. The jumpsuit was untidy and unprepossessing, but at least the bloodstains had been removed.

Sula approached a woman with the shoulder boards of a junior fleet commander and braced at the salute, chin high to expose her throat to her senior's correction. "Lady Fleetcom," she said.

"Welcome, Lady Sula. Would you like a coffee, or fruit juice?"

Lady Michi Chen hadn't seen Sula since the end of the Naxid Rebellion but had managed nonetheless to remember that Sula didn't drink alcohol. That, Sula thought, was very professional of her.

"Tea, Lady Fleetcom. With honey, or cane syrup if you have it."

One of the aides was sent to fetch tea. Michi was a stocky woman with a cap of gray hair cut in bangs across her forehead, and recent care and anxiety had jaundiced her complexion and drawn fresh lines at the corners of her mouth. Even though it was Sula who had just undergone twenty-nine days of hard deceleration, it was Michi who looked more careworn.

Yet there was good reason for her exhaustion. It might be said with perfect justice that the fate of the human race depended entirely on Michi Chen's decisions.

Michi looked at Sula's jumpsuit. "You didn't bring uniforms?"

"I traveled incognito. But I've sent my measurements to a tailor on the ring, and I'll have a complete set soon."

Michi glanced over the room. "I think you know everybody here except for the Kangas twins."

The twins, Paivo and Ranssu, were big-jawed blonds, tall and burly, with large hands and outsized knuckles. They were the sons of Fleet Commander Eino Kangas, who had died leading the Home Fleet to victory at the Battle of Antopone, and they both wore the uniforms of lieutenant-captains.

"I'm pleased to meet you, Lady Sula," Paivo said. "We've just done a brief survey of your *Striver.*"

"It's hardly *my Striver*," Sula said. "It belongs to the Ondau Company."

"It's yours now," said Ranssu. "You took it. And you killed over forty members of the Legion to do it."

"Not me personally."

"It looked like a real bloodbath," said Paivo.

Yes, Sula thought, *and I dream about it and wake up screaming.*

"It's true that an antimatter missile is more hygienic than bombs and firearms," Sula said. "In any case, if *Striver* is mine, I happily surrender it to you. I'm glad to be out of it."

"I don't blame you," said Paivo. "The smell alone—"

His brother nudged him, and he fell silent.

Paivo's words had brought a scent-memory to Sula's senses: the sharp tang of explosives, the smoky odor of propellants, and the deep throat-clogging reek of the Torminel blood that had run down the metal staircase in thick, clotting waterfalls.

Sula knew she'd have another bad dream tonight.

An aide arrived with Sula's tea and honey on a platter. For a brief instant she had a near-overwhelming urge for alcohol, for the relaxation it would bring to her strained muscles, the confidence it brought to her personality, and the obliteration it would bring to her memory.

Odd that the compulsion was so strong, when she'd only had alcohol a few times in her life, when she was a teen, and hadn't much cared for it then. But her youth had also been full of the damage she'd seen alcohol inflict on others, and she'd sworn to stay away from it.

She added a long, slow, fragrant dollop of honey to the tea, then sipped and tried to let its sweetness overcome the memory of blood and death. It failed.

The noise of the hatch opening announced the arrival of a pair of Sula's fellow passengers on the *Striver*. Lieutenant Lady Alana Haz had once been Lord Alan Haz, Sula's premiere on her frigate *Confidence*. She was tall, broad-shouldered, and— because she hadn't been traveling incognito—wore one of the superbly tailored uniforms she had brought with her from Zanshaa. With her was Captain Lord Naaz Vijana, who had made his reputation suppressing the revolt of the Yormak natives of Esley, a victory made easier by the fact that the Yormaks had Stone Age tools and Vijana modern weaponry. He was a slender man with a pointed face and caramel skin, and his alert black eyes surveyed the room and paused at each face, as if he were quietly evaluating each officer for his own purposes. Since he'd traveled incognito alongside Sula, he didn't have a uniform, but he wore neat dark civilian clothes with a Fleet sidearm strapped around his waist.

Sula sipped her tea while Michi Chen introduced the new arrivals, and then the hatch opened again, and Gareth Martinez entered. He was a larger presence than she remembered, with his lantern jaw and dark brows, and the long anthropoid torso and arms balanced atop comparatively short legs. Perhaps he'd managed to somehow inflate himself since she'd last seen him.

Hung about his neck on its black-and-gold ribbon was the brilliant disk of the Golden Orb, the empire's highest decoration. At least he hadn't brought the Orb's golden baton itself, which would have required everyone in the room to stand at attention and salute him.

She'd had weeks to prepare herself for this moment, since *Striver* had followed Martinez's ship on its escape to Harzapid. Martinez, founder of the Corona Yacht Club, had ridden to Harzapid on *Corona*, his club's yacht carrier, a plush vessel equipped with every luxury—possibly, she thought, even a ballroom. While Sula had been obliged to lead a bloody mutiny against the black-clad Torminel fanatics, Martinez had enjoyed what seemed to be a three-month-long cocktail party interrupted only by the occasional yacht race.

And along the way, with his unarmed transport vessel, he had somehow destroyed an enemy cruiser. Not that Sula would give him the satisfaction of asking him how he'd done it.

Behind Martinez came his entourage: Captain Nikki Severin in his blue Exploration Service uniform, Lieutenant-Captain Elissa Dalkeith, a Martinez protégée who had commanded a frigate in the last war, and Lieutenant Chandra Prasad, who during the Naxid War had served as Michi Chen's tactical officer.

Introductions were made. Sula was pleased that with Martinez in the room her heartbeat had increased only a little. Martinez's glance passed over her without hesitation or surprise, and Sula knew that he'd had time to prepare for this meeting as well.

Michi told everyone to take their drinks and join her in the conference room.

The conference room had only half its decor installed, with arculé wood paneling, but the ceiling was a tangle of pipes and beams with paper labels dangling on wires, and the deck was composed of metal plates enameled a grayish white. The air smelled of solvent. Rolls of paper had been laid down over the metal to dampen the clanging sound of heels striding across the deck.

The room was furnished with temporary folding tables, but they had real linen on them. The chairs were resinous and stackable. Usefully there were video displays on all the walls, enabling the conferees to see whatever data they needed to see.

Sula carefully sat where she wouldn't have to spend the meeting looking across the room at Martinez. Michi Chen called the meeting to order.

"I'd like the captains Kangas to open with a report on ship conversions."

The twins' report gave Sula a chance to appreciate Michi's achievement. While Sula had been fleeing from the capital of Zanshaa, Michi had been creating a haven for Sula to flee to. The Fourth Fleet consisted of a hundred and eighty-three warships, of which only forty had been crewed by Terrans. The ships had been under the command of Senior Fleet Commander Surang, a Daimong, and Michi herself had no ships under her command, but instead was in charge of only the dockyard. Yet once she'd heard that secret orders had gone out to disarm every Terran warship in the empire, she had managed to organize an action in which all non-Terran ships had been bloodlessly boarded, their officers confined, and their crews moved to makeshift prisons on the planet's antimatter ring.

A gratifying bonus for Michi had been the fact that Fleet Commander Surang, his staff, and his senior commanders had been arrested at a meeting where they intended to complete plans for boarding the Terran vessels and securing their officers and crews.

The Kangas twins had been put in charge of converting the non-Terran ships for the use of Terran crews. "Daimong and Torminel are shaped more or less like human beings," said Paivo, "so we can use their beds and furniture if we run out of those made for Terrans."

"Which we will," said Ranssu.

"Unless we develop more success at manufacturing new gear than we have at present," Paivo said. "But everything will be all right with what we have."

"Nonii," assured Ranssu.

"We've been concentrating more on converting the Lai-own ships," Paivo said. "The seats, beds, and acceleration couches are not compatible with human physiology, so we've had to do a complete replacement. I'm pleased to report that the Lai-own ships should be ready for new crews within the next six to ten days, depending on how many people we can add to the work gangs."

"And the Cree ships?" Michi asked.

Paivo waved a hand. "That will take longer."

Cree did not have proper eyes, but primitive eye patches that provided them only with a vague and confusing picture of their world. Lacking an effective sense of sight, they depended on acute hearing to navigate their way through their lives. The control rooms on their ships presented a cacophony of sound, buzzes and clicks and shrieks and murmurs that were bewildering to any Terran. Converting every control station, every display, and every gauge to something comprehensible by a Terran was a major undertaking.

"Fortunately there are only fifteen Cree ships," Paivo said. Fewer than any other species.

The Cree, generally speaking, were not a military species and were ill-suited to the formality and discipline of the service. They liked sleeping in a pile in the center of the room, for one thing, and had a hard time understanding why officers should sleep in separate piles from the enlisted.

Sometimes Sula thought that Cree viewed service in the Fleet as something akin to a hilarious joke.

"It will be at least a month before the Cree ships are ready," Ranssu said.

Michi turned to one of her staff for a report on personnel. Every ship had to be crewed by Terrans, of course, and, for fear of sabotage, all crucial work also had to be performed by Terrans. Since Harzapid had been the base of the Fourth Fleet for centuries, there was a large supply of retired crouch-backs who could be recalled to the service, but many were too old to endure the heavy gravities expected in combat and were relegated to support functions, to training, and to work gangs. There would not be enough trained crew to staff the Fourth Fleet fully, and ships would be obliged to set off without their full complements.

Plenty of volunteers were flooding the training camps, fortunately, but they were unlikely to be ready by the time they were needed.

The next report was offered by Martinez's friend Shushanik Severin, known as "Nikki," a commoner raised to the officer class following several unconventional exploits—one of which involved shutting off a pulsar, and another of which was his creation of a well-regarded puppet show. He looked at the room from narrow eyes over high cheekbones and reported that the Exploration Service would contribute to the Fourth Fleet his own light cruiser, *Expedition*, just completing repairs, the frigate *Ranger*, taken from its Lai-own crew during Michi's coup, and the light cruiser *Explorer*, crewed by Terrans, which was returning to Harzapid after a nine-month cruise investigating whatever was to be found on the other side of a newly discovered wormhole. Severin could also offer unarmed scout ships and transports.

This, Sula thought, was encouraging as far as it went. But

like the Fleet, most Exploration Service vessels were crewed by non-Terrans, and right now, in some meeting room somewhere, Exploration Service officers belonging to at least four other species were probably offering their vessels to the other side.

Since the Exploration Service also staffed the wormhole relay stations on either side of the wormhole gates that knit the empire together, Severin was also sending out armed Terran crews to all stations staffed by other species. The relay stations forwarded all communications between star systems, and the small part of the empire that Michi controlled was slowly expanding as information from Harzapid began to replace information from Zanshaa.

A hunched, elderly Terran in the uniform of a senior captain, clearly brought in out of retirement, reported on the status of the training camps, which were full of enthusiastic volunteers who knew nothing useful, and who would take months to learn.

"As we have an insufficient supply of line officers," Michi said, "I'm going to have to promote a great many officers into posts for which they would otherwise be too junior. For the moment we're doing training on simulators, and those who do well will have first chance at promotion."

Sula sat up and wondered if she had heard Michi properly. Had a high-ranking officer just announced that promotions in her command would be made on something like *merit*, as opposed to heredity, wealth, family influence, nepotism, and the trading of favors?

Of course, almost all Fleet officers were Peers, anyway, so

the promotions would still remain within one class, but still this was something like revolution.

But, she reflected, it went without saying that Gareth Martinez, who happened to be married to Michi's niece, would receive a very important command, so nepotism would hardly be extinguished in the Fourth Fleet. So perhaps Michi was speaking carelessly, and considerations of something other than merit would play their usual part.

This thought faded beneath the wry realization that, however well connected he might be, Martinez *deserved* high command. He was the only officer of the Fleet whose accomplishments might equal her own.

Damn him anyway. He had made her love him, then abandoned her to marry Clan Chen's heir, who came with connections that would assure promotion and a chance of command. And now she was going to have to find some way of working alongside him for the length of a long, miserable war.

Michi opened a discussion of the timing of reinforcements. Lord Jeremy Foote's Light Squadron Eight, having struck the first blow of the war with a surprise attack against two enemy squadrons at Colamote, was presumed to be somewhere between Colamote and Harzapid, and would arrive in a month or so, depending on how fast he was pushing his crews.

Sixty-three Terran ships, defectors from the Home Fleet at Zanshaa, were also believed to be en route but would not arrive for another two months.

Fifty-five defectors from the Second Fleet at Magaria, under Senior Squadron Commander Wei Jian, were also bound for Harzapid, but they had been forced into a roundabout route and would not arrive for another five or six months.

Left out of the calculations was the Third Fleet, based at Felarus at least six months' travel away. The Third Fleet was comprised of 206 ships, forty of them Terran under Senior Squadron Leader Nguyen. Nguyen knew that he had no hope of leading his twoscore ships across the wormhole net of the empire to Harzapid, not with the First and Second Fleets in the way, and so he'd buttoned his crews into his ships and announced that *no one* was leaving Felarus without being fired on. The result would have been a bloodbath fought at close range, with mutual destruction a near certainty, and so now the entire Third Fleet had been neutralized. Which was lucky, because the Third Fleet's commander, Do-faq, was one of the most talented leaders in the Fleet.

"No matter how hard I work the numbers," Michi said, "they come out the same. Once the Second Fleet joins the Home Fleet, and Supreme Commander Tork calls in the ships and squadrons on detached duty, we're going to be opposed by five hundred seventy-three warships. And once Foote and the defectors from the Home Fleet join us, and including Captain Severin's small squadron from the Exploration Service, we'll have only two hundred fifty-six. So we'll be outnumbered two to one."

Sula had worked the numbers as well, having had little else to do during her days of deceleration. The vast weight of the enemy armada was intimidating, though Sula thought she could do well against the right commander.

But the numbers themselves posed their own problem.

No one knew how to maneuver and fight fleets so vast—the largest fleet in the Naxid War, led by then Fleet Commander Tork, had consisted of eighty-seven warships. Sula had no idea how a single commander could control 256 vessels during the uncertainty and confusion of combat, and she worried that if control broke down, the battle would turn into a confused melee, which the side with the most ships would inevitably win.

Elissa Dalkeith blinked her watery blue eyes. "Once the Second Fleet defectors join us," she said, "we'll have over three hundred."

Sula had forgotten Dalkeith's lisping, piping voice, a six-year-old's in the body of a middle-aged woman.

"I dare to presume," Michi said, "that the enemy knows how long it will take those ships to reach us and will attack before they arrive." Dalkeith fell into silence.

Martinez cleared his throat. "We'd better hope that Supreme Commander Tork is going to lead the attack himself. That way we might have a chance."

Sula almost laughed. "How could he not?" she said. "He's led a private war against some of us for years—he's denied Lady Michi promotion and command, when after the last war she should have a *fleet*."

"Well." Michi's expression was grim. "Now I've *got* a fleet, and most days all I long for is retirement. Though the chance to jab a fork in Tork's eye gets me through my day."

"Tork is elderly," said Ranssu Kangas. "He should not be leading a fleet into battle at that age. Why wouldn't he assign the command to someone else?"

Sula cackled. "We have to make sure he doesn't," she said. "We should mock the hell out of him in our propaganda. Say that he's old, incompetent, overrated, and nothing more than a senile lackey to the greedy frauds in the government."

"All of which has the advantage of being true," said Chandra Prasad.

"It's true, and that's exactly why it will sting," Sula said. "Tork takes every disagreement personally—imagine how he'll react to insult and defiance aimed at his achievements and character."

"We have no way of distributing propaganda in Zanshaa," said one of Michi's captains.

"We can distribute it here in our sphere and send it from our relay station to theirs. I assume it will find its way to Tork sooner rather than later."

The gaunt, gray-skinned Tork had a unique position in the government, having leveraged his decisive victory at Second Magaria into being not only Supreme Commander of the Fleet—a rank he had invented for himself—but chairman of the Fleet Control Board, the government committee in charge of the Fleet. No one had ever before held a seat on the Control Board while also retaining active command, and to some it seemed a dangerous concentration of power in the hands of a single person.

Certainly it proved dangerous enough when Tork, in the wake of political turmoil blamed on Terrans, made the decision to proactively board and disarm all Terran ships. He had the prestige and power to carry it out in the face of any opposition. Now that his plan had backfired and spurred mutiny among the Terran elements of the Fleet, Tork had little choice but to double down on the war he'd inadvertently inspired.

"Do we *have* someone in charge of propaganda?" asked Naaz Vijana. "Is anyone trying to manage our . . . our message?"

"We have an ad hoc committee of politicians who are trying to direct operations outside of the military sphere," Michi said. "Most of them are local, but they include convocates like Lord Roland Martinez, and prominent individuals like Lord Mehrang."

Lord Mehrang was the patron of Esley, where he had brought Naaz Vijana to quell the uprising of the primitive Yormaks. Roland was Gareth Martinez's older brother, the presumed heir to Clan Martinez. Sula thought him capable, but ruthless, calculating, overambitious, and untrustworthy. She also suspected that it was Roland who had bought the Chen heir for his brother and enhanced his own fortunes by saddling Gareth Martinez with a beautiful, polished rich girl who played the harp, instead of . . .

Well. Instead of someone else.

That made for *two* members of this ad hoc committee being cold-blooded intriguers devoted to their own self-interest. Pity the rest of them, whoever they were.

"I don't like this *ad hoc* business," Sula said. "Whoever's in charge of the political side needs to get serious about running our little rump empire—keeping the economy moving, adequately supplying the Fleet, and maybe start thinking how we're going to manage things when we win. What's our political settlement going to be? The composition of the Convocation and the Fleet Control Board? What's our policy on amnesties for our enemies—who gets amnestied, and who gets the chop?"

The others just looked at one another.

"Ah. Hah," Sula said. "That's what I thought."

There was another moment of silence, and then Sula cleared her throat.

"As long as I'm raising uncomfortable issues," she said, "do we have any evidence that the two heavy squadrons at Zarafan—they'd be under Squadron Commander Rukmin, yes?—are not in pursuit of Foote's Squadron Eight? If they pushed on at high gees, they could get to Toley ahead of Foote and get between him and us."

When that smug idiot Foote had begun the war by prematurely annihilating the two enemy squadrons at Colamote, he'd altered course to dive through a succession of five wormhole gates leading to Toley, and from there to Harzapid. But the two heavy squadrons at Zarafan, either of which outgunned Foote's force, could beat Foote to Toley if they were willing to pulp themselves with high gravities. They had fewer gates to jump through, for one thing.

"We analyzed that possibility," Michi said. "Rukmin's two Zarafan squadrons *might* try to intercept Foote, but if they did, they'd almost certainly be destroyed by the Home Fleet defectors, which have to pass through Zarafan and Toley to reach us. They could cut off Foote, but the Home Fleet defectors would cut Rukmin off in turn."

"Couldn't they double back through Colamote?"

"It's barely possible, but their timing would have to be exactly right."

"Or to avoid pursuit the enemy could just fly off into space, off the wormhole routes. That would force any pursuers to choose between pursuing them, and uniting with us." Sula reached for her tea, decided against it, then retracted her hand. "We have two squadrons orbiting the Harzapid system," she said. "May I suggest that we send them toward Toley to escort Foote? It's best to be safe, I think, and we can replace them with new conversions once they launch."

Michi parted her lips and took a slow inhalation of breath. "I'll take it under consideration, but I'll have to review the timing considerations."

That was about all Sula could hope for. She sipped her tea.

"I don't see any drawbacks," said Alana Haz. "If Foote isn't being pursued, there's no danger. And if he is, we can save him from destruction."

"Nonii," said Ranssu.

The meeting devolved into topics less interesting and far less urgent. Sula twisted in her seat to relieve a cramp in her back. Eventually Michi called an end to the meeting, and Sula gratefully stood, rolled her shoulders as she heard the crackle of ligaments echo through her bones. The officers drifted back into the reception room to snack and refresh their drinks. Sula put down her tea, then went to Michi, who was talking to the Kangas twins. She waited for Michi to turn to her and then spoke.

"I'm sorry if I raised too many awkward questions," she said, "but the whole time I was strapped into my couch during the deceleration, I had nothing to think about but how to manage the war."

"While I, on the other hand, was actually managing it," Michi said. Her irony had returned. "But," she conceded, "you may be right about these things—it's very distracting here, dealing with the day-to-day issues."

"Your coup, my lady," Sula said, "was brilliant. How you managed it without a single casualty is beyond my imagination."

"I was lucky in my opponent," said Michi. "Surang had no experience with conspiracies, either running his own or detecting mine." She frowned for a moment, then looked at Sula. "Have you any more questions?"

"Just one." Sula turned to the twins. "What does 'nonii' mean?"

They laughed. "It's a quaint old word from our home world of Devajjo," Paivo said. "Our ancestors lived for centuries in this remote mountain valley called Toimi, and we were all poor but virtuous. But then one of my ancestors discovered that we were sitting on huge deposits of praseodymium, and we all became rich, and my ancestor became the first Lord Kangas."

"You're rich now," Sula said, "but are you still virtuous?"

"Of course!" Paivo said. "We are beyond reproach!"

"But anyway," Ranssu said, "nonii is just one of those old words from Toimi, and it means practically anything. It can mean 'all right,' or 'hello,' or 'we're ready,' or 'let's get going.'"

"Or 'I agree,'" added Paivo. "Or 'it's about time,' or 'you're right.'"

"Or 'Here we go,'" offered Ranssu. "Or 'I'll start now.'"

They looked at each other. "There must be more," Ranssu said.

"On Terra there was a word like that," Sula said. "It was '*okay.*' It could mean 'yes' or 'all right' or 'very good' or 'fair enough' or 'acceptable' or 'authorization' or a number of other things. But the Shaa abolished it from the language because it meant too many things and offended their sense of exactitude."

"I guess the Shaa never visited Toimi," said Paivo. "We still have our word, and a few others too."

"Nonii," said Sula, and then clenched her teeth as a back muscle went into spasm. "If you'll pardon me, Lady Fleetcom," she said. "I have to get myself to a masseuse."

"By all means, Lady Sula."

The back spasm made Sula want to list to the left as she walked, but with an effort of will she kept her spine straight as she marched from the room.

She was not going to give Martinez the satisfaction of seeing her in pain.

CHAPTER 3

"Well," Martinez said to Michi a few moments later, "it seems that Lady Sula hasn't mellowed with the years."

"No." Michi glanced at the hatch through which Sula had disappeared. "That was a little sudden."

"She's good at vanishing." Sula had fled from Martinez no less than three times and left him with a gaping hole in his heart each time.

"Maybe that's why they call her the White Ghost," Michi said.

"Maybe." He raised his glass to his lips and took a sip of his Kyowan and Spacey. Tart botanical flavors shimmered over his palate.

Martinez had steeled himself for the meeting today and had managed to sit in the same room as Sula without twitching or breaking into a sweat or otherwise embarrassing himself. He hadn't stammered either, but then maybe that was because he'd hardly spoken at all.

Michi still stared thoughtfully at the hatch. She raised her coffee cup to her lips, looked down at the murky beverage, which over time had separated into cool, unappetizing clouds of brown and white, then dropped the cup again into her saucer. "Do you think Lady Sula's right about Foote and Rukmin?"

"Would you like me to check the original calculations?" Martinez said. "They were made before I arrived here."

"Of course. I'll have them sent to you." Michi looked at Martinez, then hesitated. "I'm torn. If it looks like Foote is in actual danger, I'd like to put you in charge of the expeditionary force. But you're so damned useful here bringing crews up to the mark, I'd also like to keep you at Harzapid, and I should really give another officer the appointment, give him some seasoning."

Martinez suspected Michi was offering him a choice. He wanted to leap at any chance to win a victory over the enemy, but he thought he should at least pretend to consider the question rationally.

"The senior officer in our two orbiting squadrons is Carmody, yes?"

"Yes."

He nodded. "A brave officer. His *Splendid* did well at Magaria and Naxas."

"It did."

"And Foote served under him in *Splendid*. They might work well together."

Unspoken was the idea that ginger-whiskered Carmody was brave enough, but otherwise a mediocrity raised to his current status by family connections and an exchange of favors. If he encountered the enemy, his imagination would not extend beyond a straight-up fight, and though superiority in numbers would guarantee him a victory, he would take casualties that the Terran fleet could not afford.

"If not me," Martinez said, "who?"

"Someone who's worked with the Martinez Method," said Michi. This was the tactical system that Martinez and Sula had developed during the Naxid War, and which had been employed in three victories. One might think that this might serve as evidence that the Fleet should adopt the Method as doctrine, but the conservative Supreme Commander Tork hated innovation and had done his best to write the Martinez Method out of history, and to punish any officer who advocated its use.

Which was lucky, since Martinez hoped to use the Method against Tork and the Home Fleet when they arrived.

"Chandra Prasad, perhaps?" Michi offered.

"Chandra's a lieutenant," Martinez said. "Carmody might resent being superseded by a junior officer who's never commanded a ship before, let alone a pair of squadrons."

"Naaz Vijana? He's commanded a frigate and did well against the Yormaks."

"A drunken rigger with a shotgun could do well against Yormaks," Martinez said. "How well does he know the Method?"

Michi sighed. "Well, then. Elissa Dalkeith. She's commanded a ship, and she's employed the Method in two battles."

Martinez sipped his Kyowan and Spacey as he looked across the room at Dalkeith, who stood chatting with Alana Haz. She had been a middle-aged lieutenant when she'd come aboard his *Corona* as premiere, with no patronage and no hope of promotion; and after the victory at Hone-bar she had been made lieutenant-captain only as a compliment to Martinez, whose tactics had secured the victory.

Martinez thought her personality bland, and it had to be admitted that she lacked drive and imagination. But neither had he any reason to think she would be deficient in any task assigned to her.

"I say nothing against her," he said.

Michi looked at him sidelong. "Your 'nothing' nevertheless seems to mean something."

"I think she'll be fine," Martinez said. "But I would give her a hard-charging premiere."

Michi gave a tight smile. "It's not like we have a lot of hard-charging lieutenants to spare, either."

"Well." An aide floated by, and Martinez put his empty glass on her tray. "We'll give it more thought. And if you'll excuse me, I have another meeting to attend."

"Of course."

Martinez braced briefly in salute and then walked to the hatch and out. His steps boomed on temporary flooring, echoed off ductwork.

He was already thinking about how he was going to beat Rukmin.

SULA LOOKED FROM Martinez to his older brother, Roland. The two brothers, big and olive-skinned and lantern-jawed, strongly resembled each other. They sat with Sula around a small round table covered with wooden gaming pieces, but the game they were playing seemed obscure.

"I'm not sure how to do this," Martinez said.

"Oh, for all's sake," said Roland, "you just have to use a little more *force*."

With that he leaned toward Sula and shoved her, his palm striking her sternum. The breath went out of her in surprise and she felt herself toppling backward. There was an unnerving sense of weightlessness, and then a shock as she dropped into chill water. She hadn't realized there was a tank or tub directly behind her.

The water closed over her face. She struggled but Roland's strong hand pinned her down. Stinging water flooded up her nose.

She clutched at Roland's wrist. The two brothers were perfectly visible through the shallow, shivering water that covered Sula's face. Fire kindled in Sula's lungs.

Martinez peered down at her with a mild expression. "So that's how it's done," he said.

"It's not just *how*," said Roland, "but *when*."

Martinez shrugged. "I guess *when* is *now*," he said.

Pressure built within Sula's ribs. She pounded at Roland's arm, but he remained immobile. Both men looked at her with interest.

"Any time now," Roland said.

Sula's heart exploded in her chest. The air burst from her lungs, and she felt the agonizing inrush of the water as she drowned . . .

SULA SAT UP in bed, her heart thrashing, her lungs dragging in air. She curled into a ball on the sweat-soaked sheets and shuddered until her pulse ceased to pound and her breathing returned to something like normal.

She dreamed of drowning, she dreamed of smothering, she dreamed of blood. The dreams had slowly faded after the war, but after the battle on *Striver* she'd woken nearly every night with a shriek clawing its way out of her throat. During those last weeks of *Striver*'s escape, with the pressure of three gravities sitting on her chest, the dreams of smothering were almost real, and almost continuous.

And now she was dreaming of the Martinez family killing her. She wondered how much to trust in this omen.

The bed was a tangled mess, and the sheets smelled of sweat. She smelled, too, and her lip curled at her own stink, a stink she'd had to live with, pinned to her couch by gravity, all those long days aboard *Striver*. She rose, showered, and dressed in the nondescript garments she'd worn when she was calling herself Tamara Bycke and hiding from the Legion. She thought again about alcohol, rejected the idea, then padded into the kitchen to make herself some tea, trying to move as quietly as possible so she wouldn't wake any of the other members of her military household. Her dreams had woken them too often as it was.

Sula found tea already steeped, in a serviceable stoneware pot that waited on the table. One of her irregulars, Ming Lin, sat at the table, sipping tea and looking at figures on a portable display she'd propped against a sugar bowl. She looked up. "Join me?"

"Thank you."

Sula poured the tea, and its floral aroma whispered into the room. Lin—who knew Sula's tastes—took her portable display in one hand and offered the sugar bowl with the other. Sula put three spoonsful of sugar in her tea, then took a seat.

"Can't sleep?" Lin asked.

"Not a whole night, usually," Sula said.

"All I did on *Striver* those last weeks was sleep and eat," Lin said. "Now I'm at normal gravity, what I want to do is dance. I'll probably be up for days."

Though Sula hadn't met her then, Ming Lin had been a pigtailed teenage volunteer in Sula's secret army during the Naxid War and specialized in hurling bombs into assemblies of Naxids, a skill that had proved useful during the fighting on *Striver.* After the peace, Lin had gone for a graduate degree at the Zanshaa College of Economics, and when Sula had been co-opted into the Convocation and stuck on the Committee for Banking and Exchange, Sula had hired her as a part-time adviser charged mainly with translating specialist financial jargon into something resembling understandable prose. Once the empire's economy began to tip into collapse nearly two years ago, Lin had proved expert at predicting what shambling financial institution, or tottering sector of manufacture or trade, was going to collapse next. Neither she nor Sula had been able to prevent the worst from happening, but Lin's clear-sightedness extended to opportunities for prospering amid the wreckage, and she'd made Sula a surprising amount of money while the empire's economy crumbled into ruin.

There was a lot of money to be made in catastrophe, Sula had learned. And in war, too.

The symmetry of Ming Lin's face was disturbed by a crooked, bumpy nose, the result of a fight with one of the Legion's Torminel fanatics. Fast-healers had repaired the damage quickly enough, but between urgency, neglect, and heavy gravities, the nose hadn't healed straight, and Lin now looked more like a street fighter than an academic.

Adding to the hard-bitten affect was Lin's hair, normally worn in a tangled rose-pink updo, but during the months of transit her dark brown roots had grown, and her hair now flopped around her ears. Maybe it was time for another style.

How did the fashionable bomb thrower style her hair these days? Sula had no idea.

Lin looked at the figures on her screen. "I'm trying to catch up with what the local markets are doing," she said. "It seems to me that the situation is so unusual that all everyone can do is pretend that things are normal."

"That's good," Sula said. She sipped tea, let the sugar sweetness flow over her palate. "Do we really want them using their imaginations?" she asked.

"Maybe not," said Lin. "But we'd better use ours. We're in a war now, and we've got to figure out a way to pay for it."

"We can't just coin more money?" Sula said. "The banks have to do what we say, I assume."

"Creating money builds inflation, and the effects of inflation are always felt unequally. You wouldn't want to be on a fixed income in that situation." She brushed pink hair tips from her face. "Of course, it takes a while for the effect of inflation to be seen, so if we just create money out of nothing, we should hope for a very short war."

Sula waved a hand. "Raise taxes?"

"Naturally." Lin nodded. "But that's always unpopular, and remember also that Terrans are only a minority here. Right now the other species seem to have adopted a wait-and-see attitude as far as the war goes, but if we start asking them to pay for it, they'll get a lot less enthusiastic."

Sula rubbed her forehead. The middle of the night was not the ideal time for this conversation, a horrific nightmare followed immediately by a discussion of war finance. "Borrowing?" she ventured.

"That way the people most concerned with the war's outcome will have a chance to support it. But of course if you sell bonds or whatever, there has to be a reasonable expectation that at the end of the day the investors will get their money's worth, and that will only happen if we win. You'd know better than I how *those* odds stack up."

"We have to hope," Sula said, "that Terrans will be willing to pay a lot not to be reduced to second-class citizens. Or lumps of radioactive carbon, depending on what policy Zanshaa settles on."

"That," said Lin, "would be a strong motivator."

Sula stared at her tea for a moment, then took a deep breath. "Could we talk about something else? I'm not sure I'm at my best right now."

"Of course." Lin turned off her display and refreshed her cup of tea, then settled herself into her chair. "You're going to get a command, of course, so you'll be off fighting. What am I going to do with myself then?"

"I'd hope you'd continue in an advisory capacity," Sula said.

"But where? You won't need me on a warship, I'd just be in the way."

"The planetary government, perhaps?"

Lin rubbed her broken nose. "I imagine they have their own economists." She laughed. "Maybe I can actually do the author tour that I was supposed to do in the first place."

Lin was the coauthor of *The Cosgrove Legacy*, a history of the financial collapse that made good use of the insider knowledge available as Sula's consultant. The book provided the only counternarrative to the government's claim that the decline was the result of a conspiracy by Terran criminals, politicians, and financiers, and it had been a huge success across the empire. When she'd fled to Harzapid on the *Striver*, she'd traveled openly, as a wildly popular author on an appearance tour.

"We'd have to make sure you have guards," Sula said.

Lin raised her eyebrows. "You have a way of making everything so cheerful," she said.

Sula waved a hand. "Sorry." She sighed. "What *else* shall we talk about?"

Lin laughed. "Well," she said. "I've always wanted to ask. What is Gareth Martinez really like?"

SULA MANAGED TO drowse for a while on the sofa before she was awakened by Constable First Class Gavin Macnamara, one of her servants. Tall, with a halo of curly brown hair, he was beginning his own day and was surprised to find her asleep on the couch. He apologized and backed out of the room, but she waved him back in and told him he might as well make breakfast.

So she had breakfast with her little household, Macnamara, Ming Lin, and Engineer First Class Shawna Spence, who during the Naxid War had manufactured the bombs that Ming Lin threw at the enemy. They were the people Sula trusted the most—perhaps the *only* people Sula trusted. Macnamara and Spence had earned that trust in one deadly confrontation after another, and Ming Lin had earned Sula's respect in the fight on *Striver* as well as for her war record and her financial expertise.

Macnamara and Spence were her servants, and Ming Lin an employee, but Sula would rather share a table with them than anyone else, and Fleet protocol could go bite itself. She'd been to enough formal dinners anyway, particularly since she'd been co-opted into the Convocation.

Sula had sweetened tea, sweet pastry loaded with sweet jam, and soft cheese covered with nuts and dripping with sticky syrup; and gradually she felt her better self emerge from the wreckage her twice-interrupted sleep had left behind. Her growing contentment was fractured when the door announced a caller, and Macnamara, looking at an image from the door cam on his hand comm, announced that Mr. Braga was waiting outside.

"Oh hell," Sula said. "Let him in. And make some more tea."

She took her tea to the front room to greet Hector Braga, whom she had known long ago as Lamey. He came into the room with his distinctive gliding gait, his thickening body clothed in a braided suit of shimmering green moiré silk, bright as a peacock, with a gold-threaded cravat and a handkerchief blossoming from his breast pocket like a frozen ice cream sculpture.

"Earthgirl!" he said. "Welcome to Harzapid!"

"You welcomed me yesterday," Sula said.

Without waiting for an invitation Lamey dropped onto a chair. "True, I was there at the airlock with everyone else," he said, "but we didn't get a chance to talk."

Sula settled into another chair. "Well. Let's talk then."

Lamey smiled. "Can I have breakfast?"

"There may be some pastry left." Macnamara was still hovering protectively in the room—he disliked Lamey even more than he disliked all Sula's other male friends—and she sent him to inquire. He returned with two pastries on a plate. Lamey looked up at him.

"Can I have some coffee?"

"You can have tea," Sula said. "It's being brewed."

Lamey gave a contented, catlike smile and settled into his chair with his pastry. Macnamara withdrew to the doorway.

"I'm on this committee with Roland Martinez and Lord Mehrang and some others," he said. "We're trying to give some political direction to what we're doing. You have a lot of experience with committees in the Convocation, so I've arranged for you to join them. The next meeting is tomorrow afternoon."

"I'm not very good on committees," Sula said. "I get out-voted on everything, and then I get blamed when what I didn't vote for goes wrong."

Lamey took a delicate bite of his pastry. "That's politics, Earthgirl. What did you expect?"

"I know I didn't expect to have to flee to Harzapid. Did you?"

He shrugged. "I half expected I'd have to flee *somewhere*. But I never expected the economy to collapse and that my friends would get blamed for it." He waved his hand with a pastry in it. "But we seem to have landed pretty well. All *you* have to do is win the war, and then our side will be in charge."

"Win the war," Sula repeated. "I'll work on it."

"So you'll join our little committee?"

"I'll hate it."

"Unfortunately your questions in yesterday's meeting knocked everyone on their ear—I heard about all that from Captain Vijana—and now you're obliged to help find answers for them."

Sula rubbed the pad of scar tissue on her right thumb. "I'll attend," she said, "if Lady Michi doesn't assign me some other work."

"That's all I ask."

Macnamara returned with Lamey's tea, which he put on a side table by Lamey's chair. Lamey thanked him, and Mac-namara wordlessly withdrew.

Sula studied the self-satisfied, superbly dressed man who sat across from her. They had first met on Spannan, when she had been a schoolgirl named Gredel, and Lamey had been a young linkboy in charge of a crew who earned their living through hijackings, gambling, drugs, usury, and violence. She had been seventeen—or fourteen in Earth years, a fact she knew because once she learned the formula for converting one to the other, she now did so automatically whenever anyone mentioned their age. Seventeen or fourteen, she was not so young that she couldn't be a gangster's girlfriend.

She hadn't been Lady Sula then, but a kid from the streets, different from the others only in the obsession with Terran history that resulted in her nickname of "Earthgirl." And then Lady Sula—the real one—had turned up in their lives, blond and green-eyed and lost. Caro Sula burned through her money and her luck as fast as possible while buoyed by supplies of drugs and alcohol—and in the end she had, with a little help, suffered a convenient overdose.

Gredel hadn't spent her life on the streets without knowing when to take advantage of an opportunity. Caro Sula, suitably weighted, went into the river, and Gredel adopted a new identity, a new bank account, and a new accent, and had then gone to the Cheng Ho Academy and a career in the military. She'd assumed Lamey was dead—people in his line of work didn't live long—but then two years ago he'd turned up at her door in Zanshaa with a scheme to make her a member of the Convocation, the empire's supreme body.

Lamey was the only person who knew that she wasn't the genuine Lady Sula, and she was obliged to cooperate with his plans. They were in a pact of mutual annihilation, for while he could bring her down, she also knew enough about him to send him to the executioner.

When she'd fled Zanshaa on *Striver*, she hadn't told Lamey she was leaving—but then he'd hitched a ride here with the Martinez family aboard *Corona*. So—at least until she boarded a warship and went to battle—she and Lamey were in some kind of partnership again.

Lamey took a sip of his tea. "I've got a new line," he said. "I'm going to develop a planet."

"That'll keep you busy for a few generations," Sula said.

"Esley," Lamey said.

"Ah. Hah." Esley was the native world of the shaggy Yormaks, and until recently most of its surface had been reserved for the native inhabitants. Until the Yormaks had rebelled a few years ago, when most were killed and the survivors confined to small reserves. Now the vast empty world, under the patronage of Lord Mehrang, would be opened to settlement, but it was a cold world, with most of its water locked up in glaciers, and a lot of changes would have to be made before a suitable population of imperial citizens could thrive there.

"I'm sure Lord Mehrang had plans for Esley," Sula said. "And those plans are all on hold on account of the war."

"They're on hold because financing has dried up," Lamey said. "And the contractors who were going to do the work are blockaded. So—" Again he deployed his catlike smile.

"So you're putting together an organization to help him out?"

"Of course."

"What do you know about how to develop worlds?"

Lamey laughed. "I don't need to know anything. The Mehrang family has been sitting on the plans for generations, waiting for the Convocation's permission to proceed. All I have to do is organize people into doing the work, and if I run into trouble, I can consult Roland."

Roland Martinez and his family owned the only companies in the empire with experience in developing new worlds, but all their assets were far away, except for those on Rol-mar, and those were tied up on what for all intents and purposes was a planetwide strike.

Sula was reasonably sure Lamey was creating an organization devoted to diverting Lord Mehrang's money into Lamey's pocket, but then she didn't know Lord Mehrang and didn't care whether he lost his money or not. Lamey's project might also keep Lamey too busy to harass Sula, so that would be a bonus.

"I'm not supposed to be a part of this company, am I?" Sula said.

"No," Lamey said. "Not unless you want to be. But I'd be obliged if you'd talk to your rich friends about investing."

"My rich friends got left behind on Zanshaa," Sula said.

"Michi Chen's about to put you in charge of dozens of officers with money," Lamey said. He waved a hand and laughed. "There's no better investment than a planet! That planet's not going anywhere!"

"Ask the people who invested in Rol-mar," Sula said, "how secure they feel about their investment right now."

"Rol-mar is Roland's problem," Lamey said. He took a sip of tea, then leaned back in his chair. "We expect Terrans will invest in the war," he said. "We'll have to do that, for our own survival. But other species—with all the financial chaos going on, they're going to be looking for safe places to put their money."

"I'm not sure about your timing," Sula said, "but good luck with that. And I'll be sure to mention you to my rich friends who happen to belong to other species."

"Lady Koridun, for instance," said Lamey.

Sula had no intention of letting Lamey anywhere near Lady Koridun's money.

"I'll be sure to tell her everything about you," she said.

He laughed. "That's my Earthgirl!" he said.

After Lamey left, Sula went back into the kitchen and found Ming Lin looking once more at columns of figures on her portable display. She looked over her shoulder as Sula entered.

"Is Braga serious about starting a company to develop Esley?" she asked. "In the current climate? To say the least, that's going to be challenging."

"He's not going to develop anything," Sula said. "His company's going to be a complete fraud."

Lin's eyes widened. "Oh. Well." She turned back to her figures and nodded. "That makes sense, then," she said.

CHAPTER 4

Photos of Martinez's family floated around the perimeter of his desk display: Terza with her harp leaning on her shoulder, gaze inward as she concentrated on her music; Gareth the Younger aboard *Corona* just a couple months ago, peering at a fish in one of the carrier's tanks; and Martinez's daughter, Yaling, who for her own safety had been sent with her aunt Walpurga to live with her grandparents on Laredo, the photo caught at her fifth birthday celebrations on *Ensenada*, before Michi launched her coup and communications between Harzapid and the rest of the empire had been slashed.

Yaling, who had been sent to Laredo so that if Martinez and Gareth Junior were both killed, Martinez and Terza would still have an heir. Roland, the oldest Martinez brother, had insisted.

Good of Roland, Martinez thought, to have so thoughtfully considered all eventualities.

In the display, Martinez's family gracefully orbited the Structured Mathematics Display, where he had been working out calculations relating to the escape of Jeremy Foote's Light

Squadron Eight from Colamote, along with the presumed pursuit of the two heavy squadrons from Zarafan. The original calculations that suggested Foote was in little danger, worked up by one of Michi's staff, were sound as far as they went, but they showed evidence of haste. The suppositions on which they'd been based were sound, but alternate suppositions hadn't been considered.

The original calculations assumed that Foote would push his squadron at a constant acceleration of two gravities. Two gravities was hard on the crew, but not unendurable—but also it was unlikely a commander would keep up that pace for an entire twenty-nine-hour day. There would be breaks for meals, for bathing, for maintenance on hard-stressed ship systems.

Martinez knew that Foote was a yachtsman, and a good one, accustomed to harder accelerations. Even with meal and bathroom breaks, Martinez thought Foote might push his crews harder and turn up sooner than the calculations indicated.

But so might Rukmin and her two heavy squadrons from Zarafan. The calculations assumed that it would take Rukmin a day and a half to ready her forces for departure, and that would be very prompt for peacetime, but Martinez thought that Rukmin would be burning to avenge the two squadrons Foote had annihilated at Colamote, and get moving within hours, and burn hard once she got going. That Rukmin was a Torminel, considered the most pugnacious species under the Praxis, was another factor worthy of consideration.

Martinez looked at his calculations, and then viewed his

family as they silently orbited the display. He turned to the display on his left sleeve and called Michi Chen's office. "I'm sending the fleetcom some figures," he told the secretary who answered, "and then I'll need to see Lady Michi in person."

"WELL THEN," SAID Michi. She glittered in her dress uniform, on her way to a formal supper. "I'm promoting you to senior squadron commander, and I'm giving you *Bombardment of Los Angeles* for your flagship, with Elissa Dalkeith for your flag captain. You've successfully worked together before, and I imagine you'll do so again." She looked up at Martinez. "Walk with me, please."

An aide handed her a billed uniform cap, which she tucked under an arm. She left her suite on *Perfection of the Praxis* and made her way to the elevator. Martinez followed a half-pace behind in a cloud of her floral scent, their footfalls absorbed by soft carpeting.

"If Rukmin's pursuing Foote," Michi said, "you'll need to wipe her out with few or no casualties on our side. We can't afford casualties, and since you specialize in battles of annihilation, I'm going to have to trust that you'll produce another one."

Martinez resisted the temptation to preen. The Martinez Method had been deployed in three battles, and each had produced spectacular one-sided victories even though Martinez hadn't technically been in command at any of them.

But now Martinez had jumped several grades in rank and had his first squadron command as well as permission to use his own tactics. He almost began to hope that Rukmin was on Foote's trail.

"I'm giving you Prince Huang as your tactical officer," Michi continued.

"Prince?" Martinez asked. "He's from a world where they have princes?" Which, if true, would be surprising indeed, because anything suggestive of monarchy was forbidden. Authority under the Praxis was collegiate, shared primarily between Peers whose families had proved reliable over centuries. That's why they were called "Peers," for each was, in theory, the equal of all others, and each with proper training, doctrine, and attitude, capable of doing the same work.

Martinez felt that the fact he was considered replaceable was in itself a complete critique of the theory.

"'Prince' is his forename," Michi said. "He's a kind of cousin of mine, and he's a genius."

"Ah." Martinez didn't quite know how to respond to this declaration. *I'll be the judge of that* would have been an honest answer, but not tactful under the circumstances. Instead he said, "Is 'Prince' an allowed name?"

"Apparently."

People were required to choose from a list of acceptable names when giving a name to their children, names without subversive content. There were no children named Freedom, and no Jesuses or Vishnus or Rebels. That was one reason why names tended to repeat themselves in families generation after generation—once you found a safe name, you felt free to reuse it.

Michi reached the elevator and passed her command key

over the sensor, which would cause one of the elevators to abandon any other duties and leap to the aid of the fleet's commander.

"He's explained his tactical ideas to me," Michi went on, "but I don't quite grasp them. I think you're in a better position to make sense of them."

What if they don't make sense at all? Martinez wondered.

Well, he thought. It's not as if he'd actually *need* a tactical officer.

He could do it all.

Elevator doors opened and revealed an empty cage where the permanent floor, roof, and side paneling were yet to be installed. They entered.

"Entry hatch," Michi told the elevator, and the elevator began to ascend, girders, conduits, and crossbraces sliding past. Michi turned again to Martinez.

"You—or more properly Dalkeith—will have the best crew I can give you, but at least half the officers and most of the enlisted will either be untried in their current positions, or brought out of retirement, or both—and you won't have a full complement. But at least the rest of your command will be at full strength—Carmody and the other captains left the ring with complete crews, and if you need to, you'll be able to shift your flag to another ship once you join them."

"Yes, Lady Fleetcom."

Maybe, he thought, he *couldn't* do it all, not if it involved training a crew in addition to working up a battle plan and carrying it out.

Still, he thought. Command of two squadrons—that made

it a *fleet*, albeit the smallest fleet possible. And whether Dalkeith's cruiser was quite up to the mark wasn't going to change the outcome, which would be that Rukmin's force would be ambushed, attacked, and annihilated.

Nothing like another victory to pump our side's morale, he thought. Not to mention enrage Supreme Commander Tork and tempt him into something ill-advised.

Speaking of which . . .

"Lady Fleetcom," he ventured. "Are you planning on using the battleship as your flagship in the confrontation with Tork?"

She gave him a sidelong look. "Why do you ask?"

"Once the enemy finds the only battleship in our order of battle," Martinez said, "you'll become the focus of the most savage attack Tork can mount."

"Well," Michi said. "I think I know where you're going with this, but since you've assigned me the role of naïve interlocutor, I'll oblige you and respond as you expect, and I'll say, 'Shouldn't a commander put herself in the position of maximum danger?'"

Martinez looked at her. *No one ever said she wasn't smart*, he thought.

"I was planning to say that taking those sorts of risks should be someone else's job," Martinez said, "and that I'd put that someone in command of *Perfection of the Praxis* and use it to lure Tork into making an unwise attack on the wrong target." He cleared his throat. "But if you would rather I say something else, I'll oblige."

The elevator came to a halt, and the doors rolled open to reveal the battleship's entrance hall, all polished pale marble, recessed lighting, and a dark-paneled desk intended for a polite receptionist, but now occupied by armed guards who stood ready both to direct workers to their assigned jobs, and to repel any attack. Michi stepped out of the elevator.

"I don't have time to think of something else for you to say," she said. "But if, in between working up your new command and suffering through a long, brutal acceleration, you can work out a way to divert most of Tork's attention onto this useless, half-finished barge, feel free to send me a memo."

She cast a smile over her shoulder as she walked toward the hatch, and then was gone.

MARTINEZ HAD BEEN ready for months to assume command of *something*, so his storage space on *Corona* was filled with trunks and bags packed with the ridiculous amount of gear a commander was supposed to haul aboard his ship: uniforms, wine and spirits, coffee and tea, delicacies for the squadron commander's pantry, monogrammed crystal wineglasses, large silver boats designed to hold a half-dozen champagne bottles submerged in crushed ice, decanters, silverware, plates, and place settings for a formal dinner of up to sixteen. Multiplied, as always, by the necessity of catering to the dietary needs of all the species under the Praxis— Torminel, who preferred their flesh raw, required scrapers, specialized tools for extracting marrow, and larding needles complete with lard, whereas the Lai-own liked picks designed to clean their peg teeth, and Daimong with their complicated mouth parts preferred their food made into small packages.

Of course, given that the war at present was Humanity vs. Everyone Else, Martinez would command ships crewed only by Terrans, so conveniences for the other species could be put in storage for the now. But, in the event of peace, he could see himself obliged to host dignitaries—even Fleet officers— from other species, and in that case all the species-specific equipment would be necessary.

After leaving *Perfection of the Praxis*, Martinez went straight to *Corona* and found it deserted, discovering only a trace of Terza's vetiver scent floating in the air, and called his orderly on his sleeve display.

"Yes, my lord." Khalid Alikhan had an upright bearing, iron-gray hair, and the curled, upturned mustachios favored by senior petty officers. He was a retired master weaponer who had returned to the Fleet as Martinez's servant, as well as something of a good luck charm. In addition to brushing Martinez's uniforms and polishing his shoes, Alikhan was a conduit to the hermetic world of the Fleet's enlisted personnel and the petty officers who kept the warships running while the officers did their decorative best to pretend they were in charge.

Martinez realized he had less need for an orderly than Michi had for an experienced petty officer, so he'd sent Alikhan to the crews that were converting the non-Terran ships to human use.

"I'll need you back on *Corona* to shift my gear to the *Los*

Angeles," Martinez said. "We'll be launching sometime tomorrow, as soon as all the crew reports on board."

"Very good, my lord," said Alikhan. His lips narrowed slightly, which in his unruffled expression was the equivalent to signaling major distress.

"Yes?" Martinez said.

Alikhan took a breath, then spoke. "I am no longer young, my lord," he said. "I don't know how well I will be able to stand up to acceleration. Some days I think I would do better to remain here on the ring and continue my work with the conversion crews."

Martinez preferred not to respond to this directly. "And how is that work coming?" he asked.

"It is without doubt the greatest shambles in the history of the Fleet," Alikhan said. "Too many people don't know their jobs, and that includes the officers, and on top of it we're shorthanded. I'd hate to have to bring any of these ships into battle in anything like their current condition."

"That's precisely what I'm going to have to do with *Bombardment of Los Angeles,*" Martinez said. "I'm going to have to shake down the ship on the way to combat, and hope that I've got enough experienced crew on board to keep us from catastrophe."

Alikhan was silent. *He's going to make me ask,* Martinez thought.

"If you feel that the accelerations are a hazard," he said, "I won't order you to join me. But the situation is urgent, the job is more or less what you're doing now, and I would very much value your collaboration in the work."

Martinez saw a shimmer in Alikhan's eyes. "I will be honored to join you, my lord," he said.

Somewhere inside his chest, Martinez felt a little knot of anxiety dissolve. "Thank you," he said. "I won't forget this."

And then he thought, *What if I've just killed him?* Alikhan had spent thirty years in the weapons bays and had been with Martinez for another ten years on top of that, and he was perfectly right that he was too old to safely undergo the sorts of accelerations that might be required in combat.

Alikhan volunteered, he told himself. But Martinez knew perfectly well that he'd manipulated Alikhan into offering his services.

It's my job to keep them all *alive*, he reminded himself. And he *needed* Alikhan.

"I'm going to need a cook and a pair of signalers," he said.

"I won't be much use finding you a cook," Alikhan said. "But there seem to be two kinds of signalers available. Would you prefer an embryo or a grandparent?"

"One of each, I think," Martinez said. "One can teach the other."

"Very good, my lord." Alikhan paused in thought. "I think I can recommend a grandparent, sir. I served with Lalita Banerjee in the old *Pride*, and she was most competent. She's working here at rehabilitating old comm units, and I saw her yesterday. She retired as a warrant officer first class, though, and you may prefer a lieutenant."

"Thank you for the recommendation," Martinez said. "I'll look into her. And rank seems to me no boundary, since we seem to be handing out promotions with a liberal hand." He smiled. "Would you like a commission for yourself, by the way?"

He made the offer only to enjoy the look of horror on Alikhan's face. "Thank you, no, my lord," he said firmly.

Martinez ended the call. He thought he knew where to find a cook. *Corona's* civilian crew—those who were fit, anyway—had been absorbed into the military as soon as the carrier had arrived, and that included the kitchen staff. He could order one of *Corona's* chefs aboard *Los Angeles* and save him or her from the horror and tedium of serving uniformly bland food to the enlisted masses.

Before he could summon his personal chef his sleeve button chirped, and he answered a call from Elissa Dalkeith, who thanked him for her promotion to captain and for his requesting her as his flag captain.

Martinez had made no such promotion and no such request, but he said, "You're very welcome" anyway. "Well deserved," he added. "Though it wasn't just my recommendation, it was a joint decision by myself and by Fleet Commander Chen."

"I'll send her my thanks as well," Dalkeith said in her child's lisping voice. "Will you join me in an inspection of the ship?"

"I have to find my staff first," Martinez said.

"The ship will need inspecting before we launch."

"I'll be happy to join you, but it will have to be tomorrow."

"Yes, Lord Captain." She hesitated. "Or did you get promoted as well?"

He offered a laugh. "I seem to be a senior squadcom now."

She congratulated him, an irregularly promoted captain congratulating her irregularly promoted superior. After the conversation ended, Martinez issued orders requisitioning *Corona*'s head chef, Marivic Mangahas, and promoted her to master cook. Martinez knew he was no judge of high cuisine, but Mangahas had been praised by those who were—including his sister Vipsania, who rarely praised anyone. He sent Mangahas to purchase supplies for his personal pantry, and to bring them to *Corona* until *Los Angeles* was ready to receive them.

After he also requisitioned Lalita Banerjee, the post of second signaler was still open, but fortunately Michi had granted Martinez access to the Fourth Fleet's personnel database. He cast a look at the list of officers who had recently graduated from signals courses, found the one with the highest score, and looked at his file. There was nothing indicating potential trouble, and so he sent a message inviting Sublieutenant Santana to join him on *Los Angeles*. The reply was immediate and wholehearted.

Junior officers, Martinez thought, could be counted on to respond enthusiastically to a personal invitation from the second-most-decorated captain in the empire. (Sula, unfortunately, had more medals than he did.)

In addition to his staff, an officer of Martinez's rank was also entitled to four servants. Alikhan and Mangahas were all he really needed, so he filled his foursome with a pair of experienced petty officers that he could loan to Dalkeith, who could employ them wherever they were required.

Martinez walked to *Corona*'s bar and made himself a cup

of coffee and reflected on the last few minutes. He'd assembled his staff in a highly unusual fashion, without the standard favors and trading, and without accepting officers on the recommendations of his seniors. There had been too little time for any of that.

Martinez drank his coffee while using his sleeve display to compose a list of tasks that needed to be completed before *Los Angeles's* departure, and then, musing into his coffee, he heard Marietta Li's high-pitched laugh echoing from somewhere, and he knew he wasn't alone on *Corona*. To judge by the tone of her laughter, Marietta wasn't alone, either.

He wasn't interested in interrupting her, and he decided it was high time he talked to Terza anyway, so he retreated to his quarters and used the wall display in the lounge to call his wife. She appeared on the screen with an owlish expression and her face slightly distorted, which told him he was seeing the video feed from her hand comm.

He saw that she wasn't in her uniform, but dressed in a smart lilac crepe top with a ruffled collar. "Where are you?" he asked.

"I'm interviewing headmasters," Terza said, "trying to find Chai-chai a school."

Having a son nicknamed "Chai-chai" was a consequence of Martinez having married into a Peer family as ancient and established as the Chens, where the oldest boy was always "Chai-chai," generation after generation, while a younger sister was "Mei-mei," the names coming from an ancient language now known to no one but scholars. Only a few words had been passed down to the Chens, and Martinez had been told the nicknames only meant "Boy-boy" and "Younger Sister-younger sister." This seemed self-evident to the point of absurdity, but apparently a tradition this ancient was not to be denied, ridiculous or not.

"Good luck with the headmasters," Martinez said.

"Fortunately your reputation hasn't preceded you here," Terza said.

Martinez feigned innocence. "What reputation?"

"For hectoring teachers and administrators when your son doesn't get high enough marks."

"There is something about a teacher's education," Martinez said, "that forces their minds into rigid and unimaginative corridors. I'm just trying to pry open those corridors a little and throw in a little light."

Terza sighed. "Can you at least stay away from the schools till I get Chai-chai enrolled?"

"I will," Martinez said. "I'm shipping out tomorrow."

Terza's face froze. Then she took a long breath and spoke. "You're on *Corona*?"

"Yes."

"I'll come at once. The headmasters can wait."

"Where's Chai-chai?"

"In the hands of his aunt Michi's staff," Terza said. "He's getting a tour of *Perfection of the Praxis*."

Odd, Martinez thought, that Michi hadn't mentioned this when they'd spoken an hour or two ago. But then she'd been in a hurry to get to her formal dinner, and maybe thought he knew already.

"That should keep him busy for a while," Martinez said.

"I'll see you soon." Terza ended the call, and Martinez contemplated the blank wall screen for a moment, then decided to make himself another coffee.

There was so much to do before he left, he wouldn't be doing a lot of sleeping between now and *Los Angeles*'s departure. Anything that would aid him in staying awake . . .

When Terza arrived, carrying a crystal goblet of shimmering, silver Cavado wine, Martinez was listening to a message from Carmody, the ginger-whiskered squadron commander whose command he was usurping.

"I'm a little relieved, to tell you the truth," Carmody said. "I'm not exactly comfortable having the fate of the human race resting on my shoulders. I'm doing my best, but I'm feeling a little lonely out here."

Terza looked at the screen with amusement as she passed through the lounge on her way to an inner room of the suite. Martinez gave her a little wave of one hand—he needn't pay full attention to the video message, because Carmody was forty light-minutes away and it was impossible to have a conversation.

"I've been running constant drills using your Method," Carmody said, "and even though I don't understand it terribly well, I think the results have been splendid. If only we had some idea what we'd really be up against, I'm sure we'd be even better." Carmody straightened his shoulders and looked directly into the camera.

"You are very welcome to this force, Captain Martinez," he said. "I will look forward to welcoming you in person."

Martinez considered his response, then straightened his uniform tunic, and triggered the camera.

"Thank you for the generous welcome, Captain Carmody," he said. "We've fought together in two brilliant victories in the last war, and I have every confidence that our next encounter with an enemy will be as triumphant as the last." He nodded in the direction of the camera.

"I shall look forward to seeing you face-to-face, and in the meantime, I'd appreciate it if you could send me records of your last three drills. If you haven't already received orders from Fleetcom Chen, you should chart the most efficient course for Wormhole One and Toley. You should also prepare drills based on encountering Rukmin's force from Zarafan, both with and without the presence of Foote's light squadron."

He made an attempt to smile. "That should tell you all you need to know. I'll be in touch once my own plans are more evolved."

Martinez ended the call and sent it to its destination forty light-minutes away, turned to find his coffee, and saw Terza standing in the doorway, and his heart gave a lurch. She stood half in shadow, wearing stockings and a bed jacket of quilted white satin. Her long dark eyes were fixed on his. A little smile crossed her face, showing she was satisfied with her intended effect, and she turned to drink from the goblet of silver wine. Then she turned to him again.

"We don't have a lot of time," she said.

His breath caught in his throat. "I suppose we don't."

Terza was being unusually direct. Normally her passions came wrapped in a slightly unearthly tranquility, and she preferred in her serenity to accept and reflect his own desires before revealing her own.

But. As she said, there wasn't a lot of time.

Her vetiver perfume whispered into his senses. She took another swallow of wine. "The last time you went to war," she said, "we had seven days together. Now we've had something like nine years together, but it feels the same."

He took a step toward her. "How does it feel?"

"Like—" She searched for words. "Like anything can happen now. Worlds can end, new worlds can be born. Everything can twist and distort and change when we're not looking, and we won't know how till we look through the curtain. But . . ." She hesitated. "But we might win through, if we can hold firm to what we desire."

Thoughts flamed in his skull and turned to ash. Martinez approached her and took her in his arms. Her lips had the bright, rich taste of the Cavado wine with an earthy undertaste that was the flavor of Terza's blood and flesh and self. "I'll be back," he said.

"Of course you will. Victories are what you do." She kissed him, then rested her cheek on his shoulder. He inhaled the warm scent of her hair, felt the warmth of her body through the quilted satin. He could see past her into the bedroom, where in haste she had scattered her clothing on her way to the closet and her bed jacket.

Terza tipped her head back and finished the last of the wine. "I wish I'd skipped the wine and got some whisky or brandy instead," she said. "I want to feel the fire."

"I can try to kindle a spark," Martinez said.

"I know you will."

She took his hand and drew him into the shadows of the darkened bedroom, lit only by a pale spill of light from the half-closed closet. He closed the door behind him as she tossed the heavy crystal goblet onto a chair, where it rocked for a moment glittering, and then was still. As she undid the buttons of his uniform tunic, his sleeve display gave a discreet chime.

"I don't think this call is important," he said.

"I think you're right," she said.

In the hour that followed he didn't think of Sula once. Or so he told himself later.

CHAPTER 5

An earlier incarnation of the heavy cruiser *Bombardment of Los Angeles* had been crewed with Terrans and destroyed at Felarus on the opening day of the Naxid Rebellion. The latest vessel to bear the name had been constructed as part of the postwar building program, and it was crewed with Torminel. Since Michi Chen's coup *Los Angeles* had been hastily converted to a Terran ship. Since Terrans and Torminel had a similar physique, the conversion had been quick, and some of the Torminel furniture was deemed acceptable for human use.

Martinez's wedge-shaped dining/meeting room featured a wedge-shaped table and had chairs and a table intended for Torminel. The table was just a table, usable by any species, and the chairs were broader in the seat than those intended for humans, but they were well padded and comfortable enough.

It was the room's decoration that Martinez resented. Squadron Leader Lokan, the previous occupant, had been a booster of the martial arts, and the walls were covered with detailed mosaics of Torminel wrestling, with heavily furred participants in shorts and vests grappling, strangling, joint-locking, throwing, pinning, and sinking fangs into one an-other, all depicted in dark, muddy colors suited to Torminel nocturnal vision. The view was not one that would stimulate anyone's digestion.

Lokan's influence extended through Martinez's entire suite. His office next door still featured shelves filled with trophies won by Lokan in competition, and the bedroom featured Lokan's taste in erotica, positions that looked much the same as the wrestling except with more imaginative use of fangs.

Martinez was thankful that when Michi's mutineers stormed in to arrest Lokan, they'd been armed with guns. If they'd tried to wrestle him into submission, there would have been blood.

As for the Torminel erotica, he was unable to maintain even a clinical interest. He'd cover the walls with pictures of his family as soon as he could arrange it.

Martinez's staff were deployed around the table, each with a cup of coffee or tea and a slice of Mangahas's coconut sponge cake. Prince Huang, the supposed genius that Michi had assigned as his tactical officer, was small, with delicate, open features below a shock of black hair. Despite his being a graduate of the Cheng Ho Academy and his sublieutenant's shoulder boards, he looked no older than fourteen. Marti-nez supposed that as he was a Peer, he would be styled "Lord Prince," but that seemed too absurd.

Lalita Banerjee looked as if she could be Prince Huang's grandmother. Gray-haired, round-faced, and corpulent, she had served in the Fleet for thirty years, rising to warrant officer first class, as high as a commoner could expect, before retiring at the end of the Naxid War without having seen a shot fired in anger. She had returned to the colors soon after Michi had seized the Fourth Fleet, and Martinez promoting her to lieutenant had come as a surprise. Her officer's tunic had been stitched together by machine just that morning and was uncomfortable and stiff. Her shoulder boards were bright, and she had looked surprised when Martinez had first addressed her as "my lady." All officers were entitled to the compliment, whether they were Peers or not.

Banerjee was only a few years younger than Alikhan, but Martinez had less concern for her suffering under high gees. Studies showed that overweight women handled acceleration better than anyone, even the fittest of young men.

Sublieutenant Lord Aitor Santana was from Martinez's home world of Laredo, a burly man with full, dark brows and a thick horseshoe mustache that dropped from the corners of his mouth straight to the jawline. He looked formidable enough to stand a chance against Squadron Leader Lokan in a wrestling match.

Santana was just the age to have been inspired to join the Fleet by Martinez's success in the Naxid War, which of course had been publicized more thoroughly on Laredo than elsewhere; but Santana had even less patronage in the service than Martinez and would probably never rise past lieutenant unless he found someone to look after him. Martinez was willing to be that person, if Santana proved good at his job.

Santana watched the others carefully and spoke little, as if he were trying to work out how best to fit himself into this company. Just promoted to officer's rank, he had been finishing a communication course on Harzapid when the war suddenly made his skills extremely valuable.

"My lord, my lady," Martinez said, looking at Santana and Banerjee. "I'm going to need you to practice signals with each other. The success of any engagement depends on prompt and understandable communication, and you're going to have to communicate not with a single squadron, but with two, perhaps three." He cleared his throat. "I'm going to send you recordings of actual Command room orders given during combat in the last war. Any responses by the signalers have been stripped out of the recordings, so I'll want you to respond to those orders as if they were real. We'll see how well and clearly you can transmit orders under extreme time pressure." He picked up his cup of coffee. "Any questions?"

"No, my lord." Banerjee's soft voice indicated how intimidated she was by this company.

Santana looked somewhat doubtful, then spoke. "I haven't trained this way, Lord Squadcom," he said. "So I feel I should warn you that I'm not going to be very good at first."

That was honesty, at least. "We'll be accelerating for weeks before there's an engagement," Martinez said. "If there actually *is* an engagement, I mean. I'd also like you to practice while the ship's at high acceleration, because it's unlikely we're going to fight battles at a nice, steady one gravity."

"Yes, Lord Squadcom."

Martinez took a piece of coconut sponge cake, then turned to Prince Huang. "I've had Squadron Commander Carmody send me the records of his last three exercises. I haven't had a chance to look at the records, so I'd appreciate your analysis."

"Yes, Lord Squadcom, of course." Huang took a deliberate taste of his cake, then added, "If you think that's the best use of my time."

Martinez paused in surprise. "You have a suggestion, Lord Lieutenant?"

Huang's answer was prompt. "I think I would be best employed in acquainting officers of a new tactical system based on employing an alternative fractal dimension. If you'd allow me to use one of the displays . . ."

Without waiting for permission Huang shifted a presentation from his sleeve display to a larger screen, flanked by a pair of snarling Torminel wrestlers, on one of the walls. Martinez recognized the Structured Mathematics Display, and his eyes were dazzled by a series of complicated mathematical formulae as they scrolled across the screen.

Huang darted a cursor around the display. "You see, my lord—" he began, and was then interrupted by the alarm for zero gravity.

"Ten minutes to launch," came the announcement. "All crew to prepare for null gravity followed by acceleration."

Martinez rose from his chair. "We don't have time for a presentation now, Lord Lieutenant, and I very much doubt that we'll have a chance to drill our ships in a new tactical system by the time we meet the enemy."

"It won't take that long to learn," Huang said. "It's all in the formula, all you have to do is follow it."

"You can make a presentation to me later," Martinez said. "In the meantime, I'd be obliged if you'd spend the next day or so analyzing Carmody's exercises."

Huang seemed willing enough. "Certainly, Lord Squadcom."

Martinez addressed the whole group. "You can join me in the flag officer's station or spend the acceleration in your beds. Entirely up to you. Dismissed."

The others rose from their chairs, braced in salute, and left the study. Alikhan came in to clear the table.

"Will you be requiring your vac suit, my lord?" Alikhan said.

"I hope not." Martinez took a single forkful of the sponge cake, tasted coconut and citrus, and handed the plate and the fork to Alikhan.

"I'll just use sanitary fatigues," Martinez decided. Acceleration was hard on the bladder. "I won't be needing your assistance."

"Very well, Lord Squadcom."

Martinez changed into a jumpsuit, and with his groin gently cupped by miraculous hydrostatic technology, he left his sleeping cabin and crossed the hall to the flag officer station. Three decks forward of Command, where Dalkeith and her officers controlled the ship, Martinez's oval-shaped station held just five workstations, of which only four would be occupied. From here Martinez would maneuver the squadrons Michi had placed under his authority—or would, once *Los Angeles* rendezvoused with Carmody's force. At least the room had no mosaics of wrestlers—instead there were only bare walls of dark gray broken by large video displays. Martinez stepped through the rings on the acceleration couch, sat in his place, and let the couch swing on its gimbals once it took his weight. He reached over his head, drew down the displays, and locked them in place. As he switched the screens on, Banerjee and Santana entered and took their places.

A one-minute alarm rang through the ship. Martinez turned his displays to views of the ship's exterior—at the moment there was little to see but the long gleaming runway of Harzapid's ring—from this perspective it looked completely flat—with warships moored nose-in on either side. The planet itself was hidden behind the ring, though its glow was visible on the north and south edges of the vast station.

Another alarm clattered, and suddenly *Los Angeles* was free of the ring and floating into space—planetary rings were set just at escape velocity, so that anything released from the ring would drift into the void instead of falling toward the world below. Martinez felt a brief stab of vertigo, and then realized he was floating—he'd forgot to strap himself in. As he busied himself with his straps, he realized that he hadn't been on a warship in nearly ten years, and that it wasn't only the cadets and retirees who were going to need to polish their skills.

Through the displays he saw Harzapid's ring recede, and the relative positions of the ships, installations, and the vast spreading solar collectors move as the ring rotated beneath *Los Angeles*. Then his inner ear eddied again as the ship altered its heading, and the rings on his acceleration couch sang as his seat swung.

As *Bombardment of Los Angeles* drifted farther from the ring, Martinez could finally see Harzapid's poles emerge from behind the ring, which gave him his first glimpse of the planet that played involuntary host to the Fourth Fleet. Harzapid was a glory of brilliant color, with blue-green oceans, white clouds, and green continents snaking with silver rivers. A whole bright, brilliant world, inhabited by billions of people, that Martinez had never visited despite his time in the system.

Corona had docked nearly a month ago, but he'd spent all his time on the ring, almost all of it in the Fleet dockyard, in a frenzy of work.

Well, the frenzy wasn't going to stop any time soon.

But still he felt a powerful longing to feel a world under his feet, to breathe air that hadn't been recycled, to look up at clouds drifting overhead. His three-month journey on *Corona* had been luxurious, but he'd still been trapped on a small ship with the same people every day. Harzapid's ring was a magnificent structure, but it was still a mass of corridors and artificial light and functional design, *Corona* made gigantic. The Fleet dockyard was a vast armory, bustling and purposeful, that was nothing more than a giant machine enclosing him—it molded him to its purpose, not the other way around.

A sense-memory rose in him, the scent of his own garden on Zanshaa, the lu-doi blossoms in their sweetness.

A pair of brief hisses told him that Banerjee and Santana were using their med injectors, and again he felt chagrin that he'd forgotten an important piece of procedure. He reached for the pistol-shaped injector in the pocket on the side of his couch, drew it out, adjusted the dose, placed it to his neck, and injected himself with stew of chemicals that would keep his brain alert, his heart steady, and his blood vessels supple in the face of high gravities.

He returned the injector to its pocket just as the warning for accelerations blared out. He settled into his couch, and then felt a kick to his spine as the main engines fired. His couch swung to its deadpoint.

The screens showed Harzapid falling away as *Los Angeles* accelerated toward Wormhole One, but by then Martinez was no longer paying attention.

He was thinking of ways to beat the enemy.

SULA WALKED INTO the meeting room at the Empyrean Hotel and only then realized how she'd been had. It hadn't occurred to her to wonder who exactly was on this committee onto which Lamey had dragged her. Roland Martinez she had expected, and even though she didn't particularly like him, they'd worked together well enough in the Convocation— and she'd assumed Lamey and Lord Mehrang would be present, along with another Martinez sibling, Vipsania, who managed Imperial Broadcasting and its many outlets, and who she knew had arrived on *Corona* with the others. She assumed as well there might be local officials.

But for some reason she hadn't expected to find Terza Chen sitting perfectly composed behind the polished table, her brown uniform tunic immaculate, her black hair bound in a complicated knot behind her neck. The woman who had snatched Gareth Martinez from under Sula's nose, and then got pregnant half a second into their marriage so as to have a child to hold over her husband . . .

At the sight of Terza, Sula's breath seemed to evaporate from her lungs, and she took a little gasp that she hoped no one heard. But she kept moving into the room without, she thought, a hitch in her step, until she stood next to Roland Martinez.

The uniforms she'd ordered had arrived, and today she, like Roland, wore a wine-red convocate's jacket. Unlike Roland's, her jacket was cut like a Fleet uniform tunic, and she wore her Fleet shoulder boards and medals. She had more respect for some of her colleagues in the Fleet than she did for all the Convocation put together—now more so than ever, since the Convocation had fallen in line behind Lady Tuhon's coup to replace the Lord Senior with Lady Gruum, a more pliable figure who seemed willing to extend her grudge against the Martinez family to the entire Terran species.

If you'd just lost your money in a financial crisis, it made a certain kind of sense simply to kill a lot of people and take their cash. That seemed to be the new government's recovery plan.

"Lord Roland," Sula said. "May I present my aide, Ming Lin?"

"Aide," she thought, seemed a more impressive title than "employee."

"Very pleased to know you, Miss Lin," Roland said. "I read your book with great interest."

He was mentioned in the book, of course, as one of those who had seen the crash coming and managed to profit from it, thus becoming a criminal in the eyes of Lady Tu-hon and her faction. Roland resembled his younger brother with the same broad shoulders, long arms, big hands, and olive complexion. Like his brother, he spoke with the provincial Laredo accent that marked him, to High City ears, as an incurable rustic. Still, he had wedged his way into the Convocation and was the head of an influential faction—or had been, until he thought it wise to flee.

"Miss Lin has some interesting ideas about raising money," Sula said. "I thought she'd be a valuable resource."

"I'm sure she will be," Roland said.

Lin was looking less like a pirate today, having donned an indigo-blue silk suit of the sort she had only recently been able to afford, with peaked lapels, padded shoulders, and a double row of gold buttons. A coiffeuse had made the most out of her pink-tipped hair, and gelled it into something resembling her old updo, with the pink tips dancing over her collar. She looked very much like a well-dressed executive prepared to take charge of an unruly meeting.

The crooked nose, however, lent her a slightly sinister cast, as if she were a suspect in a Dr. An-ku mystery.

"I am happy to listen to Ming Lin on the subject of raising money," Roland said, smiling, "but I'm not sure if that's on the agenda for today."

"Perhaps we should speak to whoever's in charge of the agenda," said Sula.

Roland surrendered gracefully. "I believe *you* must be the one in charge, then. We're really very informal here."

Roland introduced the other members of her committee.

Lamey, still in his brilliant green suit. Lord Mehrang, an enormously tall, enormously obese, self-satisfied man with a pointed chin-beard and drooping mustache. Roland's sister Vipsania, who had adopted her husband's surname of Yoshitoshi, sat in an elegant brocaded gown with a high collar. Sula was moderately surprised that she hadn't brought a camera crew with her.

"And of course Lady Terza Chen," Roland said, for Ming Lin's benefit. He turned to Sula. "I assume you've met?"

"Before the last war," Sula said. She turned to Terza and did her best not to clench her teeth. "We met at a reception in the Li Palace, when we were all in mourning for the last Great Master." She took a breath and quieted the flutter she felt building in her voice. "You played your harp beautifully."

Terza looked up at Sula, her face tranquil, surprising warmth in her brown eyes. "You are very kind to remember," she said.

Roland turned from Terza to introduce others. There were, as Sula had anticipated, some local officials; and the lord governor of Harzapid was present through a video link from the planet's surface. His name was Binh, and he had been the secretary of public lands until—as a senior Terran in the planet's administration—Michi Chen had repurposed him as lord governor, with the Fourth Fleet's antimatter missiles to buttress his authority.

Roland suggested they all sit. The meeting room was unlike the half-finished room on *Perfection of the Praxis*: it had probably been unchanged for hundreds of years, with indirect lighting, dark wood paneling accented with yellow chesz-wood, a massive arculé wood table, and over all the scent of lemon polish. Celadon vases held sprays of lu-doi blossoms. Sula chose a seat for herself where she wouldn't have to look at Terza every second.

"Our latest member, Lady Sula," Roland said, "wishes to raise a point, so I've agreed to let her have the floor."

"More than one point, I'm afraid," Sula said. "Beginning with the question of what we call ourselves."

"Ourselves?" Lord Mehrang asked. "You mean this committee, or—?"

"Our . . . movement," Sula said. "Our cause. Our revolution."

Roland winced. "We can't call it a *revolution*," he said.

"That would suggest we stand in opposition to the perfection of the Praxis," said Vipsania.

"It's the worst word in our political vocabulary," Roland said.

"We're going to hear a lot of bad words thrown at us," Sula said. "*Rebel. Bandit. Pirate.* When they get tired of those, they can always go back to *Terran criminal.* My question is: What words can we throw back at *them?*"

"We've always said that the Gruum government is illegitimate," Vipsania said. "We've said that all we want to do is return to the government of Lord Saïd, and to a policy of equality between the species."

"Except, of course, for the Naxids and the Yormaks," Sula said.

"Well." Vipsania looked uncomfortable for a moment, then shrugged.

"Can we call ourselves the Saïdists?" wondered Lord Mehrang.

"I think we might try to find something a little more universal than that," Vipsania said. "I'm not sure whether we want to tie our movement to one particular politician." Her voice was as polished as the arculé table—unlike her brothers, she had managed to drop her Laredo accent in favor of the fashionable accents of the High City.

"We were Loyalists in the last war," said Mehrang.

"So were our enemies," said Sula. "And they're already using that word for themselves."

"The Purifiers," said Lord Mehrang. He offered a grim smile. "The government could do with a little purification."

"A little too frightening, perhaps," Roland said. "If I had no other stake in the matter, I know how I'd choose between a Loyalist and a Purifier."

"Legitimists?" said Terza in her soft voice. "Because we're trying to restore the legitimate government?"

"That's more like it," Vipsania said. "I think—"

"Restorers!" said Lord Governor Binh. He had not meant to interrupt, but his contribution had been delayed a few seconds by its transmission from the planet's surface.

Vipsania made a face. "That sounds like we're refurbishing an old building."

Sula grinned. "Aren't we?" No one else seemed to find that amusing.

"The Restoration, then," said Roland.

There was a brief debate between the Restorationers and

the Legitimists, before the committee settled on Restoration for the name of their faction. Sula turned to Vipsania.

"Lady Vipsania," she said, "do you think you could compose and broadcast a Restoration manifesto?"

"Of course," she said. "But as soon as Zanshaa found out that Lady Michi had taken the Fourth Fleet, I was cut off from Imperial Broadcasting in most of the empire. I can only broadcast the manifesto in those systems we can control."

The Restoration had fifteen inhabited systems under its umbrella, and many of these were controlled only tenuously, on Michi's side only insofar as they had not openly declared for the Zanshaa government. Terra, with its human majority, had shown enthusiastic support for Michi, as had Lord Mehrang's Esley, and three other worlds that happened to have human governors. The newly discovered world Rol-mar, where Nikki Severin had destroyed the cruiser *Beacon* before the war had quite started, was in a state of rebellion against— apparently—*everybody,* and in any case was so sparsely populated that there was little point in trying to secure it or use its resources.

Michi had armed several small ships and sent them to worlds that seemed less enthusiastic for her cause, and their antimatter missiles were expected to bring them into total compliance.

"Broadcast to everyone you can," Roland said. "Wormhole stations outside our sphere will pick up the messages and may send them on to *somewhere.*"

"Nonii," Sula said, "so that's resolved." She looked around

the table. "I have another issue to raise, having to do with how we're going to pay for this war. And to that end I'd like to introduce my aide, Ming Lin, the author of *The Cosgrove Legacy.*"

Lin walked the committee through the same options she'd mentioned the other morning, and then came to a conclusion. "If we can sell bonds to finance the war, it's by far the best option. The purchasers' gratification will be delayed, but if we win, they'll make a profit."

"If we win," muttered one of the locals.

"Miss Lin!" boomed Lord Governor Binh, his voice distorted by speakers to wince-inducing levels. "My government has most expert advice, and we have considered all these issues. In fact we're preparing a bond issue through the local branch of the Imperial Bank."

"I'm aware of that, Lord Governor," Lin said. "But what I fear is caution on the part of the public, even the Terran public. Not everyone will want to invest in what might be viewed as a treasonous enterprise, and be subject to penalties if we should lose."

Sula looked over the table and saw that the possibility of losing the war was making most of the committee uncomfortable. She took pleasure in the thought of politicians facing the same grim prospect of death as the military.

It took a few moments for Lin's words to reach Binh, and his reply to reach the ring.

"We'll know how well the bonds sell when we put them on the market."

"I'll be buying them," said Lord Mehrang.

"And I," said Vipsania.

"We all will," Terza said.

"I hope everyone else is as committed to success as we are, Lord Governor," Lin said. "But if some people are reluctant for whatever reason, I thought we might make use of the Bureau of Arrears and Obligations." She tilted her head as she looked at the camera pickups. "Have you considered using the bureau, Governor Binh?"

The committee watched Binh's doubtful expression as he listened to the transmission, then made a reply.

"Use it how, Miss Lin?"

The Bureau of Arrears and Obligations had been set up at the start of the fiscal crisis, as the arch-speculator Cosgrove's empire collapsed. The bureau was established to buy Cosgrove's businesses and wind them up, but as the crisis spread, many businesses in which the Imperial Bank had an interest also failed, and the bureau found itself saddled with them as well.

"The bureau has acquired stock in *thousands* of businesses," Lin said. "We can sell the stock at face value, with the assurance that our government will buy it back at the end of the war. The stock isn't a bond with our name on it, it's not treason to buy it, it's just a piece of stock in an insolvent company. The purchaser has a choice of selling the stock back to us after the war, or to try to make the business a success— which isn't as hard as it sounds, since a lot of these businesses went down because the Imperial Bank increased reserve requirements at every bank throughout the empire, and suddenly money wasn't available even for businesses that were turning a profit." Lin paused for a moment, then added. "I'd also suggest decreasing those reserve requirements. War calls for easy money and a booming economy."

Governor Binh took a few moments to absorb all this and decided to address the last issue. "My advisers fear inflation."

Sula laughed. "If you don't mind a little advice, I think your greatest fear should be that we'll lose the war."

The room fell silent while the transmission bounded down to Harzapid's surface, and then Terza's soft voice rose into the silence. "I think we have reached the point where we must simply try *everything*."

Governor Binh pondered this for a moment, and then said, "I am willing to try anything you suggest, my lady, but I cannot both raise and lower reserve rates at the same time."

Now it was Roland's turn to laugh. "Lower them, by all means!" he said. "Haven't you read Miss Lin's *book*?"

Binh conceded, and Roland turned to Sula. "Do you have any other issues, Lady Sula?"

"Yes. I'm afraid that I do." Sula paused a moment while she wondered just how tactfully she could state the obvious.

Fuck tact, she decided.

"We're called the Terran criminals," she said. "And in the short time I've been here, I've seen very few people who *aren't* Terran. There are only Terrans at this table, and only Terrans left in the Fleet. Yet we say that once we win, those we displaced will be welcomed back into their former roles. Why should they believe us? How many Daimong are carrying our message? How many Torminel?"

"We are a bit short of volunteers among the other species," Roland said. "It's the Terran race that is being threatened. Others may offer their sympathy, but they're unwilling to risk their lives for us. We have very few allies, and most of them are in places controlled by the enemy. They have to be cautious."

"There's Lady Koridun," Sula said. "She isn't cautious at all. On *Striver* she strangled an enemy commander with her own belt, and she's as committed to the Restoration as any of us."

Lamey grinned. "I remember her coming off the *Striver* with her mirrored gown and pistol," he said. "Quite a picture!"

Roland frowned. "How do you suggest we employ her?" he asked.

"Get her some first-rate speechwriters and put her on video," Sula said. "You need her to reach the non-Terrans in our sphere and tell them why the Restoration is worth fighting for."

"I can do that," Vipsania said.

"On second thought, she may not need the speechwriters," Sula said. "Her conviction is genuine, and she's eloquent enough putting forth her ideas. But she may need a little help keeping on point."

"My people are used to helping inexperienced people look good on camera," Vipsania said. She looked at Sula and raised an eyebrow. "We helped *you*, if you recall, with *The Naxid War*."

"Hah," Sula said. "And here I thought my success was down to my poise, intellect, and rhetorical gifts."

Vipsania smiled. Sula didn't trust her—she didn't trust *any* Martinez—but Sula thought Vipsania could be relied on to follow her own self-interest, and right now her self-interest was definitely aligned with the Restoration.

"I'd also recommend that Lady Koridun be appointed to some high office," Sula said. "It would show she's trusted."

Roland looked at her. "What office do you have in mind?"

Fuck tact, Sula thought again. "Lady governor of a planet," she said. She looked at the video screen. "Not necessarily *your* planet, Governor Binh."

There was another delay before Binh's reply arrived. "I didn't ask for this job," he said. "And if you, or Lady Michi, or whoever is actually in charge up there so decides, I would step aside for Lady Koridun or anyone else." The sentiment seemed heartfelt.

"Lady Koridun is very young for such a senior post," Terza said.

"I'd recommend support from a very experienced staff," Sula said.

"That's assuming we can find anyone experienced in handling insurrection on this scale," said Roland. "And we won't."

"Naxids," said Sula.

Vipsania frowned. "That isn't very amusing," she said. "And even if true, the Naxids here remained loyal."

"I'll be happy to be on Lady Koridun's staff!" Lamey said. His smile was a brilliant white. "I've become experienced at outsider politics, and I'm more acceptable than a Naxid."

Sula resolved to warn Lady Koridun about Lamey sooner rather than later.

Beyond deciding to call themselves the Restoration,

nothing was actually resolved at the meeting, though Sula managed to get Ming Lin installed as a permanent committee member, and her sense of the others was that Lady Koridun would soon be appointed to an important post.

Constable First Class Macnamara waited in the corridor outside the room and escorted Sula and Lin through the hotel to the electric car that would take them back to their residence. As the car whispered to life, Sula found herself thinking about the Naxids. After the failure of the Naxid Rebellion, the Naxids had been reduced to second-class status. They weren't allowed in the military, or in many posts associated with internal security. There were still armed Naxid police, but these were mainly intended to police other Naxids. There were still Naxids in the Convocation, but their numbers had dropped by about two-thirds.

All this despite the fact that the Naxid Rebellion had controlled at best a third of the empire, and that the vast majority of the Naxids had remained loyal, or at least quiescent.

Sula wondered if there was any path to rehabilitate the Naxids. As Harzapid was the base for the Fourth Fleet, a great many former Naxid military resided here. Some had retired before the rebellion started, and some had been on active duty and interned until the war was over. There were other Naxids who were skilled at manufacturing and shipbuilding.

All Sula had heard since her arrival had been of the lack of skilled personnel in critical positions. She wondered if Naxids could be quietly slipped into some of those posts.

Yet she, herself, was renowned as a killer of Naxid rebels.

She wondered if there was any chance that the Naxids would trust her.

Only one way to find out, she decided.

DALKEITH KEPT BOMBARDMENT *of Los Angeles* accelerating at a steady one gee for an hour, to make sure all shipboard systems were properly functioning, and then the warning sounded again and *Los Angeles* gradually accelerated to two gees. Martinez began deliberate, slow abdominal breathing— he was a yacht racer, was in very good condition, and he had endured many more gravities than this. Two gravities wasn't torture, it was an inconvenience. But when Dalkeith increased to three gravities, he began to feel as if one of Lokan's Torminel wrestlers was sitting on his chest.

If a ship's projected course called for high gravities—and *Los Angeles*'s certainly did—it was best to do as much acceleration as possible right at the start. The crew was fresher and could stand more punishment, and of course the more acceleration undergone early, the greater the distance traveled in a given amount of time.

The oxygen content of the air had been increased to over thirty percent to make breathing easier, and to help heal the sprains and pulled muscles that high gee would inevitably cause.

Martinez heard gasps and grunts coming from Santana and Banerjee, mixed with muttering and the occasional exclamation. They were gamely continuing the exercises Martinez had assigned them, responding to commands recorded in actual combat. Both were stumbling over their transmissions, but Santana was letting his frustration build into anger, and his responses were getting more garbled, not less.

Martinez considered interrupting and telling Santana to take a breath and calm down, but he decided against speaking out. Santana had to find his own way, and besides, the three gravities sitting on his chest would calm him down sooner or later.

In any case they had weeks before any possible encounter with the enemy.

Martinez shifted one of his displays from the rapidly retreating planet to a view of Dalkeith and her command crew. They seemed to be operating with perfect confidence; but then the ship was flying in a straight line, without maneuvering, and they hadn't been given any challenges as yet.

Martinez would have to assign an exercise in the next few days, if Dalkeith didn't do it first.

Miniwaves pulsed from the acceleration couch, to keep his blood from pooling and prevent chafing and bedsores. Accelerations would not ease for another three hours, when there would be a one-hour break at half a gee for supper before acceleration was resumed.

He felt a shimmering to his inner ears as *Los Angeles* began a series of yaws back and forth, both to test if the engines were gimbaling properly, and to train the crew in the sort of gyres used in combat, to avoid being a predictable target and falling prey to an enemy's antiproton beams.

Martinez saw something flash out of the corner of his eye, and he managed to twist his head away just as a large bolt, rolling in response to one of the ship's yawing maneuvers, plummeted from a light fixture overhead at three times its normal weight. It clipped the corner of his couch, striking sparks, and then bounded into a corner of the room, where it hit the floor with a crack. Banerjee and Santana fell silent, and Santana spun his cage around to see if he could locate the source of the disturbance.

Martinez's heartbeat and adrenal glands caught up with the danger too late to be of any use, and he lay on his couch gasping for a moment while he stared up at the light fixture to see if the whole thing was about to wrench itself from the ceiling and cudgel out his brains, but the light dazzled him and he could see nothing.

I could have lost an eye, he thought. He might even have been killed.

He configured one of his displays to control the lighting in the room, and he turned off the light over his head, only to have ghost lights bloom on his retinas. He took command of the lights in the room, then tracked some spots to illuminate the fixture over his head, then peered at it with one of the room's cameras. Even at high magnification the installation seemed completely stable.

Some workman had let a bolt fall, or set it in place atop the fixture intending to use it, and then forgot where he'd put it.

Martinez wondered how many other bolts were rolling free in the ship, ready to turn into bullets at high accelerations, and how many storage lockers or compromised fixtures lay ready to drop and crush unwary crew or smash some important control station or power connection.

In the next few days they'd find out.

THE OPEN-TOPPED SUN Ray automobile provided little protection, and the explosion pummeled Sula's ears and gut. Concussion blew her hair in her face, and it was a moment before she could make out what was going on ahead. She saw smoke and sprawling figures and debris bounding down the road, and she realized that what had blown up was a checkpoint that separated the Fleet dockyard from an industrial area farther down the ring—and she saw Daimong with rifles sprinting through the smoke and wreckage, and she heard the crackle of fire.

Macnamara had already braked to a stop. "Back up!" Sula shouted so that her words would penetrate Macnamara's stunned eardrums.

There was a time in her life when she was called the White Ghost and explosions such as these ruled the night—and the reflexes of the White Ghost hadn't faded apparently, because everyone else was staring at the lost checkpoint while her vehicle was moving in reverse, away from the attack. She half crouched on the back seat and turned to look over her shoulder as her car dodged another vehicle and swerved into a new lane. Beside her, she saw Shawna Spence looking at the checkpoint with narrowed eyes as the engineer calculated lines of fire, angles of attack, the size of the explosive that had just gone off, all the elements of her own volatile domain.

Around the vehicle, people were still staring, or turning to confer with each other. Sula reached into her holster for her sidearm and waved it. "Run!" she shouted. "Enemy attack!" Still looking over her shoulder, she saw the gold-on-brown ornament of the officers' hostel coming nearer.

"Fuck!" she said. "They're after the officers' quarters!"

The Restoration's command had far too few officers available. A strike on the officers' hostel could deal the Fourth Fleet a deadly blow.

Sula scanned the structures across the road, saw a narrow building with a canteen on the ground floor, and high windows on the stories above. She slapped Macnamara on the shoulder. "Park here!"

The vehicle lurched over a curb and bent a traffic sign. Sula jumped out onto the road. "Follow me!"

She sprinted for the canteen, which she now saw was called Rahul's Cafe. It had an automatic door that began, very slowly, to open, and out of frustration she punched the door glass with her fist.

Shots crackled in the air. People were starting to run now.

Sula tried scraping through the opening door, caught a button on her tunic, and wrenched it free. The silver button sang as it struck the floor. The warm, humid air of the canteen was filled with cooking smells. Fleet personnel and civilian dockworkers stared at her, forks half raised from their plates. "Enemy attack!" she shouted and waved her pistol again. "Who here is armed?"

Two Terran females stood, both young cadets. "Good!" Sula said. "You're coming with me!" She made a general wave at the rest of the room. "The rest of you run out the back door, if there is one! If you've got access to a gun near here, get it and come back! Otherwise, report to your units!"

Macnamara and Spence burst into the canteen after her, and Sula turned to see the door begin its agonizingly slow close. She turned to the room, looked at a waiter frozen with plates balanced on his forearms.

"We need to lock this door!" she said. "Who can do that?" The waiter stared, then dumbly looked over his shoulder toward the kitchen.

Gunshots sounded, close by. Then there was a ripping, hammering sound that Sula recognized as an automatic weapon cycling caseless ammunition very fast, at least fifty rounds per second, and she hunched into her shoulders as she half expected the window to collapse into shards behind her. But she hadn't been the target, and the bullets had gone somewhere else. *They're going to run out of ammunition at this rate*, she thought and ran up to the waiter. "How do I get upstairs?" she said.

The waiter had lost the ability to speak. Wide-eyed, he rolled his eyes in the direction of the door to the kitchen. Sula ran for the door, kicked it open, and then looked over her shoulder at the roomful of stunned, motionless diners.

"*Run*, you idiots!" she said.

The kitchen was full of bright lights and old, worn machines doing basic tasks: chopping vegetables, washing dishes, stirring pots. Two obese humans in aprons and caps stared at the armed intruder. One held a whisk poised above a cast-iron skillet, dark roux dripping.

"Enemy attack!" Sula said. "You need to lock the front door *now*!"

"Ruin my fucking roux," said one of the humans. She dropped the skillet to a tiled countertop, walked to a control panel, and punched the lock button.

Sula walked farther into the kitchen, saw a door, and shouldered it open, revealing a kind of foyer with a door leading to the road behind the canteen. A staircase of dark composite stretched up to a narrow landing above. "This way!" she called and sprinted up the stairs. Muffled shots pursued her as she ran.

The floor above the restaurant seemed to be private apartments, and so was the floor above that. Sula found the door to the apartment overlooking the avenue, knocked, then lost her patience and threw herself against the door. Pain crackled through her shoulder, and the door barely trembled.

A bitter laugh escaped Sula. They could hardly fight the enemy if they let a door defeat them.

"If you'll step aside, my lady." Macnamara studied the door for a brief moment, then took a step back, hurled himself forward, and kicked with both feet at a part of the door adjacent to the lock.

The door came open with a crash, pieces of the frame flying through the air to land on the floor with a clatter. Sula hopped over Macnamara's prone body and ran into the apartment.

The apartment was stuffy and filled with old, sagging furniture. She saw a credenza full of framed photographs of a man in a Fleet uniform, ranging in age from a young recruit to a graying petty officer on the verge of retirement, and Sula suspected the man was in the dockyard now, having been called back to service. From amid the photos two white long-haired cats stared at Sula in horror with blue eyes, and then their claws scrabbled as they panicked. One of the photographs crashed to the floor as the cats leaped from the credenza and disappeared into another room.

Good idea, Sula thought, as she moved to the windows overlooking the front. They released with a simple lever, and Sula unlocked one window and pushed it open. The sound of shots was much louder, and Sula looked across the avenue at the officers' hostel and saw a group of men in front, peering down the avenue. Most were in uniform, and some at least carried pistols. Among them Sula recognized Lieutenant-Captain Alana Haz, who had been her first lieutenant on *Confidence*, and who had fled with her to Harzapid. Haz sent the others scurrying back into the hotel, took one last look down the avenue, and then sprinted for the door.

Well, good. They wouldn't be caught completely by surprise.

Spence had already opened the other of the two windows. "How many spare magazines do you have?" Sula asked.

"One spare," Spence said.

"Me too."

Sula took a quick survey of her whole party, which by now included Macnamara and the two cadets from the canteen. Between them they had a total of five pistols, all unsuited for the sort of fight that was developing, and a total of ten full magazines. Sula pictured them plinking down from their

windows while the enemy emptied two-hundred-round magazines of caseless ammunition in response. *We'll just have to
be very clever*, Sula thought.

She looked at the cadets. "I don't suppose either of you is
a crack shot?" she said.

One shook her head. "No, my lady," said the other.

"Macnamara, take the window on the right," Sula said.
"I'll take the one on the left." She turned to the others. "When
Macnamara uses up his ammunition, one of you pass him
your pistol and your spare magazine."

Macnamara was by far the best shot, having most recently utilized his talents in dispatching a Naxid assassin in
New Zealand, on Terra. Sula had emerged from that encounter covered in blood, but Macnamara's uniform remained
spotless.

Sula looked at the two cadets. "One of you stay by the
stairs, in case they try to come up behind us."

"Yes, my lady."

"Let's get ready here." Lamps and tables were shifted out
of the way. The one light in the room was turned off. Drapes
were drawn over the window, leaving slits for the shooters
to fire through. Macnamara crouched behind his window,
his pistol resting on the sill. Sula, standing, peered out to see
the Daimong attackers coming up the avenue.

Like all Daimong they were tall and gangling, gray-
skinned and expressionless, with round fixed eyes and a round
fixed mouth. They seemed comfortable with their weapons,
but Sula saw they weren't moving like an experienced combat
team. They kept hesitating, then urging each other forward,

and they'd stop to blast anything that looked threatening, or anyone who seemed to be in uniform. Their officer, if they had one, wasn't keeping them focused on the mission, and they were burning through a lot of their ammunition.

Sula had seen a lot of that in the war, with her untrained Secret Army volunteers willing to fight, but uncertain how to go about it. Sometimes they'd come back from a raid having fired every single bullet, mostly at shadows. Fortunately Sula had managed to recruit a hard core of violent criminals to put some drive into her operations.

The Daimong apparently hadn't thought to bring gangsters with them.

The Daimong came up the avenue in little rushes, taking cover behind vehicles they'd shot into immobility. Sula got a first glimpse of the officer, who wore black body armor and a helmet. Most of his team were in civilian gear, and the armor didn't give Sula a positive impression of the officer's courage.

"Officer at thirty-five degrees low," Sula told Macnamara.

Macnamara answered without shifting out of his shooter's crouch. "Shall I shoot him, my lady?"

"He's armored. Find a softer target, and wait."

A few shots popped out from the officers' lodge—apparently the defenders weren't any better armed than Sula's group. The response was overwhelming—at least a half-dozen rifles returned fire, some burning through two-hundred-round magazines in a few seconds, but some firing a more measured response. Other Daimong simply dived for cover. The gold-and-brown façade of the lodge seemed to fly into the air, and windows were hammered in. The brass medallions were shot off the walls and bounded into the road. Through the windows Sula saw sparks fly from shattered light fixtures.

The shooting ended in an abrupt silence that left Sula aware of the ringing in her ears. Sula felt a mild surprise that the officers' hostel remained intact, its front heavily scarred but apparently sound. The attackers scurried forward, calling to one another in their melodic Daimong voices, and Sula saw one attacker run to cover behind the wheels of a windowless Sun Ray van. Sula saw him reach into a pack he was carrying and knew at once what he was reaching for.

"Bomber in front of the yellow Sun Ray," Sula said. "Shoot him before he can throw."

She dropped into a crouch, holding the pistol with both hands, the butt resting on the window sill. Macnamara made a small adjustment in his posture, acquired his target, and fired twice. Sula saw sparks as one bullet hit the vehicle, but the other seemed to have hit the bomber, because he slumped, one hand clutching at the Sun Ray for support. Sula lined up the bomber in her sights, but by that point Macnamara had fired twice more, and the bomber flopped onto the rubberized road, dead or dying.

The scent of propellant stung the air. Sula widened her attention to the whole group of attackers, who seemed not to have yet realized there was an enemy behind them. The officer called another attacker to run up to the Sun Ray, and the attacker just stared at the officer, then replied in a complaining tone. For a few seconds the combat paused while the two had what seemed to be an argument, and then a third Daimong decided to take the mission on herself and ran toward the van. A couple shots from the hostel pursued her, and the whole body of attackers replied with another massive volley.

"Take out the bomber," Sula said, and Macnamara fired two pairs of shots that sprawled the second bomber over the body of the first.

"Find another target," Sula said, and then she found another herself. As long as the Daimong were burying the hostel in fire, they weren't going to notice someone shooting at them from an unexpected angle.

Sula fired three measured shots at one of the attackers firing from behind a vehicle, which resulted in the Daimong dropping her weapon and sagging against the car; and Macnamara picked off two more before his magazine ran dry and he had to reload. By this point the officer had apparently won his argument with his reluctant subordinate, and the third bomber sprinted forward, crouched over his rifle as if protecting an infant from a hailstorm. He dived for cover behind the Sun Ray, threw down his weapon, and began to dig the explosive satchel out from beneath the two corpses.

Sula took aim at the bomber and began to fire deliberately. The bomber's movements grew more frantic as bullets punched into the van behind him. He pointed in Sula's direction and squalled out a piercing shriek that could only come from the Daimong vocal apparatus, and Sula saw heads begin to turn in her direction.

The bomber rose to his feet, satchel in hand, and began to make a clumsy run around the Sun Ray toward the officers' hostel. At best, Sula knew, the bomb would blow out the door of the hostel and let the attackers enter to begin a massacre. At worst it would take off the whole front of the building. So Sula did her best to track the bomber in her sights and kept pulling the trigger until a light shone on the back of the pistol to tell her the magazine was empty. Return fire smacked into the wall of her building, twitched the curtain above her head. She dropped the magazine out of her pistol, slapped in her spare, and saw the light wink out. But she'd lost sight of the runner, and then she heard the thrashing sound of one of the rifles on full automatic, and the open window frame dissolved into flying metal splinters while bullets hammered the wall and plaster and dust filled the air.

Sula rolled back onto the floor as bullets began to fly through the window and chop out pieces of the ceiling overhead. She glanced over the room and saw that everyone else was flat on the floor as plaster and resinous laths came raining down. Sula rolled onto her stomach to keep from inhaling debris, her mind spinning while she tried to come up with a new plan. Extreme cleverness had taken her only so far.

The flash and sound came simultaneously, and Sula felt the kick as the floor bucked and tried to throw her off. The torn window curtains were blown horizontal, debris filled the air, and the photographs all spilled off the credenza.

Sula felt her heart sink. The explosion was certainly enough to have blown in the front of the officers' lodge, perhaps destroyed it completely, and if that were the case there was very little she could do to help anyone trapped in the building. In the dusty, dazed silence that followed the blast,

Sula uncertainly rose to a crouch and crunched over rubble to look cautiously out the window. She could look into the front of the hostel without exposing herself to fire from the road below, and to her surprise the battered exterior was largely intact. She stepped forward with care, revealing more of the avenue, and saw the crater that had dug through the ring's floor to the thick layer of lunar and asteroid material that armored the ring against radiation. Flames still licked upward from the crater.

The bomber hadn't reached his target. Maybe one of Sula's bullets had dropped him, or someone else's had, or the bomb had gone off prematurely. In any case the officers' hostel still stood like a proud, battered fort above the carnage scattered in its moat.

The Sun Ray van had been hurled across the road and was lying on its side, acrid fire now shooting from its battery packs. Sula's own car had been flipped on its back. A number of the attackers had been knocked flat and were only now picking themselves up.

Sula heard a hiss, and fire retardant began to fall onto the scene in a gentle rain.

"Macnamara," Sula said. He rose to his feet and came to his window. Sula stepped to her own window, steadied her pistol on the sill, and fired on one of the stunned Daimong struggling to his feet.

That started the firefight again. Return fire came through the window or slapped the wall, but the volume was nothing compared to what had come before. Shots came also from the officers' hostel, and though the pistols were inadequate weapons they at least had the advantage of catching the attackers in a cross fire.

Then there was a rapid *chug-chug-chug* from the hostel, and Sula felt her heart lift. It was the sound of a Sidney Mark One, a homemade weapon that Sula's army had used in the fight for Zanshaa City. In fact it was probably her own personal weapon, taken from her suite by some enterprising officer. She wanted to cheer.

The *chug-chug-chug* died away in a blizzard of suppressive fire. Sula emptied her second magazine and one of the cadets slapped a pistol into her hand. She risked a three-second look through the shredded curtains, didn't find a clear shot at a target, and drew back.

The firefight had slowed down. Sula figured the attackers were running out of bullets and had pretty well lost direction after their bomb went off at the wrong instant and in the wrong place. The attackers' chances of perpetrating a massacre at the officers' hostel had faded, and they didn't know what else to do. A retreat was doomed to failure and fatality, and the Daimong seemed to have given up trying to advance. The officer was as baffled as the others and had stopped giving orders.

As for the defenders, all they had to do was hold in place until rescue arrived. There was a lot less reason to expose herself at the windows now, and Sula took advantage of it.

Alarm sang in Sula's nerves as she saw the silhouette of something dark and crablike move on the other side of the window, and then there was a gushing noise, and Sula realized that it was a remotely operated fire-control robot in the act of deploying. Fire was a terror in an artificial environment such as the ring station, and there were elaborate safety measures, including large robots that glided over the ceiling on a series of tracks, and that featured a nozzle on a long boom that could direct fire-suppressing chemicals to the danger spot.

And so the crater and the flaming Sun Ray batteries were drenched, and then the boom swung slowly out over the avenue, took careful aim, and covered one of the attackers with fire retardant. A second fighter had been drenched before the attackers woke to their new situation, and they began directing fire at the boom. The boom, undamaged, shifted over to where the officer was frantically directing his men to shoot the robot and smothered him in frothing goo.

Sula laughed aloud. Whoever was operating that boom, she decided, was going to get a medal.

The quality of light shifted, shadows appearing where there hadn't been shadows before, and Sula slipped to one side of the window and peered along the avenue. The overhead illumination had been switched off farther down the road, which argued that something was happening there that the authorities didn't want the attackers to see.

A lethal response deploying, presumably.

"Shouldn't be long now," Sula said. "Don't expose yourself unnecessarily." Her words were punctuated by the roaring sound of the firefighting robot drenching another attacker.

The counterattack launched a few minutes later, Military Constabulary soldiers in helmet and full body armor carrying a variety of lethal weaponry. They came hunting down the avenue from out of the dark, moving from doorway to doorway, weapons trained on Daimong illuminated by the overhead strips and pinpointed by the robot boom.

"Rescue's here," Sula said. "Take cover and stay safe. Our part's done."

A growing fusillade echoed her words, followed by the shrieks of terrified Daimong.

The firing continued, and eventually the shrieks faded.

THE AVENUE WAS a wreck, slick with fire suppressant, covered with debris and shattered vehicles, and littered with bodies. The lighting strips overhead burned at maximum intensity, and every piece of wreckage, every shard of window glass, and every corpse, was rendered brilliant and unnaturally distinct. Ambulances gave priority to the wounded, and the dead lay sprawled where they had fallen.

The chemical reek was searing, but Sula preferred it to the scent of dead Daimong, who smelled like corpses even when alive. Fleet constables moved uneasily though the ruin, weapons poised, alert to any possible threat.

"Your rifle, Lady Sula." Lady Alana Haz presented Sula with her Sidney Mark One. "I don't know if I hit anything with it, but at least I kept their heads down."

"Thank you." Sula hung the rifle over her shoulder on its strap. She stepped on something soft and looked down to discover that she had just put her foot on a flayed Daimong arm, presumably that of the bomber. Her stomach turned over, and she looked away.

Through the shock of revelation Haz's words were per-ceived dimly. "I had to kick your door down to get your gun. But other than the broken door, I think your suite suffered no damage."

"Let's go inside," she said.

They walked to the sturdy, scarred doors of the hostel, which had survived surprisingly well. Spence and Macnamara followed, along with the two cadets, who apparently could think of nothing more useful to do.

"Lady Sula! Wait!"

Sula turned to see Captain Naaz Vijana hurrying toward them. He wore a helmet and body armor and carried a rifle over one arm.

"You were part of the counterattack?" she asked. Vijana was a warship commander and had never served in the constabulary so far as Sula knew.

"I sort of led it," Vijana said. "I have some experience, after all."

He had fought in the capture of the *Striver*, and before that had annihilated the Yormak uprising along with most of the Yormaks. Sula supposed he was as experienced at this kind of warfare as anyone who hadn't served in the Secret Army.

"Thank you for rescuing us, then," Sula said.

"You were in the hostel?"

Sula gestured toward Rahul's Cafe. "I was across the road," she said. "Setting up a cross fire."

Vijana was impressed. "Good work, my lady," he said. "I wondered how so many bodies ended up on that side of the road."

"Macnamara is a very good shot," Sula said.

Vijana viewed the constable. "I know. I've seen him at work." He glanced over the scene, the bright overhead light outlining his sharp features. "We've got three wounded prisoners," he said with satisfaction. "Once they've been stitched back together, we'll find out who they are and who's behind it." He snarled. "I'll interrogate them myself, if I can stand the stink."

"There are professionals for that."

"The professionals?" Vijana grinned. "How good can they be, if they didn't stop us from taking the Fourth Fleet?"

Sula didn't have an answer for that. Vijana glanced over his shoulder at the ambulances.

"One of the Kangas twins was wounded," he said. "Now we won't have so much trouble telling him apart from his brother."

"Does his brother know?"

"They were together in the ambulance."

Sula's nerves leaped at a pair of shots that echoed down the road, and the constables all instantly went on guard, their weapons trained in the direction of the sound. Vijana busied himself with his communications systems, then turned to Sula with a look of apology.

"Shooting at phantoms, probably," he said. "But I'd better go calm them down."

"See you at the meeting tomorrow," Sula said.

Vijana was surprised. "Meeting?"

"There's bound to be one."

He laughed. "True." He waved good-bye and trotted off.

"You know," said Alana Haz, "I think Vijana enjoys this sort of thing too much."

"Some people do." Sula knew that she'd have nightmares about this for weeks, her dreaming senses choked with the acrid reek, the hard edges of rubble gleaming in the blazing light, the flayed arm of the bomber.

"I'm going to take a shower," she said. "And then get started on my report, because someone's going to ask me for one. Then I'll be asked for recommendations, all of which will be ignored."

Haz looked at her. "You seem to have a very good grasp of Fleet procedure," she said.

"I wish it didn't have such a grasp on *me*," Sula said, and she reached for the scarred hostel door.

CHAPTER 6

"Some may say that I am too young to accept this appointment as lady governor of Harzapid." The blue-eyed Torminel, visible on Severin's sleeve display, glanced out over an audience that was out of the camera's frame. "But I am not too young," she said, "to fight for the Restoration!"

She paused while applause washed over her. She was dressed in a governor's formal purple robes, brilliant with gold-and-scarlet brocade that glittered in video lights. Behind her stood a row of solemn officials, representing a cross section of all the species beneath the Praxis. Severin wondered how many of them actually wanted to be there.

"Some claim we are rebels!" the new governor said. "We *disdain and reject* the term!"

More applause. Captain Shushanik Severin glanced from the sleeve display to the entry port twenty paces away.

In most ring stations the Exploration Service used the Fleet dockyards for their ships and paid the Fleet for their support, but Harzapid was large enough for the Exploration Service to have a dockyard of its own. Station crew bustled around one of the entry ports, readying it for traffic. One gray-haired woman peered at a screen while manipulating a joystick, guiding the docking tube to *Explorer*'s main personnel hatch. A pair of armed guards stood waiting to check the passes of anyone boarding the ship. The walls were covered with artwork featuring the Exploration Service surveying new worlds, or crewing the wormhole relay stations that knit the empire's communication network.

"The Restoration seeks to return the empire to the Peace of the Praxis!" said the new lady governor. "We wish to reinstate our proper government, and to drive out those who have usurped power in Zanshaa!"

More applause rang from Severin's sleeve display. He adjusted the collar of his dark blue dress Exploration Service uniform, then stretched in his seat. He waited in an electric car painted in the viridian green of the Fleet, and which he'd borrowed from the other service. As he relaxed from his stretch, he absently rubbed his wrists and hands and popped every finger joint.

When he had taken up puppeteering, the unnatural hand positions produced aching joints and muscles. Since his *Expedition* had blown up the cruiser *Beacon* at Rol-mar several months ago, Severin had been continually occupied in keeping his wounded ship alive on the journey to Harzapid—and once he'd arrived, in putting his ship through a major refit in the briefest time imaginable. As the refit had approached its conclusion, he'd found himself thinking of his puppets again and longing to work out some of the stories that had come to him before the fight with *Beacon*. So he'd unpacked the trunks in which he'd stored his puppets and begun to develop a new serial, with predictable effects on his tendons.

His working out of plot and dialogue, refreshingly free of any pressures from the real world, had been a welcome, relaxing change from the frenzy of work.

At least until he'd received a message from the inbound ship *Explorer*, and the ship's captain—Lihua, Lady Starkey— had told him that she needed an urgent conference on her ship as soon as she docked and would not explain why.

"I don't want a whiff of this to get out," she said. "I daren't even send it in code. I'm going to request that you come on board *Explorer* and receive a briefing—" She offered a nervous smile. "After which, as the senior officer, *you* can decide what to do with the information."

Explorer had been on a seven-month voyage exploring what was coming to be known as the Terran Reach. Terra had long lived on the fringe of the empire, the home world of the human race but a backwater planet. It had only a single wormhole gate connecting it to civilization, and so it was literally a dead end in the wormhole network. Over the centuries billions of its natives had emigrated to more prosperous parts of the empire, and Terra itself had languished in a kind of shabby neglect. But six years before, a new wormhole gate had been discovered in a distant corner of the system, and that gate was discovered to lead to two more systems that contained a total of three habitable planets, all now in the early stages of survey and development. The new discoveries could only be reached through Terra's system, which had now turned from a dead end into a gateway.

Explorer had gone beyond the newly discovered worlds and was literally returning from the unknown.

"Lady Starkey," Severin said, "this concerns something you found in one of the new systems?"

"I don't want to say, my lord," Lady Starkey said. "Please come aboard as soon as you can. I can only say that this is very . . . disturbing. I'm not allowing any of my crew off the ship until we can come to some kind of resolution about— well, you'll find out in the briefing."

"Does this have any bearing on the war?" Severin asked.

Starkey looked uncertain. "I don't think so. Nothing direct, anyway. Not unless there are weapons and warships that we don't know about."

Well, *that* was ominous enough. So now, rubbing his aching forearms, Severin sat in his car, listened to the inauguration of Lady Governor Koridun, and waited for the crew around the entry port to signal that *Explorer* and its docking tube had finally mated.

Severin watched as the tube was pressurized and the crew ran tests to make certain that the seals were holding. The tests were successful, and floodlights came on to illuminate the port. The name *Explorer* appeared on a display above the door. Severin turned off his sleeve display, cutting off Lady Koridun in the midst of a tirade on the perfidy of the enemy, and then eased himself out of the car and made his way to the gate.

As the planetary ring spun to generate gravity, *Explorer* was actually docked nose-in below Severin's feet. The entry port led to a very large elevator, inset with mirrors and polished brass ornament, capable of transporting forty crew at a time. This descended to the level of the docking tube, which itself was quite plain.

An entry party saluted Severin as he stepped off the docking tube into the ship. The air on the cruiser had a stale odor, which told Severin that *Explorer* was not yet receiving its air from the dockyard.

Lihua, Lady Starkey was the result of a successful marital merger between the Hua and Starkey clans, both of which had long histories of providing officers to the Exploration Service. When her mother had died in the Naxid War, she had inherited the Starkey title when she was still in her teens. A lifelong commitment to the Service was a part of her heritage, but the timing was less than ideal: the war left Lady Starkey junior to all those officers who had advanced during the conflict, including Severin. Despite generations of Service tradition in both branches of her family tree, she had only received this, her first command, ten months ago, and then only because the Exploration Service was undergoing a major expansion as the empire was opening new worlds to settlement.

Lady Starkey was a small, lithe woman with an expressive face and dark hair worn past her shoulders. After Severin told her and her party to stand at ease, she introduced her officers and led Severin to her dining room, where the air carried the scent of spiced coffee.

"Please be seated, my lord," she said. "We've arranged a presentation for you."

Severin was not a Peer, but all officers were called "my lord" out of courtesy, since just about all of them were. Severin's wartime field commission made him about as exotic an officer as the Service possessed, a commoner with what had by now become high seniority.

"Thank you, Lady Starkey," he said. "May I have some of that coffee? The scent is tempting."

"Of course."

Stewards in white gloves served coffee and tea in fine porcelain, the cups so thin and delicate as to make Severin wonder how they had survived any kind of acceleration. The porcelain was the deep blue of the Service uniforms, with gold ornament in the form of linked Hua and Starkey crests. The dining room itself was richly paneled, with polished brasswork and portraits of Lady Starkey's ancestors in their blue uniforms. The chairs were covered with soft, velvety aesa leather and adjusted themselves to their occupants. The room seemed like it belonged in a private club on Zanshaa, one of those to which Severin would normally not be admitted. Fortunately Lady Starkey was more broad-minded than the doorman at the Seven Stars.

"Would you like any other refreshment, Lord Captain?" asked Starkey.

"No, thank you. I've just eaten."

Lady Starkey ventured a smile. "I'm very glad to see you, my lord. I was worried I'd find you in prison after the fight at Rol-mar."

"I managed to record my dealings with Captain Derin-uus," Severin said. "And the recordings were enough to exonerate me. And also—" He picked up his coffee. "When Lady

Michi assumed command of the Fourth Fleet and our Service's dockyard, she dismissed all the officers senior to me. So as the senior officer remaining, I was able to exonerate *myself*. Fortunately Lady Michi agreed with my decision."

The other officers seemed uncertain whether it was proper to laugh. Lady Starkey raised her eyebrows. "Very sensible of her, my lord."

"I'd like to think so." He sipped the coffee—it was excellent, the perfect combination of spice and bitterness, and if it was a foretaste of Lady Starkey's kitchen, he might regret turning down her offer of a meal. The Exploration Service traditionally ate well, a compensation for long voyages and many months crewing wormhole relay stations.

He put down his cup. "Well," he said, "let's see this presentation."

Starkey's premiere called a map onto the wall display, showing Terra with its newly discovered gate, the two systems and three worlds that lay beyond, and the wormhole, at a considerable distance from its primary, through which *Explorer* had plunged into the unknown.

"We thought we'd struck it lucky, my lord," Starkey said, "because we'd only been in the system four days before we found an ideal planet." The planet itself appeared on the display, blue oceans, polar caps, swirling white clouds, green land. "It orbits a main-sequence star. Twenty-two percent oxygen in the atmosphere, almost all the rest nitrogen. Three-eighths of the planet's surface is open water. Life is obviously abundant." She looked at the planet with a kind of wistful admiration, as if she were recalling a hope that had faded over time. "The wormhole was so far out that it took us almost a month to reach the new world—we had a catalog name for it, but we were calling it Garden."

"The name seems apt," Severin offered.

"Well, I suppose it is. But we should have called it *Trouble*." She frowned. "Because on our approach, we found *this*."

Severin recognized it at once—a boxy structure with mooring for ships, lacy solar panels, the jagged structures, reminiscent of battlements, that could lock additional counterweights to the station if they were needed, and most importantly the long black foreshortened cable descending to the planet below.

"A space elevator," Severin breathed. Through his shock he looked at Lady Starkey. "You found a *civilization*?"

Lady Starkey met his eyes. "We found the *remains* of a civilization," Starkey said. "There hasn't been intelligent life on that world for thousands of years."

Severin stammered. "They—what?—they evacuated?"

"We think most of them died," said Morales, the blond premiere lieutenant. "But the Great Masters all left."

Severin stared at him, mind flailing.

"The terminal looks like one of ours because it *is* one of ours," Morales said. He gestured at the elevator terminal parked for eternity in geosynchronous orbit. "There are four of them still, and we think there was a fifth that was destroyed or was released somehow."

If the wealth of the world justified it, the five skyhook stations would have been expanded to make a planetary ring to generate the antimatter that powered Shaa civilization. Apparently the Shaa hadn't been in residence long enough to take that step.

"The stations are no longer functional," Lady Starkey said. "The solar panels are perforated by micrometeorites, power storage is dead, the seals failed long ago, and there's no longer any atmosphere. But we suited up and explored them all, and we documented the search with video."

What followed was video patched together from recordings made by helmet and handheld cameras. Lady Starkey led a party to one of the station's personnel airlocks, which lacked power but was cranked open manually by a pair of crew sweating and panting in their vac suits. The surface of the station was pitted, and if there had been any labels or instructions on any of the entry ports, they had long faded from sight, or had been obliterated. But once inside the station, the labels, information, and warnings were all visible and were perfectly familiar. Each was written in the Shaa alphabet, and the words were in the language of the Great Masters themselves. The cavernous corridors were built to accommodate the monumental bodies of the Shaa, nearly twice the height of a human.

Lady Starkey led her party right to Station Command, because Station Command was in the same place in all the older stations in the empire. There were two sets of controls, one sized to the mammoth Shaa and the other to a smaller species. A shaking camera zoomed into a plaque set on one end of Command, with an incised inscription.

LORKIN ELEVATOR TERMINUS NUMBER ONE
PROUDLY DEDICATED IN THIS, THE YEAR OF THE
PRAXIS SIX

"Year of the Praxis *Six*?" Severin said. "Year One was
the establishment of the Great Masters on Zanshaa. So this
place—Lorkin?—was settled at the same time as *Zanshaa*?"

"We think this place was earlier," Starkey said. "We think
the Year One was declared here *first*, and then the Shaa altered the calendar once they settled on Zanshaa and declared
a new Year One. We think this place was written clean out of
our history."

According to the official story, the primitive tribal Naxids
were the first species to be conquered by the Shaa, in Year
437. Certainly there was no mention of another species before the Naxids, nor any adjustment to the calendar.

"What happened here?" Severin said.

"We'll walk you through it, my lord, if you don't mind."

The elevator terminal was bare of ornament compared to
Harzapid's ring, but still there were murals on some of the
walls, not faded at all, showing the vast forms of the Shaa
directing labor. The laborers were mostly other Shaa, though
there was another species so strange-looking that Severin at
first took them for some kind of plant, or possibly just an ornamental motif.

The creatures—Starkey called them "Lorkins"—had
snakelike bodies topped by a head dented by a cavity on its
crest, and a collar of tentacles just below the head. Other than
the tentacles, there were no visible limbs. It took Severin a

while to work out that the cavity atop the head was in fact a mouth that dimpled the head like the caldera atop a volcano. Perhaps the Lorkins were more worm than snake.

Near Station Command was a kind of concourse separating work areas from crew quarters, and in it was a sculpture showing one of the Great Masters brandishing a tablet at a group of Lorkins, who reared back in attitudes of astonishment and awe. It was, Severin realized, an early version of the famous group of figures on the Boulevard of the Praxis in Zanshaa High City, *The Great Master Delivering the Praxis to Other Peoples*, with a titanic Shaa revealing the Praxis to the varied species of the empire, all coiled in attitudes of wonder, terror, and admiration.

The video went on to the Shaa quarters, segregated from the rest of the station by an impressive set of metal shutters. "It's lucky the gates were left open," Starkey said. "We'd have had a hard time getting past them otherwise." Furniture suitable for the Great Masters was still in place, as were conduits for delivering air and water. Quarters for the Lorkins had no great gateway, but featured furniture suitable for their snake-like anatomy, including low round beds—apparently they liked to coil into circles while resting.

"Did you find any bodies?" Severin asked.

"No, my lord," Starkey said. "Neither here, nor on the planet. The stations were very thoroughly cleaned before the Shaa departed, and as for the planet, it's wild now. We don't have any archaeological training, because nobody thought we'd ever need it. It's possible that once proper excavations can be done, we'll find cemeteries or tombs."

"Or not." Morales frowned. "It's occurred to us that the Lorkins might not have had anything like a skeleton, or bones or teeth, and so even if we find cemeteries there wouldn't be anything in them."

"Did you find station records?" Severin asked.

"All carefully removed," said Lady Starkey. "The Great Masters were so thorough I'm a little surprised that they even let the elevator terminals remain."

"Of course a proper excavation might reveal records buried in ruins on the surface," Morales said. "If they haven't decayed completely, of course."

"Would you care for more coffee, my lord?" said one of the stewards. Severin looked down at his cup with his cold, forgotten coffee trembling at the bottom. The spices that had seemed so inviting had turned bitter on his tongue.

"I'd like some water, please," he said.

"Of course, my lord."

He and *Explorer*'s officers had been discussing what should be a state secret in front of Lady Starkey's servants, but it wasn't as if the entire crew hadn't known how staggering were the finds at Lorkin. Every crouchback on the ship had months to digest this information—the only ignorant person on *Explorer* was Severin himself.

"We conducted two investigations simultaneously," Lady Starkey said. "While crews were exploring the elevator termini, we were also conducting ultra-wideband radar surveys of Lorkin's surface. Here's a map of the second-largest continent."

The oblong continent appeared in garish enhanced color, and Severin gasped at what the survey had revealed. *Explorer*'s radar had penetrated tree cover and dipped, depending on the nature of the local soil and stone, below the surface of the ground. But depth of subsurface penetration hardly mattered, because the principal discoveries were very near the surface, and the principal discoveries were an entire civilization, revealed in brilliant detail. Cities, a road network, ports, terraces for agriculture carved into the sides of hills and mountains.

"It's all broken foundations and rubble now, completely overgrown," Morales said. "But it's clear enough what was once there."

"There were billions on this world," Severin said.

"The Lorkins had an advanced society before the Shaa ever arrived," said Lady Starkey. "We don't know if they ever got into space, but it's not unlikely they had some kind of primitive spaceflight systems, just as Terra did." She zoomed in on certain features, and cursors pointed out geometrically shaped ruins. "We think we can identify certain structures for which the Shaa were responsible. These absolutely straight roads radiating from the elevator termini, for instance. They look like the kind of supersonic rail transport we have on every developed planet in the empire."

"So what happened?" Severin asked. "Where are they all now?" The crawling sensation on the back of his neck told him he already knew the answer.

"We don't know *why*," said Lady Starkey, "but it's clear the Shaa wiped the Lorkins out. Background radiation levels are higher in urban areas, consistent with antimatter bombardment from orbit thousands of years ago. Judging from a layer of carbon the survey shows in some areas, it seems as if forested areas were targeted, presumably to set them alight."

"Just like Dandaphis," said Morales.

Dandaphis had been destroyed by the Shaa as an example to others. A group of human biologists on the planet had been caught attempting to breed a Shaa-killing plague, and executing only the conspirators hadn't seemed a grand enough lesson. Dandaphis had been bombed from orbit, and the smoke from fires and explosions had smothered the planet for years and blocked out the sun. No crops could grow, and anything that could freeze had frozen, including the inhabitants.

There had been no survivors. And no one had tried to kill the Shaa in the years since.

"Your water, my lord." The steward placed a crystal goblet before Severin. Absently, he lifted it to his lips and sipped.

"There's more, isn't there," he said. It wasn't really a question.

"We took our shuttles to the surface," Lady Starkey said. "Landed on the ocean and went to the sites of what had been port cities. Though we aren't equipped to do archaeology, we managed some very elementary digs and confirmed what we thought we already knew. What seem to be the slightly radioactive ruins of cities are in fact radioactive ruins of cities. There's a layer of ash practically everywhere we looked. We looked for the remains of one of those high-speed railways, and we found one. The rails are in poor condition but they're recognizable as the same configuration as those we use now."

As Starkey spoke, Morales paged through images of artifacts, broken foundations, twisted rails, broken stone, fused glass. Every object had in some way been destroyed, if not by celestial bombardment, then by time.

"We brought thousands of objects back with us," he said. "They're in our holds now, along with soil samples and so on."

"And we have *masses* of documentation," Starkey said. "This presentation just scrapes the surface of what we've learned." Her dark eyes turned to Severin. "But what should we do with it all? We've discovered a world that's perfect for settlement, except for this huge secret that's concealed just under the surface. A secret that's so huge that the Great Masters rewrote history to keep it hidden."

"If so," Severin said, "it's odd that they allowed the wormhole to continue to exist."

"I think they never discovered our particular wormhole," Starkey said. "Remember it's a considerable distance from the primary. I think they entered through a different wormhole, and after they evacuated they hurled enough matter through it that they unbalanced it and caused it to evaporate. That we found another route into the system was purely chance."

"We tried to find evidence of another wormhole," Morales said. "We initiated a search for any wormhole relay station remaining in the system, but that's a lot of space to cover, and the survey wasn't completed when we left."

Severin frowned at the display, which was showing bits of fused glass along with the display of a radiation counter. "The Shaa were ashamed, weren't they?" he said. "Or at least embarrassed that they'd failed. That's why they were so thorough in hiding the catastrophe. If they were proud of what they'd done, they'd have boasted about it."

Lady Starkey seemed relieved that he'd said such a thing out loud.

"It might have all been the Lorkins' fault," Morales said, his tone a little defensive. "They might not have been teachable. They might have been naturally rebellious and willful."

"They might," Severin said.

"The Shaa kept the peace among *us* for over twelve thousand years," said Morales. "And now they're gone, and just *look* at us—two civil wars in a little over ten years."

"Our record hasn't been good," Severin said. "But what about the record of the Shaa? What can we say about it?" He realized that he was rubbing his sore right forearm and desisted.

Morales looked stubborn, ready to continue in defense of the Great Masters.

"We may be recapitulating the Great Masters' early mistakes," Severin said. "We don't know how many wars they fought among themselves, or how many other planets and species they wiped out before they met us." He repressed an impulse to pound his fist on the table. *How dare they not tell us?* he thought. "Maybe they just killed anything they couldn't understand."

Morales seemed about to object, then decided against it. Severin found himself getting angry and made an effort to calm himself. "I don't know how much you know about the battle I fought with *Beacon* at Rol-mar, but I was trying to prevent its captain from doing to Rol-mar what the Shaa did to Lorkin. The scale was different—there were only three hundred thousand settlers on Rol-mar—but I think I should admit a personal prejudice and say that I'm opposed on principle to annihilating masses of intelligent life. And not only am I opposed, but I'm opposed to lying about it once it's done."

Ideas and images battled in his mind: *Beacon* blazing up as its own missile detonated; the dark, deserted station with its Shaa-sized corridors; bright flashes over cities. He rubbed his chin and tried to make sense of it all.

"You know, I never thought of the Great Masters as *liars,*" he said. "They always seemed sincere, even if they were dogmatic and unimaginative. But now everything we know about them is in doubt, and I am inclined to wonder if this sort of mass extermination is built into the Praxis somehow. It's not there in so many words, but maybe it's *implied.* Because now we're engaged in a war to keep Lady Gruum and the others from killing Terrans the same way the Shaa killed the Lorkins."

"Or Lord Mehrang killed the Yormaks," said Lady Starkey.

"The Yormaks rebelled!" Morales said, almost defiantly.

"The Yormaks were primitives with stone-tipped spears," said Lady Starkey. "There were ways of dealing with them that wouldn't have left two-thirds of them dead and the rest penned up on tiny reserves." She turned to Severin. "So we're in the age of massacre now?"

"I hope not," said Severin. "And the best way to make sure we're *not* is to make sure that massacres aren't rewarded."

Lady Starkey threw out her hands. "And if we release the information about Lorkin, does that increase the killing or decrease it?"

Severin raised his goblet of water to his lips, contemplated it for a moment, then returned it to the table. "The war complicates everything," he said. "I think I want to take some counsel before releasing this information."

"That's sensible," Starkey said, "but in the meantime what do I do with my crew? Right now I'm not allowing anyone off the ship, but denying the crew leave after a seven months' survey will make people wonder why we're shutting them up."

Severin thought about this for a moment, then shrugged. "Let them have their liberty," he said. "Just ask them not to tell anyone what you found. Some of them are bound to talk, but it's not as if they'll be broadcasting the news to all Harzapid. They'd be starting rumors here on the dockyard, but the dockyard is bound to be full of rumors anyway. Lorkin might be just one rumor among many."

Lady Starkey was relieved. Severin looked down at his crystal goblet, considered picking it up, then decided against it. Fused glass from the video display reflected in the goblet's facets.

Lady Starkey reached into her tunic pocket and took out an envelope with her seal on it. She pushed it across the table toward Severin. "Here is a foil with a copy of all our data," she said.

He took the envelope. "Thank you. And now I think I'll seek some of that advice I just mentioned." He rose, and the others jumped to their feet and braced. He waved them at ease, and then Lady Starkey escorted him to the *Explorer*'s entry port.

"Thank you for being so . . . reasonable," she said, as he turned to say his farewell.

"Reasonable?"

"I half expected to be arrested," she said.

Severin was taken aback. "Can't afford to do that," he said. "We need your ship."

"Well." She let out a breath. "It's good to be needed." He saw a tremor in her left cheek, and he realized she'd been terrified. She forced a smile.

"I'm a fan of your puppet shows, by the way," she said.

"Oh." He was surprised. "Thank you."

"I was watching your *Alois* serial when we went through the wormhole into the Lorkin system," she said. "I haven't seen anything past Episode Six."

"Aren't they on the feed here?" Severin said.

Her brown eyes widened. "I haven't looked! I've been so preoccupied I didn't think about *Alois* until just now."

"Well," Severin said. "I'll send you the missing episodes, with my compliments."

"Thank you, my lord," she said and braced.

Why was she afraid of me? Severin thought, as the elevator carried him back to the dockyard. *One look at my puppet theater and she'd know I'm harmless.*

And then he remembered that he'd destroyed the *Beacon* along with all its crew; perhaps he was a little bit frightening after all.

ONCE HE'D RETURNED to the dockyard, Severin realized he didn't quite know who to approach with his problem. Gareth Martinez was a good friend and supporter, but Martinez was off in *Bombardment of Los Angeles* and probably wouldn't be back till the war was over. Severin therefore went to the next person in line, Roland.

Roland Martinez had requisitioned an entire floor of the Empyrean Hotel, the most luxurious hotel on the ring, where all the important officers and dignitaries stayed. Roland was doing his best to run the Restoration from there and was as frantic and busy as anyone on the station, but when Severin sent him an urgent message, Roland told him to come at once.

The Empyrean Hotel was set back from the rubberized floor of the ring, secure behind an elaborate gilded fence and a screen of orange trees. Severin parked his green Sun Ray on the wide avenue, then crossed to the entrance. The hotel towered above him, a façade of gleaming white ceramic broken by a swooping abstract black pattern, like elliptical orbits superimposed on one another. The empty chairs of the lobby were guarded by armed Military Constabulary, their rifles carefully pointed at the floor until needed. One of the guards accompanied Severin up the elevator to Roland's floor.

The doors opened to reveal Lady Sula's friend Ming Lin, dressed formally in a high-collared suit. Severin greeted her, and she went into the elevator with the guard and, presumably, to her next appointment. A constable first class, in dress uniform and carrying a holstered sidearm, took Severin to a large office—one grand desk, ferns, and cream-colored poufy chairs—where Roland waited. Severin accepted Roland's offer of a golden Comador wine, and he drank without tasting as he told Roland what *Explorer* had discovered. Roland listened intently, his head cocked, his thoughts shifting like shadows behind his eyes.

"We've declared the intentions of the Restoration to return to traditional government built on the foundations of the Praxis," he said, "and now you bring information that calls those foundations into question. I think we'll have to keep this secret for a while."

"It shouldn't be a secret *forever*," Severin said. "This is of crucial importance."

"Agreed," Roland said. "After we win the war, this information should become a part of a discussion on the future of the empire."

"And if we lose?" Severin said. "I don't want all this wiped out with us, or suppressed by the Zanshaa government."

"If the crucial battle is lost," Roland said, "I will see the data is distributed as widely as I can. My sister can send it to millions via Imperial Broadcasting."

"In that case she'll have to have the data, and a presentation to explain it."

"Lady Starkey already has a presentation, doesn't she?"

"Do I brief Lady Vipsania first, or you?"

Roland sipped his wine. "You and Lady Starkey should brief both of us, I think. And now, if you'll forgive me . . . ?"

No one escorted Severin on his way out. He made his way to his viridian Fleet car, then reached into his pocket to touch the envelope with the data that might unmoor the empire.

As if it weren't unmoored already.

He returned to his office on *Expedition*, where his puppets were draped over the furniture or hung from hooks, and down-loaded all *Explorer*'s data into *Expedition*'s computers, then put it under his own captain's seal. He called up the signals board onto his desk to send a message to Lady Starkey, then paused for a moment and attached the complete *Alois* serial.

CHAPTER 7

The meeting on *Perfection of the Praxis* combined two committees: around the arculé wood table were the officers who made up Michi Chen's steering committee, and some of the politicians—Lord Mehrang, Roland Martinez, Terza Chen—who were trying to guide Restoration policy. Lamey wasn't present, so Sula assumed he was off raising his money for his planetary development scheme. Once she entered the room, a fierce solvent smell seemed to clog the back of Sula's throat, and she wanted to somehow hawk it up. Because of the urgency of the meeting, there was no reception with drinks and pastry beforehand, just a hissing urn of strong black tea with no sweetener next to a stack of cups. Sula let her tea cool untouched on the table.

To Sula's surprise, the first item on the agenda was not the attack on the Fleet dockyard, but something far more ominous. "We've been monitoring enemy news broadcasts," Michi said. "And currently the news readers are boasting of an antipartisan operation on Chijimo."

"Partisan?" someone said. "We have partisans on Chijimo?"

"According to the news readers," Michi said, "we do." She looked more drawn and jaundiced than ever, the whites of her eyes now pale yellow and surrounded by reddened lids.

Terrans in the Kalpana and Brake districts of Chijimo's capital had supposedly attacked government workers and other loyal citizens, and now police and what were called "volunteers" had surrounded the districts and were going through them house by house to root out subversives. Despite what was called "desperate resistance," progress was stated to be good. Video showed Terran corpses lying on rubble, huddled civilians being marched off, and the news reader promised interrogation for all and execution for those deemed guilty.

"This may set a pattern for future actions," Michi said. "A general purging of Terran neighborhoods."

Paivo Kangas spoke up. He had been with his wounded brother, Ranssu, in the hospital since the attack, and he sagged in his chair from weariness.

"I was on Chijimo with the Home Fleet during the war," he said. "I've stayed in Kalpana. It's a rich district with beautiful views of the river. Apartments there can go for twenty thousand or more. Brake is farther up the river and middle class, but it's still desirable real estate."

"Do we have any estimate of the population?"

"The capital's urban area holds about six million. So figure that at least a million of them are Terrans, though of course they're not all in those two districts."

Naaz Vijana's bearing was the opposite of Paivo's—even though he'd been fighting the previous day and presumably spent the intervening hours bossing the constabulary and setting in motion some kind of investigation, his activities seemed only to have stimulated him. His black eyes burned with savage intensity, and his words came in a rush.

"My lord, are you saying that this is a naked attempt to seize valuable property under the cover of suppressing rebellion?"

Paivo's lips twisted into a mirthless smile. "Of course."

It's the new fashion, Sula thought. Vijana had started it himself, when he and Lord Mehrang had killed most of the Yormaks and opened their land for settlement.

"Well then," Vijana said, "we have to make sure the enemy get nothing but rubble for their pains."

"I agree," Sula said. "This demands retaliation."

Everyone in the room knew what *retaliation* meant: missiles with antimatter warheads accelerated to relativistic speeds to race to Chijimo ahead of any warning, then plunging through the atmosphere to strike their targets. They were next to impossible to shoot down, the massive release of radiation would kill tens of thousands in an urban environment, and if the missiles were tungsten-jacketed, the resulting fireballs would set whole districts aflame.

"This has to be done carefully," Michi said. "Two can play at this game."

Once unstoppable relativistic missiles were targeted at planets, or at the antimatter-generation rings, billions could die, maybe even tens of billions. An exchange could become a war of annihilation, and that was to be avoided at all costs.

"We should make it clear that this is a specific response to a specific outrage," said Terza Chen.

"And we should target those trying to *profit* from this specific outrage," said Roland. "If Chijimo has an equivalent to Zanshaa High City, it should go up in flames, along with the governor."

Vijana was scrolling through something on his sleeve display. "Lady Michi, I'd be very pleased to help choose the targets. I assume demographic data for Chijimo is available . . . ?"

Michi sighed. "Captain Vijana, you are so appointed, along with Captain Haz." She turned to Terza. "Lady Terza, if you would assist these officers with, ah, the political aspect."

"Of course, Lady Fleetcom."

Michi turned her gaze upward to the unfinished ceiling, the tags hanging from the tangle of pipes, the frame for the ceiling that had yet to be installed. She appeared to be steeling herself for further effort. "As for that affair yesterday," she said, "I'd like to thank Captains Sula, Haz, Vijana, and the Kangas brothers for their part in suppressing the enemy attack. But now we have to decide what information we're going to release about it."

"What information do we *have*?" Sula asked.

"I've asked Captain Kai of the Investigative Service to make a report." She turned to her aide. "Lieutenant Yuen, could you ask Captain Kai to join us."

Captain Kai was a solid-looking man with bushy white hair and eyebrows. His beefy face had a benign expression, and his mellow baritone broadcast reassurance. "We have identified all of the attackers," he said.

The individual but immobile faces of the Daimong were easily identified with recognition software. The leader of the attack had been a Captain Voday, and his followers were all members of his Twenty-Ninth Company of the Legion of Diligence—who, supposedly, had been arrested, disarmed, and sent to the planet's surface in the aftermath of Michi's coup.

"*Disarmed*?" Vijana said, scorn in his voice.

"We're trying to trace the weapons," Kai said, "but it seems the serial numbers have been removed from the record."

"So that means there could be more guns out there," Vijana said.

"Yes, possibly. We are trying to locate and confine all remaining members of the Twenty-Ninth Company."

Vijana waved a hand in anger. "Why were they allowed to go free in the first place?" he demanded.

"That was not my decision, Lord Captain," said Kai.

The attackers had a good plan: assemble just before the attack on the checkpoint, then storm the officers' hostel with the aid of a large bomb. To prevent the officers from fleeing by the hostel's rear exit, a fire team had been emplaced on the avenue behind the hostel and shot at anyone trying to leave.

But, Sula thought, they were Legion of Diligence. These were the feared black-clad political police, tasked with arresting those who stole from the government or defied the Praxis. They were accustomed to confronting corrupt bureaucrats or terrified dissidents and hauling them to the interrogators, and while they had trained with their weapons, they hadn't trained for a firefight against people who shot back. They were police, not an army. Their hesitation and lack of coordination during the attack had been a result of a training regimen inadequate for their new role as terrorists.

Despite a successful infiltration, appropriate weapons, and a solid plan, the attackers hadn't succeeded in killing a single officer, though nearly twenty had been wounded, some seriously.

"Did Captain Voday command the entire unit," Sula asked, "or was there someone over him?"

"The Twenty-Ninth Company was part of a division commanded by Colonel Dai-por, a Lai-own who headed all investigations in the Harzapid system. We are trying to locate him as well."

"Arrest them all when you find them," Michi said.

Captain Kai's tone seemed designed to sooth jangled nerves. "I have already given that order on my own authority, Lady Fleetcom."

"How did they get onto the ring in the first place?" asked Roland Martinez.

Vijana's black eyes burned with anger. "How did they get into the *dockyard*?"

Kai was unruffled. "I'll answer those questions in order, if I may."

Because security cameras monitored all public areas of the Fleet dockyard, and because many areas of the civilian areas were also surveilled, the Investigative Service was able to track the attackers backward in time from the moment of the attack. The Daimong had traveled to the ring in twos and threes under false identities over the period of a week. They

had gotten into the vicinity of the checkpoint using maintenance corridors and areas under construction or renovation,
which indicated a profound knowledge of the ring's architec-
ture. Since Voday had served on the ring and had arrested
people smuggling Fleet supplies and equipment out of the
dockyard, perhaps he and his associates knew the routes by
which the smugglers operated.

"Or he had a *guide*," Vijana said. "A guide who's still at liberty to shepherd more attacks."

Captain Kai conceded this possibility. "The investigation
is in its first hours," he said. "We'll know much more by tomorrow."

Michi thanked Kai, and the man made his way out.

"That man needs to be sacked," Vijana said, "and replaced
with someone competent."

"Are you suggesting yourself?" Michi asked.

Vijana gave a savage laugh. "I could hardly do worse!" he
said. "I'd track those animals down to their lair!"

"I need you on your ship when it's ready," Michi said. "So I
won't be sending you to the IS. But what I really need to know
now is how we're going to release the information."

"We can't hide the news of an explosion and firefight right
on the Avenue of the Praxis," Roland said.

"Tell the truth," Sula said. "Say that a pack of fanatics attacked the dockyard and were all killed."

"They *weren't* all killed," Vijana said. "We took prisoners."

"The world doesn't have to know that."

Vijana nodded. "Yes," he said. "You're right."

Terza raised a hand. "Lady Michi," she said, "most of

those killed on our side were civilians who just happened to work in the dockyard. Let the story emphasize *them*. Release information about them, about their families, about their orphaned children. The attack was a tragic waste of life and resources, and it accomplished nothing from the military point of view, and the people behind it were brutal incompetents."

Sula liked that idea, turning what could have been a horrific loss into a video melodrama, complete with weeping children. She grinned. "Mention the operator of the fire-suppression robot," she said. "His contribution was decisive, and he should get a medal. Lady Michi, I'd suggest you pin that medal yourself."

Michi was puzzled. "Robot operator?" she said. "Who?"

Apparently the Military Constabulary had appropriated all the credit for defeating the Legion. "Ah," Sula said. "You see—"

"Excuse me, Lady Fleetcom." One of Michi's aides, an olive-skinned cadet with a heavy jaw, had stepped into the room. "We've received an urgent message, and Captain Shimizu wanted to make sure you saw it right away."

The aide approached Michi and handed her an envelope on a salver. Michi opened the envelope and found both a data foil and a written transcript. She unfolded the transcript and looked at it.

"Well, my lords and ladies," she said, "we've finally heard from Captain Foote and his missing Light Squadron Eight. And it seems they are in trouble."

THERE WAS A crackling in Martinez's chest as he inhaled, his ribs newly released from the constraints of heavy gravity. He deliberately inflated his chest and felt a liberating expansion as ligaments popped and loosened. Alikhan placed his dinner in front of him, and he had the sense that his casserole, like his chest, was in the process of expanding from a somewhat crushed condition.

A diet of soups, stews, and casseroles was the inevitable result of high acceleration, because they could be secured in the oven for hours while the cooks were safely strapped in their acceleration couches. He'd eaten his share of uninspired casseroles during the course of his service and had nothing against them except their monotony.

"Wine, my lord?" asked Alikhan.

"Certainly." A golden wine was poured into his crystal goblet, a goblet engraved with the crest of his former command, the heavy cruiser *Illustrious*. Between the wars he'd commissioned table settings that reflected his career, with the intention of playing host to the officers of his next command, but it had been nine years since the end of the Naxid War and his going aboard *Bombardment of Los Angeles*, and during that time the polished crystal and brilliant porcelain had languished in storage. Since there was plenty of room on *Corona*, he'd carried all the dinnerware and all his other gear with him to Harzapid, and now he was pleased to see it gleaming on the table before him.

"Wine?" asked Alikhan of Martinez's guest.

"No, thank you," said Prince Huang. "Could I get a Citrine Fling?"

"Of course, my lord."

Martinez reflected that Huang didn't look old enough to drink alcohol in any case. Huang looked down at his plate. "The lemon sauce has such a refreshing scent, don't you think? And is that carri fish?"

"Please," said Martinez. "Feel free to begin." He picked up his own fork by way of example, and he wondered whether that actually was lemon he was smelling, and whether the bit of protein he could see amid the vegetables and sauce was carri fish or something else. He certainly couldn't tell by looking. He took a forkful, and the casserole tasted fine to him. Less bland than the usual casserole, anyway.

Alikhan returned with Huang's Citrine Fling and poured it into his goblet. Martinez took a moment to look carefully at Alikhan, to see if he'd suffered from the high gravities of the last day and a half. He seemed much the same as he always had, his wavy iron-gray hair and waxed mustachios in perfect order, his uniform immaculate, his dignity intact.

"This dish is superb!" Huang said. "Please give my compliments to the chef."

"I'm sure Chef Mangahas will be gratified," said Alikhan.

"How has the carri fish been preserved?" Huang asked. "It's not rehydrated, is it?"

"I shall inquire, my lord," said Alikhan.

Martinez looked at his guest. "You're interested in cooking?" he asked.

"Cooking is the application of formulae to real life in order to produce a near-infinite series of results," said Huang. "That's what I'm *really* interested in."

"Ah. I see." Martinez raised his glass. "My lord," he said, "to the everlasting glory of the Praxis."

Huang raised his glass. "To the Praxis," he said and took a polite sip.

Alikhan drifted back into the room. "Chef Mangahas says she used salt carri," he said.

A delighted smile spread across Huang's face. "Classic!" he said. "I would never have imagined salt fish could be so tender."

"It was cooked for a long time, my lord," said Alikhan.

"A whole shift at least," Martinez said. He sipped his wine, which he thought tasted much as wine was supposed to taste. Vipsania had assured him it was a glorious vintage, and he supposed he had to take her word for it.

"Lieutenant Huang," Martinez said. "Shall we look at Carmody's exercises while we eat? We have limited time."

"Certainly, Lord Squadcom." Huang was paying full attention to his meal, but looked up when the recordings of Carmody's exercises were put on the wall displays. Around the displays, the frescoes of Torminel wrestlers continued their ferocious exercise.

Huang offered his analysis as the recordings ran. Carmody's two squadrons ran through three scenarios: a battle in which he employed the Martinez Method against a superior force, a similar battle in which both sides employed the Method, and a fight in which his own squadrons fought each other, both employing the Method. The first two were fought in a virtual environment, with a computer maneuvering the enemy forces and with simulated missile flights, but in the last the squadrons separated and maneuvered against each other, and the missile launches were real, with only the impacts simulated.

"On the whole, they've done well," Huang said. "Not surprising, because they're all veteran crews, though the Method is still a bit new to them. Squadron Commander Carmody— or his tactical officer—is developing a good practical understanding of those uses of the Method, and its limitations."

Limitations? Martinez thought. Though up to the mention of alleged limitations, his analysis and that of Huang were in agreement.

The battles themselves went as Martinez would have expected. In the first fight the Method beat the enemy despite their superior numbers. In the second, where both sides used the same tactics, the superior force won—though not as well as they might have, because the computer-guided enemy employed its tactics with less imagination. In the fight between Carmody's two squadrons, the winner had only two ships remaining after a general annihilation.

Huang pointed out a few missed opportunities, and Martinez agreed. Martinez took a last sip of his wine and tried to get a grip on his nerves.

"You mentioned the Method's *limitations . . .*" he began.

Prince Huang brightened. "Of course, Lord Squadcom," he said. "The problem lies in the fact that both sides, whatever their tactics, are inhabiting the same fractal dimension, whereas . . ." He busied himself with his sleeve display. "May I use the Structured Mathematics Display? I'd like to point out some of the features of—"

The wall display he'd chosen remained blank. Huang worked to bring it to life, but it turned out to be another victim of the series of electronic and mechanical faults that had plagued *Los Angeles* since its hasty refit. As he switched to another display, there was a knock on the door, and Sublieutenant Santana came in without waiting for permission to enter.

"My lord," he said as he brandished an envelope, "an urgent message from the fleetcom."

Martinez held out a hand as the wall displays lit up with lines of complex mathematical formulae. The envelope contained both a data foil and a printout: he glanced at the printout and then rose from his chair to slot the foil into one of the wall displays.

"My apologies, Lieutenant Huang," he said. "But I'm going to have to view the message." As Santana turned to go, Martinez held out a hand. "Please stay, my lord. You're both going to have to know this."

The message had been carried to the Harzapid system on a missile fired from the light cruiser *Vigilant*, flagship of Light Squadron Eight, commanded by Senior Captain Lord Jeremy Foote. Foote and his squadron had actually begun the war at Colamote, with a surprise attack on two enemy squadrons, both of which were annihilated without firing a shot in return. Despite its tactical success, Foote's attack had been illtimed and started the war before the Restoration had all its assets in place.

The missile bearing Foote's message to Harzapid had been accelerated to relativistic velocities, making it nearly impossible to intercept, and had entered the Harzapid system at over ninety-six percent of the speed of light, which allowed it to broadcast a vastly blue-shifted message to Michi Chen before passing through the system and into the void beyond. Michi had forwarded the message to Martinez by more conventional methods.

Martinez returned to his chair and signaled for Alikhan to refill his wineglass. He had never liked Foote, and wine might make viewing him more tolerable.

When Foote appeared on the room's video screens, though, Martinez couldn't help but feel a degree of sympathy. Foote lay in an acceleration couch, his expression strained, his exhaustion plain in the pallid skin that contrasted with the deep blue blooms beneath his eyes. Broken veins had turned his eye whites pink.

"Captain Lord Jeremy Foote to Squadron Commander Lady Michi Chen, or to whoever commands the Fourth Fleet." Foote was under hard acceleration and had to pause to gasp in air every few words. "I hope your ladyship has succeeded in taking command, because otherwise . . ." He gasped several times. "Otherwise, Footeforce is in a bit of trouble."

Footeforce? Martinez thought. Just like Foote to name his command after himself.

Through gasps and pauses, Martinez pieced together Foote's story. After obliterating the unsuspecting enemy at Colamote, Foote had piled on the gee forces and burned for the crossroads system of Toley en route to Harzapid, hoping to outrun Rukmin's two squadrons from Zarafan. Though

Rukmin would have to begin from a standing start, she needed to pass through only three wormhole gates to reach Toley, whereas Foote would need to pass through five.

Foote had arrived at Toley after weeks of acceleration but had been surprised to discover that Rukmin's heavies had arrived ahead of him. "They must already have been moving," Foote gasped. "Supreme Commander Tork must have put them on alert ahead of time and got them some delta-vee." Even so, Martinez thought, Rukmin's crews must have suffered serious casualties to stroke and accident as they burned for Toley and vengeance against Footforce.

As soon as Rukmin's ships had seen Foote enter the Toley system, they'd spun about and began a heavy deceleration, intent on letting Foote's squadron fly straight at them. So Foote had turned his own ships around and began his own deceleration, maintaining the distance.

Both sides, having been accelerating for weeks, were by now traveling slightly in excess of 0.3 c (speed of light), and though they were now burning in the opposite direction, they would still have to leave the Toley system, then make yet another wormhole jump, and then another, before they reduced their already-established momentum and began to crawl toward Toley again . . .

And that's where I'll meet them, Martinez thought. He'd been sent to rescue Foote, and that's exactly what he'd do. He'd catch Rukmin unawares and squash her like an insect caught between two rocks.

"Lieutenant Huang," Martinez said, "I'll need you to create a list of tactical options, and then work with Squadron

Commander Carmody to create exercises based on those scenarios."

Huang blinked. "Yes, my lord." He gestured at the wall display. "My presentation on fractal dimensions, my lord?"

"Not now, I'm afraid. We've got to act on this news immediately."

Huang was unable to conceal his disappointment. Martinez's sleeve display chimed, and Captain Dalkeith's bland face appeared on the sleeve's chameleon weave. "Is your meeting finished, my lord?" she asked. "Acceleration is scheduled to begin again in seventeen minutes."

"Hold the acceleration at seventeen," Martinez said. "I'd like you in my dining cabin, if you please."

Dalkeith either was incapable of registering surprise, or maybe everything surprised her equally, because her expression didn't change. "Very good, Lord Squadcom."

Martinez only just restrained himself from rubbing his hands with glee.

Other than the victory itself, he most looked forward to rescuing the smug, overprivileged Jeremy Foote—and once he'd done it, he'd enjoy rubbing it in Foote's face every time they met.

BOMBARDMENT OF LOS Angeles had scheduled a luxurious two and a half hours for their supper break, with the acceleration reduced to 0.8 gravity before a long night of merciless acceleration. Cook First Class Mangahas had produced a casserole of chicken flavored with cinnamon and other spices, the taste of which surprised Martinez, but which was praised by his guests.

He had invited his own staff, along with Elissa Dalkeith and Dalkeith's six lieutenants. Only four of the lieutenants were able to attend, for the most junior had been assigned to monitor the ship from Command, while the premiere—a white-haired onetime retiree made first lieutenant on the basis of decades of seniority—had been made practically comatose by the heavy accelerations and now rested in his own cabin under sedation, with an oxygen mask strapped to his face.

Hardly the hard-charging premiere that Martinez had once recommended for Dalkeith.

This was definitely a job for the young, Martinez thought. *And fortunately, I'm still young.*

When everyone was on their second drink—except for Huang, who still nursed his first lemonade—Martinez called up the recordings of the last several exercises. All exercises were now designed to reflect the tactical situation as Jeremy Foote had reported it, with Rukmin's forces sandwiched between Foote and Martinez's onrushing command. Martinez was unsurprised to discover that the best possible outcome was achieved when Rukmin was unaware of Martinez's approach and was annihilated by missiles that she didn't see coming.

But Martinez couldn't count on Rukmin failing to look behind her—Martinez certainly would have, knowing there was an entire hostile fleet somewhere between Rukmin and Harzapid—and when Rukmin was aware of Martinez's approach, the tactical situation grew more problematic. Though all scenarios ended with Rukmin's force being wiped out, the fact that Rukmin and Martinez were racing toward each other at a considerable closing velocity increased the danger for Martinez's command, and it seemed clear he was going to lose ships. Yet, as Michi had said when appointing Martinez to command, the Restoration couldn't afford to take any casualties at all. And so he offered hospitality to Dalkeith's officers in hopes they might be able to contribute ideas for future scenarios.

This they did, but Martinez thought these ideas were mere variations on what had already been tried, and he signaled Alikhan to refresh the wineglasses in hopes it would spur creativity.

"If the squadcom will permit," said Prince Huang, "I have a variation on that last exercise that might interest you."

Martinez looked at Huang carefully. Huang's wide-eyed expression was guileless, but Martinez suspected he had picked his moment carefully.

"Proceed, Lieutenant," he said.

Angry Torminel wrestlers watched from the frescoes as Huang's scenario shone from the wall displays. The display showed a fight that had begun the same way as the last exercise, which had ended with Rukmin's force obliterated at the cost of Martinez losing five ships. The battle remained similar until the ships neared range, and then the Restoration forces began to make mad accelerations, zooming around and over the enemy. Missiles accelerated as well, impacting Rukmin's ships well before they should have.

"Wait," said Santana. "*What?*"

He had echoed Martinez's thoughts exactly. Seeing the furious dancing accelerations of his forces, Martinez could only think that everyone on his ships had been mashed to scarlet jelly.

The scenario ended with the destruction of Rukmin's squadrons and no ships lost to the Restoration—though presumably all crew belonging to both sides were dead.

Huang, a triumphant expression on his face, looked from one officer to the next.

"That," said Dalkeith in her lisping voice, "was . . . *interesting.*"

Santana was less charitable. "What's your plan, then?" he asked. "Turn the ships over to control by computer before we all get pulped like cassava?"

"No, not at all," said Huang. "The Praxis forbids machines that think like a person, so our computers aren't smart enough to execute those tactics. Humans will be required to conceptualize and execute these ideas."

Martinez was annoyed and knew it, but he suspected he should also be impressed. "Explain how it works, then, Lieutenant," he said.

Huang smiled with bright white teeth. "Of course, Lord Squadcom." Once again, the Structured Mathematics Display flashed onto the screen and filled with calculations. "Our ships were able to move so remarkably because they were moving through an alternate fractal dimension." He looked from one officer to the next. "Are you all familiar with the High City boundary paradox?"

Martinez's memory of the paradox was vague, but he recalled it had to do with the size of the units of measurement applied to a complex natural boundary. He looked at the others and saw a few expressions of complete bewilderment, so he turned to Huang. "Perhaps you'd better refresh our memories."

"You see," Huang said, "Zanshaa High City sits on an old volcanic plug, a natural formation. Now, suppose you want to measure the boundary of this formation, so that you know exactly how big the High City is." He raised a finger. "But it turns out the measurement is very *complex*. The volcanic plug isn't an artificial structure laid out in easily measured straight lines. The boundary is full of jigs and jags and complexity that grows ever more complex as you begin to look at smaller and smaller structures."

Huang gave another of his triumphant smiles. "The length of the High City boundary is dependent on the size of the unit by which the boundary is measured." He gestured at the table. "Let's say we choose the length of this table as the unit of measurement, and we lay out the table from point to point along the whole circumference of the plug, and we'll get an answer in terms of the table." His fingers dabbled on his plate and came up with an ochoba bean. "Let's say we use this bean as a unit of measurement," he said. "We lay the bean out along the edge of the High City and measure the whole boundary in bean units—and when you compare them to the table units, the length of the boundary has radically increased. And if you use even smaller units as a basis for measurement—a human hair, say—the length of the boundary can grow *massively*."

"Because you're taking closer measurements of the smaller irregularities that your longer measuring stick simply jumps over," Santana said.

"Yes. And if the unit of measurement gets small enough, the High City boundary approaches infinity." Huang looked up at one of the screens, and the battle began to reenact itself in reverse, the ships leaping away from one another. "This offers us two exciting possibilities: first, hiding our ships in a fold in that infinite space." His giggle grated on Martinez's nerves. "What are the odds the enemy finds us?"

He pointed at the screen. "The second possibility is what I've done here," he said. "I've shifted the unit of measurement in the other direction—I've made it *larger*—which means the ships travel faster because the length of each unit of their journey has increased."

"How did you accomplish that exactly?" Martinez said. "Those aren't real ships on the screen, they're simulated."

"I altered the programming," Huang said. "I increased the amount of delta-vee for the same amount of acceleration."

The others just looked at him. Martinez felt his simmering annoyance turning to anger. "Just to make this clear, Lieutenant," Martinez said, "you changed the programming of the simulation so that the simulated ships would behave as you wanted them to."

"Exactly!" Huang grinned.

"But," Martinez said, "simulated ships *have* to do what you tell them. How do you give this benefit to real ships in what, for the sake of argument, we shall call the real universe?"

Huang waved a hand. "I'm not a specialist in impulse," he

said. "But I should think that once the theory is understood, a competent engineer could set to work on it, and our ships would be scaling up our delta-vee in no time."

Santana had clearly had enough. His words came out as something like a snarl. "We have engineers in this room," he said. "Does anyone feel *competent* to address this issue?"

There was a moment of silence, but Martinez ended it. "Real ships don't behave the way you want them to, Lieutenant," he said. "They deal with real issues of mass, motion, and acceleration across real spacetime."

"Yes, of course!" Huang said. "But—"

"Lieutenant, you want a competent *magician*, not a competent engineer," Martinez said. "You can't change the parameters of reality the same way you can change them in a simulation. I called this meeting to develop practical solutions to a real dilemma, and you have wasted our time with a theory that can't be realized in the real world." He glared at Huang. "Confine your suggestions to the practical from now on, Lieutenant."

"Ah." Huang blinked several times, and Martinez had the sensation that each blink marked the passing of an argument that Huang wanted to make, but decided against. Huang took a breath and then conceded. "As you wish, Lord Squadcom."

Martinez looked over at his silent guests. "Does anyone have a *practical* suggestion?" he asked. There was no reply. "In that case," he said, "I wish you a pleasant shift."

The others stood, braced in salute, and made their way out. Martinez watched them go with a stony gaze, then jumped to his feet and threw his napkin onto the table. He turned to

Alikhan, who stood impassively by the door, the wine bottle in his hand. "By the all," he said, "I'd like to clip that puppy's ears. But he's some kind of relation to the fleetcom, so I can't."

"I have not served dessert," said Alikhan, who stood by the door. "Some form of strudel, I believe with cheese."

"Sounds *delicious*," Martinez snarled.

"Cook Mangahas worked particularly hard on dessert, to complete it in time," said Alikhan. "It's a shame that it will go to waste."

"Don't waste it, then," said Martinez. "Give it to deserving members of the crew."

Martinez wasn't quite certain how this happened, but he ended up consuming two desserts even though he wasn't hungry, then sent his compliments to Mangahas and went to his sleeping cabin so that Alikhan could clean up the remains of the ill-starred feast.

He was running one of the battle simulations on his wall display when there was a knock on the door that led to the corridor outside.

"Enter," he called. Lalita Banerjee opened the door, a message in her hand. Her expression was tentative, as if she feared he might explode at her interruption.

"My lord," she said. "From the fleetcom."

"Thank you, Lieutenant."

She handed him the envelope and returned to the corridor. Martinez glanced at the transcript, then straightened and read it again.

The message was a caution, informing him that three missiles would be fired from Harzapid's ring, and pass *Los Angeles* en route to Wormhole One. He was not to be alarmed when this happened.

There was no explanation of when the missiles would be fired, why they would be fired, or where they were bound once they passed through Wormhole One. Apparently Michi did not consider it necessary for Martinez to know.

Because there was nothing else to do, he logged the message into the day's instructions, so that any officer standing watch would see them as he came on duty. Then, because Michi hadn't indicated whether a duplicate message had been sent to Carmody, Martinez forwarded Carmody the message.

If Michi was blowing things up, he thought, she probably had a good reason. He only wished he knew what it was.

CHAPTER 8

Ranssu Kangas had lost some of his good looks in the attack, having been shot while he was firing out the window of the officers' hostel. He'd been hit on the gun hand, losing two of his big knuckles, and then the rifle bullet had gone on through his right cheek to shatter his upper jaw and take off part of his right ear.

He seemed about as cheerful about his injuries as possible. "Nonii," he said past a jaw that could barely move. "This won't keep me from my new ship." He waved his undamaged hand. "Some rehabilitation, some surgery to patch me up, and I'll be all right. I never needed those two fingers, anyway."

"You're far from the most incapable commander in the Fleet," Sula said.

"That's what I've been telling him," said Paivo.

"Well," Sula said. "Apparently he believes you."

The officers' wing of the Fleet hospital was a pleasant, purposeful place filled with soft, vaguely floral odors and murmuring tranquility. Even the nurses and aides, men and women, seemed chosen for their physical attractiveness, perhaps with the intent of raising the officers' morale.

Sula suspected she might find a less ideal hospital if she visited the wing with casualties drawn from among the enlisted.

Ranssu lay on pastel sheets in a well-lit room. He was surrounded by gifts from friends, most of which seemed to be bottles of liquor. At least no one had offered sweets to an officer whose injuries would prevent him from tasting them.

Sula hadn't come to visit Ranssu purely out of compassion, but because she thought she needed information from Paivo in hopes of getting a better idea of how the dockyard's conversion was progressing, and what was needed to ready the Fourth Fleet for action. Since Paivo now spent practically all his time with his twin, Sula was obliged to visit the hospital.

Ranssu gave her an amused look. "I took a few shots at you," he said. "I'm glad I missed."

Sula was surprised. "Why were you shooting at *me*?" she asked.

"I saw gun flashes from the building across the street. I didn't know you were on our side, I thought you were one of the attackers." Ranssu grinned with his deformed mouth. "Lucky I'm a bad shot, hey?"

"Now I'm glad I didn't bring you a present," Sula said.

Ranssu's grin broadened, and then he winced. "Nonii," he said.

"I actually have some questions," she said, "which I think

Paivo can probably answer, while you lie on your bed and nod in agreement."

Ranssu waved the uninjured hand. "'Okay,'" he said, with audible quotes around the word. Sula laughed.

Ranssu pressed a button on his bed's control panel to give himself a dose of painkiller, administered through a cuff on his arm. In answer to Sula's questions, Paivo told Sula that the conversion of the ships for human use had absorbed practically all available personnel, even as more Terran workers were being shipped up from the planet below. The shortages weren't so much in work crews for the warships, as for the smaller support vessels and the routine tasks of the dockyard, maintaining equipment and shifting supplies and armament.

"What if we brought in help from members of another species?" Sula asked. "Workers that were familiar with the Fleet and the jobs at hand? Would they be accepted by the Terran workers?"

She decided not to mention that the species she had in mind were Naxids.

"Depends on how many bring guns and bombs with them," Paivo said. "I'd say the dockyard workers are on edge right now, and not inclined to trust outsiders."

"Suppose we put the other workers in barracks when they come up," Sula said, "and don't let them out until the war is over. That way they'd be under supervision and kept in isolation from . . ." She searched for a word. "Malign influences," she decided.

"They could still conduct sabotage," said Paivo. "Even a

small ship would make a formidable weapon if it were put on a collision course with the dockyard."

"And where will these barracks be found?" Ranssu asked. "Fleet facilities are full, and anyplace outside the dockyard isn't secure."

Sula didn't have an answer for that. "There must be a place to put people," she said, and then the answer blazed into her head. "Put them on a *ship*. We have immigration ships in the civilian dockyards that aren't going anywhere right now, and they can hold *thousands*."

"Aren't they full of immigrants?" Paivo asked.

"Most of the immigrants would have been bound for Rol-mar," Sula said, "but Rol-mar's in a state of mutiny and no-body's going there. The worlds found on the far side of Terra aren't accepting large groups of newcomers yet. The immigrants might still be on the ships, but I'll find out."

Ranssu's painkiller had made him sleepy, and he'd been drowsing while Sula had been questioning Paivo. He opened one eye, looked at Sula, and croaked out a word.

"Ghost," he said.

Sula looked at him, and then at Paivo. "Ranssu is remind-ing me to ask you a question," he said. "We've heard about the Martinez Method, and we understand that you prefer your own Ghost Tactics, and a few people have even talked about the Foote Formula. They all seem similar to an outside ob-server, and we were wondering why you prefer your method to the others."

In fact the systems weren't similar, they were identical: Sula and Martinez had developed their tactics early in the last war, and Jeremy Foote, in his position as a military censor, had eavesdropped on their conversation. But still, Sula thought, why should she give credit to the other two?

"If you ask me," Sula said, "Ghost Tactics are simply superior."

LORD NISHKAD WAS a senior squadron commander in the Fleet when the Naxid War broke out. He had been in charge of a procurement office on Chijimo, hadn't known about the mutiny in advance, and hadn't participated in it—so far as anyone knew, he was one of the vast majority of Naxids who had remained loyal to the legitimate government, or at least hadn't done anything to subvert it. Shortly after the war began, Nishkad and all other Naxid personnel were retired from the military and some of the security services. Those entitled to collect pensions were allowed to do so. Nishkad had been able to use his Fleet experience to start a procurement agency of his own, and the success of that venture had taken him to Harzapid.

Sula met him in his own apartment in a Naxid district of Harzapid's ring. So as not to be recognized she wore civilian clothing, a conservative blue suit with satin lapels, and a wide-brimmed hat to conceal her bright hair. She'd put Macnamara and Spence in civilian clothing as well, cut so as to conceal their firearms.

Sula felt uneasy stepping from the monorail in the Naxid neighborhood. Naxids zoomed along the sidewalks and down the platform, their four legs thrashing at the paving as they hurled themselves along, their flat heads darting atop their short torsos, eyes locking on one subject after another as if in search of prey. But if any of them marked Sula as a target it wasn't obvious, and the Naxids politely made room for her on the pavement.

A servant in Nishkad livery met Sula at the door and escorted her to a parlor. Spence and Macnamara were whisked away to be entertained by the servants.

A bright herbal scent, like rosemary, wafted through the parlor. Succulents rose in spears from polychrome pots. The centauroid Naxids were shorter than humans, so their ceilings were often low; but Lord Nishkad's residence had been built with guests of many species in mind, and the tall ceilings had a distinctive horseshoe arch, tucked in slightly at the bottom.

A door opened and Lord Nishkad entered. Naxids had two speeds: *fast* and *dead stop*, and Sula tried to avoid flinching as Nishkad hurled himself at her like an onrushing bullet, then came to an abrupt halt right in front of her.

"Good morning, Lady Sula," he said. "I am honored by your presence."

Sula nodded. "As I am honored by your hospitality, Lord Squadcom."

There was a pause. "I have not been called by the title in a long time."

Nishkad looked up at Sula from black-on-scarlet eyes. His dress was dignified, gray with a tall stock that restricted the possible movement of his flat head. His age was showing: Sula could see that his black, beaded scales were dull and graying, and some were missing, showing pale weathered flesh.

"Please be seated, Lady Sula," Nishkad said. "May I offer refreshment?"

"Tea would be welcome," Sula said.

A human-scale chair had been placed across a low table from Lord Nishkad's settee, and Sula sat while Nishkad coiled his four-legged body on his couch. His scarlet eyes turned to her.

"How may I help you, Lady Sula?"

"I was hoping we might help each other, my lord," Sula said. "I was hoping to offer employment to some of your old comrades who lost their places in the last war."

If Nishkad was surprised, he didn't show it. "What sort of employment, my lady?" he asked.

"I was hoping to find people with experience at supplying ships, and at converting ships from one purpose to another," Sula said. "Ultimately, for building new ships."

Because, she thought, every shipyard in enemy hands would be receiving contracts for new ships, and it was time the Restoration began to plan new warships to replace inevitable losses.

"You wish Naxid dockworkers to assist this Restoration?" Nishkad said.

"Yes, Lord Squadcom," Sula said.

"You realize that I am not a spokesman for all Naxids, and that other Naxids are in no way obligated to follow my suggestions in any matter whatever."

"That is understood, Lord Squadcom. No one expects you to produce miracles." Sula did her best to radiate sincerity. "But you have stature, influence, and respect. You would know who to talk to, and what arguments to employ."

There was a moment of silence in which Nishkad's red eyes remained fixed on Sula, and then he spoke. "There would be a certain amount of danger associated with this course," he said. "What would happen to these workers if the Restoration lost the war? And would not Naxids elsewhere in the empire be put in jeopardy?"

"We could agree that these workers would be conscripted," said Sula. "They could not be blamed if they were acting under compulsion."

"I think you have an overoptimistic view of the Zanshaa government." Lord Nishkad considered for another moment, long seconds that seemed to fall in slow motion from the arched ceiling of the parlor. "Assuming for a moment that this is even possible," Nishkad said finally, "what benefit might these workers obtain?"

"They would be paid well for work in which they are . . ." Sula's next word was chosen after some consideration. "Underutilized," she said.

"You mean they are now forbidden from taking such employment," said Nishkad. "But if my people assist the Restoration in their efforts, will the restrictions on Naxids be lifted?"

Sula had already decided not to promise anything she couldn't deliver. "I can't guarantee such a thing," Sula said. "We don't know what form the government will take after the war. But I can say that the government would be in your debt, and I would personally work to lift as many restrictions as possible."

"Ah. Thank you for your honesty." Again Nishkad spent a long moment considering his reply, until the door opened and a liveried servant entered with Sula's tea. Tea was poured, and a delicate floral scent filled the room. Sula added three lumps of sugar and stirred.

"Well," Nishkad said finally, "let us say that, somehow, all barriers to this plan were overcome. What exactly would you need?"

Sula sipped at her tea while a song of triumph rang out in her mind.

She thought she had her workers. Now all she had to do was convince Michi that they were a good idea.

LAMEY'S OUTFIT MAINTAINED his tradition of extravagance, with its blue watered silk jacket and burnt-orange facings. In polished half-boots he glided over the walk like a prince. "You haven't sent me any of those rich friends of yours," said Lamey. "Have you talked to them about my project?"

"You overestimate the number of rich people I can influence," Sula said. "And in any case I'm trying to get them to put money into Restoration bonds."

"They can put money into Esley as well," Lamey said.

"All the people who could really use defrauding are still on Zanshaa," Sula said.

"Defrauding?" Lamey said innocently. "I'm not defrauding anyone!"

"You could try Naaz Vijana. He was awarded property on Esley after he defeated the Yormaks, and the faster Esley's climate is altered, the faster his property will increase its value."

Lamey made a scornful sound with his lips. "Vijana's broke. He lost his money at tingo, mortgaged his property, then lost that, too."

Sula was not completely surprised at this, as she'd known Vijana was a gambler, but still she found herself startled at his recklessness. His victory over the Yormaks had made him a hero well placed to advance, but in the Fleet even heroes needed money, and now he was without funds.

But then during the fight at the officers' hostel he'd led the counterattack personally, so possibly he wasn't addicted to gambling per se, but to thrills. Plenty of thrills in war.

As they came near the gate of the Empyrean Hotel, they could smell the scent of the orange trees that lined the front of the building. "How about Lady Koridun?" Lamey asked. "With all those relatives of hers getting killed, she has to have inherited several fortunes. Surely she can spare at least one."

"You can go down to the planet's surface and pitch your scheme to the governor yourself," Sula said. "Though I think she's got enough on her hands running the planet she's already got."

"Will you give me an introduction?" Lamey asked.

Will I ever, Sula thought. She'd give Lady Koridun a warning to send Lamey packing.

"Of course I will," she said.

The guards at the hotel gate recognized them and let them

pass. The guards at the elevator insisted on thumbprints. Lamey was annoyed, but Sula approved of the guards taking no chances of a saboteur slipping in under false pretenses.

Outside the meeting room she met a member of the Fleet constabulary carrying out the remains of a celadon vase, along with the gladioli it had once contained.

"I hope that wasn't thrown at someone's head," Lamey said.

"No, sir," said the constable. "It just fell off a table."

"That's what they tell us, anyway," said Lamey.

In the meeting room Sula found Ming Lin, Lord Mehrang, Roland Martinez, and a waitron who provided drinks and pastry. Sula was pleased to discover that her host by now knew her well enough to provide her favorite brand of cane sugar syrup. By the time Sula had sweetened her tea and collected a puff pastry with a honey-butter glaze, Terza Chen and Vipsania Martinez had arrived.

The meeting began with a report by Ming Lin on the first issue of Restoration bonds, which had exceeded expectations. Humans were more motivated to support the rebellion than had been assumed.

Ming Lin had also been working with the Bureau of Arrears and Obligations for an issue of defunct stock, aimed at those who would be less than happy to be found with Restoration bonds in their portfolios. She was pleased to report that interest among banks, brokers, and investors was high.

"We're issuing the stock only of the most viable businesses," she said. "Fortunately for us the crash wrecked a *lot* of them."

Sula had grown used to the way the economic wreckage

that had ruined so many people could be used to generate income for those who were lucky or well placed, but this was her first experience of a *government* making money off a catastrophe. She wondered if the Zanshaa government was doing the same thing.

Under Lady Tu-hon, and with the avaricious Lord Minno in charge of the Treasury, Sula was fairly confident that they were. Except in Zanshaa, those running the government would benefit personally.

Terza Chen spoke next. Sula frowned down into her tea, but the announcement made her look up.

"Lady Michi wanted me to announce that this morning three missiles were fired from Harzapid to Chijimo, in retaliation for the slaughter of Terrans in the capital. The targets were chosen to cause maximum damage to those who would have ordered the attacks or benefited from them." She raised her hand comm. "I have targeting information if you care to review it, as well as estimates of casualties. One missile has been targeted specifically at the government district, with the hopes of catching the governor and his administration within the fireball."

"There will *be* a fireball?" Sula asked. "The missiles aren't being used only as a radiation weapon?"

"Lady Michi says the warheads have retained their tungsten jackets," said Terza. "The intention is to create as much destruction to property as possible."

There was a moment of silence as everyone pondered this news, and then a smile spread across Lamey's face. "The propertied classes are going to lose a *lot* of property," he said.

"We'll broadcast a statement explaining our actions," Terza said. "I have the text available."

They examined the text, which was a bland statement that ended with the promise not to use further radiation weapons on populations unless the persecution of Terrans continued.

"I'd like to suggest one addition," Sula said. "Which is to state that if the persecutions continue, we will assume they are directed by the Zanshaa government and will act accordingly."

There was another moment of silence. "I don't think threatening Zanshaa will raise our popularity," Roland said. "Zanshaa has been the capital for over twelve thousand years. The original Tablets of the Praxis are there. Neither side attacked the capital in the last war, because it's too symbolically important. Zanshaa is sacrosanct."

"I think it's time our leaders were held responsible for their decisions," Sula said. "Those *fucking idiots . . .*" Sula took a calming breath and continued. "Those imbeciles in Zanshaa have allowed two civil wars to start in less than ten years. How many more can the empire stand?" She waved a hand. "*Wipe them out,*" she said. "I don't care if they live on Zanshaa or in a mining habitat on Comador. Kill them all, and then maybe we can find some intelligent people to run things."

The others stared at her in shock—except for Lamey, whose face was split by a delighted grin. Sula looked back at her audience in defiance, despite having succeeded in shocking herself—she was surprised at the depth of her feeling, of her rage. She hadn't realized she hated so thoroughly.

"This is your own class you're talking about," said Lord Mehrang.

And a class to which Mehrang aspired—he might be a patron to a world, but to the high-caste Peers of Zanshaa High City he was still a provincial lord.

"If it's my class," Sula said, "then I know all the better how much happier we'd be without them."

Terza Chen looked away. Sula had just proposed her annihilation, and clearly Terza hadn't decided how or whether to respond.

"Perhaps we should take a vote on Lady Sula's addition to the statement," said Roland.

Sula's addendum was voted down, which was nothing less than what she'd expected. She shrugged and took a bite of her pastry.

"This discussion leads into another issue I hoped to raise," Roland said, "which is the question of how we return to something like normality after victory. Once we get to Zanshaa with the Fleet, for all intents and purposes we'll be military dictators, and we'll want to ease away from that kind of arbitrary power and return to a situation more . . . conventional."

Sula was quick to answer. "What's wrong with being military dictators?" she said. "It's what the Shaa did, after all—one day, Earth was running its own affairs, and the next a few dozen major cities had been destroyed and the Shaa were not only demanding submission, but that Terrans abandon their own civilization and adopt that of the Shaa."

"Did Terrans *have* civilization?" Vipsania asked. "I thought our ancestors were barbarians who lived in tents, rode horseback, and whacked each other with clubs."

"Terra had a great many civilizations," Sula said. "We had space travel and installations in space."

"Did we?" Vipsania was surprised.

"The Shaa didn't really want us to know any of that, so the history hasn't been taught. And as for barbarism, the Great Masters killed more humans in the first day than the Terrans had managed in their entire history."

Vipsania contemplated this. "Surely a single civilization is better," she decided.

Sula suppressed a smile. An ambitious woman like Vipsania could climb to the top of a single culture, but would be hard put to reign over a dozen at once.

"In any case," Sula said, "I don't see why, once we're in charge, we don't keep on running things." She waved a hand. "Handing power back to the Convocation is madness. A six-hundred-member committee running an empire? No wonder they ran straight into disaster."

"A lot would depend on who's going to be dictator," said Lord Mehrang. "Pick the wrong person, and—"

"I didn't intend just a single leader," Sula said, and then smiled. "Though if you insisted on nominating me, I wouldn't decline."

Lamey laughed. Lord Mehrang looked puzzled. "And if not a single dictator, then who?"

"We could continue more or less as we are now, a small committee, with some additions to make it more representative of the population. But *small*—not an unwieldy beast like the Convocation."

"No one's saying the composition of the leadership wouldn't

have to be altered," Roland said. "Even the Convocation." He was looking at Sula as if he were reevaluating everything he'd ever thought about her. "But what would you suggest?"

"The Chinese empire chose their officials through competitive examinations," Sula said. "And they lasted a few thousand years."

Ming Lin looked thoughtful. "I don't think there's anything in the Praxis against that idea," she said.

"That's a profound change to our entire society," Roland said, "and we can't impose that kind of change instantly. We're going to have to depend on Peers to carry out our program—there really isn't anyone else in a position to do it."

"In that case," Sula said, "we should make sure the Peers are neutered. The Peers were designed to be a class of collaborators who could be relied on to carry out the program of the Shaa. But once the Shaa were gone, the Peers tried to think for themselves, and that led to disaster." She raised both hands in an offering gesture. "That's why *we* should stay in charge. Make the Peers work for *us*, and for all's sake make them stop *thinking*."

Terza was looking at her now through narrowed eyes. "How is it that you're so virtuous that you should be running the empire?"

"I'm not virtuous," said Sula. "I'm *competent*. It's the one quality that is never rewarded in our culture." She waved her teacup. "When someone's proposed for a position, someone might say, 'Who's her family?' or 'Where in the High City does she live?' or 'Who's his patron?' They *never* ask 'Can he do the job?'" A mischievous idea occurred to her, and Sula surrendered to it, and nodded toward Terza. "I'm sure your husband can testify to *that*, Lady Terza."

Lamey could barely restrain himself from laughing. An angry flush threatened to rise in Terza's cheeks, but it was checked—no doubt, Sula thought, by her breeding.

Roland once more glided into the conversation, his soothing tone marred only slightly by his Laredo accent. "I think we should confine ourselves to the art of the possible," Roland said. "We and our friends might be competent to run things for our lifetimes, but the legacy we'd leave will be a degenerate tyranny."

How is that any different from what we have now? Sula wanted to ask, but decided she'd probably filled her quota of outrage for the day.

"We want to establish some kind of *structure*," Roland said. "Something that will survive us, and that will address the problems that brought about our current crisis. To that end, I've been working out some ideas with Mister Braga."

With Lamey the fixer? Sula's surprise turned to interest as she wondered exactly how Lamey planned to cash in on his ideas.

"One difficulty is that our leaders are isolated in Zanshaa," Lamey said. "They're dependent on receiving information from a limited number of people in the empire, and often those people are out for their own advancement and don't give a hang for the policies they're supposed to be enacting."

Sula wondered if Lamey realized he was very much describing himself.

"The Praxis mandates a clear line of direction and control,"

Roland said. "From superior to inferior all the way down the line. But when the subordinates are months away, the superiors often receive an incorrect idea of the situation. So our thought is to create other entities entitled to report up the chain of responsibility."

"Create independent committees with different areas of expertise," Lamey said. "In finance, in production, in labor, in agriculture, in resources, in security."

"How are you going to choose the membership?" Sula asked. "If local officials make the choice, they're just going to pack the committees with their clients and cronies."

Roland spoke cautiously. "We had thought," he said, "that the choice of membership would be more of a bottom-up procedure."

"Inferiors choosing their superiors?" Sula said. "Isn't that *democracy*? And isn't democracy absolutely forbidden by the Praxis?"

"I'm not quite sure what democracy is, exactly," said Lord Mehrang. He scratched one ear. "Isn't it the same thing as anarchy?"

"Democratic choice of those in authority is forbidden, yes," said Roland. "But the committees won't have any actual authority—they won't create legislation, or issue or enforce decrees—but they'll have the right to *appeal*. If they feel their interests are being neglected, they can appeal further up the line of authority, to the Convocation if necessary."

Sula considered this notion in light of her study of Earth history, then inwardly smiled. She turned to Roland. "Have you heard the term '*workers' soviet*'?" she asked.

Roland was puzzled. "No."

"You should probably look it up. And in any case you should stress firm party discipline."

Sula suspected that Roland's committee scheme would cause little but chaos, but then Roland and Lamey might want chaos for reasons of their own. Whether there was chaos or not, Sula intended to make the most of any victory before Roland and his clique gave up their power to the Convocation, their industrial committee system, or some other useless entity.

Certain people were going to disappear. Others were going to be tucked away in positions where they could do no harm. And others were going to find themselves promoted into positions of power.

Roland might object to some of her plans, but then she had no intention of asking his permission before she set her friends to work.

She had her own sources of power back on Zanshaa—and once upon a time, they had called themselves her army.

MICHI CHEN'S JAUNDICED face, shot from an unflattering low angle, appeared in Sula's sleeve display. "I'm putting you in charge of Division Three," Michi said. "That's twenty-six ships, light cruisers and frigates, in three squadrons, all just completing refit."

"Thank you, Lady Fleetcom," said Sula.

"You'll be promoted to senior squadron leader," Michi said. "You'll have your choice of flagship, and of flag captain."

Sula had been expecting this appointment for some time, and her only real question had been to what rank Michi would promote her. She had been tempted to make a bet by buying a set of squadron leader shoulder boards but had restrained herself.

"I'll take Alana Haz for flag captain," Sula said. "She was my premiere on *Confidence*, and we work well together."

"Very good." Michi consulted a list offscreen. "Captain Haz has tentatively been assigned to *Defense* and has been working up a crew in simulation, though I can send her to another ship if you prefer."

"If I can inspect the ships available?"

"I'll alert the captain of the dockyard to expect you."

"Thank you, Lady Fleetcom."

Michi appended a file with details of ships, officers, and crew. Sula thanked her again and signed off.

The call had come early in the morning, and Spence and Macnamara had just joined Sula in the kitchen, where she had been quietly drinking tea since a savage, bloody nightmare had jolted her awake a few hours earlier. Ming Lin, exhausted with shuttling to the planet and back for meetings with bankers and investors, was still asleep in her room.

Spence and Macnamara had heard Michi's message, and they looked at her expectantly, as if they expected Sula to charge to the dockyards immediately.

"We can finish breakfast," Sula told them. "And I want a shower before I go climbing through ships under construction."

She was on her way to the shower when she got a call from one of the guards on the hostel's newly installed security gate.

"My lady, there is a former lieutenant Shankaracharya who wishes to see you."

Shankaracharya? Former lieutenant? The name tickled Sula's memory. She was confident he'd never served on one of her ships, but she couldn't swear she hadn't met him at some point in her career.

"What does he want?"

"He won't say. But he's here with his wife."

That tickled another memory, but again Sula couldn't place it, and her shower was calling.

"Well," she asked, "are they armed? Do they have a bomb?"

"No, my lady."

"Let them wait in the lobby."

Twenty minutes later Sula arrived in the lobby, her skin scrubbed and aglow. She wore a Fleet jumpsuit suitable for climbing around in half-converted ships, and a soft undress cap to keep her hair clean. Spence and Macnamara followed. They both wore sidearms, and Macnamara carried Sula's Sidney Mark One over his shoulder.

Damage from the Legion raid still scarred the lobby, with broken light fixtures and pictures of distinguished Fleet officers shot full of holes. Sula's visitors sat on a sofa placed beneath a pattern of bullet marks, and they rose as she came down the stair. Memory returned as soon as she saw their faces.

"Mister Shankaracharya," Sula said, and then nodded at his wife. "Sempronia," she said. "I'm afraid I don't know whether you use Shankaracharya or Martinez these days. Your family doesn't talk about you."

"I don't talk about them, either," said Sempronia.

Sempronia was the youngest and least conventional of the three Martinez sisters. Her siblings shared a certain look—olive skin, dark hair and eyes, sturdy, mesomorphic bodies. But Sempronia had light brown hair, hazel eyes, a slim silhouette, and a lively disposition.

Too lively for some tastes. Before the war her social-climbing family had figured to jump several grades in the High City hierarchy by engaging Sempronia to PJ Ngeni—colorful, useless, and indigent, but a member of the powerful and prestigious Ngeni clan. Sempronia had kept him at arm's length, but PJ had managed to fall hopelessly in love with her anyway, and he'd been crushed when Sempronia had run off with Nikkul Shankaracharya, one of her brother's officers.

The Martinez clan had offered up another sacrifice, the middle sister, Walpurga, and there had been a sham wedding to PJ before Walpurga fled Zanshaa ahead of the Naxid advance. PJ stayed behind, and Sula assumed it was because he preferred the company of the invading Naxids to those of his wife and in-laws.

Sula, working undercover in the capital, had found PJ only too willing to join the Secret Army. He was so well placed that he was able to provide valuable intelligence, but he yearned for action, apparently with the intention of proving to Sempronia that he was worthy of the love she had no intention of giving him. Sula had kept him out of the fighting until the very last, and he died on the day she stormed the High City, carrying a rifle he never had the chance to fire.

As for Nikkul Shankaracharya, he was something of a mystery. He'd served under Gareth Martinez, but he'd left

Martinez's ship under some kind of cloud, and then Sempronia had promptly married him.

Not that he wasn't worth a second look. Slightly built, with smooth cocoa skin, liquid dark eyes, and curling hair that hung in ringlets to his collar, he looked like a slightly bruised angel, and Sula could understand why Sempronia might turn protective on his behalf.

"I'm a Shankaracharya," Sempronia said. "That other name I never use."

A Martinez who so comprehensively despised her own family could only earn Sula's admiration. "What can I do for you, then?" Sula said.

"My family manufactures electronics," Shankaracharya said. "In fact, we manufacture the sensor suite that's standard on all the new Exploration Service ships, and which is being retrofitted into the older ships as they come in for refit."

"Congratulations?" Sula offered.

Shankaracharya hesitated. Sempronia spoke out.

"It's better than the suite the Fleet uses," she said. "But we can't get a hearing here—Michi Chen's turned us down without giving us an interview."

At the bidding of her in-laws, Sula assumed. "I sympathize," she said. "But I'm not sure what I can do to help you."

"Just look at the performance statistics!" Sempronia urged. "The lidar can be tuned to specific frequencies, and that will help in penetrating the plasma bursts caused by missile explosions. You'll be able to see farther into an enemy screen and spot more missiles coming at you."

"Plasma frequency decreases as the burst expands and

cools," Shankaracharya said. "Our lidar will compensate automatically and seek the frequency best suited for penetrating the screen."

Sula considered this. "I can see it would be useful," she said. "Can you give me the specifications for the sensor suite? And more importantly, do you have tests?"

"We didn't test it against missiles, no," Shankaracharya said. He seemed almost embarrassed to admit it. "But it is designed to—"

"You could ask Captain Severin!" Sempronia said. "And Lady Starkey, who's just used the suite on a long exploration journey."

"I'll do that," Sula said. "But they haven't tested it against missile bursts either, I suppose."

"I can't imagine that they have," Shankaracharya said.

"Perhaps a test would be in order, then. But in the meantime, if you have the specifications?"

Shankaracharya passed Sula a data foil, which she pocketed. "I'll review the data," she said, "and see where I can go from there. But no promises."

Shankaracharya bobbed his head in thanks. "We appreciate it, Lady Sula."

Sula looked at Sempronia, and thought, *And if I can make your family look bad, all the better.*

Sula's car, an ovoid in viridian green, had already pulled to the curb under its own guidance. The car had a hard top, which made Sula feel a little less exposed when on the move. She took her Sidney from Macnamara and sat in the rear seat, and Macnamara and Spence shared the front, with Spence behind the controls. She took the vehicle off autopilot and steered the car into the sparse traffic, heading for the dockyard and *Defense*.

As they neared the docks proper, Sula saw that almost everyone on the street was wearing some kind of uniform. For some time her car was stuck behind a cargo carrier pulling several trailers full of Fleet supplies, but this drew away into a warehouse district, and then the vast expanse of the docks opened before them, a smooth dark plain dotted with moorings that stretched into what seemed to be the infinite distance.

"Is that Lady Michi?" Spence asked, and Sula craned her neck to see another viridian-green car, a Hunhao limousine, traveling in the opposite direction, toward the warehouse area. The long vehicle was open, and Michi Chen was visible in the back, surrounded by members of her staff. Sula raised a hand as they passed, but Michi was intent on a conversation with her aide Sandra Yuen, and Michi's car sped by.

"*Defense* is the third mooring," Macnamara said, and then suddenly a flash seared the dockyard and a thunderous blast hammered Sula's ears. She turned to look behind her and saw only wreckage and billowing smoke covering the warehouse district.

"Find us some cover," Sula said, and Spence accelerated as she spun the car around. Sula's ears rang, and she could barely hear the bolt of her Sidney as she yanked it back, then put the weapon on safety.

The nearest cover was a truck that was waiting in a line to load from one of the warehouses, and Spence stopped the car in its lee. Sula was out of the car before it had quite stopped, moving to the front of the truck body and crouching low. The acid reek of explosives stung the air. Sula peered from the front of the truck, the rifle at her shoulder, expecting at any moment to hear the rattle of firearms and see the Legion in their black uniforms appear through the smoke and debris.

No gunfire was heard. No black uniforms were seen. The gouts of flame from a warehouse were suppressed by remotely operated firefighting robots deploying from the gridded ceiling above. And then, as the smoke faded and the dust settled, Sula saw a warehouse with its façade collapsed, and before it a vehicle clipped over, and viridian-clad bodies lying over the dark surface of the road.

"Shit!" Sula said. "That's Michi's car!"

CHAPTER 9

Bombardment of Los Angeles was in the middle of combat when a priority message arrived from Harzapid. "Your eyes only, my lord," said Lalita Banerjee. "Your key is required to decode it."

Martinez wore a vac suit and helmet, the better to repel any loose hardware that tried to knock him on the head. A glance at the battle plot told him he had a few moments before he would be required to make another decision. He pulled up the message onto his screen, decoded it from the command cipher, and then experienced a soft compression of his nervous system, not unpleasant, as Caroline Sula's face materialized before his eyes. Her silver-gilt hair was pulled back from her drawn face, and a resentful fire seemed to glow behind her jade eyes.

"This message is to all squadron commanders and captains," Sula said. "I regret to report that Fleet Commander Chen was injured this morning, the victim of a bombing. Two of her staff were killed. She is in the Fleet hospital in stable condition, but she's lost a leg and it will be some time before she can resume her duties. A full recovery is expected in time. In the meantime I've assumed command of the Restoration forces here at Harzapid."

Her tone was flat, but behind her words Martinez heard grim fury. "I wish to assure you that continuity of mission will be maintained," Sula said. "I'll leave it to you to decide when or if to inform your crews of this development, but if so, please emphasize that we are doing everything possible to track down the saboteurs and that we expect a resolution of the case very soon."

The orange end-stamp filled the screen, and Martinez realized he'd forgotten to breathe. He pulled in air against one and a half gravities, then tried to come to grips with what Sula had just told him. Michi had lost a leg, and they would grow her a new one and attach it, but that would take time, and then there would be months of rehabilitation. So Michi was effectively barred from any active part in the war.

And now Sula was apparently in charge. But Martinez knew that she was far from the most senior captain on station, and he wondered if Michi, lying in her hospital bed, put Sula in command or whether Sula had staged some kind of coup.

It wouldn't be the first time, after all.

"My lord," said Prince Huang. "Recommend course shift to zero-four-four by zero-one-seven relative."

Martinez shifted his attention to the tactical display. "Agreed," he said. "Signal the squadron to begin the maneuver in one minute."

"Zero-four-four by zero-one-seven relative," repeated Aitor Santana. "Commence in one minute."

Of course it was not a real battle. *Los Angeles* was engaged in a simulation for training purposes, with the computer playing the opposing forces as well as other friendly ships in the flagship's squadron. The scenario was a simple one and would probably end with massive casualties on one side and the utter annihilation of the other.

It wasn't a full-blown exercise, with *Los Angeles* maneuvering, firing its engine, and launching missiles—instead the cruiser was accelerating at a steady one point five gee toward Wormhole One. Simulated accelerations and movement were probably all the inexperienced crew could handle.

The heavy accelerations of the first ten days had been reduced, in part because it was now known where Foote and Rukmin actually were. There was an ideal place to ambush Rukmin's force, and a lower rate of acceleration would see the Restoration forces there on time.

While he waited for the change of course to take place, Martinez let his thoughts return to the situation on Harzapid. He wondered how many other people were injured or killed by the bomb, and if it was as bad as the attack on the officers' hostel, or as bad as the hostel attack *could have been*. Martinez knew there was censorship in place, and so he couldn't trust any official casualty figures that had come out of Harzapid.

And he also didn't know how to view Sula being in command. He called up the video again and looked closely at Sula's shoulder boards, which showed her as a senior squadron commander. That was his own rank, and he felt thankful that at least he had seniority. Unless of course Sula was self-promoted, in which case she could further promote herself all the way to Supreme Commander and Vice-Ruler of the Universe.

Well, there was nothing Martinez could do about it from the swiftly receding *Bombardment of Los Angeles*, so he returned to the tactical problem he'd set for *Los Angeles*'s crew and began to plan when he would release his simulated missiles.

TWO HOURS LATER, the exercise had ended—Martinez had been mildly gratified by *Los Angeles* and its simulated squadron having wiped out the simulated enemy while losing only half their number. The crew had secured from general quarters and were being given their supper. Much preferring the scent of sesame oil to that of his vac suit seals, Martinez finished a noodle dish in his dining room while reviewing video of the exercise.

At the end of the meal Alikhan appeared with a small glass of mig brandy and then began to clear the table.

"How do you think the exercise went?" Martinez asked him.

"I think the crew handled their panic fairly well," Alikhan said.

Martinez nodded. "I suppose that's the best we can hope for," he said.

Alikhan cleared away the dishes and left Martinez contemplating his glass of brandy. There was a knock on the door, and Aitor Santana entered.

"Another eyes only message from Harzapid, my lord," he said.

"I'll take it." Martinez froze the video and looked up at

his signals lieutenant. "You did very well this afternoon, Lord Aitor."

"Thank you, Lord Squadcom." He hesitated. "I've learned a lot. Lieutenant Banerjee is a good teacher."

Martinez thought he might as well turn pedagogue himself and ask for Santana to analyze the day's experiment. "How do you think the exercise went, Lieutenant?"

Santana gave the question a few seconds' thought before making his reply. "Very smooth, Lord Squadcom," he said. "But the exercise wasn't particularly challenging. Those weren't real ships we were maneuvering."

"True," Martinez said. "But there were no significant errors, and that's something we can be satisfied with. More challenging exercises will come."

Once *Los Angeles* united with Carmody's two squadrons to complete Division Two of the Fourth Fleet, more complex exercises would be possible, and all would be aimed at crushing Rukmin in an ambush.

"Well," Martinez said. "I should view the message now. Thank you, Lord Aitor."

Santana handed Martinez the envelope containing the message on its data foil, and Martinez deployed his squadron commander's key to unlock the command cipher and view it.

Martinez found himself bewildered by the message. Though it originated in the fleetcom's office, it was delivered by a female cadet Martinez had never met and ordered *Los Angeles* to fire two antimatter missiles toward Harzapid, one thirty-one seconds behind the other. The first would explode short of Harzapid, and the other would pass through the ex-

panding plasma cloud, decelerate, and be recovered by another vessel. No explanation of the exercise was given.

The missiles were to be fired in just under sixteen hours,
time enough for a query to be sent from *Los Angeles*, and a
reply to reach him.

"Squadron Commander Martinez to Fleet Commander
Chen, personal, eyes only," he said. "I have been ordered to fire
two live missiles toward our dockyard, which I find puzzling. I
would be obliged if this order were confirmed. End message."

He coded the message and sent it, and early the next
morning received his reply from Sandra Yuen, one of Michi
Chen's staff. Yuen was a mess, with two black eyes, a splint
on her broken nose, and a full assortment of cuts and bruises
spattered across her face. Her message merely repeated the
instructions from the first.

At least the order came from someone he knew. Dutifully
Martinez fired the two missiles on schedule and watched as
the first exploded and the second, presumably, didn't.

What was that *about?* he wondered, but he clearly wasn't
going to be told, and so he turned his attention to the more
urgent matter of destroying Rukmin's squadrons.

IT WAS ELEVEN days before Michi Chen felt able to resume
her command of the Restoration. Most of her injuries had
healed, and her new left leg was growing in a vat of nutrient
solution in the Fleet hospital. Her stump had been slathered
in a gel that would ready it for the attachment that would put
Michi on her feet again.

During those eleven days, Sula had moved quickly and quietly. The test with live missiles had demonstrated the superiority of Shankaracharya's sensor suite, and she had ordered enough for the entire Restoration armada. Unfortunately most conversions couldn't be made right away—she had ordered all warships capable of flight to depart the station, because broadcasts from Zanshaa featured commentators raving about the antimatter attack on Chijimo and what was termed its "innocent civilian population." Sula worried that Zanshaa might retaliate for Chijimo by sending a barrage that would wipe out Harzapid. Since she'd sent the ships on a trajectory toward Wormhole One, she ordered them to launch a barrage of decoys, and hoped that if Zanshaa decided to strike, the warships might be able to shoot a few missiles down, or that the decoys would absorb some of the barrage.

The warships, now on the move, would have to acquire their new sensor suites on the run, and that meant support ships would have to bring the new electronics from Harzapid, along with enough personnel to efficiently install them. Shankaracharya agreed to provide technicians.

Those warships remaining at the station were the two squadrons adapted to Cree crews, which required extra work because all displays had to be shifted from auditory to visual perception. During the course of their refit, they would receive the Shankaracharya sensor suite while still in dock.

Sula decided to equip support vessels with the new electronics and use these to supplement the warships, staying out of the battle while using their sensors to probe for the enemy.

How they would actually accomplish this in practice was a problem yet to be worked out.

While all this was in train, two large immigration ships were requisitioned, then shifted from civilian to Fleet docks, while Naxid dockworkers, traveling in secret and under false names, were moved into them. Lord Nishkad, procurement specialist that he was, organized them into work parties, and they quietly went to work converting, arming, and loading support vessels that would be needed for the Restoration fleet to resupply and to extend its influence into enemy-controlled space. They also began to work in areas of the supply chain that were experiencing blockages due to lack of trained personnel.

After the Fourth Fleet had finished its conversion, Sula planned for it to begin an expansion. New warships would be laid down, and Terran and Naxid workers would compete to finish them ahead of schedule.

Fortunately there was money to pay for all this. Ming Lin had masterminded the first sale of stock from the Committee for Banking and Exchange, and it had gone well, buoyed by the fact that the economy of Harzapid was showing signs of robust growth. Once the regulations on bank reserves were eased, the banks could make loans and the recovery could begin in earnest.

In fact the recovery was progressing throughout the area controlled by the Restoration. The only element of the economy that was lagging was interstellar shipping, and that was because shipowners were worried that if they sent their vessels to Harzapid, the Fourth Fleet would requisition them for its own purposes.

As long as the money kept coming in, Sula concluded, she'd let Michi Chen worry about the merchant economy.

But now Michi Chen was seated in an aesa-leather chair in her new office at the Empyrean Hotel. Though the walls were paneled and the floors deeply carpeted, the place still smelled like a hospital. Michi wore a fleet commander's viridian tunic, and a coiffeuse had arranged her hair while a cosmetician applied cosmetics. A desk had been wheeled up to her, in part to conceal the fact that below the waist she wore only a hospital gown, with her stump and her surviving leg propped on a footstool. The camera would show a poised, smiling commander receiving congratulations from her subordinates— but like most public relations, it was all a matter of angles.

Still, Sula thought that even without the cosmetic Michi looked better than she had twelve days ago. Enforced bed rest, proper nutrition, and a diet of fast-healer hormones and antibiotics had brightened her eyes and warmed her jaundiced complexion. Now, Sula concluded, Michi would be in much better condition to begin once again to work herself to death.

The Fleet public relations techs set up cameras and lights. Once the cameras began recording, Sula marched to Michi's desk, braced in salute, and formally surrendered her temporary command to the head of the Restoration.

"Cut!" said the director. "Lady Sula, you stepped out of your light. One more time, please."

Sula repeated her brief scene, but one of the cameras hadn't triggered, and she had to do it again. This time there was too much noise from someone walking along the outside corridor; and the next, someone coughed at the wrong moment.

When the seventh take failed due to a technician tripping over a cable and plunging the room into semidarkness, Sula turned to the director.

"Which side are you on, anyway?" she demanded. "Has Tork sent you here to commit sabotage?"

The director stared at her wide-eyed. "Sorry, my lady!" he said. "I don't—"

"Why don't you make sure everything is working *before we start*?" Sula snarled. "And then tell everyone *not to fucking move*!"

"Ah—yes, my lady."

The scene came out right on the eighth take, and then more scenes were shot as Roland Martinez, Lady Governor Koridun, and a parade of subordinates came forward to offer Michi their congratulations. Among them were the Kangas twins—Ranssu had been released from the hospital on the same day Michi was admitted, having only lost two fingers as opposed to a whole leg. Part of his face was encased in a protective sheath to hold his broken jaw in place, and to protect a skin graft, but he was already mobile. He'd decided against having his fingers replaced, which would delay his taking command of his frigate. "I only need one finger to push buttons," he'd said, and waved a blithe hand. "Nonii."

Following the congratulations ceremony came the medal ceremony. For their actions in defense of the officers' hostel, Sula, Lady Alana Haz, the Kangas brothers, and Naaz Vijana received medals—Vijana remotely, since he was somewhere between Harzapid and Wormhole One in command of a light cruiser squadron. Sandra Yuen pinned the Medal of Merit,

First Class on Sula's tunic while Michi read the citation, and Sula idly wondered whether she'd decisively pulled ahead of Martinez in the medal race.

Not till she won the Golden Orb, she decided.

Other rewards were scattered about, to recipients not present: Spence and Macnamara, and various officers concerned with the hostel's defense. Sula had made certain that the operator of the fire suppression boom, who had drenched the attackers with fire retardant, received the civilian version of the Award for Valor. That she was a Lai-own acting in defense of the Restoration made the award all the more important as propaganda.

After the ceremonies Michi was carried to her bed for a rest, and the various guests lunched in the hotel restaurant. Lady Koridun sat next to Sula and kept urging her to tell the story of the battle at the officers' hostel, interrupted constantly by Lamey, who kept trying to sell Koridun on his planet-development scheme. Koridun, warned ahead of time by Sula, did her best to ignore him. Afterward Sula returned to Michi's suite and found there Captain Kai, the Investigative Service officer who had been abused by Naaz Vijana for not finding Colonel Dai-por, the presumed mastermind behind the attacks. During her period of command Sula had received Kai's reports and had realized that Vijana was mistaken.

Well, *mostly* mistaken.

Sula and Kai were called into Michi's room to find her propped up in bed, her eyes bright, her hand comm in her lap. She was dressed in a luxurious embroidered bed jacket of silk, and the remains of her lunch sat on a tray by her bedside. Elaborate bouquets of flowers were arrayed on either side of the bed and filled the room with their fragrance.

"Captain Kai wanted to report on the search for the bombers," Sula said, "and I wanted to give you a briefing on some items too sensitive to have included in my formal report."

"Sit, if you please," Michi said, and her eyes turned to Kai. "Captain Kai first, I think. I have to say that my interest in the matter is very personal."

Kai's beefy face, as always, radiated confidence and reassurance. "Lady Sula already knows that we've located Colonel Dai-por and have been keeping him under surveillance for three days now."

Michi seemed startled. "He hasn't been arrested?"

"We're keeping him under close observation, and monitoring his communications, to find out who he's talking to while we map the extent of his organization." His pleasing baritone nearly sang the words.

"There's no way he can get away?"

"He was located in a rather remote resort area, occupying a hunting cabin in the off-season. There's a lake on two sides of him, and only one road in and out. We've taken care to make sure he can't get away on foot, and he doesn't have a boat."

In spite of Kai's reassuring tone, Michi seemed a little suspicious. "And how is your mapping of this organization faring?"

"We've identified his couriers and tracked them on their

rounds." Kai grinned and seemed so pleased with himself that he was practically bouncing in his seat. "And he's been—well—a little careless with signals communications. He's got some false identities and comm accounts attached to those identities, and he knows the words that would get the automated security algorithms interested in his conversations, so he's developed a crude substitution code, 'cake' for 'bomb' and so on. But really, he's making too many calls and sending too many instructions. He should rely on couriers, but he's too impatient."

"I'm afraid he's following the playbook I developed in the Naxid War," Sula said. "He's got a little bomb factory going, and he started with a store of weapons that he's trying to expand with homemade weapons and ammunition. He's trying to organize his group in cells, but of course all the Legion personnel know each other, so that won't get him far until he starts recruiting outside his sphere."

"I don't think he's doing very well at recruiting," Kai said. "After all, everyone on the planet knows that if they prove troublesome, we can just drop a bomb on their heads."

Michi raised her eyebrows. "We have that consolation, yes," she said. "When do you anticipate making the arrests?"

"At your command, Lady Michi," said Kai. "But I would recommend waiting at least another day. Dai-por's communications indicate he's got an important courier visiting tomorrow, one we haven't yet been able to identify. After we track that one to her destination, we can wrap up the whole ring within a matter of hours."

"I'll take your recommendation, then, Lord Captain," said Michi. "But I want your operation to go off without a hitch, do you understand?"

Kai favored her with his benign smile. "Of course, Lady Fleetcom."

Michi's eyes tracked to Sula. "Your report, then, Lady Sula?"

Sula indicated Kai and the members of Michi's staff who had been silently hovering around her bed. "If we could have privacy, Lady Fleetcom?"

The others were sent from the room, and Sula began with some candid evaluations of some officers and personnel. She then mentioned her test of the Shankaracharya sensor suite, and how it had proved superior to those on Fleet vessels for detecting enemy missiles. Michi's lips tightened as Sula explained her plan for reequipping all Restoration ships with the new hardware, but she made no comment.

Then Sula told Michi about Lord Nishkad and the Naxid workers she'd brought onto the station and watched horror rise on Michi's face like a pale dawn.

"IN VIEW OF the fact that I will be unable to take command of the Fourth Fleet against Lord Tork," said Michi, "I hereby promote you to the rank of fleet commander. Congratulations—and we could really use a victory about now, so please give us one."

Martinez stared at the video, his nerves in something akin to a state of shock. He had anticipated that he'd receive an expanded commission following Michi's hospital stay, but he hadn't imagined a formal promotion, let alone full tactical control of the Restoration forces.

Still, being a fleet commander would help in dealing with the defecting squadrons of the Home Fleet when they arrived, and maybe that's what Michi had in mind.

"I'm sending you a report on the current status of the Fourth Fleet," Michi continued. "I'm also promoting Lady Sula junior fleet commander, so she'll be able to prepare the ships here for your use against Tork, after which she'll continue in command of Division Three." This was said with a slight hint of distaste, as if Michi were reluctant to make the promotion. Martinez wondered how Sula had gotten up Michi's nose.

"I'll remain in the dockyard to coordinate supply and support elements," Michi continued, "and I'll decide issues of policy. Let me know if you need anything, and I'll do my best to provide it." Her face relaxed, and she offered a hint of a smile. "Good luck with all this," she said, "and make Terza proud." The orange end-stamp filled the screen.

The message had arrived when Martinez was in his office, doing administrative work while eating his breakfast of coffee and jellied mayfish, the dose of protein he liked in the morning. He called for Alikhan.

"Ready my full-dress uniform," he said. He should dress formally to send his thanks back to Harzapid. As Alikhan turned to leave, Martinez called him back.

"I don't suppose you've got a fleet commander's insignia somewhere in your stores, do you?" he asked.

Alikhan's smile spread beneath his curling mustachios. "I believe I do, my lord," he said.

"Attach it to the tunic later," Martinez said.

To send his thanks while wearing the insignia, he thought, would be a sign of egotism and self-promotion.

He would, he hoped, avoid all that.

CHAPTER 10

Division Two of the Restoration Fleet had worked on its plan for the Battle of Shulduc for nearly a month. They had drilled every conceivable scenario, and after Martinez and *Los Angeles* had joined Carmody's squadrons on the far side of Harzapid Wormhole One, the scenarios had been as realistic as possible, with the ships maneuvering against each other in real time, the crews being subjected to real accelerations and real gee forces. To develop the weaponers' skills, missiles were actually fired and maneuvered against each other, and point-defense systems, operating at less than lethal levels, had tried to hit the missiles on their way.

"The crew handled their panic fairly well," Alikhan had said of one early drill, and over time *Los Angeles*'s holejumpers had handled their panic better and better, and eventually most of the panic faded away in spite of Dalkeith's pedestrian leadership and the first officer lying in a near coma. In terms of performance, *Los Angeles* lagged behind the other ships of Division Two, but the other ships' crews had served together for years and knew each other and their ships inside out. *Los*

Angeles would do well enough. It would not embarrass itself in action and would not offer itself as a target any more than the other ships in the division.

Martinez knew a lot about the forthcoming Battle of Shulduc—he knew both sides' orders of battle, the number of missile launchers on each side, and the names and histories of the captains; he knew where the battle would take place and where each element of each fleet would be in relation to one another—and he knew beyond any doubt that he would win—but when all was said and done, there was a lot he *didn't* know, and all that had to do with the enemy.

He knew that Rukmin's two heavy squadrons had arrived at the crossroads of Toley ahead of Jeremy Foote's light squadron, after which both forces had flipped over and begun a deceleration as fierce as the acceleration that had brought them to Toley in the first place. Instead of trying to race Foote to a destination, Rukmin was now in a race to catch him, but they were still moving toward Harzapid because they were unable to decelerate quickly enough.

And this meant that Division Two, when it flashed through Shulduc Wormhole Three, would appear *behind* Rukmin, and because of the deceleration would overtake Rukmin swiftly, which meant that several things were happening at once. From the perspective of an objective observer, Foote and Rukmin were flying toward Harzapid but decelerating, where Martinez was accelerating from Harzapid to overtake them. From the perspective of Rukmin, she was accelerating to overtake Foote, who was likewise accelerating to maintain his distance. Martinez's perspective showed him accelerating to overtake Rukmin and Foote, who were flying ahead of him as quickly as they could.

Because the trajectory and acceleration of the various fleet elements were known, it was known that the Shulduc system would be the site of the battle. Shulduc was a system in which a number of gas giants battled for gravitational dominance, and any small rocky planets had long since lost the war and been turned to rubble. There were no habitable worlds, and the system's only residents were the crews of the system's wormhole relay stations.

When Division Two emerged from Wormhole Three into the system, it was possible that Rukmin wouldn't know they'd arrived. Martinez's Plan One was based on this possibility, and he intended to keep Rukmin as ignorant as possible. Division Two would launch a hundred missiles and a couple dozen decoys before entering Shulduc, and then go dark before passing through the wormhole, shutting down all active sensors as well as the engines. The ships would make the transit in a particular order, at particular angles, so as to arrive in something like battle formation. There would be no missile or engine flares to alert the enemy. Even without the engines lit, Division Two and Rukmin would rush toward each other with furious speed, and with luck the first warning of Martinez's arrival would be a hundred missiles making their final course corrections as they zeroed on a target.

Michi Chen had asked for a battle of annihilation, and Plan One would give her one. The only problem with Plan One was that it required the enemy's cooperation, and it assumed that Rukmin wouldn't be scanning behind her. This seemed unlikely, given that Rukmin knew perfectly well that there was a hostile fleet somewhere between Shulduc and Harzapid, and that it might appear at any moment.

Martinez had decided to give Rukmin a distraction that might rivet her attention in a different direction. He and Foote had been in occasional communication, via missiles shot through the wormhole system to broadcast messages, which was how each knew to fine accuracy where the other was. Martinez had ordered Foote to simulate a malfunction aboard one of his ships, one that would shut down the engine. The appearance of this helpless target was designed to attract Rukmin's attention, as would the series of maneuvers undertaken by Foote's squadron, before to all appearances Foote would decide to rally around the crippled ship and engage in battle, right at the moment when Martinez could soar in to save him.

Rukmin would have seen the missiles going back and forth to Harzapid, so she'd know that Foote had been in contact with someone. But Martinez tried to time his replies so that they plausibly could have come from Harzapid, which might help Rukmin rest easy. Martinez hoped that the prospect of fighting the outnumbered, outgunned Foote would keep Rukmin focused on the enemy in front of her, and not what might be sneaking up behind.

There were other plans than Plan One, but they all depended on how Rukmin reacted once she discovered the two squadrons racing up her tail, soaring behind a barrage of missiles flying at her like a swarm of fierce, lethal insects.

ON THE DAY of the battle, Martinez was in the flag officer station well before he had to be, in his vac suit and carrying his helmet in one hand and a flask of coffee in the other. Lalita Banerjee, on duty at the signals station, stiffened as she saw him enter, the closest she could come to bracing while lying on her contoured acceleration couch. Martinez waved his coffee flask in reply as he made his way to his own acceleration couch, where he stashed his helmet in the web pocket, strapped himself in, and pulled down the displays to lock them in front of him. He stretched the elastic of his fleet commander's key over the wrist of his vac suit then pulled it off and inserted it into the slot of one of his displays. The displays lit, and he lost himself for a time in reviewing plans for the upcoming battle, his mind filled with trajectories, accelerations, possibilities. Prince Huang and Aitor Santana entered and took their places in silence. Martinez paid them no attention until Prince Huang spoke.

"Fifteen minutes to transition, Lord Fleetcom."

Martinez blinked as he returned to the small, bare room with its displays and consoles. "Thank you, Lieutenant," he said. "Signals, message to division from flag: 'Proceed as per plan. See you on the other side.'"

"Very good, my lord."

Martinez took his helmet from the mesh bag and put it over his head. The scent of suit seals rose in his perceptions, and the constant murmur of the ship's engines dimmed. He felt cool circulating air on his face.

"My lord," said Prince Huang. "Missiles launched from every ship in the division."

"Thank you, Lieutenant."

Martinez watched on his display as the missiles raced toward the wormhole, then cut their engines just before they transited to the Shulduc system and vanished from the display. Ships and decoys began to make minor course adjustments to take them through the wormhole on the schedule, sometimes only seconds apart.

Martinez triggered a virtual display, and a schematic universe appeared in his senses, projected on the optical centers of his brain. The virtual display was confined to ships, missiles, trajectories, and nearby astronomical objects, and it eliminated anything that might distract him from the task at hand: he saw no distant stars, the bare walls of the flag officer station faded away, and the others in the room became mere auditory presences, words only.

Another auditory presence intruded: the warning sound for zero gravity. A few seconds later the engine rumble faded completely, and Martinez floated free in his harness.

Ships vanished from the display as they made their transitions through the wormhole. The abstract symbol for the wormhole, a whirling spiral, came up very fast in the virtual display, then the spiral engulfed *Los Angeles*—and suddenly a whole new universe appeared, and arrayed before him were Rukmin's sixteen ships, all blossoming on Martinez's visual cortex like burning flowers, with Foote's eight ships some distance beyond. One of Foote's ships had ceased its acceleration, and the others were maneuvering in a somewhat confused manner.

"We're being painted, my lord." Aitor Santana sounded disappointed.

"Those may be Foote's lasers," Martinez said. "Wait till we see if Rukmin reacts." But even if those were Foote's ranging lasers painting Rukmin and incidentally lighting up Division Two as well, the echoes would still be reaching Rukmin's sensors. Plan One depended entirely on Rukmin paying no attention to those echoes that would be appearing on her sensor screens in just a few minutes.

Long seconds ticked by, and then Rukmin's ships cut their engines, which told Martinez he'd been spotted. He felt a brief moment of disappointment, followed instantly by a fury of calculation.

"Lots more lasers painting us, my lord," said Santana.

"Flag to division," Martinez said. "Accelerate one gee. Commence evasive maneuvers."

"Accelerate one gee. Commence evasive procedure."

The point-defense lasers on smaller ships could be used offensively, but Rukmin's heavy cruisers had far more dangerous defensive armament in the form of antiproton beams, which could blast whole chunks out of the Restoration ships if they didn't dodge out of the beams' path. A few seconds after Martinez's order, *Los Angeles*'s engines ignited, and Martinez's acceleration cage fell to its deadpoint, then lurched a bit, the deadpoint swinging to a new bearing. *Los Angeles* had begun its swooping series of evasions, and since it was currently traveling at 17.9 percent of the speed of light, each swerve left plenty of space between it and any beam weapon firing at where it used to be.

Martinez's inner ear registered the movement, but he kept his eyes riveted on the display. What Rukmin had just seen was Division Two's sixteen ships plus thirty decoys, which were missiles configured to appear on radar and lidar as a warship. Rukmin's first view of Division Two was of thirty-six vessels bearing down on her, more than twice her number and enough to assure her annihilation.

But a few seconds' reflection would show her that many of those blips were decoys. Encouraging, but it wouldn't change the fact that an enemy force of unknown numbers was coming straight at her with all the confidence in the world.

She could accelerate on her current bearing and hope to engage Foote before Martinez could intervene, but Foote could easily keep his distance. Or Rukmin could rotate her squadron and charge Martinez and hope to engage in a head-on battle of mutual annihilation.

Martinez had plans to avoid anything resembling mutual annihilation, but what really worried him was the possibility that Rukmin would simply accelerate at a lateral angle, off into deep space. She could blast away at ten gees or more, which would force Martinez and Foote to chase her, and though Rukmin would eventually be run down and destroyed, it would draw the Restoration forces far off their intended track.

But Rukmin was more aggressive than that. Her ships swung on a track for Wormhole Three, and her big antimatter torches ignited. At the sight Martinez heard a singing in his nerves.

Challenge issued!

Challenge accepted!

Rukmin was going to go down fighting.

"Flag to Captain Dalkeith," Martinez said. "Fire missiles at Wormhole Stations One and Three."

The two wormhole stations on the far side of the battlespace were in the hands of the enemy and would report the progress of the battle to the government on Zanshaa. Martinez had tactics he preferred not to reveal to eavesdroppers, and so he would wipe out the observers before the battle reached its climax.

The station at Wormhole Two, leading to Harzapid, had been recrewed by the Restoration and would be reporting the news of Martinez's triumph to Harzapid.

Unless, of course, Rukmin chose to blow them up.

"Dalkeith to flag," Banerjee reported. "Missiles fired."

Martinez had already seen the missiles on his display, fired from their tubes on chemical rockets, then lighting their antimatter torches once they were sufficiently clear of the ship. They raced off on a looping trajectory to avoid Rukmin's counterfire and arrowed for the stations at an acceleration that would have pulped any human passenger and that would assure the destruction of the stations before the light from the battle reached them.

Foote, Martinez saw, had flipped his entire squadron and was charging after Rukmin at something like four and a half gee, which would ensure that he, or at least his missiles, would be in at the finish.

But in the meantime Martinez and Rukmin were hurtling toward each other at something in excess of 14 percent of the speed of light. With the ships closing that fast, and the space between them soon to be filled with hundreds of missiles,

Rukmin's tactic of bringing on a battle of mutual annihilation seemed perfectly plausible.

Martinez didn't want the annihilation to be mutual, and he'd planned to avoid that.

"Lord Fleetcom," said Prince Huang, "recommend Plan Two commencing in six minutes. I also recommend lighting off our missiles to provide cover for the maneuver."

A glance at the display showed that the timing was plausible. "Very good," Martinez said. "Signals, send to all ships in Division Two."

The message went out, and the engines of Division Two's advance guard of missiles lit, and the missiles tore straight for Rukmin and her ships. A swarm of countermissiles raced from enemy batteries, and the two began to close with one another.

Foote opened fire as well, a wave of missiles blazing out from the light squadron. Rukmin was going to be hit from both sides.

"Flag to all ships," Martinez said. "Another volley."

Detonations erupted in the space between the two forces, overlapping balls of fierce hot plasma, and Martinez's view of Rukmin's ships faded in the radio blaze. Martinez watched the second wave of missiles racing toward the enemy with tails flaming, and then there was the urgent sound of the zero-gee warning, and Martinez floated for a brief moment before his acceleration cage swung as *Los Angeles* rotated to a new heading. Then there was an acceleration warning, and Martinez was punched into his seat as the cruiser's engines lit.

Division Two of the Restoration Fleet consisted of two squadrons, each of eight heavy cruisers, which made a total of seventeen once *Los Angeles* had been added to the order of battle. The concept of a "division" was itself new and was an attempt to better organize the expanded Fleet that had come into existence after the Naxid War. During that war, the squadron was the largest maneuver unit, but with so many squadrons in the expanded Fleet, maneuvers—not to mention real battle—had threatened to degenerate into confusion. So in hopes of better organizing the Fourth Fleet, Michi had created a unit called the "division," which would contain two or three squadrons.

Division Two had been led by Squadron Leader Carmody of Heavy Squadron Eleven, the senior of the two squadron leaders in the unit. Martinez had replaced Carmody in command, then had attached his own ship to Heavy Squadron Twenty, commanded by a Junior Squadron Leader Khalil, who—though formally polite—Martinez suspected resented his usurpation of the unit.

Plan Two involved Squadrons Eleven and Twenty separating, allowing Rukmin to pass between them and thus avoiding the head-on collision that was bound to be disastrous for both sides. Martinez envisioned Division Two opening wide like the jaws of a monstrous animal, preparing to swallow its prey.

Once the maneuver was complete Rukmin would be effectively surrounded, with missiles homing in from all sides. Rukmin would be flying through sensor-confusing plasma bursts, while other plasma bursts grew closer and closer. Fire control would grow confused, defensive fire would be less effective, until eventually Rukmin's defense collapsed altogether and her ships would be turned to ionized gas drifting on the solar wind.

"Flag to all ships," Martinez said. "Free to fire pinnaces."

Pinnaces were small vehicles carrying a big engine and configured to carry a single crew. They had been designed to be fired along with missile volleys, to guide the missiles to the target. Missiles of course could accelerate at rates that would turn a human being into scarlet mash, but it was hoped that the pinnaces could at least get closer than the warships that had fired them, and might be able to view weaknesses in the enemy defense and exploit them. Prior to the Naxid War, the cadets who crewed the pinnaces held the most glamorous posts in the service, in part because the pinnace pilots were dashing blades who had volunteered to fight alone in the great missile-filled dark, and in part because the pinnaces were considered an introduction to the even more glamorous world of yacht racing.

But losses among pinnace pilots in the Naxid War were on the order of 80 percent, which made the assignment less glamorous in a hurry. At the start of the war, nearly all pinnace pilots had been high-ranking Peers; but by the end, most pinnaces were crewed by commoners.

By that point, however, the Fleet had begun firing pinnaces not with missile salvos, but in directions lateral to the flight of the warships, in hopes that from their unique perspective they might be able to see around the bursting plasma screens that shrouded the battle, locate the enemy, and be able either to send information to the flagships or to take command of missiles and drive them through the enemy's defense.

Dalkeith fired her two pinnaces immediately. It was best to do this at once, while Rukmin's ships were shrouded, because firing a pinnace would identify *Los Angeles* as a warship, and not a decoy. That was why Martinez had chosen not to launch pinnaces while Rukmin was in a position to observe the little ships take flight.

While Division Two split and the pinnaces were fired, the Restoration forces kept pumping missiles in Rukmin's direction, to keep her blind to the division's maneuver. Martinez kept his attention focused on the display, on the enemy ships hidden behind the roiling hot plasma shroud. Data began to come in from the pinnaces, and the image seemed to grow a bit more clear.

Martinez felt a jolt to his heart as he saw a phantom enemy squadron appear for just a few seconds, the ships standing on their tails of fire, and then the antimatter torches vanished, followed by the ships themselves. Martinez knew that Rukmin had seen at least something of what Division Two was doing and had cut engines while maneuvering to a new heading.

But which heading? He found himself peering into the display until his eyes ached—useless, because the display was unfolding in his brain and his eyes had been, in effect, switched off.

Gradually ships appeared, grainy and indistinct in the display, haloed by the brilliant flame of their torches. Quickly Martinez made estimates of their course and speed, and then he felt the hair on his arms prickle as he realized that Rukmin had shaped a course to intercept Martinez and his nine ships, presumably with the hope that she could overwhelm Martinez before the other elements of his command could interfere.

"Flag to Squadron Eleven and Squadron Eight," Martinez said. "'Engage enemy more closely.' Flag to Squadron Twenty: 'Alter course to . . .'" He paused while his fingers danced over a virtual keyboard as he made a calculation.

Prince Huang's boyish, excited voice piped into Martinez's headphones. "Suggest one-sixty by ninety-two, my lord!"

That seemed right. "Alter course to one-sixty by ninety-two. Accelerate to one point eight gravities. Execute in two minutes."

Martinez would alter course and fly from Rukmin, which would give the other two squadrons a chance to enter the fight and crush her between them.

Rukmin's ships appeared more clearly on the display as the plasma shells dispersed, and there seemed to be more enemy ships than there had been at the beginning of the engagement. The Restoration ships had been concealed from Rukmin, but she had been concealed from them as well, and she'd taken the opportunity to fire decoys.

Martinez was beginning to feel admiration for his enemy. She'd been undergoing heavy accelerations for nearly two months, and her brain and body had been so beaten down that she shouldn't have a functional synapse still working; but instead she was fighting aggressively and with intelligence.

Pity to have to kill her.

Time, Martinez thought, to keep the pressure on the enemy. While the zero-gee alarm rang and the ships ceased acceleration while they rotated to a new heading, he ordered more missiles launched, and they sped from their tubes and raced toward Rukmin. Best, he thought, to keep her flying into fog as much as possible.

Carmody's squadron adjusted their course and began an acceleration toward Rukmin—and after a brief pause, Foote shifted to a new heading as well. All units in the Shulduc system were now heading for a meeting at a single point in space, but one side or another would be annihilated well before that meeting took place.

Rukmin's best chance was to destroy Martinez and Squadron Twenty before the others could get within decisive range, and she knew it, so when she saw that Martinez was trying to escape her, she increased her own acceleration, and Martinez pushed his own acceleration to two and a half gees.

Two and a half invisible Torminel wrestlers sat invisibly on his chest. The miniwaves pulsing from his couch hummed in his bones. He tightened his abdomen and began a series of deliberate breaths and kept his mind focused on his display.

However bad this was, it was bound to be worse for Rukmin and her crews, who were accelerating at four gees or more.

He didn't want to outrun Rukmin. Division Two had come into the Shulduc system with a lot of momentum that it couldn't shed in time, and so he and Rukmin were bound to shoot past each other no matter what maneuvers they underwent in the meantime. He wanted only to delay his fatal encounter with Rukmin until his other units were able to enter the action.

Right now Rukmin was flying through a blazing cloud of plasma that was blinding her sensors, and the faster she accelerated, the more swiftly his missiles came at her. Enemy missiles flew out of the plasma cloud, looping toward Squadron Twenty, their courses jittering to avoid defensive fire.

"Flag to Squadron Twenty," Martinez said. "Adopt starburst pattern one. Commence in forty seconds."

Up till now all ships in Shulduc had been arranged in loose order around their flagships, far enough apart so that their antimatter torches wouldn't cook one another, but close enough for the flagship to maintain control over each ship. Early in the Naxid War, the disadvantages of this formation became apparent, for while the ships were in formation, they remained an excellent, close-packed target for an enemy. The alternative had been to starburst, with each ship racing away from another, but in this case the ships lost contact with one another and ceased to act as a unit.

This was where the Martinez Method came into play. With Sula, Martinez had worked out a type of starburst in which the ships would fly in an ever-shifting mathematical relation to one another, flying along the convex hull of a chaotic dynamical system, a fractal pattern calculated to maximize defensive weapons' effectiveness while keeping the ships at a safe, and completely unpredictable, distance from one another.

Now the question was whether Rukmin would use the Method herself. Even though Supreme Commander Tork had denounced it as an innovation that insulted the perfect tactics of the ancestors, and forbidden its use within the

Fleet, the system wasn't a secret, and Martinez had done his best to disperse knowledge of the Method to as many officers as seemed open to the idea. He wondered if Rukmin was one of the officers who had received the formula, and whether she would consider employing it in a situation that found her at a considerable disadvantage.

She hadn't yet, as far as he could see.

Checking his display, Martinez confirmed that the enemy-held wormhole relay stations had been blown up and wouldn't be able to send information about Martinez's tactics to Supreme Commander Tork.

Martinez watched as the ships of Squadron Twenty drew apart from one another and began maneuvering within their pattern. Antiproton beams flashed from his warships, setting more of space alight as they burned enemy missiles. Counter-missiles were fired against the missiles that had evaded the antiproton weapons. Martinez was ordering more missiles fired when Prince Huang's voice came into his headset. "Lord Fleetcom, I recommend some tactical adjustments. If you would care to view my plot . . ."

Martinez took several grunting breaths to clear his head, then triggered Huang's simulation. For a moment it seemed as if Huang was recommending increased acceleration, enough to render everyone in the squadron unconscious, but then he realized that he'd seen a simulation of these sorts of darting, leaping ships before, when Huang had demonstrated his fractal boundary theory. Anger simmered in his brain.

"What is this, Lieutenant?" he asked.

"You've got to shift the unit of measurement larger!" Huang

said. "You can run right ahead of those missiles, then jump back closer to the enemy to fire, and then get away again!"

"*It can't be done!*" Martinez said. He wanted to lunge out of his couch and yank the microphone connections out of Huang's helmet. "Lieutenant," he said, "in the future, confine your suggestions to the possible!"

"*This is too important!*" Huang said. His boyish voice searched for a higher register, and found it. "If we do this, we can *save lives*!" he shrilled.

Martinez wondered if Huang was genuinely crazy, or if the sight of missiles heading for *Los Angeles* had driven him mad with fear. "*Not now!*" he said. He shifted back to his virtual display of the battle. "Signals," he said. "Please cut Lieutenant Huang out of the flag station circuit."

"Gladly, my lord!" Santana sounded furious, even though the two and a half gravities that sat on his diaphragm had reduced his anger into a croak.

"No!" Huang said. "This is import—"

Martinez gasped with relief as Huang's voice vanished from his perceptions. He was trying to make sense of the virtual combat plot that showed Rukmin still coming on at four or more gravities, largely invisible behind a churning sea of plasma. Some of the enemy's missiles had been hit by point-defense weapons, and the rest were on the verge of being annihilated by countermissiles. Foote and Carmody were closing with the enemy, and firing steadily.

"Message from Captain Dalkeith, my lord," Banerjee said. "We've killed one of the enemy."

"Confirmed?" Martinez said.

"Sensors indicate enough radiation for a cruiser's anti-matter store blowing up—wait!" Excitement glittered in Banerjee's voice.

"What is it?"

"Another ship destroyed! Confirmed! And there was a third hit, but apparently it was a decoy."

Martinez would have laughed if he could have spared the energy. "Flag to squadron: 'Congratulations and keep firing. Only fourteen enemy to go.'"

A shift in course sent Martinez's acceleration couch swinging, and before it returned to its deadpoint, Martinez glimpsed Prince Huang and saw that his gloved fingers were rapping out a message on a keypad. Foreboding crept into Martinez's mind.

"Santana," he said. "Take a look at what Huang's doing, will you?"

"Yes, Fleetcom." There was a moment of silence, and then the cruiser's engines shut off without warning, and the air rang with a belated zero-gee alarm. The weight on Martinez's chest vanished as he floated in his harness. He was aware of Santana shouting, the words buried under the sound of the alarm. He stared at the displays in front of him. These showed the rest of the squadron accelerating on without the flagship, leaving *Los Angeles* drifting in space with two enemy squadrons bearing down on it.

"What's going on?" he said. "Contact Dalkeith!" And then, "Santana, please repeat!"

"Huang's sent his damned plan to every one of our ships!" Santana snarled.

"Send out a cancellation. And cut Huang out of every communications circuit!"

"Yes, Lord Fleetcom," said Santana. "But I think I'm going to need your commander key to do that."

"Send it to my board, then, and—"

"Captain Dalkeith reports she doesn't know what tripped the engines," Banerjee interrupted. "But the engine crew's tracking it down."

Martinez glared at the display that showed his ships madly accelerating away from him. "Banerjee, send from flag to Squadron Twenty: 'Re-form, starburst centered on flag.'"

Santana gave a growl of frustration. "My lord, Huang's sent the order *again*."

Banerjee called out. "I've just received an inquiry from Squadron Commander Carmody asking which set of orders to follow, my lord."

"Damn it!" Martinez could see a torrent of enemy missiles flying toward him out of the plasma cloud. "Right," he said, "put me on video. I'm going to broadcast to the division personally." Martinez waited until his own underlit, harried face appeared on one of his screens, and he took a breath and spoke.

"This is Fleet Commander Martinez to all Restoration ships. A panicked crew member on *Los Angeles* has seized control of some of the communications apparatus and is sending out conflicting instructions. Disregard any orders requiring absurd or impossible accelerations, and accept orders only from me, in person, transmitted by video. Thank you."

Martinez ended the transmission and wondered why he'd added the polite *thank you* at the end. He had no reason at this moment to be thankful for anything, the more so because he saw that Huang was still tapping on his keyboard, sending who knew what insanity out into the world.

"Lord Fleetcom," said Santana. "I'm afraid I do in fact need your commander's key to take Huang out of the system. I've sent the appropriate screen to you."

Martinez had already put his commander's key into the slot on his command board, and so he brought Santana's signals screen onto his displays and ran his fingers down the list of communication and data privileges from which he was barring Huang. Once all the lights shifted over to *Privileges Revoked*, he pressed the *Confirm* button.

Huang, he saw, kept on pressing keys for a while, then hesitated, jammed more keys for a while, then gave up. He put a hand on one of the struts of his acceleration cage, then swung it around to face Martinez. Martinez could see Huang's murderous glare through the visor of his helmet.

"Captain Dalkeith wishes a private channel, Lord Fleetcom."

Now what? Martinez wondered. "Put her through," he said.

Dalkeith's child's voice lisped in his headset. "We've tracked the cause of the engine trip, my lord," she said. "It's the first lieutenant—he's had a stroke."

Which made sense. High accelerations could cause strokes or other cerebral accidents, and the suits worn by crewmen at quarters monitored their physical condition. Under peacetime conditions a stroke suffered by any crew member would be enough to cause an emergency shutdown, but during combat or an emergency, a different priority took hold, and only the most critical members of the hierarchy could cause an engine trip.

Which, normally, would include the first lieutenant. That *Los Angeles*'s premiere had been incapacitated in his bed since early in the voyage had apparently not changed the computer's priorities.

"I could page a stretcher team to his cabin," Dalkeith said, "or—"

Martinez looked at the flood of missiles heading toward *Los Angeles* and clenched his teeth. He didn't like Dalkeith passing this responsibility on to him, not when it was her ship and her officer and her decision.

"No, Captain," he said. "The premiere's on his own. Override the computer, ignite the engines, and accelerate at four gees until we catch the squadron."

There was only a slight hesitation. "Yes, Lord Fleetcom."

The premiere was a genial man, gray haired, who had come back to the Fleet twelve years after retiring, and Martinez imagined that he ruled the wardroom with a benign, fatherly hand.

Martinez realized that he was already saying good-bye to him.

Next time, he mentally told Dalkeith, *kill your own damn lieutenant.*

He saw that Huang was struggling with his webbing, trying to get out of his acceleration couch. He was inexperienced at moving in zero gravity and kept getting himself caught in the webbing or bouncing off the bars of the cage.

"Sit down, Huang!" Martinez said, and then the acceleration warning sounded, an insistent whoop that warbled up and down the scale, telling the crew to get to an acceleration couch before the engines lit. Huang ignored it—he flailed free of the webbing, and then braced himself against two looping bars of the cage, and pushed himself off directly toward Martinez.

"What the *hell*!" Martinez tried to shove Huang off, but his hands couldn't quite clear his own acceleration cage. The cage began a slow tumble as Huang seized it, and then Huang was climbing into the cage, hands reaching for Martinez's displays. If Huang couldn't broadcast from his own station, he apparently intended to use his commander's.

"My lord!" Santana's voice roared in Martinez's headset. "Hold on, I'm coming!"

Blazing fury ignited in Martinez. "No!" he said. "We'll be under acceleration soon!" He tried to shove Huang away, failed, then tried a vicious punch to the floating ribs. Strapped in the couch, and lacking gravity, he was too cramped to throw an effective punch, and the vac suit absorbed much of his force. A new wobble was added to the cage's spin. Huang was thrown against one of the bars of the cage, but he bounded back and reached for the displays again.

"My lord!" called Santana.

"Get out of there!" Martinez could barely hear his own voice over the whooping alarm. He punched again, failed to accomplish anything, and then doubled up in the cage, got the toe of one boot under the locking ring of Huang's helmet, and then kicked as hard as he could. Huang hit the cage bar again and rebounded, but now he was perfectly positioned for a clean kick, and Martinez lashed out with every ounce of his anger. The cage went into a rapid spin. The kick hurled Huang headlong into a corner of the room just as the engines fired.

Los Angeles didn't go from zero to four gees instantly, but it happened quickly enough, and the floor rose to flatten Huang like a flyswatter crushing an insect. Huang's helmet hit with a rattling thud. Martinez's cage crashed to its dead-point, swung, crashed again. Acceleration built, and Martinez found himself gasping for breath. Huang moved slowly, gathering himself, and then with slow determination pushed himself upright. He got one foot under him, the knee raised, and then looked ready to push himself to a standing position when the increasing gravity proved too much, and he slumped to the floor.

"Good job, my lord!" Santana said.

"Flag to Dalkeith," Martinez gasped, forcing the word out from a rib cage now four times its own weight. He remembered that he was supposed to give all orders on video and triggered the camera. "Flag to Dalkeith," he said. "When we go to a lower acceleration, page two constables to the flag officer's station. I need to place an officer under arrest."

Dalkeith was too overcome by the fight for air to register surprise. "At once, Lord Fleetcom."

Martinez battled for breath and shifted to the more useful virtual display. The deluge of missiles hurtling toward *Los Angeles* was being thinned by defensive fire, and Martinez could assume much of that fire was coming from the rest of Squadron Twenty.

The surviving missiles came on. Defensive missiles launched, joined by a swarm of defensive missiles from Squadron Twenty. *Los Angeles* was beginning to enter the effective defensive zone of the rest of the squadron, and Martinez was gratified to see rippling blooms of plasma in *Los Angeles*'s wake, detonations overlapping one another.

Yet the detonations were getting closer, missiles dodging and spiraling to avoid counterfire, moving through the blooms of hot plasma to make their detection more difficult. Calculations sped through his mind.

"Flag to Dalkeith," he said. "Set defenses to automatic and increase to twelve gees for fifteen seconds."

He forgot to trigger the video that would confirm the order, but Dalkeith saw the sense of the order anyway, and the gravities began to increase. Each breath was a battle, and Martinez's vision closed down, narrowing until there was only a constricted tunnel focused on a display that seemed very far away.

He didn't think he actually passed out; and when the gravities fell away, he felt relief surge through his body like a flush of hot blood mantling his skin. Four gravities had once been distressing, but now they seemed like an element of paradise. He waited for his vision to clear and tried to make sense of the display. *Los Angeles* was now entering the very midst of Squadron Twenty and might well shoot through and leave the rest behind. The other ships were maneuvering so as to form on the flagship and were in slight disorder as a result.

Enemy missiles were still coming, leaping out of the plasma flowers that marked the deaths of other missiles.

Martinez felt a burst of horror as he realized how close the missiles were. A drumfire of bursts reached toward *Los Angeles* like a giant finger thrusting at a point between Martinez's eyes, the finger flying at incredible speed, and then Martinez's display filled with fire, and the rest of the universe vanished behind a wall of superheated plasma.

When the display went white, the first thing Martinez felt was relief. *Los Angeles* had not been annihilated, but a near miss had burned out every sensor on the ship. That was of little concern, because warships carried replacements, and these would be deployed as soon as the outside environment grew a little less fierce.

What was far more important was that *Los Angeles* had survived. And as soon as the flagship replaced its sensors, it was time for Martinez to plan the battle's endgame.

"Flag to Dalkeith," Martinez sent. "Reduce acceleration to conform to the rest of the squadron."

A couple of Torminel wrestlers climbed off Martinez's chest, and he filled his lungs with a welcome breath of air. Automatic mechanisms replaced sensors on the outside of the hull, and the world slowly began to restore itself on the display. In *Los Angeles*'s wake a wall of cloud and fire obscured Rukmin's ships, and through the electromagnetic hash he caught only glimpses of shadowy hulls and burning antimatter torches. Carmody and Foote continued their charge toward the enemy, hurling walls of missiles ahead of them. Both had starburst, their ships moving along the unpredictable paths of the Martinez Method. Carmody's missiles were boring straight in, Martinez saw, but many of Foote's missiles were taking a looping trajectory toward the enemy, hiding behind the cooling, expanding plasma shells created by the missiles fired by Rukmin and Martinez. Martinez was reluctant to give Foote credit for much of anything, but he had to think that was clever.

"Lord Fleetcom? You called for us?" There was a respectful tap on his faceplate.

Startled, Martinez let the virtual display fade from his optical centers and looked up to see a pair of Military Constabulary looming over him, large men bulky in their vac suits. The Constabulary were normally recognized by their red armbands and belts, but neither were suitable to their vac suits, so the belts and armbands were painted on.

It took Martinez a moment to remember why the constables were here. He looked for Huang and saw him still crumpled on the floor. Martinez raised his faceplate and pointed at Huang.

"Arrest that officer, please." He spared a glance for the displays locked down in front of him and saw that the drumroll of missile bursts continued. He turned back to the constables. "We may have some violent maneuvers coming up soon. If you can get the prisoner on his feet, march him to confinement as quickly as you can. If he can't stand, secure him in his acceleration couch. One of you take the spare couch here, and the other should get to a couch as soon as he can."

The air outside his suit smelled hot, and Martinez wondered how far the hull temperature had been raised by the near miss.

More than twice their normal weight, the two constables

lumbered to Huang and tried to help him rise. Huang's feet kept folding under him, so the constables gave up and heaved Huang onto his couch. Since he too was more than twice his normal weight, it was lucky that he was small, otherwise they might not have managed. As it was, it seemed as if one of the constables badly strained his back.

Huang was secured to his couch, and one of the constables—the one with the strained back—limped to the spare cage, while the other plodded out of the room.

"Two more enemy destroyed!" Lalita Banerjee could not contain her glee. "It happened while we were at twelve gees—the sensor operators have just gone back through the data!"

"Starburst, my lord!" Santana's words came fast on the heels of Banerjee's report. "Rukmin's starburst!"

Martinez shifted back to his virtual display, and through the blaze of erupting antimatter he could see enemy torches pointed in different directions as the enemy ships flew from each other like bits of a bursting shell. By chance he happened to be looking directly at one of the enemy ships when it blew up, leaving a larger, brighter flare that briefly outshone the missile bursts.

That's eleven left, Martinez thought. At this rate Squadron Twenty might be able to finish the fight on its own.

That would depend, however, at how Rukmin was managing her starburst, whether her ships were parting to operate on their own, or whether she was re-forming into the shifting, unpredictable array of the Martinez Method.

It appeared that she wasn't. Rukmin's ships weren't moving in any pattern that Martinez could detect.

"My lord!" Santana's tone was urgent. "*Compliance* has ceased acceleration!"

"Query Captain Kim," Martinez said, and then he turned on the video to record himself. "Flag to Squadron Twenty," he said. "Re-form on *Compliance*."

The squadron buzzing around *Compliance* would mean bringing on a general engagement faster than Martinez had intended, but he had every confidence that he'd win it. He wasn't going to sacrifice *Compliance*, not when he was on the verge of victory.

"Captain Kim reports a hit on one of his engines," Banerjee said. "He can't fix it, and the engines are out of commission for the present."

It must have been an antiproton strike on the engine, Martinez thought. No enemy missile had come close.

The zero-gee warning sang out, and the engines cut as *Los Angeles* rotated to a new heading, maneuvering to aid the helpless *Compliance*. The acceleration warning whooped up and down again, and then the engines kicked on. By chance *Los Angeles* was heading straight for the wall of fire that represented Rukmin's squadron—which, Martinez calculated, would actually pass through Squadron Twenty in ten or twelve minutes.

The battle didn't last that long. The starburst had shattered Rukmin's defensive cohesion, the missiles kept raining in, and the enemy ships were buried in fire. The end was swift, the surviving enemy wiped out in a matter of seconds, and then all the sensors could find were expanding, cooling plasma shells and aimless missiles searching for an enemy to attack.

"Flag to all ships," Martinez said. "Well done, and congratulations to all officers and crew. Recall all missiles and
pinnaces. Division Two, shape your course for Shulduc Wormhole One and reduce acceleration to point five gee."

Reduced gee came as another relief to his bones. He saw
Santana and Banerjee spinning in their cages with their arms
uplifted, rejoicing in their victory and their survival.

"Congratulations, Lord Fleetcom!" Santana said.

The constable unwebbed and bounded in the light gravity toward Prince Huang, who remained motionless on his
couch. His face, partly visible through the faceplate, was expressionless and fixed on the ceiling. The other constable arrived, and the two of them together marched Huang off to
confinement. Martinez found himself without any comment
on the matter. He'd deal with all that later.

Division Two had spent weeks under heavy acceleration
to get to Shulduc, and now they were going to have to go
through the same amount of deceleration before they could
begin their journey back to Harzapid. But this time there was
no enemy at the end of the journey, but a friend: the sixty-
three defecting ships of the Home Fleet, who had been heading to Harzapid for almost two months.

Martinez wrenched off his helmet and stowed it in the net
bag on the side of his couch. He looked at Santana and Banerjee, who were still grinning at each other.

"I need to send a message to Fleet Commander Chen,"
he said. "When you have a moment."

The two looked startled and a little guilty, and both returned their attention to their displays.

"When you're ready, Lord Fleetcom," Banerjee said.

"Fleet Commander Martinez to Fleet Commander Chen," Martinez said. "I am pleased to report a complete victory at Shulduc over Squadron Commander Rukmin. The enemy lost sixteen heavy cruisers, and the Restoration suffered one ship damaged. All captains and ships performed to my complete satisfaction, and all deserve credit for this victory." *Except for your cousin Prince*, he added mentally, and then finished his bulletin. "A more detailed report will follow. End message."

The message itself might be a little belated, for the Restoration-occupied relay station would have recorded the battle and forwarded it in real time to Harzapid. Martinez could imagine Michi and her staff sitting in a semicircle about a big wall display while missiles and explosions were reflected in their eyes.

There's your battle of annihilation, Martinez thought. *That's what you asked for, and that's what you got.*

And then he thought, *Tork's fleet will be a lot harder.*

AS LIGHT SQUADRON Eight shot past Division Two on its way to Harzapid, Martinez called Jeremy Foote. He'd been waiting for Foote to contact him, a junior reporting to a senior, but then finally decided he was done with waiting.

Martinez had climbed out of his vac suit, showered, and put on a fresh uniform before making the call. He spoke from his office while waiting for Alikhan to deliver his dinner.

On video Foote appeared pale and wretched, with bruise-like purple blooms beneath his eyes, and new lines on his

face. Though his ship was now under a very light deceleration he lay on his couch as if pasted there and unable to move.
Even his cowlick had been beaten flat by hard gravities.

"Congratulations on your survival, Captain Foote," Martinez said. "Do you have a report or any other message I can
forward to Fleet Commander Chen?"

Even after two months of high gees, Foote's High City
drawl hadn't lost any of its self-importance. "I haven't had the
chance to compose a report," he said, "having been involved
in a rather thrilling fight for existence."

"Glad I was able to help you with that," Martinez said.
"But now you can maintain a nice, gentle deceleration until
you meet the rest of the Restoration fleet somewhere this side
of Harzapid."

Foote raised an eyebrow. "Restoration?"

"That's us," Martinez said. "The enemy is still 'the enemy'
as far as I know."

"They'll remain the enemy until they become the dishon-
ored dead," Foote said.

"That's the spirit!" Martinez grinned.

"So Lady Michi is a fleet commander now," Foote said.
"I imagine you've been promoted as well?"

"I'm a fleet commander, too. Feel free to salute me when
next we meet."

Foote nodded. "I'll make a note to do that."

"Don't worry," Martinez assured him, "you'll get a promotion as well. And it will be based on merit, not the schemes of
your high-placed relatives, so it will be deserved."

Foote's mouth started to smirk, but he was too exhausted

to fully carry it out. "I think all my promotions were deserved," he said.

"It's so endearing of you to believe that!" said Martinez. "If you want to send messages of your continuing existence to Fleet Commander Chen or anyone else, the relay station ahead of you is in friendly hands."

"I'll do that. Thank you for your consideration."

"You're welcome. I'll leave you to your well-earned rest. End transmission."

As the orange end-stamp filled the screen, Martinez grinned, reached for his crystal wineglass, and offered himself a toast.

Having an advantage over a rival was a pleasure, but having a rival owe you his life was a sensation far more sublime.

CHAPTER 11

Martinez kept Division Two's deceleration at a half gravity while ships were checked for damage and repairs were made, and anyone injured by high accelerations could be tended by one of the medics—or, if they were lucky, by an actual doctor. *Compliance* reported that it had lost a piece of one of its four main engine nozzles, possibly due to a flaw, possibly due to a strike by an antiproton weapon, but that its captain felt that with care it could limp along on its three remaining engines.

In any case *Compliance* would require a visit to the Harzapid dockyards before it would again see action, and so Martinez ruthlessly raided the damaged cruiser for useful officers, warrant and petty officers, and a few of her more experienced enlisted. Dalkeith's first officer had survived whatever cerebral accident had caused *Los Angeles*'s engines to shut down, and he and the other injured were transferred to *Compliance* for transport to Harzapid and treatment. The premiere was replaced officially by Dalkeith's second officer, who had performed well, and her place was taken by a replacement from *Compliance*.

Prince Huang, under guard, was shifted to a holding cell on the wounded cruiser. Martinez didn't feel the need to see him off.

After a day and a half of light gravity and general celebration, Martinez ordered everyone strapped in and worked his command up to three gravities' deceleration. *Compliance* managed well.

During the dinner break, when deceleration was reduced to a single gee, Martinez sent Michi a confidential message detailing Prince Huang's behavior during the battle. "You could court-martial him and have him shot," Martinez said, "but I'd be just as happy if you kicked him out of the Fleet and let him wreak havoc on some other elements of the population." He took a breath. "And in the meantime, I need a *real tactical officer.*"

He hoped that for a tactical officer Michi might this time look outside her own family.

SEVERIN DREW THE sleeve of the puppet up his forearm. "I don't know why," he said, "but I decided to build a Lorkin."

He brandished the puppet, his fingers tugging at the network of interwoven strings that triggered the movement of the tentacles around its head. He aimed the mouth at Lady Starkey.

"I'm just a harmless life-form," he said in a plaintive, rather dim-witted voice. "I don't even have a skeleton! Please don't drop a bomb on me!"

Lady Starkey smiled. "You realize you've just turned the Great Masters' biggest secret into a play toy."

"It's better than the Great Masters playing with the Lorkins by turning them into radioactive dust," Severin said. "Would you like some more chocolate?"

"Not now, thanks." She looked at the puppet and its dancing tentacles. "How do you make the tentacles work?"

Severin explained that there was a kind of mesh net inside the puppet, and that tugging on the strings with his fingertips produced random movements in the tentacles. "The movements look more purposeful than they are," he said. "And of course the fingers have to manipulate the mouth as well."

"May I try it?"

"It may take a little practice." He took the puppet off his hand and passed it to Starkey. She undid her cuff buttons, rolled the sleeve of her tunic up her forearm, and put the Lorkin over her hand. She experimented with manipulating the tentacles, then pointed the mouth at Severin, bobbed the puppet up and down to simulate movement, and adopted a squeaky voice.

"I'm as pretty as a flower! Watch me bound over the green fields of my native land!" She stopped, then feigned surprise. "What are those big gray beings come down from the sky?" she said. "I wonder if they'll be my friends!"

Severin found it charming that her mobile face unconsciously adopted the same expression she was attempting on the puppet.

"Very nice," Severin said. "But you're closing the mouth

when you speak instead of opening." He demonstrated with his fingers. "You must *e-nun-ci-ate*. Make the vowel sounds *biiig*." He held open his fingers by way of example.

"Oh." Starkey blinked. "Sorry."

"No worries. Lots of people make that mistake."

Severin had just given a dinner to the captains of his squadron. Michi Chen had promoted him to squadron commander, first grade, the highest rank in the Exploration Service and equivalent to the Fleet's rank of senior squadron commander. This was particularly generous of her, because five of his eight-ship squadron belonged to the Fleet, not the Exploration Service. He had wondered if the Fleet officers would resent his being placed over them, but they were all lieutenants who had been promoted to lieutenant-captain and given their first commands, and they seemed so overwhelmed by their new responsibilities that it hadn't yet occurred to them to take offense at his superior status.

Their attitude, however, might change over time, and so Severin worked hard to place himself beyond resentment. He had a lot to learn about combat and maneuvers—the ships of the Exploration Service were so often on detached duty that Severin hadn't had to worry about unit formations since the last war, and at that time he was a lieutenant and had only to follow orders, not give them.

He had a lot of catching up to do, especially as Lady Sula, who now commanded the entire Fourth Fleet during Michi Chen's recovery and Gareth Martinez's absence, was ordering daily drills. The Fleet, minus the two Cree squadrons that had not yet completed conversion, was advancing to a rendezvous with Martinez at a steady one gravity. There was no reason to hurry, and the leisurely pace allowed for a lot of time for training.

Lady Starkey dropped her hand and rubbed her wrist. "It's hard to keep my hand in that position for long," she said.

"Puppetry is pain," Severin said cheerfully. He poured himself another steaming cocoa, and filled her cup as well.

Dinner with his captains had gone well. Severin had reminisced about his own surprising promotion to the officer class—he'd been a warrant officer first class when Michi Chen had promoted him lieutenant for his service in the Naxid War, and he'd moved from the world of the commoner into the grand milieu of the Peers. His shock was not unlike those of his newly promoted captains at finding themselves removed from the clublike atmosphere of the wardroom to lonely positions of command, and he tried to offer them the benefits of his experience. The Exploration Service was a good deal less formal than the Fleet, where the officers were expected to be uniform, obedient, correct, and more or less interchangeable; and the Service's informal traditions allowed Severin to offer a degree of support that would have been alien amid the pomp and ceremony of the Fleet.

The other captains returned to their ships after dinner, but Lady Starkey had asked to see the puppets, and Severin had taken her into his office. The puppets and their theater had been packed away against heavy accelerations, and he'd had to dig them out of boxes. She'd enjoyed seeing the characters from his *Alois* series, and also some of the characters that he'd been developing for a new serial that had been interrupted by the war.

"But I haven't been thinking about that story much," Severin said. "I've been thinking of developing a satirical series based on the war."

Starkey was surprised. "*Our* war?" she asked.

"Well, yes. The opposition, mostly." He took a Daimong puppet from one of his boxes and drew it over his arm. "Let's say this one is Supreme Commander Tork." He then dipped his free hand into another puppet, this time a Lai-own, and brought the puppet up to face the Daimong. He adopted a worshipful tone.

"Supreme Commander, how do you plan to defeat the Terran insurgency?"

Severin rounded his tones to imitate the melodious voice of a Daimong. "I am the greatest commander in the history of the Fleet! There will be a vast and bloody battle, and I will achieve victory by being one of the very few survivors!"

He returned to his Lai-own voice. "Isn't Michi Chen a more successful commander? After all, she wiped out a Naxid fleet and took very few casualties." He clacked his teeth together to imitate the sound that Lai-own sometimes made when they clapped their mouths shut and their peg teeth snapped against each other.

Severin raised his voice to the grating roar of Tork in full tirade. "I'm *far superior*! I can easily take *three times* the casualties of Michi Chen!"

Lady Starkey was laughing. "You've got Tork's voice exactly!" she said. "Not to mention his attitude."

"He's an easy target," Severin said. He raised the Lai-own puppet. "Let's say this one's Lady Tu-hon." He raised his voice to a well-bred screech. "This war is taking too long! How many Terrans do we have to kill before I can *stop paying taxes*!"

This time Starkey's laughter was less enthusiastic. "That's a little too close to reality," she said.

"I could argue that keeping close to reality is the whole point of satire," Severin said.

Starkey still seemed dubious. "At least you're making vicious fun of our enemies."

"Unfortunately any series would be unlikely to be seen in Zanshaa," Severin said. "Where it would do the most good."

"You could at least show it to our side," Starkey said. They discussed the possibilities of the series for a while, and Starkey made a few suggestions, including a scene featuring Zanshaa's minister of finance, Lord Minno, who—according to Gareth Martinez—had before the war been part of an illegal pump-and-dump scheme. The scene featured Lord Minno trying to hide stolen cash during a visit by Lady Gruum, the Lady Senior—who, fortunately, was too haughty and well-bred to notice the sacks of money stuffed under the sofa cushions.

"That would work," Severin judged. "I'd give you cowriting credit, if it wouldn't put you on Minno's enemies list."

Starkey shrugged. "We're on that list already, aren't we?"

"I suppose we are."

"It seems perfectly just that we mock the people who are

trying to kill us." She took her cup from Severin's desk and sipped her cocoa. "Very frothy," she judged.

Severin looked at her. "You know," he said. "I—*we*, if you like—could create a few shows for the amusement of the Fleet. If we can find the spare time to do it."

"Let Tork rant on at greater length."

"Yes. A full comic scene would require more than a couple jokes."

She smiled. "I'm willing to help, but I have no experience in puppetry or drama."

"You could contribute scenarios and jokes—I'd work them into a story."

"I'm not much of a joke writer, either. But I'll do my best."

They discussed satire and its possibilities for a while, and Severin ordered another pot of frothy cocoa. Lady Starkey tried on a series of puppets and enjoyed learning to manipulate the special triggers on some of the puppets—the components that would roll the puppet's eyes, or make its eyebrows wriggle, or cause its hair to stand on end.

Severin's clock gave a discreet chime to signal the change of a watch. Lady Starkey looked surprised.

"It's late," she said. "I'm sorry to have taken up so much of your time."

"It was a pleasure," Severin said.

She stood, and Severin rose from his chair and maneuvered around the desk and the boxes to his office door. Suddenly in the crowded office they seemed very close together.

"You're still wearing Alois," Severin pointed out.

"Oh. Sorry." He took the puppet by its head and drew it off

her arm. She looked up at him with attentive eyes. Her breath was scented with chocolate.

"I can't ethically kiss you good-bye," he said. "I'm your superior officer. Whereas—"

She wrapped her arms around his neck and kissed him fiercely. A gentle shock passed along his nerves. As he responded to the kiss, a stray thought wandered across his consciousness.

Well. This is a pleasant surprise.

"**AFTER WE THRASH** Tork," said Lord Naaz Vijana, "we'll have to purge the Convocation. We can execute those who led the war against us, and others we can threaten with execution if they won't resign. Whatever happens, we need to keep a Terran majority in Convocation, otherwise we're done for in the long run."

"I urged our political leadership to consider dictatorship," Sula said, "but they were reluctant."

Vijana looked impatient. "Why win a war and then give away the spoils?"

Sula was playing host to the Fourth Fleet's captains, one squadron at a time. Vijana, on the strength of his slaughter of the primitive Yormaks, had been raised to the command of Light Squadron Six, eight frigates with a light cruiser as a flagship. Counting Sula, that made ten officers around the table, which made dinner more intimate than Sula would have liked. The captain on her left was fond of broad gestures that threatened to upset Sula's crystal glasses. The captain on her right, Lord Ahmad Husayn, wore a scent that made him smell like an entire grove of patchouli.

The formal gatherings were traditional and probably even necessary, but she didn't enjoy having to endure so many, one every day in which she played host to one or another group of officers, or in which she was invited to dine on another ship, or in the company of *Defense*'s wardroom. She now cherished her time alone more than ever, and she counted the minutes until she would be free of the cloud of patchouli.

"I think there will be plenty of spoils," Sula said.

"No doubt," Vijana said. "Though that's not why I'm fighting. I just want to put the animals in their kennels." Fury burned in his eyes.

Sula couldn't understand why Vijana, or anybody, would waste so much energy on hatred, particularly for whole classes of people he'd never met. She had hated very few people in her life and preferred to despise or dismiss those who got in her way. When she'd killed people, it was because they were trying to kill her, or because they were stupid and useless and obstructing something that was necessary.

She'd hated Caro Sula, but the hatred had faded. At the end, with Caro lying dead on the couch, and Caro's money shifted into Sula's account, all Sula had felt was weariness that warred with a determination to see the thing through.

And so she'd seen it through, and now here she was, at a gathering of glittering high-caste officers she was leading to war. She rubbed the scar tissue on her right thumb.

"Let's have one last toast," she said, "and then you can return to your ships. Remember we'll be having a drill tomorrow."

A drill in which the Fourth Fleet would face off against Tork's augmented Home Fleet, which would outnumber them nearly two to one. Sula imagined that even with the best tactics, her side would not fare well.

"To the Restoration," Sula said and raised her lemonade. The others raised wineglasses, and they all drank. Then Sula rose, and the others rose with her. "I'll walk with you to the airlock," she said.

Sula's rank entitled her to a smart little cutter, currently mated to *Defense*, and she'd sent the cutter to pick up the other captains and offer them hospitality on the way. Trailing the scent of patchouli, the party walked down a companionway that took them down two decks, and then to the airlock that an honor guard held open.

"Good night, my ladies. My lords."

First through the airlock was a portly captain who had been promoted from being a portly lieutenant. Since the cutter's airlock was small, and the portly captain was a little drunk, and exiting the cutter's small airlock involved turning around and making one's way down a ladder to the deck below, the operation took a while, and the others had to wait.

"I hope the exercise doesn't take too long tomorrow," said Naaz Vijana. "They're executing Colonel Dai-por in the afternoon, and I want to watch it live."

Sula had seen enough executions in the last war, when she'd forced herself to watch the deaths of her colleagues in Military Governor Pahn-ko's stay-behind army.

"I expect I'll be enjoying a nice shower," Sula said. "And maybe tea and cake afterward."

"At least that imbecile Kai finally caught the man," Vijana said. "It took him long enough."

Sula smiled inwardly. "Oh, Kai found him quickly enough," she said. "Dai-por was kept under observation for several weeks so that we could track his network."

Vijana seemed nettled, perhaps because he'd thrown away his hatred on an unworthy target.

"There were less than thirty arrests," Sula continued. "Dai-por couldn't persuade very many people to join his cause, which is good news for us."

"The other species aren't *entirely* stupid," Vijana said. "They know it's absurd to fight when there's a fleet in the sky above them. They'll wait till our backs are turned before they stab us."

"Let's guard our backs, then," Sula said. It was finally Vijana's turn to go through the airlock, and he wished Sula good night and stepped over the sill. The honor guard closed the airlock door. Sula let out a long breath, unbuttoned her collar, and turned to make her way back to her own cabin when she saw another officer standing quietly in a corner of the room. The officer was looking toward the airlock with an expression of fixed hatred, her jaw grinding in anger.

"Is something wrong, Lieutenant Gao?"

Gao's hazel eyes were frozen, unblinking in their hatred.

"Vijana," she said, and then she seemed to shake herself out of her fury and realized who she was talking to. She braced. "Apologies, my lady," she said. "I shouldn't have bothered you with my personal concerns."

"If there's a problem with one of our officers," Sula said. "I need to know it."

Lady Xia Gao was a middle-aged woman and the second officer aboard *Defense*. She had served fifteen years in the Fleet, but lack of patronage had obstructed any hope of promotion, so she'd resigned her commission and sought work in the civil service. The Naxid War had brought her back into the Fleet, where she'd commanded a tender ferrying supplies to the warships of Tork's fleet, but she'd resigned after the war and returned to her job with the Ministry of Forestry and Fisheries. Now she was back in harness again, serving in a Fourth Fleet where traditional restrictions on place and promotion were relaxed.

She was an officer with a lifetime's experience, and a background in both the military and civilian realms. She didn't seem the sort of person to hate someone without a reason.

Sula could see calculation speeding behind Gao's hazel eyes. "I'm reluctant to share my opinion, my lady," Gao said. "Squadron Commander Vijana is a decorated hero of the empire."

"All the more reason—" Sula began, and then the words *Ministry of Forestry and Fisheries* rose to her mind, and she understood.

"Ah. Hah," she said. "You were on Esley."

Again rage hardened Gao's features. "He killed my people," she said.

Sula nodded. "You were one of those assigned to look after the Yormaks."

Gao nodded. "The Yormak Bureau. I spent years with the Yormaks, studying and surveying, learning their language. I protected them from other species who wanted to take their lands and poach their game—the other species blamed the Yormaks' special status for Esley's lack of development and economic progress." Her lip curled. "Vijana shot them down from aircraft. He dropped bombs that killed their cattle and left them to starve over the winter."

Sula considered this and found herself unsurprised. "The Yormaks were supposed to have rebelled," she said.

Contempt snarled in Gao's voice. "*Rebelled*. Have you seen the videos? They show the Yormaks *upset*, because someone off-camera was provoking them. But the Yormaks never raised a hand in violence to a member of any other species, not in all their history. They had no technology more advanced than a stone-tipped spear, and yet they were supposed to have coordinated a rising that attacked members of the Yormak Bureau across the whole world, and *on a single day*?"

"You think it was Vijana who faked the rising?"

"No, that would be Lord Mehrang and his cousin the lord governor. They would have coordinated the goons that drove the Yormaks to protest, then killed my colleagues and blamed the Yormaks for it." Gao took a deliberate breath. Her lips worked as if she wanted to spit on the floor. "Vijana was the butcher they called in to finish the job. He must have been part of the plot, but he didn't *start* things. He just destroyed one of the intelligent species living under the Praxis, and he did it for a promotion and some grants of prime real estate."

Land that Vijana had already mortgaged, Sula thought, *to feed his gambling habit.*

"Do you have evidence for any of this?" Sula said.

"Those fuel-air bombs were being deployed within days of the start of the action. As if they were already built and ready for action. That's suspicious." Gao shrugged. "But I have no real evidence, just my knowledge of Yormaks and the way the other species on the world hated them. A serious investigation would have uncovered a great deal, but no one on Esley investigated, thanks to the lord governor being a part of the Mehrang family and able to direct the police. I'm sure the thugs who started the conflict have been boasting about it in every bar on the planet."

Sula considered this. "Who else have you told?"

Gao waved her hands. "Practically everyone—everyone we can get to listen."

"*We?*"

"Those of us in the Yormak Bureau. They rounded us all up during the actions and put us under guard—'*for our protection.*'" This was said with withering scorn. "We all know what happened, but we weren't a witness to anything. We can't get anyone to hear us, or to do anything!"

Sula considered Lord Mehrang and thought that perhaps it was lucky that Lamey was doing his best to take all his money.

"Any action will have to wait till after the war," Sula said. "We can't start a second civil war inside the Fourth Fleet."

Gao's voice hardened. "I know," she said. "But it's hard to stop thinking about it, especially when Vijana has been so rewarded and comes here blithering about killing other species."

"One thing at a time, Lieutenant," Sula said.

But returning to her quarters, she wondered why she should care about the Yormaks in any way. The Yormaks were insistently primitive, refusing such items of technology as were offered them, and learned the language of the Shaa only under compulsion. The Shaa themselves had given up trying to advance them and given them large reserves on Esley where they could follow their cattle and practice their traditional life.

The Praxis was strong on advancement through natural selection, which was one reason why improvement through genetic modification was forbidden. If you wanted a better human, you *bred* them, which of course was what the Peers thought they were doing within their own caste. But it could be argued that the Yormaks, with their refusal to change, were an evolutionary dead end. There was a case to be made that their extinction was inevitable.

But it had been accomplished by fraud and conspiracy, and the agents of evolution, Mehrang and Vijana, intended not to rectify nature's mistake, but to make themselves rich. The level of corruption tolerated among the ruling classes had always offended Sula, and she considered her gangster friends honest by comparison.

But first things first. If the Restoration lost the war, then Vijana and Mehrang would die along with Sula, all her friends, and the Yormaks.

It was her job to make sure that Vijana and Mehrang survived the war long enough to be tried for their crimes.

"THE WAR COULD have picked a better time to start than my transition," said Alana Haz.

"If the war consulted you on its timetable," Sula said, "then it would have to let *everybody* mess with it. Next thing you know, there wouldn't be a war at all."

Sula stirred another lump of sugar into her tea. Haz took a sip of Kailas, her favorite dessert wine. Its honeyed scent enriched the air, and Sula wondered what it tasted like. If it tasted anything like its scent, it would be glorious.

But, Sula reminded herself, Kailas had a lot of alcohol, and she didn't drink. So she'd have to confine herself to enjoying its bouquet.

Lord Alan Haz had been Sula's premiere on *Confidence* during the Naxid War. He had been a vigorous, square-shouldered man, adept at sports and at encouraging the crew to greater exertions. After the end of the war Sula had lost touch with Haz, until she discovered that in the intervening years Haz had married, fathered two children, and then transformed, not quite completely, into Alana. Her wife, in whom Sula detected a dogged determination, had joined Alana in exile in Harzapid and brought the children with her.

Sula dined in Haz's quarters, as her guest. *Defense* had been a Daimong ship, and its captain had decorated his quarters with hand-painted tiles showing scenes of oceans, islands, and sea life, scenery as far removed from the howling vacuum outside the ship as could be imagined.

"Fortunately the role of a military officer is somewhat stereotyped," Haz said. "I know how to do that. I'm not quite sure yet how best to be myself."

Sula was not very interested in discussions of the self but was willing to be a courteous interlocutor if courteous interlocution was called for. "The war aside," Sula asked, "would you rather be doing something else?"

"Probably," Haz said, "but I don't know what that would be." She sighed. "I thought that once I'd done my transition, my problems would be over, but all I'm seeing is more complications on the horizon. I'm changing, but I don't know what I'm moving toward. Myself, I hope."

"Let's hope we all live long enough to find out," Sula said. The morning's Fourth Fleet exercise had not gone well for the Restoration, who had inflicted vast damage on a virtual enemy fleet, but in the end had been overwhelmed by numbers. *Defense* had spent a lot of time jinking at high accelerations in a futile effort to avoid enemy missiles, and Sula's muscles were sore, she had a backache, and nevertheless she had to exert herself to be a pleasant dinner guest.

"The whole empire is in transition," Sula said, "and we don't know what it's becoming. Sometimes I think absolutely anything is allowed."

"We may be more ruthless now than the Shaa," Haz said. "Who would have thought that was even possible?"

There was an uncomfortable silence. Haz took another sip of her Kailas. "Perhaps we could change the subject," she said.

"Have you seen Squadron Leader Severin's video of Puppet Tork?"

"No," Sula said, "but I like the sound of 'Puppet Tork.'"

"I can call it up if you like."

Sula considered the matter. "If it's not too long."

It was something like twelve minutes, and it was hilarious, particularly if you knew Supreme Commander Tork. Puppet Tork stormed about the stage proclaiming his own greatness, bellowed at his interviewer for leaving her collar unbuttoned, and demanded painful death for traitors. He offered absurd defenses of Lady Gruum and other members of the Zanshaa administration. "Didn't you like my stadium show?" he demanded. "It was the best ever, just as my victory at Magaria was the best ever—until the next, which will be even bester!"

Sula's muscles, sore from accelerations, ached even more from laughter.

"I've never seen Severin's stuff," she said. "Is it all as good as this?"

"The humor usually isn't as pointed," said Haz. "But I'm devoted to his oeuvre. You could start with *Lord Quisp*, for example."

There was a soft knock on the door, and one of *Defense*'s signalers entered with an envelope. "Pardon me, your ladyships," she said. "But there's a priority message for Lady Sula from Harzapid."

Sula held out a hand, and the signaler handed her the envelope. The signaler withdrew, and Sula drew a data foil out of the envelope. "If I may use your display?" she said.

"Of course."

Sula put the foil into one of the wall displays along with her commander's card. Michi Chen appeared on the display. She was looking a little drawn, having only a few days before endured the surgery to attach her new leg.

"This is Fleet Commander Chen," she said. "I'm delighted to report that there has been a battle in the Shulduc system, and that Fleet Commander Martinez, aided by Captain Lord Jeremy Foote, has destroyed sixteen heavy cruisers at the cost of a single ship damaged. A full recording of the battle is attached to this message, so that you can use it in formulating your own tactics. In celebration of the victory, the Restoration has declared a holiday in thirteen days' time. Please participate if your schedule permits." The orange end-stamp filled the screen.

"Sixteen enemy ships destroyed," Sula said. "That leaves only five hundred and fifty-seven available to Tork. We should be able to beat those without any trouble at all."

"And a big party in thirteen days' time," said Haz. "Such fun to organize."

"At least we won't have to organize it ourselves," Sula said. "Which of your lieutenants will you name party control officer?"

Haz laughed. "Pity Vonderheydte has been promoted to captain. He would be perfect."

Vonderheydte, who had run off with Marietta Li, and whose war thus far had mostly been a kind of extended honeymoon—at least until his *Declaration* frigate had departed Harzapid, and even then Sula couldn't be entirely sure he hadn't smuggled Marietta on board.

Haz looked at her. "Will you send a message of congratulations to Fleet Commander Martinez?"

Sula took a sip of her tepid tea. "I'm sure he's been congratulating himself every minute since the battle," Sula said. "Anything I'd send would be redundant."

Haz seemed curious. "I remember you and Martinez from the last war," she said. "When you seemed to like each other."

"With age comes wisdom," Sula said, and then frowned. "I should announce the victory to the Fourth Fleet. And you should make your own announcement to the crew."

"Yes, I suppose I should."

Sula rose. "Thank you for your hospitality," she said. "I'll make the transmission from my office."

Alana Haz rose to her considerable height, a head taller than Sula, and braced. "Thank you for joining me, Lady Fleetcom."

"Always a pleasure," Sula said.

On her way to her suite, Sula thought, *Sixteen enemy ships, no losses. Martinez will be insufferable.*

THREE DAYS LATER Sula lay on her bed, her eyes closed, doing her best to think of nothing. Her mind had run at full speed all day, running a fleet exercise, analyzing the Battle of Shulduc, and playing host at yet another supper for yet another set of squadron captains. Now she desired nothing but silence and peace.

At least the nightmares had faded. It's as if her system was so exhausted that it could no longer devote much energy to generating horrific dreams. Reality, perhaps, was scary enough.

There was a brief tone from the wall comm. "No outgoing video," she said. "Answer."

"Beg pardon, Lady Fleetcom." The voice was that of Ricci, one of her signals lieutenants. "Priority, eyes only, from Fleet Commander Chen."

Sula pulled herself out of bed, dragged on the tunic she'd thrown on a chair, and opened the door. Ricci braced and offered an envelope. Apparently the message had arrived when he was shaving, because half his face had dark stubble and the other half didn't, and there was a bit of soap on his collar. Sula was too weary to laugh.

"Thank you," she said and closed the door. She put the data foil in the wall video, slotted in her captain's card, and told the display to play the dispatch.

The stern look on Michi's face told Sula that she wasn't going to like the message. Michi put on that face when she was issuing orders that might encounter resistance, and she wanted to preempt that resistance by being implacable from the very start.

"I want to begin by congratulating you on the way you've shaken down the Fourth Fleet," Michi said. "You are doing a fine job of turning inexperienced, incomplete crews into models of efficiency, and you are giving me increasing hope for a victory in the upcoming battle against Tork."

Oh, this is going to be bad, Sula thought. If Michi felt it necessary to butter up Sula to this extent, Sula absolutely knew that she was really not going to like the orders that followed.

"I have received a request—a demand, really—from Fleet Commander Martinez, for a competent new tactical officer." Michi seemed to have to gather inner strength before delivering the next part of her message. "To that end, I have decided to appoint you to that position."

Sula felt every molecule of her body vibrate with outrage. Michi hastened through the next part of her message. "I know that you don't want or need a staff position right now, that after so many years of waiting you finally have a command worthy of your talents. But the need is great, and quite frankly you're the best. At Naxas I saw the two of you work together, and together you're better than you are apart."

Michi took a breath. The hard part of her message was now over. "There's no need for you to hurry on to join Division Two. You can remain with the Fourth Fleet until such time as Fleetcom Martinez rejoins, but I'd appreciate it if you communicate with him in the meantime. Message ends."

Weariness and exhaustion had vanished. Sula paced her sleeping room in fury, shrieking at the silent screen a comprehensive series of rhetorical arguments crucially demonstrating that Michi was an idiot for thinking that she and Gareth Martinez could possibly work together again.

Not to mention that she'd finally got a command of her own where she could succeed on her own terms, and if she became tactical officer she'd become just another Martinez sidekick. No matter how much she contributed, he'd take credit for her ideas just as he'd take credit for the victory.

But of course Michi wouldn't have a problem with that. Martinez was married to Michi's niece, and the greater the glory that accrued to Martinez, the greater the reflected glory for Michi's family as well as the Martinez clan. Sula could maybe expect a little sympathy from Michi, but it would be the kind of sympathy that wouldn't change anything.

Yet her own self-respect demanded that she respond.

"What?" she sent. "Martinez can't find anyone in his All-Victorious Division of Immortals capable of serving as a tactical officer? What does that say about his training methods?"

She snarled at the camera. "If I've got to pull his chestnuts out of the fire, I want full recognition for my contribution to any victory." Sula drew her lips back in a parody of a winsome smile. "The Golden Orb would be nice, don't you think?"

MARTINEZ SAW A fleet blossoming out of a wormhole gate on the other side of the system—there seemed to be *hundreds* of them, advancing like a great sparkling wave, their drives boosting them at a steady one gravity. For a moment his heart lurched, and he thought Tork's Home Fleet had arrived, and he was about to face a fight of his sixteen ships against hundreds.

But then he realized that it *was* the Home Fleet, but only the Terran part of it, and that Kung had surrounded his sixty-three ships with a hundred or more decoys.

He sent a message welcoming Kung, but the message would take over nine hours to reach its destination. Kung's own signal arrived just before his own message would have reached Kung's flagship. Kung's message was brief and to the point.

"This is Senior Squadron Commander Kung, to unknown warships. Please identify yourselves, or I will blow you to bits."

To Kung, the sensor image of Division Two would have looked identical to Rukmin's squadrons, and so his declaration was understandable. And since Martinez had identified himself in a message sent nine hours earlier, Martinez wasn't worried about the threat.

Division Two was locked in a heavy deceleration just as draining as the acceleration that had brought it to Shulduc. It had shot through the Shulduc system, then through Toley, and was now two systems beyond. Another few days should bring it to the point at which the deceleration would end, and an acceleration toward Toley, Shulduc, and Harzapid could begin.

The damaged *Compliance* had been unable to decelerate at the same rate as the rest of the squadron, and as a result had shot half a day ahead of the rest of the division.

Every inhabited world within reach of Division Two's communications arrays had been informed that it had been liberated by the forces of the Restoration and were obliged to broadcast to their population messages from Michi Chen, Roland Martinez, and Lady Koridun welcoming them to the legitimate rule of the empire. Martinez also said that anyone, Terran or not, who felt they were being discriminated against by the Zanshaa government was welcome to contact him.

There was considerable response, mainly from Terrans who had been dismissed from their posts in government. Martinez, relieved there had been no wholesale evictions and arrests as on Chijimo, suggested to the leaders on these worlds that the Terrans be reinstated. As those on the inhabited worlds were staring up at close to five hundred rocket launchers, the suggestion was obeyed.

Martinez sent Kung congratulations at his successful escape from Zanshaa and asked if he knew where Tork and the Home Fleet might be.

"Tork has been joined by the Second Fleet and left Zanshaa system three days ago," Kung said. "His combined force has been named the Righteous Fleet for Suppression of Dissension, which you have to admit is very much in his style. It'll be over a month before he reaches here, I'm sure."

This time Kung had sent his message by video, which showed a well-groomed square head, with brushy white hair and a mustache that spread like wings. His expression was benign and amused. Martinez, exhausted with weeks of deceleration, could hardly rise to such perfection.

Martinez sent Kung the latest news. "I'll also send you our latest codes and ciphers, but I'll wait until an enemy-held relay station isn't directly behind you."

Through that station, the enemy had just heard for the first time the results of the Battle of Shulduc. There was no reason to keep it secret any longer, and Martinez hoped the news might damage enemy morale.

Since the Righteous Fleet for Suppression of Dissension wasn't going to show up any time soon, Martinez ordered Division Two to reduce its deceleration. His ligaments crackled as they broadcast their relief.

Thirty hours later Kung and Martinez came close enough to have something like a normal conversation.

"I'm sending you recordings of the Shulduc fight," Martinez said. "I hope they'll be useful to you."

"I'm sure they will be," said Kung. "We've been drilling the Foote Formula ever since we left Zanshaa system, but it's always useful to see the formula being applied."

Inwardly Martinez winced at the mention of Foote.

"I see you're not accompanied by *The Sublime Truth of the Praxis*," Martinez said. *Sublime* was the battleship built for Terran crews on Zanshaa's ring.

"It wasn't complete, and we couldn't take it," Kung said. "But we wrecked it good and proper before we left. Destroyed every piece of electronics, smashed every working part on the engines, and punched holes in the hull. It'll be months before they can get it in service again."

"Very good work, my lord. Were the other battleships complete?"

"They are by now," Kung said. "I'm sure Tork is commanding from Battle Squadron One, for all it has only three ships now. I don't know whether the Second Fleet's battleship was ready or not—I rather think not."

"Do you know if Tork has developed any doctrine for use of the battle squadron?"

"None that he ever articulated to me."

Martinez wasn't surprised. He had always assumed that the battleships had been Tork's vanity project, the floating palaces in which he could parade his own grandeur.

"We also took every Terran-crewed support vessel with us," Kung added. "So we have a full complement of tenders, supply ships, and courier vessels." That explained the large number of ships with Kung, many of which Martinez had first mistaken for decoys.

"Excellent, my lord." Martinez was beginning to feel intimidated by Kung's unblemished record of success and annoyed by his method of announcing it.

"Along the way," Kung said, "we also plundered Zarafan. Wrecked the dockyards, stole all the military supplies, and took every ship we could crew or that was willing to join us."

"Congratulations, my lord."

"The ships I detailed for that work are some distance behind us," Kung said. "Please don't shoot at them when they come through the wormhole."

"I'll do my best not to."

"When we beat Tork, any enemy survivors will have to run all the way to Zanshaa to resupply," Kung said. His benign expression was beginning to look more like self-satisfaction.

"I'm not planning on there being any survivors," Martinez said.

"By the way, Lord Gareth," he said, "I see that you're calling yourself 'fleet commander' these days."

"Lady Michi Chen was kind enough to promote me," Martinez said.

"But yet—" Kung seemed to be making some kind of thoughtful internal calculation. "Yet I have always been superior to you in rank. Not your fault, of course, but—"

So *that* was what this litany of self-praise was about, Martinez thought. Kung was angling for command of the Fourth Fleet and was hoping to so impress Martinez with his accomplishments that Martinez would be intimidated into stepping down.

"So," Kung said, apparently drawing some kind of conclusion, "if I were to give you an order . . . ?"

"I don't believe your lordship has any reason to give me one," Martinez said.

"Hmm. Really?" It had to be admitted, Martinez thought, that Kung's well-groomed performance, pretending all this analysis was spontaneous, was really quite superb.

"You can take this up with Lady Michi, of course," Martinez said. "But before you do, you might want to ask yourself a question: *How many battles have I won?* Because when I ask *myself* that question, the answer is *three*, with a fourth won by the Martinez Method though I was not present." Martinez thought that perhaps it was his turn to offer a little self-satisfaction. "Whereas," he continued, "I know you had a desk job in the last war." He smiled, then added, "Not your fault, of course."

"Well, Lord Gareth," Kung said, carefully avoiding speaking Martinez's rank aloud. "You have certainly given me a great deal to think about."

"Please give my best regards to Lady Michi when you speak with her," Martinez said. "And we have a whole series of dispatches, along with mail, that I hope you will transmit to Harzapid when you have the chance."

"Of course, my lord."

Nothing, Martinez thought, *like putting a rival in the role of postman.*

A few hours later, Division Two finally ended its long

deceleration, and began its acceleration in the direction of Harzapid. Nothing really changed—the ships flipped but were on the same bearing, and acceleration and deceleration felt alike to anyone having to endure them. But this time the acceleration was less ferocious, and the crews all got a chance to sleep without having to fight for every breath.

It was eleven days later, when Division Two finally entered a system that had a friendly transmission link to Harzapid, that Martinez received Michi's transmission about his new tactical officer. He stared at the screen for a long time, and then was aware that his mouth was hanging open, and closed it.

This is going to be awkward, he thought.

CHAPTER 12

Nikki Severin had been advancing the Restoration's controlled wormhole network as quickly as he could, sending out shuttles full of armed Exploration Service crews to the relay stations to relieve the existing crews. Martinez and Division Two had moved beyond the relay station network after Shulduc and had gone out of communication, but since then the network had grown, Martinez was now one system out from Toley, and should again be in communication with the Restoration.

Time, Sula thought, *to face the enemy.*

She wore full-dress uniform, with the high collar, the double row of silver buttons, and her junior fleet commander's shoulder boards. She wore more cosmetic than usual and wished she could have used more to create a perfect mask to hide behind.

Sula sat upright behind a desk that smelled faintly of lemon polish, with the camera directly in front of her. Behind the camera her wall screen showed the notes she'd made for her transmission. She hadn't written a speech, exactly, but she'd put her talking points on the screen. She didn't want to miss any points and have to send a follow-up message as a kind of embarrassing appendix.

"Junior Fleet Commander Lady Sula to Fleet Commander Martinez, personal and private," she began, then paused. *Begin*, she thought, *with the disclaimer.* "I'd like to make it clear that I did not seek the job of tactical officer. This was Lady Michi's idea, ordered over my objections.

"I'd also like to state that I have no intention of wearing staff tabs on my collar. A junior fleet commander is not on anyone's staff."

Set out the terms, she thought. *Then get to the actual message.*

MARTINEZ WATCHED SULA, stiff and formal and expressionless, behind her desk. His chest seemed to be full of flapping butterflies. Ablaze with resentment, the emerald-green eyes bored straight into him.

"I'm enclosing the records of all the exercises I've been running with the Fourth Fleet," she said. "The earlier records are full of inexperienced crews learning their jobs, so if I were you, I'd look at the later ones." She took a breath. "The results are not encouraging. Fighting odds of nearly two to one, we can hurt the enemy badly, but eventually we're overwhelmed. Even if we win, we're so badly damaged that we'd have a hard time mustering the numbers to advance to Zanshaa."

Great news, Martinez thought. He was half reclined on his bed, fresh from his morning shower and drinking his breakfast coffee. Large pictures of his family, Terza, Gareth the Younger, and Yaling, were arranged to obscure the erotic contortions of the Torminel on his walls, and they added a pleasing note of domesticity to his decor.

He wasn't looking at his family. He was looking at Sula. He wasn't thinking domestic thoughts, either.

"One thing we're learning," Sula said, "is that our initial dispositions are critical. Our fleets are now so large that shifting deployments on the run is next to impossible. This was even more obvious once Kung's forces joined ours—our fleet is increasingly difficult to maneuver." She raised a hand. "Of course, with double our numbers, that problem will be even greater for Tork. Once the engagement starts, he'll be stuck with whatever disposition he starts with. If we could work out ways to increase our maneuverability, we could try to take advantage of his static positions."

She took a breath. "We can make certain assumptions about Tork's intentions. He'll come in slow and deliberately, as he did at Magaria. And because they worked for him once, he'll use the same tactics he used at Magaria. And he won't *care* what tactics we use, because he'll know that his tactics are right and ours are wrong, and he won't think beyond that. But his officers *might*"—she made a fist and shook it, once, at an invisible enemy—"so if Tork lets them off the leash they could really fuck us." Sula let the fist fall to her desk. "So we have to make sure that Tork stays in control of his forces up until the very end. And *that* means *we have to keep Tork alive*—he should be the last person to die in the entire Home Fleet. And we should also give him what he's looking for— we should deploy our forces in the most conventional way possible, and then change it up and hope he can't react quickly enough."

It wouldn't be hard to find Tork amid his vast battle fleet, Martinez thought. His flagship would be a part of Battleship Squadron One, and the battleships would be looking for the enemy flagship so that Tork could thrash the rebellion out of Michi Chen in person.

Which meant, Martinez realized, that Tork would be going after *Perfection of the Praxis* on the assumption that it would be Michi's flagship. He wouldn't know that Michi wasn't with the Fourth Fleet, or that Martinez would be commanding from *Bombardment of Los Angeles*. Which in turn meant that *Perfection of the Praxis* might be used to lure Tork into a deadly mistake.

Sad, Martinez thought, *for whoever was commanding* Perfection. *Conyngham, wasn't it?*

"So we use *Perfection* as a decoy," Martinez said, in his reply to Sula later that morning. He imitated Sula's style of on-camera delivery, wearing full dress with the disk of the Golden Orb around his neck, and recording from behind the desk in his office, with its background of Torminel wrestlers. "We'll have to make it look good by supporting *Perfection* with a couple squadrons of heavy cruisers, but if we do it right, we can draw Tork and his battleships out of position. And then *Perfection* won't engage, just keep pulling away . . . and in the meantime we can concentrate on the rest of the Home Fleet and wreck them."

He could *see* it, and he knew that Sula, when she received the message, would see it as well. Every time they had worked together—on developing the Method, on fighting at Naxas—their minds fell into an eerie synchronization, even if they were in separate star systems. Different as their personalities were, their brains saw some kinds of problems in complementary ways.

"As for the difficulty maneuvering such a large fleet," he said, "try experimenting with mobile reserves to give us some flexibility. But what I'd like to start working on *now* are ways to keep Tork and the Home Fleet under pressure. Constant small ambushes, the same sort that Chenforce encountered at Arkhan-Dohg in the Naxid War. That will mean setting up radars and lidar ahead of time, preferably unmanned, because if they had people on board it would be suicide for them. I'm afraid you're going to have to organize that, because I don't have the resources out here. Understand?"

He knew that she would understand. He knew that she would be superb at this.

Tork wasn't going to know what hit him.

LAMEY GAVE AN earnest look at Sula through the video screen. "I hope you're telling your rich officers about the investment opportunities available to them," he said. "'Investment as solid as the mountains of Esley.' That's our slogan."

Oh, Lamey, Sula thought. She could only shake her head. At Harzapid he had a whole planet of possible victims, and he wanted the Fourth Fleet, too?

"Seriously, Earthgirl," he said. "I could use some help. Mehrang's getting on my back about lack of progress, and I'm cut off from my own sources of funds at Spannan." He grinned. "I'll offer you a twenty percent commission on any investments you bring me."

Sula snorted, then took a sip of her honey-sweetened tea while considering how best to reply. *I'm not going to recommend dubious investments to anyone I count on to preserve my life* might well express her feelings, but an inner voice suggested that she shouldn't take the risk of making Lamey angry. He knew too much about her, and though he couldn't denounce her without running a risk of being denounced himself, he might in his anger let something slip.

Your job is raising money, my job is fighting a war. Still too blunt, she decided.

She was trying to phrase another rebuff when her cuff button chimed, and Lieutenant Ricci's face appeared on her sleeve display. "Message from Fleetcom Martinez, my lady," he said.

"Is it in my queue?"

"As soon as it's decoded, my lady."

"Right. Thank you."

She forgot about Lamey and looked at her message queue. Another few dozen messages—"Personal and private"—had appeared since she'd answered Lamey's message. She sighed.

The flagship was currently receiving in excess of twelve thousand messages every day, messages from subordinates, from Harzapid, routine reports, urgent queries about supplies or dispositions or clarification of a ship's part in the next maneuver. Most of these could be handled in a routine manner by members of the staff or the signals department, but still a disturbing number of Sula's subordinates seemed unable to resolve even minor problems without guidance from the flag officer in command.

She was looking forward to Martinez's arrival, if only because then all the correspondence would be directed to *him*, and she could take a rest.

The decoded message from Martinez popped up in her queue, and she triggered it.

Use Perfection *as a decoy. Mobile reserves. Ambushes.*

Oh yes. Her heart shifted into a faster rhythm, and she tasted metal on her tongue, as if she'd completed a circuit in her head. Scenarios unfolded themselves in her mind, and she saw the battle complete, from the opening moves to Tork's blazing destruction.

Sula picked up a stylus and jotted notes to herself on her desk display, and then she wondered who she could call on to help her ideas come into better focus.

There was a knock on her office door, and Spence entered, carrying Sula's dress uniform on a hanger.

"Your guests are on their way," she said. "You need to dress for dinner."

Another damned dinner, Sula thought. She reviewed the guest list and found them all uninspired.

"Right," she said, rose from behind her desk, and began to unbutton her undress tunic. "Let's get this over with."

She'd forgotten Lamey entirely.

※

BEFORE THE WAR broke out, Martinez's sister Vipsania had produced a video documentary, *The War of the Naxid Rebellion*, which had been broadcast throughout the empire on her own Imperial network. The video succeeded in turning Martinez into a celebrity, and Sula into a public hero.

Sula had assumed the video was intended solely to glorify Martinez and his family, but to her surprise it provided actual history, as well as going to some effort to track the contributions of individuals to the victory over the Naxids. Sula's contribution to the new tactics had been acknowledged, and Chandra Prasad had been given credit for anticipating the Naxid ambush at Arkhan-Dohg.

Prasad had been promoted to squadron leader and now commanded Division Twelve, the two light squadrons that hadn't finished their conversions when the rest of the Fourth Fleet departed Harzapid. Division Twelve had finally completed its modification from Cree- to Terran-crewed ships and had pulled hard gees to catch the Fourth Fleet. Now that she'd arrived, Sula invited Prasad to a welcoming supper, along with half her captains. The other half would have to wait for another occasion, or for *Defense* to install a much larger dining room.

Lady Chandra Prasad was a Martinez protégée, and Sula knew her only casually from when they'd encountered each other on Harzapid's ring. She had a pointed chin and long dark eyes and braced at the hatch with her shoulders flared back, her long hair—a bright, highly artificial shade of red—turned to a scarlet halo by a light behind her in the airlock.

"Welcome, Squadcom," Sula said. "Will you introduce your captains?"

Sula already knew the small, delicate Vonderheydte, another Martinez protégé, and again wondered if he'd managed to sneak Marietta Li aboard his *Declaration* frigate. Of course she knew the Kangas twins and saw that Ranssu wore gloves, presumably so as not to call attention to his mutilated hand. The fresh skin on his cheek stood out by virtue of its not being as weathered as the rest of his face. The improbably youthful Lieutenant-Captain Lord Pavel Ikuhara had served with Sula on the *Confidence* and later helped capture the *Striver* on its way to Harzapid. He had grown a goatee in an attempt to look more mature, but instead he looked as if a child had scrawled over the lower half of his face with a crayon. The other three captains were middle-aged lieutenants promoted out of retirement. Sula introduced her own Captain Haz and led the others to dinner, sitting them at the wedge-shaped table in the wedge-shaped room. Spence and Macnamara poured wine and served starters of cashment flavored with tart chuchu berries.

Division Twelve had been equipped with the Shankaracharya sensor system, and Sula asked whether the operators had been able to detect a difference in their readings.

"Hard to say," Prasad said. "We see more detail in certain structures, but so far nothing that has to do with our mission. If we were Exploration Service ships scanning a newly discovered planet, or looking for asteroids or wormholes, we'd do very well. But aside from that one experiment you ordered, we lack data concerning how the sensors will behave in combat."

"Speaking of newly discovered planets, Lady Fleetcom,"

Ikuhara said, "can you clarify what it is that *Explorer* found on its last expedition? I've heard they found an entire alien civilization that the Shaa wiped out in the far past."

Sula blinked in utter surprise. "I've heard nothing of the sort," she said.

"Our officers visit back and forth from ship to ship," Ikuhara said. "And apparently some of the Exploration Service officers talked about it once they got some liquor on board—though of course I don't know whether it's even *supposed* to be secret."

"I should imagine it would be," said Alana Haz.

"Now that you've brought it up," Sula said, "you'd better tell us what you've heard."

"Not much more than what I've told you," said Ikuhara. He touched his wispy beard in a self-conscious way. "The planet is either called Garden or Lorkin—I've heard both. It's suitable for settlement, a bountiful world, but it's absolutely packed with old ruins that have been bombed to bits, and there are Shaa installations both in space and on the surface."

"Well," said Prasad. She leaned back in her chair, a look of cynical amusement on her face. "It seems the Shaa were keeping secrets."

Haz looked thoughtful. "The Great Masters may have had good reason for keeping secrets, I suppose," she said.

Chandra Prasad snorted with laughter. "Because they fucked it up!" she said. "They fucked it so badly they blew up everything and left!"

At that moment Sula found herself liking Prasad. Neither of them were afraid of raising uncomfortable possibilities.

"What this means," she said, "is that the annihilation of entire species was built into the empire from the beginning. It's not something we've invented since the death of the last Shaa."

Vonderheydte was dubious. "Is that supposed to make us feel better?"

"Wait a minute," said Paivo Kangas. "Isn't Severin using a character called 'Lorkin' in his puppet shows?"

"That thing with the tentacles?" said Ranssu.

"Ah. Hah," Sula said. In Severin's last few satirical programs, a being called "Lorkin," supposedly a member of a recently discovered species, was always interrogating members of the Zanshaa government and trying to make sense out of their narcissistic, nonsensical replies.

"I think that Squadcom Severin may have an agenda," she said. "And I think we should avoid speculating until I have a chance to see Severin and ask him what it is."

It wasn't that there weren't other things to talk about. Sula spoke to the four captains she didn't know and tried to draw out details of their careers. She wasn't interested in the captains themselves, exactly, but she wanted to form an idea of what each might be good at, in case she had to make specific deployments or send someone on a special detail, and there was always the possibility that one might be promoted into a higher position of trust.

It had to be admitted that the captains disappointed her— they seemed to be undistinguished mediocrities promoted into their places because they were the only officers available. They were probably suited well enough to their current assignments, but none struck her as the Fourth Fleet's next tactical wonder.

After the meal, when her guests were lingering over their desserts and their sweet trellin-berry liqueur, Sula brought up the way that Chenforce, with Chandra Prasad as tactical officer, had survived the ambush at Arkhan-Dohg. The Naxids had painted Chenforce briefly with a ranging laser from within the system, which served to light it up just as hundreds of missiles, accelerated to relativistic velocities, shot into the system through a wormhole gate. Chenforce had only seconds of warning, but managed to survive without a loss.

"I was lucky enough to anticipate the attack," Prasad said. Wine had relaxed her—she lay semireclined, one shoulder overhanging the back of the chair, the shoulder itself overhung in turn by her red hair. "I demonstrated how devastating the attack could be with an exercise, and then Lady Michi was good enough to alter our dispositions so as to be able to anticipate the arrival of the missiles." She took a sip of her dessert wine and looked thoughtful. "Though of course the enemy were observing us as we advanced, and they saw us alter our dispositions. I've often wondered if they worked out why we shifted our formations and launched more decoys, and that suggested the attack to them. If I hadn't run that exercise, they might never have attacked us."

"I've been thinking how best to make such an attack on Tork," Sula said.

A dry smile touched Prasad's lips. "I've been thinking about sending you a memo about that very possibility."

Sula picked up her goblet of Citrine Fling and viewed the

cloudy liquid as it rolled around the glass. "Well then," she said. "We'd better conspire."

Chandra laughed. "Yes. I think we should."

It proved a fertile conspiracy indeed.

"I THINK YOU'LL be pleased with the latest experiments," Sula said. "I've been working up some ideas about your mobile reserves, and I think they can be used to give us local superiority if they can be brought into the battle at the right moment. I'm not sure when that is yet, but I'll try to have an answer for you soon."

Sula was a good deal more relaxed than she'd been in her first dispatch. The masklike cosmetic was gone, and the bristling ramrod posture had eased somewhat. A cup of tea was visible on her desk.

And now and then she allowed herself a smile. Martinez appreciated the smiles.

Martinez viewed the message from behind his own desk, an inadvertent mirror image of Sula's video likeness, only without a teacup and with Torminel wrestlers in the background.

Sula continued her analysis of maneuvers, and afterward appended the daily status reports and forwarded any dispatches from Harzapid.

"One other question," Sula said. "Have you heard any information about what might have happened to Wei Jian? She's overdue at Harzapid, but if the enemy had wiped her out, they'd be boasting about it."

Wei Jian had fled Magaria at the start of the rebellion with the fifty-five Terran-crewed ships of the Second Fleet, apparently bound for Harzapid, a five- or six-month journey along a wormhole route filled with barren and barely inhabited systems. Jian should have turned up at Harzapid by now, or at least sent word, but nothing had been heard from her. Martinez had heard nothing, either from Kung or any mention of her in enemy dispatches.

Another fifty-five ships would be useful against Tork, Martinez knew. But they seemed to have vanished completely.

"Message ends," Sula said, and the orange end-stamp filled the screen.

Martinez paged through the status reports and the messages from Harzapid, which all concerned matters of supply and the progress of the six cruisers under construction in Harzapid's yards—some, apparently, by Naxids, as part of an arrangement that Sula had made before she'd left with the Fourth Fleet.

A text from Lalita Banerjee appeared on his desktop. *Urgent high-priority message from Kung just arrived. Will be added to your queue after decoding.*

Kung had been promoted to junior fleet commander on joining the Fourth Fleet, with seniority below that of Sula. This probably hadn't pleased him, but Martinez hadn't heard that he'd complained. That was why the Kung who appeared on the decoded video startled him.

"The news of Lorkin is leaking through the Fourth Fleet," Kung said. His face had reddened, and his broad mustache was unbalanced, one wing turned up, the other down. "This is provoking unwholesome and subversive discourse on the part of the officers, and now it's oozing down to the enlisted. It may be too late, Fleetcom Martinez, but I'd recommend quarantining the Exploration Service ships at once, along with any other ship where these sorts of rumors are prevalent. Severin and Lady Starkey should be put under arrest."

The orange end-stamp flashed onto the screen. *Lorkin?* Martinez thought.

He wondered if Kung was drunk. But even if he were, the message demanded a reply.

Martinez buttoned his collar, faced the camera, and recorded his reply.

"Thank you for alerting me to the existence of a problem," he said. "I regret to say that I'm unfamiliar with the situation you describe. Perhaps you could send me more details."

Then he forwarded Kung's message to Sula, with the title *What the Hell?*

SEVERIN'S SLEEPING CABIN was cluttered with trunks, puppets, and puppet-making materials, with grotesque, cartoonish faces hanging off furniture or dangling upside-down from fixtures. The puppet stage had been set up in his neighboring dining room, and that meant that furniture from the dining room had been shifted to the sleeping cabin. There was only a narrow path from the door to the bed, but fortunately the narrow path was all he and Lady Starkey needed.

"I'll edit tomorrow afternoon, fleet exercises permitting," Severin said. "And then you can let me know how you like it."

Lady Starkey grinned. "I could let you know in person," she said.

"I hope you will."

He thought the latest puppet satire one of their better efforts. It involved Lady Tu-hon, Lady Gruum, and Lord Minno all madly bribing one another, passing the exact same sum from one to the next while crowing about how rich they were getting.

"Do we have a title?" Starkey asked. "How about *The Science of Economics*?"

He kissed her. "Very nice."

She snuggled next to him, her head lying in the hollow between his head and shoulder. Severin's bed was large for a single person, but cozy for two.

"I should shift back to the *Explorer*," she said. "We've got another fleet exercise scheduled just after breakfast, and I want to check with each department head to make sure we won't embarrass ourselves."

Severin inhaled the warm scent of her hair. "You can stay a little longer," he said.

"Without embarrassment? I hope so."

Presumably everyone on *Explorer* and *Expedition* knew their captains were lovers, and that word would be spread through the Fourth Fleet as crew visited one another, but so far Severin hadn't felt in the least embarrassed. There was nothing in law or custom against what he and Lady Starkey were doing. The Shaa conquerors had been bewildered by the variety and vigor of human sexuality, and in their perplexity had chosen not to privilege one hormonal prejudice over another, but instead laid down only a very few commonsense regulations, chief of which was a mandatory contraceptive implanted in every female at puberty. An adult female could have the implant removed at any time, but in the meantime was protected against both accidents and malice.

That attitude was reflected in both the Fleet and the Exploration Service, and in ship designs that included "recreation tubes," for which there was also another, more vulgar name. Severin and Lady Starkey both had private cabins and hadn't required a tube, but the tubes were in frequent use by others, particularly in long voyages.

The Exploration Service frowned on relations between officers and enlisted, and by superiors and their inferiors. It was difficult in the present situation to tell whether Severin or Starkey was of superior rank—Severin was Starkey's superior in the Service, but in terms of social standing Lihua, Lady Starkey was a high-ranking Peer, and Severin a mere commoner.

They were exploiting each other equally, Severin decided.

Severin's eyes drifted over the puppets and stage equipment, the dangling faces, stocking bodies, and limp hands. "I need to put everything away before the exercise tomorrow," he said. "Can't have the puppets slamming around in high accelerations."

"I'll help you," Starkey said.

She slipped out of bed and the two of them, naked, began packing away the puppet gear. Lady Starkey, Severin observed, seemed to treat the puppets with genuine affection and folded their bodies carefully before putting them into their travel cases.

Since his elevation to the officer caste Severin had enjoyed the company of a number of high-status women—most of them rich, restless, and married, by arrangement, to someone else—but his experience had never encompassed anyone quite like Lady Starkey. She seemed to find delight in so many things—not least the puppet and puppeteering—that his spirits rose simply by being in her company.

He had become a puppeteer because he'd had an idea for a show and was then compelled to carry it out. He hadn't allowed himself much of a choice in the business. The puppets themselves were a means by which he could produce the show economically, because he couldn't afford actors or even professional puppeteers. They were tools that helped him realize his vision. But Lady Starkey seemed to love his tools for themselves.

It would be misleading to describe Starkey's affection for the puppets as "childlike"—she wasn't anything like a child except, perhaps, in her capacity for delight. Severin wondered if anyone in either branch of her family had ever undertaken a hobby quite so out of the ordinary for Peers.

There were Peers who had abandoned the life considered suitable for their station and had become actors or other performers, and they were roundly disapproved of when they did. But a puppeteer? That was unheard of.

He watched Starkey pick up a sock puppet, brush some lint off its absurd face, then wrap it in gauze and pack it in its trunk.

He admired both her care for the puppet and the play of muscle in her haunches as she bent over the trunk—thousands of hours of conditioning to withstand heavy gravities had produced muscles and haunches well worth admiring.

"What would your family say if they could see you now?" he asked.

She straightened and gave him a grin over her shoulder. "They'll say whatever I tell them to. I'm the head of Clan Starkey, and if they say anything unpleasant they risk my displeasure."

"So they're not hectoring you over—I don't know— marrying some grizzled old Peer with two ex-wives, nine children, and a palace in the High City?"

The grin broadened. "If they're hectoring, I can't hear them—most of them are in corners of the empire that our side doesn't control." She approached Severin and put her hands on his shoulders. Her eyes were very close to his. "Why have you developed such an interest in my marriage prospects, Nikki?"

He considered his words carefully. "I thought you might want to continue our double act after the war, if your family and the whole Order of Peers doesn't object."

"Well." She smiled. "That's quite an offer. And my family has no say in the matter, because I'm Lady Starkey and I'm in charge."

"There's the Hua side," Severin said. "They hardly married your mother to your father without some expectation that you would marry higher still."

She narrowed her eyes and looked at him. "Is it marriage we're talking about, Nikki?"

Was it? He didn't think he'd quite intended the discussion to take that direction. "If you want," he said. "I won't *make* you talk about it."

"Well," she said. "I *would* be marrying higher. You're the Service's biggest hero *now*, never mind what happens in the war. You shut down a pulsar. You moved a wormhole. You saved Rol-mar from bombardment. No one else has ever done anything like that."

Severin tried to respond but found he'd somehow lost his words. *Is that really me?* he thought. He didn't think of himself that way.

He'd just encountered a series of problems and worked out solutions to them. That was all.

"And another thing," Starkey said. "If we win the war, we get to write the rules. So let's win the war."

"All right," Severin said. "Let's do that."

He took her in his arms and kissed her. Her scent danced in his senses. The kiss grew fierce, and then became intensely interesting. The sleeve button of his tunic chimed to let him know there was an incoming communication.

By the third chime he decided he'd better answer it, but then he had to find his clothing amid the disorder of his sleeping cabin and it took another few chimes before he located his tunic and slipped his arm into the left sleeve. "No picture," he told the display. "Identify caller."

The chameleon weave on his sleeve formed the letters JUNIOR FLEET COMMANDER LADY SULA.

"No picture," he repeated. "Answer." And then, just as Sula's impatient face appeared on the display, he said, "How may I help you, Lady Sula?"

Defense was a couple light-seconds out, so there was a moment before the response came.

"Squadron Commander Severin," she said. "I want you to report to me in person tomorrow, immediately after the exercise."

"Yes, my lady."

Sula's intent eyes stared out of the screen for the four seconds it took for her response to reach him. "Why have you blanked the screen?" she asked.

"I'm getting ready for bed, my lady."

"Is Lady Starkey with you? I contacted *Explorer* and was told she's visiting you."

At the mention of her name Severin saw Starkey's eyes widen in alarm.

"Lady Starkey just left," Severin said.

"I want the two of you together," Sula said. "I'll leave a message with *Explorer* that she's to join you tomorrow."

Severin wanted to ask what the meeting was about, but the orange end-stamp filled the screen before he could compose his question. In the sudden silence, he and Lady Starkey stared at each other.

"I'd better get on my shuttle," she said.

He helped her find her clothes while she dressed at speed. "I have a feeling we're going to get chewed out," he said.

"No. Really?" Irony laced the words.

"What did we *do*?" Severin asked.

"Maybe she didn't like that last show about the financial crisis." She slipped on her shoes and kissed Severin on the cheek. "See you tomorrow."

"Right." The door closed behind her. Severin looked around the room, still crowded with crates, stacked dining room chairs, and a half-disassembled puppet stage.

So am I getting married now? he asked himself. He didn't know the answer.

He sighed, then picked up a stack of chairs and moved it to the dining room.

"WELL, SEE, I'D made the Lorkin puppet," Severin said, "and so I thought I'd use it."

"The story needed someone to ask the important questions," Lady Starkey said.

"It's a naïve voice," said Severin. "It's useful. The Lorkin can accept what someone like Lady Tu-hon says at face value, and then ask a follow-up question that makes Tu-hon look ridiculous."

Sula couldn't believe what she was hearing. "So you just put the Lorkin in your playlets because it was *useful*? Or *fun*? You have no other agenda?"

Severin looked blank. "Agenda?" he said.

Sula tried to restrain her impatience. "The discovery of Lorkin has profound political consequences for the entire empire. Either the Shaa began their rule by destroying an entire intelligent species, or . . ." Sula suppressed a snarl. "There is no *or*. But was it a war, a deliberate massacre, a rebellion?"

"We can't know," said Lady Starkey. "We can't know until we can properly survey Lorkin. We'd need archaeologists and—"

"I *know* you can't know," Sula said. "We can suppose that the Shaa had reasons for what they did, but we don't know if they were good reasons, bad reasons, or reasons that were completely beyond our comprehension. But my point is that our entire civilization is based on the foundation the Shaa laid in the Praxis, and this is not the time to question whether or not the Praxis is based on massacres, equivocation, or lies."

Severin had been surprised at first, but as Sula continued he turned grim, skin taut over his high cheekbones, narrow eyes narrower still. "With all respect, Lady Sula," he said, "we haven't done anything like that. We told some jokes, and the jokes weren't about the Praxis, they were all at the expense of the sad clowns that are trying to run the empire."

"You put a Lorkin in your videos. That's making a statement about the Lorkins whether you know it or not."

Severin's anger still simmered. "And what statement is that, exactly?"

"It's a statement," said Sula, "that has a fleet commander demanding your arrest on a charge of subversion. And I don't know whether justice in the Exploration Service is different than it is in the rest of the empire, but let me assure you that if you were arrested on that charge by an officer of the Fleet, the only thing that would delay your execution would be the amount of time it would take to put the correct signatures on the correct documents."

Defiance burned in Severin's eyes. Lady Starkey looked horrified.

"I am recommending against charging you," Sula said. "But I'd advise you to drop the Lorkin from your plays and concentrate on ways to kill the enemy." She lifted a hand. "You may return to your ships."

What have I become? Sula wondered after the two had left. She had always hated the sorts of officers who placed themselves in positions of moral superiority in order to deliver pompous lectures to their subordinates, and now it seemed that she was one of them. And with the threat of execution, no less.

Way to make friends, she thought.

"I'M AFRAID, MY lord, that the good ship *Lorkin* has already left the dockyard," Martinez said. "There are too many people, officers and enlisted, who have heard about Lorkin to enforce any kind of blockade now. And as for conducting some kind of purge while in the face of the enemy—" He waved a hand. "Well, that's impossible."

He and Kung were at last in the same system, Shulduc in fact, though it would take Martinez's transmission twelve hours or more to reach its recipient. Division Two was decelerating to allow the rest of the Fourth Fleet to catch up with it, after which Martinez would at last be united with his whole command.

"Part of the problem," Martinez continued, "is that so little is known about what happened on Lorkin that all sorts of disturbing rumors may be in circulation. In that case, a full disclosure of what *is* known may serve to quell the more outrageous speculations. I look forward to any views you may have on the matter."

He sent the message confident that he wasn't the least bit interested in any of Kung's opinions, but that in order to assure Kung's future cooperation he was willing to humor the man as far as he could. He could only hope that Kung wouldn't demand any heads.

Since *Los Angeles*'s reappearance in Shulduc, thousands of queries and reports had flooded the flagship, and Martinez had set his staff to making sense of them all. Most were trivial, but each had to be assessed in some way, then answered. Martinez and his staff found themselves overwhelmed and ate their meals at their desks while trying to wrangle their correspondence.

Martinez called up his queue, looked at the long list of queries that his staff had forwarded to him, and felt a vast weariness flood his being. He decided to ignore all his official business and view the day's message from Terza.

She appeared in her usual perfection, sharing a sofa with Gareth the Younger. She wore a long black jersey dress that Martinez remembered from their trip on the *Corona*, and he could almost smell the vetiver heart-notes of her perfume. Her message was cheerful and essentially free of content, a fact Martinez appreciated. Harassed every second by issues of war, life, death, and logistics, he was happy to bask for a few minutes in the inconsequential.

He knew that Terza was working furiously to hold the

Restoration together, but her messages mentioned this only in passing. Learning the details of Terza's struggles would only add to Martinez's anxiety—and possibly his indignation—and as he was weeks away from Harzapid there was nothing he could practically accomplish to relieve these sensations. Likewise he tried not to burden Terza with the frustrations of his own existence.

After Terza's message, Young Gareth reported on his day at school and sent copies of several of his latest drawings with long explanations of what, exactly, each picture was intended to represent. People who thought the Lorkins were strange, Martinez thought, had very little experience with the mind of an imaginative child.

As he watched the video he reached into his desk drawer and drew out a bottle of Laredo whisky, poured himself a shot, and let the whisky fire ooze over his palate. The need to relax at the end of his working day was threatening to make him the best customer of his father's distillery.

A pleasant sense of well-being began to hum through his senses. He watched the video a second time, then put his bottle away and recorded a reply.

"If there's one thing I've learned since the return to Shulduc," he said, "it's that a fleet this size needs a much larger staff. I've been sent over ten thousand messages just today, most of them requiring some kind of answer. My staff is trying to sort them out and forward only the most urgent, but when the captain of a warship needs an answer, it's got to come from me."

His fingers itched to retrieve the bottle from his drawer. He repressed the impulse.

"That's averaging over thirty messages a day coming from each ship," he said. "It's complete madness, and it's a waste of, well, *me*." He raised his hands helplessly. "Yet I suppose you must be coping with similar problems, and you and your little committee have a whole planet to manage, along with a pack of other worlds. I shouldn't even be mentioning this problem, except that it caught me so completely by surprise. And speaking of surprises . . ."

He laughed. "Have you heard about Lorkins? They are being openly discussed here, and some of the senior officers are seriously upset." He considered the matter for a moment. "Yet if you *haven't* heard of Lorkins, that's probably a good thing. You should pretend I haven't mentioned them."

Martinez devoted a few moments to evaluating and praising his son's artwork, then signed off and reached for the whisky again. There was a knock on the door from his dining room, and Alikhan entered, carrying the nightly cup of hot cocoa on a salver. Martinez returned the whisky to the drawer and took the cup.

"Have you heard of the Lorkins, Alikhan?" he asked.

Alikhan showed neither surprise nor interest. "No, my lord."

"Good." Apparently the infection hadn't yet reached Division Two. "Is there anything happening I should know about?" he asked.

"Nothing requiring your attention, my lord. Though

Captain Dalkeith will have some interesting disciplinary hearings tomorrow."

"Fighting," Martinez asked, "or alcohol?"

"Both together, my lord. Along with sex."

"Of course." Martinez raised his cup in salute. "It could be worse," he said.

"Absolutely true, my lord. Will you be needing me for anything else tonight?"

"I don't think so. Thank you, Alikhan."

"Sleep well, my lord."

Alikhan withdrew. Martinez drank half the cocoa, then topped the cup with whisky. The results were not completely awful.

In less than a week, Sula would be aboard his ship. He couldn't imagine that ending well.

"EARTHGIRL, YOU NEVER answered my last call."

Lamey looked as if he'd just returned from a banquet or a fancy party, with his green-and-gold-striped coat thrown over the back of a chair, and his ruffled shirt half unbuttoned. "I hope to hell you've been selling some of my fine investments," he said. "Mehrang's on my back every minute, and nobody here is interested in long-term financing, like planetary development. With the economy here starting to boom again, everyone's rushing after immediate profits. I hope it all goes bust again."

Sula wanted to laugh at Lamey's woebegone expression. The proud fixer hadn't been able to fix his way out of trouble.

Lamey's expression turned angry, and Sula felt the hairs on her neck prickle. She knew that anger, and when she'd been Lamey's girlfriend she'd been on the receiving end of it.

"Look, I need you to get on my side and sell some damn investments," he said, "because I'm not going down alone. Understand?"

Well. There was the threat direct.

Clearly she was expected to make some kind of conciliatory response.

Damned if she would.

"Perhaps this message will find you sober," she began, glaring at the camera. "I hope so. Because if you are, you might remember it's *not my job to sell investments*. It's my job to kill a lot of enemies and make sure we both stay alive. If I fail in *my* job, you won't survive long enough to fail in yours."

She took a breath. "Assuming we both live through the next year, you might find me more useful in my role as a high-ranking Fleet officer and a member of the Convocation than as a salesman." She smiled thinly. "It's all up to you, of course."

She sent the message, and then wondered if Lamey would be so furious that he'd go straight to the authorities with a denunciation, and worry about the consequences afterward.

Sula rubbed the scar tissue on her right thumb. Everything would all come down to who was more valuable, she decided. She was more valuable now; but after the victory, Lamey's political skills might be of more use than an imposter in a uniform.

She'd have to work on maintaining her value.

CHAPTER 13

The airlock door eased open, and Martinez gave a nod to the petty officer who served as band leader. She turned to her crew, raised a hand, and gave a downbeat. *Los Angeles*'s band crashed into "Glorious Arrival" from An-tar's *Antimony Sky*. In the cruiser's small anteroom the sound was enormous.

Martinez had decided to give Sula a big welcome, and that included the ship's glittering officers lined up in full-dress uniform, as well as the band, which unfortunately hadn't had enough time for rehearsal. But they charged into the tune with enthusiasm and were backed by a small chorus of singing cadets, equally unrehearsed, in the corridor behind.

At the sight of Sula he felt a tingling, inexorable tsunami flood slowly through his nerves. Sula wore an expression of bemused surprise as she stepped through the airlock door, and then she saw Martinez and braced in salute, her chin lifted, exposing her throat for any punishment her superior might see appropriate to inflict with his ceremonial knife.

Sula had left her submachine gun in her baggage, just as Martinez had left his knife in his trunk—but after some internal debate he'd chosen to carry his Golden Orb. The Orb was an inconvenience, not for Martinez but for everyone else, because its presence required everyone to salute it. But then Martinez was the superior officer on the ship, so everyone had to salute him anyway, and the Orb wouldn't make any difference, except that everyone would know that he had decided Sula was worth the most extravagant and formal welcome he could arrange.

The Orb was a golden baton with a transparent ball on the end, a ball that contained a mixture of liquids, all different shades of gold, that swirled in beautiful streaked patterns like the clouds on a gas giant. Only two had ever been awarded in the last thousand years, one to Martinez, and the other to Supreme Commander Tork.

Martinez intended to blow Tork's Orb to atoms in the next few weeks.

Sula was followed on board by her staff and her servants, all of whom braced in turn. Martinez recognized Spence and Macnamara, having met them in the last war. He might encourage Alikhan to make their acquaintance, and perhaps get a little information, from day to day, on Sula's mood. He knew she would blow up sooner or later, and he preferred not to be in the vicinity when it happened.

He made a benign gesture with his Orb to encourage the party to stand at ease, but even at ease they still had to wait for the song to end. Standing without being able to move or speak, Martinez felt a taut, invisible string stretched between himself and Sula, vibrating to whatever spiky music snarled between them.

Martinez was relieved when the final chords thundered out, and he was able to step to introduce Captain Dalkeith— who knew Sula perfectly well, though the formalities had to be played out nonetheless—and Dalkeith then introduced her officers. Sula introduced her staff and then the welcoming party was dismissed, and Martinez and Dalkeith escorted Sula up two companionways to her quarters.

"I hope you will be comfortable, Lady Sula," Martinez said. "And I hope you will be able to join us for supper tonight."

"I'll look forward to it," Sula said, looking up at him with a fair approximation of sincerity, and then Martinez and Dalkeith left Sula, and Martinez—his taut nerves beginning to relax one by one—went up one deck to his cabin.

Alikhan helped Martinez remove the full-dress uniform and put the Golden Orb in its case. Martinez had once served on a ship where formal dinners among the officers were customary, and he'd hated the rigid manners and the benumbed conversations. When he played host, he tried to keep his dinners informal and the wine flowing.

Of course Sula wouldn't be interested in the flowing wine, but then she was never at a loss for conversation, so it probably wouldn't matter.

He took a vow to restrict his own wine intake. No point in seeming a drunken fool in front of a smart, sober woman with a savage sense of humor.

He was very glad he'd invited Dalkeith.

The dialogue might require a referee.

SULA WASN'T SURE why Dalkeith had been invited. Sula had always found her insipid and thought she had been lucky in latching on to Martinez's star early on to follow him up the line of promotion. But Sula knew nothing against her, nothing but the childlike voice that just had to be endured.

Martinez's servant Alikhan had told Macnamara that supper wouldn't be formal, so Sula knew to wear undress. She was glad to be free of the stiff collar and stiffer manners that had followed her through too many formal dinners on the *Defense*.

As she left her cabin she felt her senses expanding through the environment, like a wary cat probing the air with its whiskers. She went up the curving stairs to the deck above hers and found Alikhan standing like a sentry outside Martinez's door. He braced, then opened the door for her and ushered her inside.

Cooking smells greeted her. Martinez and Dalkeith were already present, each with a goblet of something that sparkled, and both rose as she entered and braced.

"Please sit," Martinez said, and she took the seat reserved for her. The large banquet table that would normally fill the room had been broken up, and three leaves had been arranged in a triangular formation. *Informal*, she thought. There was no head of the table for Martinez to preside from, and as she wasn't directly opposite she didn't have to spend the whole meal looking at him. She wondered if he had deliberately arranged the room that way, and then invited Dalkeith as a chaperone, to testify to Terza that his virtue was secure.

As if he hadn't sold his virtue years ago, she thought. The Chens had a mortgage on his soul.

Though even if she didn't have to look at him every minute, he was still very difficult not to notice. He was a tall, broad-shouldered man with a body sculpted by the weight of fierce accelerations, and even if he wasn't waving his Golden Orb, he was in authority here. Sitting, his big hands and long arms made him seem more imposing, and he wasn't as ungainly as when he was standing atop his short-by-comparison legs. He had presence, and Sula could almost feel that presence prickling across her skin.

Trying to ignore that presence, she looked at the murky murals on the walls, plump-bottomed Torminel grappling, snarls on their faces. "Are those *wrestlers*?" she asked.

"Squadron Leader Lokan was a martial arts enthusiast," Martinez said. "His trophies are still in the office."

"I saw those grapplers on the wall behind you when I viewed your dispatches, and I couldn't quite make out what they were. I wondered if it were some kind of pornography."

"That's in the bedroom," Martinez said.

"Really?"

"I'm afraid so. May I offer you something to drink?"

She turned to Alikhan, standing politely by the kitchen door. "Mineral water will be fine," she said.

"My lady." Alikhan bowed and withdrew to the pantry.

"Lady Sula," Martinez began. "I wonder if we might discuss how best to employ your staff."

As a captain she was entitled to four servants, and as a division commander a pair of staff signals specialists to help her send and receive orders. But a tactical officer was normally on a fleet commander's staff and wouldn't need staff of her own.

"Ricci and Viswan have been handling the signals traffic for the Fourth Fleet," Sula said. "They're experienced and know what they're doing."

"May I employ them in the same assignments?" Martinez asked.

It was pleasant of him to ask her permission. He could have just drafted them into his entourage.

"Yes," she said. "By all means."

Alikhan returned with mineral water and poured it into Sula's crystal wine goblet.

"I'm discovering that the signals traffic here is overwhelming," Martinez said. "How have you been coping?"

Sula spread her hands. "I haven't. I sent out instructions to send only urgent and imperative messages, but it seems that 'urgent and imperative' includes news of malfunctioning laundry facilities and complaints from half-trained officers about other half-trained officers assuming some privilege to which they aren't entitled."

"Not to mention half-trained captains trying their best to poach qualified personnel from other ships," Martinez said.

Sula shrugged. "Except for your division and Foote's squadron, everyone's understaffed. It's to be expected."

"I'm thinking of—Oh, thank you, Alikhan."

Alikhan handed out starters, some kind of fritter served alongside a little bowl of sauce. Sula looked at hers with suspicion—by this point in the voyage, fresh food had run out, and the cooks were usually running out of imagination. But the fritters turned out to contain eggs that had been preserved in some way that turned them bright blue and that gave the eggs a sharp, vinegar-like taste that contrasted well with the richness of the fried batter and the semisweet sauce.

Sula was savoring the first bite when Martinez spoke again.

"I'm thinking of putting restrictions on the number of messages. Say five each day, not counting messages sent during the exercises, and sent by commanding officers only."

"They'll resent it," Sula said. "And that's still over twelve hundred signals per day."

"But when they complain, it will be to Michi, not to me."

Sula was amused. "I'm sure she'll be grateful for all the signals. It'll show she's needed."

Strange that the first conversation they'd had in years dealt with such a pedestrian topic. Yet that was probably for the best. Their relationship had been equal parts ecstasy and catastrophe, and it was better that their words carefully threaded between the two.

They talked about inconsequential Fleet business for a while, and for the first time Dalkeith spoke, offering opinions on some officers she'd served alongside. Since these ideas confirmed Sula's own judgment, she found herself conceding to Dalkeith a measure of sagacity.

"By the way," Sula said, "I'm on the verge of recommending that we break up Division Twelve."

"Chandra Prasad's light division?" Martinez was surprised. "Why?"

"To make better use of the frigates' superior sensor suites. We might want to spread them out through the Fourth Fleet rather than concentrate them in a single place."

Martinez seemed to be probing this idea carefully. "How are these sensors superior?"

She tried to suppress her smile as she spoke. "They're made for the Exploration Service by your brother-in-law, Nikkul Shankaracharya."

Sula had half hoped that Martinez might explode with rancor and indignation, but he took the news without visible emotion.

"Well," he said. "Good for Nikkul."

"I didn't know whether I was allowed to mention his name."

Martinez waved a hand. "I knew Sempronia would break with PJ sooner or later. She ran away prematurely, but it was never my idea that she marry PJ."

"She seems to think otherwise."

"My idea wasn't for her to marry, it was to *fake an engagement*. But then she ran off with Nikkul, and Walpurga married PJ in her place, and that was completely insane."

"It got PJ killed," Sula said.

Martinez considered this. "My understanding is that *PJ* got PJ killed."

"There was a reason he wanted to die."

Are we having an argument now? Sula wondered. That didn't take long.

Dalkeith watched them with an expression that mingled surprise and horror, her blue eyes leaping from one speaker to the next as if she were watching a game of tennis played with a live grenade. Seeing her, Sula wanted to laugh.

I remember you and Martinez from the last war, Haz had

said. *When you seemed to like each other.* Perhaps at this moment that very thought was going through Dalkeith's mind.

I guess we are *having an argument,* Sula thought. But she knew it wasn't just about PJ Ngeni, it was about all the history she and Martinez shared now boiling up around them, ready to vaporize them both.

Martinez tilted his head and regarded Sula. "You liked PJ?" he said.

"I did," Sula said. "He was the most ridiculous person I've ever met, but I liked him."

"I did, too, for all I didn't want him for a brother-in-law." Frowning, he nodded to himself. "His family considered him disposable. He was a pawn to be used, handed off to inferiors, and certainly by the time he was dragged into marrying Walpurga he must have worked that out."

A pang touched Sula's heart. She also had used PJ, used him as a spy and his home as a base from which to launch her attacks on the Naxids, and then when he was of no further use, she let him do what he'd probably wanted to do all along, which was to die. He'd taken a rifle and gone to the war. He hadn't lasted five seconds.

Maybe we're not having an argument, Sula thought. It looks like we just decided to blame the Ngeni family.

"Chandra won't be happy," said Martinez, "that you want to break up her division."

Which was a shrewd way of skating away from the shared tension, Sula thought. Good for Martinez.

"Chandra won't object if she gets another division out of it," Sula said. She explained that what she had in mind was a straight swap, in which Prasad would lose one of her squadrons in exchange for another. "We can station the new divisions some distance from each other, so the sensor suites can cover as much extent as possible."

She had considered splitting up the squadrons and assigning one or two ships to each of the other formations, but thought it would be too disruptive to a force that would be engaging the enemy in a matter of weeks.

"I'll give the idea my consideration," Martinez said. "But I'd like to see data on these sensor suites." An idea struck him. "Is that why I was requested to fire two missiles in the direction of Harzapid? To provide data?"

"That's correct," Sula said. *Clever of him to put that together,* she thought.

Alikhan quietly refreshed the party's glasses, whisked away the starters, and laid down platters before them. The scent of coconut milk rose in the air.

"Your fish, my lord and ladies," he said.

Sula contemplated the platter with pleasure. Her own cook had efficiently produced all those dinners in his little kitchen, but his repertoire was limited, and the pantry had been stocked in an unimaginative way. By now fresh vegetables were all gone, and everything came out of cans or the freezer. Sula's meals had grown repetitious, particularly those where she was hosting a large party, with roasts and sauces followed by roasts and sauces. Nothing like this sweet-smelling fare of coconut and spices.

Perhaps, she thought, her chef could learn a few things from Martinez's cook.

The talk turned inconsequential until dessert, ices made with honey-sweetened melon, when the subject of the Lorkins came up.

Lorkin and its vanished inhabitants were no longer a secret in the Restoration Fleet. Lady Starkey had delivered a video documentary about her discoveries, a somewhat expanded version of the video she'd shown to Roland back on Harzapid, and this had been broadcast to the Fourth Fleet. So while ships' crews were still talking about the Lorkins, at least their speculations were based on what was known. Though what was known was little enough, and probably the speculations were no less wild than before.

Still, some officers like Kung were appeased by the release of the information. Though Sula suspected that Kung would rather have just shot or beheaded everyone who knew anything about Planet Trouble.

"If the Great Masters were human," Martinez said, "one could conclude that they botched whatever they were trying on Lorkin, panicked, killed everything in sight, and then out of shame or embarrassment wrote it out of history. But that's if they were human, which they weren't."

"That's very diplomatic," Sula said.

"I'm practicing for Kung," Martinez said. "I've invited him for supper tomorrow. I hope you'll join us."

"I was planning to stay away from formal suppers for a while," Sula said. "It's half what I've been doing, and the other half is responding to messages, and what I'd *really* like to be doing is thinking of ingenious ways to deploy the fleet."

"There are only three people in the Fourth Fleet with the rank of fleet commander," Martinez said. "It would be a good thing to get us all in the same room."

"I've had Kung to dine myself," Sula warned. "It's worse than having to endure Jeremy Foote for a whole evening. Kung's as dull as a doorknob, and you'll have to be careful to hide your yawns."

"You can amuse yourself by watching me do that," Martinez said. "Won't you come?"

"How can I resist?" Sula laughed. "Kung's got his own way of eating, you know."

"Really? It's . . . it's not disgusting, I hope."

"No, it's just . . . strange. When he picks up some food on his fork, he tilts his head back and opens his mouth. The fork then has to do a kind of swooping movement to lodge the food in his mouth properly. But the thing that makes it a little eerie is that even though his head is tilted back, his eyes remain directed straight at you." She demonstrated with her dessert spoon, her eyes flared and fixed on Martinez. "And of course that huge mustache makes him look even more uncanny."

"That is too unsettling," Martinez said. "Please don't do it again."

"You're going to have to sit opposite Kung and see it again and again. You might as well get used to it."

"I'm not sure I can."

Sula was startled to realize that over the course of the dinner she had managed to relax in Martinez's company and seemed to be having a pleasant time.

What surprised her more than anything was that she was less shocked by this discovery than she imagined she'd be.

IN HER VIDEO image, Ming Lin looked as if she'd aged ten years, her face drawn, her lower eyelids red-rimmed. Her pink-tipped hair had been replaced by a practical brown bob combed over her ears. Her crooked nose no longer looked jaunty or sinister, but a reminder that she was too harried and discouraged to care what she looked like.

Running the economy of a rebel empire wasn't easy, or so it appeared.

"Lady Sula," Lin said. "I hope your work goes well. I don't want to take up too much of your valuable time, but I'd like to say—if you haven't heard—that we're growing the hulls of six cruisers here at Harzapid, and that the . . . the *allies* . . . that you've brought into the dockyard are doing their work very well. The cruisers are ahead of schedule, and after they're done, we can lay down even more."

The fragrant odor of her tea drifted through Sula's office as she viewed the video message. She was aware of the cruisers, of course, but it was good to know that Lin thought her alliance with the Naxids was working well.

Lin paused for a moment, then shrugged. "I don't know if you've been hearing from your friend Hector Braga, but I think you should know that he's claiming to potential investors that you've put a lot of money into his Esley development scheme. I'm inclined to doubt his word since you've told me that his scheme was an outright fraud, but I thought I'd better hear from you before I spoke out on the matter. Please let me know at your earliest convenience."

There was another hesitation, and then she said, "I don't think I've really had a suitable time to thank you for all the opportunities you've given me, and the chances you've given me to help during the crisis—" A smile broke across her face. "*Crises,*" she corrected. "I don't know if you fully realize the scope of what I've been able to do, but it's improved the life of tens of millions, and it's all down to your support. So thank you." She smiled again. "End message."

Sula basked in the pleasure of Lin's thanks for a moment, and then realized, *She thinks I'm going to die.*

Ming Lin could read a balance sheet better than most, and she knew the odds against the Fourth Fleet. And of course even if the Fourth Feet somehow beat the odds, they wouldn't manage it without taking heavy casualties, and Sula might not survive even a victory.

So Ming Lin had decided to offer her thanks to a doomed woman, while she still had the chance. And of course if the Fourth Fleet lost the war, Lin wouldn't survive Sula by more than a few months, so the thanks were sent from one doomed woman to another.

This revelation was powerful enough to keep Sula from thinking about anything else for a long while, and then she gave a start as she remembered the message had really been about Lamey. She took a sip of her tea, then recorded an answer.

"Thank you for thinking I'd want to know what Braga is up to," she said. "And thanks also for your kind words of appreciation. We're all so busy that the civilities often escape us, and it probably hasn't escaped your attention that I'm not very good at civilities in the first place."

She gazed at the camera for a moment, choosing her words, and then spoke. "You should feel at liberty to tell people that I haven't invested a fraction of a minim in Hector Braga's development plan. At this distance from events," she added, "I don't care to say more. Just feel free to make the correction when necessary."

And maybe Lamey won't get so angry he'll denounce me.

Though she was running out of hope where Lamey was concerned. He had mistimed his criminal venture, and the results of fraud were going to catch up to him earlier than he'd expected.

For the first time Sula wondered if it were possible simply to make Lamey disappear. But she didn't have the friends on Harzapid who could make that possible: Macnamara and Spence were with her on *Los Angeles*, and the Secret Army veterans were back on Zanshaa, where they were probably fighting for their lives.

But still. It deserved some thought.

THE FOLLOWING MORNING Sula marched into the flag officer's station in her vac suit and swung herself into the acceleration couch assigned to the tactical officer. In her ungloved hand she held an envelope containing the foil with the parameters of the day's exercise.

She slotted the foil into one of her displays and reached into a pocket for a med patch to do her prep for high gravities.

She ignored the pistol-shaped med injector holstered on the side of her couch, because each time she held one in her hand her heart lurched and her hands began to tremble. The sight of injectors brought back a memory she never wanted to revisit.

Sula peeled the backing off the patch and stuck it to her neck.

Sula didn't know if Martinez had a policy for how thoroughly an officer in the flag officer's station had to suit up, so she had brought her gloves and helmet in a mesh bag even though she hated wearing them. She particularly loathed the helmet, which obliged her to exist alone in a closed space with only the sound of her breath and the stench of the suit for company. When she was obliged to wear a helmet, she kept the visor up unless someone with seniority told her to close it, and up till now she'd been the one with seniority.

Martinez entered trailing a faint astringent aroma of aftershave. He wished Sula a good morning and went to his own acceleration couch in the center of the room. He wore his helmet with the faceplate up, and she took that as permission to keep her own helmet open. Martinez's staff followed, the maternal-looking Banerjee and the scowling Aitor Santana, who looked like a particularly ferocious bouncer displaced from his dive bar. One of her own signals lieutenants, Ricci, followed and took the fifth and last couch in the room.

This would be Martinez's first attempt to maneuver the entire Fourth Fleet, two hundred fifty-six warships not counting the "Fleet Train" of support ships stretching all the way to Harzapid. Sula knew how difficult it was to wrangle all those ships, having done just this job for the last few months while Martinez was off with the Division Two.

The exercise was intended to test Martinez's idea of mobile reserves, the questions being how large the reserves would be, and how and when to commit them to the fight.

"Communications test." Martinez's voice sounded through her headset. Sula winced at the volume and nudged it down. "Can everyone hear me?"

Everyone in the room checked in. "The simulation is loaded and ready," Sula said.

"Let's establish the communications array," Martinez said. The simulation would run in *Los Angeles*'s computer, and an interlinking web of lasers would loop every ship in the Fourth Fleet into the simulation. Tork's fleet would exist only in the simulation, and the Fourth Fleet's maneuvers, accelerations, and missile launches would be real.

Once each ship reported in, Sula loaded the simulation, and Tork's Righteous Fleet for Suppression of Dissension appeared on her displays. Sula had assumed that Tork would attempt to reenact his victory at the Battle of Second Magaria, his greatest triumph, and so the enemy fleet, its reality consisting of nothing but electrons, appeared stretched out in a long line. Within each squadron ships were loosely clumped about the flagship, but the squadrons themselves were arranged as nose-to-tail as possible. The enemy fleet appeared even more formidable because at least a third of their number were decoys. Since Fleet records revealed the capabilities of every ship in the Home Fleet and Second Fleet, the virtual ships were designed to reflect their actual capabilities and armament.

The battle got off to a slow start as Martinez shifted his own formations to match those of the enemy and discovered just how hard it was to alter his dispositions. Nevertheless he succeeded in stretching out his own formation so that the enemy couldn't wrap around him and smother him in a blaze of fire. Sula was far more experienced at this and gave as much aid as she could, and once the ships were sorted, the battle proper began as the lines closed.

Fire erupted up and down the line as computer-generated explosions flared around perfectly genuine missiles. *Los Angeles* had a good view of the action, because Division Two was half of the mobile reserve, the other being a division commanded by Kung. Kung's force from the Home Fleet, Foote's light squadron, and Division Two were the elite units of the Fourth Fleet, because the crews were regular long-service veterans who had served together for years. The rest, the majority of the ships of the Restoration force, had only been aboard their ships for, at most, a few months.

Missiles lanced out. Simulated radio hash from explosions obscured the action. Under pressure, friendly squadrons whirled into the elusive, shifting alignments of Ghost Tactics. Ships, friends and enemies, were ruled destroyed by the computer and vanished from the display.

Sula sensed a growing mental pressure that signaled the battle's arriving climax, the moment when the reserves would have to be committed if they were to be used at all. Her job as tactical officer was to point this out, but she wanted to know if Martinez could discover the moment on his own.

"Message to Division Two," Martinez said. "Assume

Method formation, engage enemy on heading zero-four-zero by zero-zero-one. Execute in one minute. Message to Fleet Commander Kung—'permission to engage at will.'"

Sula felt heat racing through her veins. Martinez had spotted the moment, and he had acted.

Her acceleration cage sang as the ship reoriented, then dropped back to its deadpoint as the engines lit. Missiles leaped from tubes. Sula searched the enemy formation, located a place where an attack might unhinge the enemy alignment, pointed it out to Martinez. He adjusted the division's course and sent flights of missiles reaching for the enemy.

Sula and Martinez worked in close consort for the rest of the exercise. It was almost as if they sat with their heads together, whispering into each other's ears, tasting each other's breath, smelling the other's sweat. Their minds leaped from one point to the next, thoughts overleaping each other in dizzying array.

The result was a victory for the Restoration, with the enemy's virtual armada wiped out, and the Fourth Fleet reduced to twenty-three survivors, including the Los Angeles.

The best result so far, with casualties of only 85 percent.

As the Fourth Fleet began the quotidian business of securing from general quarters, recovering missiles, and sorting itself into its cruising formations, Sula allowed herself to sag into her couch. Her skin felt warm and flushed, and a strange elation sang in her mind despite the gravity-induced kinks and aches in her muscles. For the first time she felt convinced that the Restoration was going to win a decisive victory, and that she and Martinez would do it.

The air filled with the happy, relieved chatter of the signals officers reliving the crucial moments of the battle. Though Sula badly wanted a shower to scrub off the suit smells that clung to her, there was no point in leaving her couch, because *Los Angeles* was maneuvering and the air was full of alarms for weightlessness and then the resumption of gravity. Eventually the ship settled into Division Two's cruising formation and began a gentle acceleration of .6 gravity in the direction of Zarafan. Sula unwebbed, sat up, and wrenched off her helmet and then the soft elastic cap that held her headphones and virtual reality rig. Fresh air cooled the sweat that prickled her scalp.

Martinez, seen out of the corner of her eye, rolled off his couch onto his feet, and carefully stepped out of the acceleration cage. He looked down at Sula.

"By the way," he said, "I've decided to follow your suggestion about breaking up Chandra's squadron. I've looked at the data concerning those sensor suites, and you're completely right about them."

She looked at him narrowly as he left the room, helmet tucked under his arm. She suspected she'd heard a hint of condescension in his voice, that he'd offered agreement and praise as a way of keeping her both docile and useful.

I am just here to make him look good, she reminded herself, and then rose to her feet and made her way from the room.

CHAPTER 14

Scout craft of the Exploration Service first spotted the Righteous Fleet for Suppression of Dissension two wormhole jumps from Zarafan, a system called Roda two-thirds of the distance between Zarafan and the crossroads system of Toley. The Exploration Service had previously sent armed parties aboard the wormhole relay stations in Roda and had sent the original non-Terran crews to Toley to be interned. But since Tork was expected along with his combined fleet, the relay stations had been abandoned, and the crews had returned to their shuttles and shifted to very precise locations on the fringes of the system. Using communications lasers, they were able to send messages through the wormhole to similarly placed shuttles in the Toley system, thus maintaining contact with Harzapid and the Fourth Fleet. Though their engines were shut down, the ships were running on minimal power, and the crews shivering in their winter clothing, continuous use of the comm lasers would generate a lot of heat, and the craft would blaze like a comet in the sky were anyone scanning the system in infrared. To avoid this, communications were kept at a minimum until the arrival of Tork's ships, after which their position and appearance were reported almost continually. No active scans were employed, no lidar or radar, and only passive sensors recorded Tork's track.

Apparently Tork wasn't bothering to scan the system's outer reaches, because the feed from Roda came to the Fourth Fleet without interruption. Martinez watched the enemy advance with a sensation of grim tenacity. There were at least eight hundred engine flares advancing across Roda toward Harzapid, and though Martinez knew that nearly half of them were decoys, the very sight of the enemy was intimidating. They outnumbered his own fleet two to one.

His staff—and officers on every ship in the fleet—were studying the feeds carefully, to try to separate warships from decoys. Decoys became less convincing over time, and Tork took several days to cross the Roda system, providing observers with massive amounts of data.

Finally, as the Righteous Fleet was only a few hours short of its wormhole transit to Toley, a drifting, distant Restoration shuttle painted the entire fleet with its lidar, and seven hundred missiles, accelerated to relativistic velocities, shot through the Toley wormhole on target for the enemy.

Tork had been expecting this—the tactic, anticipated by Chandra Prasad, had been deployed by the Naxids in the last war—and so point-defense lasers and antiproton cannon were set on automatic, and Tork's own radar and lidar was pounding out to make sure the way ahead was clear.

Both the missiles and countermissile batteries had mere seconds to choose targets. Space between the wormhole and the Righteous Fleet blazed with antimatter flares, and the bursts leaped toward the enemy fleet and flamed among the warships.

The missiles had been programmed to avoid any enemy previously identified as a decoy, and to avoid as well Battleship Squadron One, the three huge vessels that were presumed to include Tork's flagship. Martinez would have liked to have destroyed the huge vessels, but even more he wanted to preserve Tork. Tork was predictable, and any successor might not be.

Martinez knew all too well the panic the missile attack would produce, the officers scrambling for their stations while the ships' engines burned in unpredictable, mad evasions, the Command crews staring in terror at their displays, crew knocked off their feet or thrown from their beds by sudden maneuvers, the sudden, horrific knowledge that death was right before them, hurtling toward them at a speed nearing that of light, and that whether they would live or die was a decision entirely out of their hands . . .

Martinez gave them a few minutes to recover from their shock and catch their breaths. The next missile barrage was timed to hit the Righteous Fleet just as it was passing through the expanding fireballs of destroyed missiles, when sensors might be confused. This barrage consisted of nine hundred missiles, and Martinez was gratified by what seemed to be a series of secondary explosions flaring in the fireball haze.

The shuttle that had painted the Righteous Fleet with its lidar shut down immediately after the second strike, but the rangefinder had blazed away long enough for Tork's staff to get a bearing. Tork dispatched a missile and destroyed the shuttle, but no lives were lost—the shuttle was empty and had been operated remotely by another shuttle a safe distance away.

Between the two attacks, Martinez's staff concluded that at least twenty-one enemy warships had been destroyed, and several more were having difficulty maneuvering and had presumably been damaged.

A third missile attack hit the Righteous Fleet a few minutes after it passed through the wormhole into Toley. Their defense was somewhat more coordinated this time, ships and decoys had been swapped around, and there were only two probable hits.

Martinez wasn't disappointed. He had plenty of missiles left. The government at Harzapid had got very good at producing them, and the Fleet Train of support vessels had got equally good at delivering munitions where they were needed.

Once Tork's ships emerged from the fireballs of this last attack, they got their first glimpse of their enemy. The Restoration Fleet was visible across the system, stretched out in textbook battle formation and accelerating away from Tork to prevent the Righteous Fleet from overrunning them. Martinez hadn't bothered sending out any decoys, because Tork knew exactly how many ships he had, and to Tork they must have looked like a morsel that would be gobbled with ease. Tork still had over five hundred warships.

Toley was the system to which Foote and Rukmin had raced at the very beginning of the war, Foote flying from Colamote, Rukmin driving from Zarafan. Rukmin had won that race and the result was her annihilation at the Battle of Shulduc.

Martinez had deliberately shown his ships to bait Tork into pursuit, and pursue Tork did, preceded by one of his pompous declarations, sent in the clear so that everyone in the system could admire it. To impress his audience with his majesty he wore his full-dress uniform, with the double row of silver buttons, and the disk of the Golden Orb around his throat.

"In the name of the Praxis and the Convocation," he said in his chiming, modulated Daimong voice, "I command all rebel fleet elements to surrender. Your piratical and murderous actions threaten order and decency, and society demands the most rigorous justice. You will fire all missiles into the interstellar void and submit to boarding and arrest, after which you will meet the severe penalties that your traitorous actions deserve."

Tork's cadaverous features looked ancient. His black lidless eyes were dull, and strips of dead flesh hung from his gray, expressionless face. His voice was as beautiful as ever, but his tone lacked the fiery conviction that had marked many of his speeches.

He seemed so skeletal and emaciated that Martinez wondered if he'd survive long enough to fight a battle.

Martinez was in his office when the message arrived, trying to cope with the message traffic. He'd issued instructions that only captains should signal him, and only five times each day, but the results had been that some captains sent fewer but longer and more detailed messages. Still, signals traffic had been reduced and left him more time for sleep.

His cuff display chimed, and he answered to see Sula with her jade eyes glittering.

"May I respond to Tork?" she asked. "Or do you want to do it?"

"Tork thinks Lady Michi is in command here," he said. "If either of us responds, he'll know that Michi isn't here."

"I don't see why that matters, but I can say that I'm speaking with Lady Michi's permission."

How much does *it matter?* Martinez wondered, and he decided it didn't matter at all.

"Permission granted," he said. He realized he was looking forward to viewing the message.

It was a few minutes before Sula sent her message, either because she was making notes or rehearsing. When it came, Sula appeared in her undress tunic, a deliberate contrast to Tork's formality. Her porcelain face was flushed with fury, her eyes ablaze.

"This is Caroline, Lady Sula, speaking with the permission of Lady Michi Chen, who had more important things to do than to respond to the nonsensical message sent by that ancient wheezebag, Lord Tork."

That's *making a good start*, Martinez thought.

"Message follows," Sula said, and her tone changed. "How *dare* you invoke the Praxis, you senile, witless box of turd! How *dare* you make demands! You *started* this war, you imbecile, with your demented order to arrest every Terran crew in the Fleet, and your smug conviction that *somehow we wouldn't find out about it*! Your security was so perfect that we knew within *hours*!"

Which was, Martinez knew, a bit of an exaggeration.

Sula's lips curled in a snarl. "You were so dim-witted that when we responded, you could do nothing but *stand there* and gobble about pirates and Terran criminals! You were *surprised* that we took action to defend ourselves! You *turned* us into enemies with your *stupid fucking order*! You're so self-satisfied and swollen with vanity that you had to invent the office of Supreme Commander and award it to *yourself*! You're allied with the worst and most corrupt politicians in Zanshaa, and you think they share your principles, when in fact they're just robbing the state while you provide them protection." She laughed again. "Lord Minno, a cheap con man and a member of a stock fraud gang. Lady Gruum, a desperate bankrupt. And Lady Tu-hon, greedy and psychotic."

Sula grinned. "And what have we done since we sailed out of your clutches? We've got a working government, our economy is soaring while yours is prostrate and in the hands of thieves, and more important than that, we keep *winning*. Rukmin and her command were *wiped out*! Force Orghoder was *wiped out*! An-sol and *Conformance* were *wiped out*! Lord Oh Derinuus was so stupid that he practically blew *himself* up!"

Sula paused for a moment to collect her thoughts while she glowered into the camera. "Now you've arrived in person with thousands of crew who you're willing to sacrifice for your own vanity." She laughed. "I'm here to tell you that you *still haven't realized who you're dealing with*. We're going to cut up that fine fleet of yours, take it apart piece by piece, and we're going to do it on *our* time, not yours. You'll watch your fleet's life's blood drain away drop by drop, and there won't be a thing you can do about it. In the end, there will be just you, alone, in your flagship's magnificent ballroom wondering why no one else has come to the dance."

Sula took a breath, then offered a smile. "But there's a way out. You don't have to sacrifice the thousands of brave crew that you're leading to certain death." She raised a hand and pointed a finger directly at the viewer. "So I order *you*, Lord Tork, in the name of the Praxis, to surrender yourself and your command at once. Shoot all your missiles into the void of space, and permit your ships to be boarded by forces of the Restoration. We promise that any who surrender will be treated fairly, and if they have not committed crimes against the Praxis, they will retain rank and status in the Fleet."

Martinez was startled. *Can we* do *that?* he wondered.

Sula dropped her hand and looked at the camera, her expression now quizzical, "I'd like to address now the officers and crew of the so-called Righteous Fleet, and I'd like to ask a simple question: *Why are you fighting us?* Why are you risking lives and honor to defend a gang of hack politicians and a senile, criminal commander? You *know* what's going to happen. If I were you, I'd start thinking about how to gracefully escape your fatal situation." Her lips quirked in a smile. "I'm attaching some entertainment to this message, which I hope you will enjoy. I know that after dodging our missiles, you're probably in dire need of a laugh." She favored her audience with a sweet smile. "This is Lady Sula. Message ends."

Martinez looked at the attachments to the signal and saw

that Sula had included all of Severin's satiric puppet shows lambasting the Zanshaa government, along with the documentary about the discovery of Lorkin.

He told Alikhan to open a bottle of champagne, then contacted Sula on his sleeve display. She was half reclined in her office chair, her top tunic button undone, her face glowing with exhausted gratification.

"That must have been satisfying," he said.

Sula gave a weary laugh. "There's nothing quite so gratifying as not giving a fuck," she said.

"Oh? Yet somehow I had the impression you cared."

Sula gave a weary laugh, and a half-hidden light gleamed in her eyes. "I'm just a terrific actor."

"I've got to agree with you."

Like Tork's, Sula's message had been sent in the clear. Which meant that every signals crew in the Righteous Fleet had seen it, and that meant so had every captain and most of the officers. Presumably none of them—unless they'd served with Sula before—had ever been addressed in this manner in their lives. Certainly Tork hadn't.

Probably has done wonders for their morale, Martinez thought.

"I've just opened a bottle of champagne to toast your message," Martinez said. "If you drank alcohol, I'd invite you to share it with me."

He spoke with care. Over the last weeks he and Sula had managed a relationship that stayed within certain well-defined limits. They worked together during exercises, and

in the freewheeling postmortems afterward, which typi-
cally involved most of the ship's officers. During that time
Sula was brilliant, eyes flashing as she followed some train
of thought or overleaped Martinez's train of logic to land on
the place he'd only glimpsed, dimly, somewhere in his mind.
She was less exuberant in the obligatory formal dinners that
Martinez hosted for his captains: she only came when invited, ate little, said less, and returned to her cabin as soon
as the decencies permitted. She never wore the red staff tabs
on her collar.

Otherwise he never saw her. She had a life of her own, it
seemed—sometimes he was aware that she played host at
her own events, with old comrades like Alana Haz, Rebecca
Giove, and Pavel Ikuhara, as well as new friends like the
Kangas twins. Martinez was never invited, and he felt ob-
scurely jealous of those who were.

Alikhan told him that Sula's chef was learning recipes
from Marivic Mangahas and serving them to Sula's guests.
That raised Mangahas's cooking in his estimation.

Sula looked at Martinez and sighed. "Even if I drank alcohol, I'd have to turn down your champagne. I need sleep, and
we're sort of on vacation as long as the enemy is in sight."

Which, oddly, was true. The Fourth Fleet couldn't stage
any of its realistic fleet exercises as long as Tork was watching and taking notes on the tactics employed. Everyone could
sleep late if they wanted.

"I understand," Martinez said. He wasn't entirely sure
what he expected to happen even if she'd joined him and

matched his champagne with her Citrine Fling. Perhaps he just wanted to explore more thoroughly the walls they'd erected around themselves.

He looked at her. "Should you have really offered amnesty to the enemy?" he asked. "I take it you haven't consulted with Michi or Roland on the matter?"

"Tork demanded that we surrender so that he could kill us," Sula said. "That seems a self-defeating strategy to me. I thought we ought to offer our enemies a more generous settlement—especially as the Fleet, outside of Tork and his immediate circle, hasn't been involved in any of the outrages against Terrans. That was all the civilian government."

"We'll see if we get any defectors," Martinez said.

"I'll settle for enemies who are less enthusiastic about torturing us to death," Sula said.

Alikhan brought the champagne in its silver bucket, then placed a glass in front of Martinez. With a series of precise, economical gestures, he wrapped the stopper in a towel, popped the stopper open, and poured. Sula, unable to view all this from Martinez's sleeve display, gazed out of the screen with an arched eyebrow.

"Well," she said, "I believe this is my cue to say good night."

"Just a moment."

He took the glass, foam spilling down his fingers, and raised it to the image on his sleeve.

"For Lady Sula," he said, "and her impeccable eloquence."

She grinned. "Thank you, Lord Fleetcom," she said and ended the message.

Martinez contemplated the champagne, its aroma dancing in his senses, and drank.

APPARENTLY TORK WAS stunned into silence by Sula's message. He, who so enjoyed his own ranting, pompous speeches, could think of no response.

A day later, the Fourth Fleet passed through the wormhole gate into the Sennenola system, a system of pedestrian gas giants and barren, rocky planets devoid of breathable atmosphere. Martinez had left behind more than a dozen uncrewed shuttles in the fringes of the Toley system, each ready to paint Tork's ships with lidar in support of an attack. These he unleashed almost at random, or whenever he suspected the enemy had begun to relax. Another half-dozen enemy ships were blown to atoms, but Martinez was hoping that the primary effect would be to enemy morale, to their nerves blasted by alarms at frequent intervals, to their bodies as they lurched to action stations, then were hurled in all directions while their ships made unpredictable evasive moves.

Inevitably the Righteous Fleet got better at avoiding missile attacks. They shifted course frequently to frustrate missiles coming too fast to maneuver, and they set out a line of constantly shifting decoys ahead of the main body to absorb the initial impulse of attacks. The attacking missiles had been programmed to ignore the decoys and go straight for the warships, but they had only brief seconds to find a target, and sometimes they got it wrong.

The Righteous Fleet also got better at looking for hostile observers. The uncrewed ships were difficult to locate, because they were dark until they deployed their laser rangefinders, but the uncrewed ships were controlled by other ships, which, because they had live Terrans on board, were easier to find. Some of these were splashed by enemy missiles, and one of the lost ships was crucial to the grand coup that Martinez intended.

This was just before the Righteous Fleet's transition to the Sennenola system. Another uncrewed shuttle was triggered at the last minute, and the Righteous Fleet was painted just a few seconds before twelve hundred missiles came racing through the Sennenola wormhole.

As the antimatter blooms filled the display, as warships jinked and fired countermissiles, as laser and antiproton beams twinkled across the black of space, another three thousand missiles tore into the enemy from behind.

Toley was a crossroads system. Martinez had sent the extra missiles through Toley Wormhole Three, in the direction of Colamote. They had ghosted into the system, turned around, decelerated, and waited, hovering in space—until the signal came to accelerate to relativistic speeds and race into Toley to hit the Righteous Fleet from behind.

The Righteous Fleet's response was uncoordinated due to the ongoing attack through the wormhole, but they *did* have sensors pointing behind them, and they saw the second strike coming in time to shoot most of them down. But there were a gratifying, dazzling series of antimatter bursts through the Righteous Fleet, a necklace of fire opals scattered throughout its long line.

The double attacks had sufficiently disorganized Tork's forces that they came through Wormhole Two in scattered groups, unable to mount a coherent defense against the hundreds of missiles boring straight at them. More fire opals blossomed in the night.

When the staff finally managed to analyze the data, Martinez learned that the three attacks had killed no less than fifty-seven of the enemy.

Unharmed, glowing bright in the center of the enemy formation, were the three vast ships of Battleship Squadron One, spared because the Restoration missiles had been programmed to spare them. Aboard one of them was Tork, who had witnessed his fleet's brief, violent agony, helpless to prevent it.

Good, Martinez thought.

SENNENOLA'S TWO WORMHOLES were unusual in that they were directly opposite each other on the fringes of the system, which meant that traveling from Wormhole One to Wormhole Two would involve passing directly through the sun, a course normally to be avoided. Fortunately three of the system's gas giants were positioned such that a close approach to each would allow the Fourth Fleet to make a gentle curve around the system's sun. Martinez had taken advantage of this by parking hundreds of missiles in the shadow of each of these worlds, or hidden them behind moons or within their rings. These would leap out to intercept the Righteous Fleet as they passed, the same trick Martinez had used to destroy the *Conformance* during *Corona*'s escape to Harzapid.

He also parked a large number of missiles very close to the sun, in hopes the enemy wouldn't be able to see them against the sun's glare and radiation.

By the time Tork's disorganized forces emerged from Wormhole One and were slapped with the third missile attack, they found the Restoration Fleet two-thirds of the way across the system and decelerating. The deceleration was an invitation to engage, though because established momentum would take them all through another wormhole, the engagement would take place in another system. Tork put his jumbled survivors in order, began his own deceleration, and began a search of the system for the small observation vessels Martinez had parked in the system's outskirts. The search was more thorough than it had been in Toley, but then the Fourth Fleet had grown better at hiding its observers, grappled to the far sides of asteroids or planetoids and only revealing themselves when, on a predetermined schedule, they briefly unmasked to take action against the enemy. Still, a few observers were detected and destroyed.

The Restoration's greatest success in Sennenola took place at the first gas giant, a dark, dingy-looking world with eight moons and a near-invisible set of tilted rings. Martinez, by that time in the Shulduc system, launched a barrage timed to strike just as the Righteous Fleet passed the wormhole, and in the confusion and flashes of near misses, the missiles hidden near the gas giant launched for the enemy. Nine warships were destroyed.

By the time the Righteous Fleet approached the second gas giant, they worked out what had happened, and sent their own missile barrage curving around the planet to seek out and destroy Martinez's missiles lurking in ambush. The few missiles remaining were easily destroyed by point-defense systems as the Righteous Fleet passed by. Missiles waiting by the third gas giant were likewise destroyed.

When Tork passed through Wormhole Two into Shulduc, he found his entire fleet illuminated by rangefinders—painted not by scout ships in the reaches of the system, but by the Fourth Fleet decelerating in combat formation, barring Tork's way to Harzapid. Their missiles were already incoming at greater than 90 percent of the speed of light.

The usual scenario played out—flashes in the darkness, expanding bubbles of radio hash, antiproton beams sweeping across the battle space. The Righteous Fleet had plenty of practice by now, and lost only a pair of ships—and then another set of missiles swarmed on them from the rear, and suddenly the darkness was torn by one blinding explosion after another.

These were the missiles that had been parked in the glare of the Sennenola system's sun. As soon as the Righteous Fleet vanished through Wormhole One, a scout ship gave the missiles the order to accelerate to relativistic speeds and pursue the enemy.

This tactic had caught Tork completely by surprise at Toley, but he was surprised again at Sennenola because Sennenola wasn't a crossroads system, with no wormhole to Colamote to send missiles through. Tork thought he was safe, was caught flat-footed again, and lost another twelve ships.

He re-formed his ships one more time, this time with a

significant change. More decoys were deployed to the rear, which was to be expected, but more importantly Martinez saw that four squadrons now hung back from the battle line.

Apparently he wasn't the only commander on the scene to think of mobile reserves. Damn.

Martinez calculated his odds. So far as the staff had been able to compute, Tork had set out from Zanshaa with 538 warships, which meant he'd left a couple squadrons behind to guard the capital against an end-run sneak attack by way of Colamote. The campaign of attrition had killed over a hundred ships and left Tork with 433, of which an unknown number had suffered damage.

Martinez's fleet constituted 253 warships not counting *Compliance*, now docked at Harzapid for repairs. If he accepted battle now, he would engage with the odds against him being 1.7 to one, no longer two to one but still bad enough.

Yet by now he was out of tricks. Planets in the Shulduc system were in inconvenient places in their orbits, and there were no suitable moons or gas giants to hide missiles behind. There was a sun, and Martinez put a few hundred missiles on its far side, but without a lot of hope. Continuing the war of ambush would result in insignificant damage to the enemy while moving the scene of battle closer to Harzapid itself. Martinez preferred to keep his family a safe distance from any action.

The magazines of the Fourth Fleet were full. The Fleet Train had done its job of bringing resupply forward, and to save time hadn't bothered to rendezvous with the warships, but instead kicked the missiles out of cargo holds one by one, then accelerated them toward the Fourth Fleet, where they matched velocities and were recovered by the warships. The Fleet Train of support vessels was now racing toward Harzapid ahead of the Fourth Fleet. They would resupply with more war materiel, or—if the battle went badly—they could try to pick up refugees from Harzapid and carry them toward Wei Jian and the Second Fleet defectors, who were still assumed to be en route for Harzapid. Nearly all the Fleet Train had cleared the Shulduc system, and the rest were fleeing the scene of combat as fast as their engines could safely drive them.

Martinez felt his stomach swoop as *Los Angeles* shifted its heading to avoid enemy antiproton fire. He thought it unlikely that Tork would open fire at this long range, but with the odds against him he couldn't afford to lose a single ship before the battle began, and he was taking every precaution that he could.

Both fleets were now decelerating, with Tork piling on the gees so as to match velocities before engaging. If Tork retained his delta-vee, he would overshoot Martinez and have a clear path to Harzapid, whereas Martinez could have gone on straight to the empire's capital at Zanshaa. Tork was right in thinking this an unacceptable trade, and if not for the threat to his family, Martinez would have accepted it in an instant.

Fight or continue the attrition battle? The decision needed to be made soon.

Right, Martinez thought. *Time to be brilliant.*

THE CABIN LIGHTS had been dimmed, and soft shadows filled the corners of the room. Severin's senses were alight with the warmth of Lady Starkey's body, the soft texture of her hair, the taste of her skin, the comforting scent of sexual satiation.

"I should get back to *Explorer*," said Starkey. "We've got a battle to fight in the morning."

Which they did, with Tork's fleet still engaged in bone-straining deceleration so as to engage within the next ten or twelve hours, their flaming antimatter torches pointed at the Fourth Fleet like so many loaded pistols.

"If we're not ready by now," Severin said, "we'll never be."

"But still," said Starkey, "we should set an example for the other officers."

"We *are* setting an example," said Severin. "I hope they *all* fall in love."

Starkey swung her legs off the bed and sat up, and Severin leaned forward to kiss her bare shoulder as she reached for her clothing.

His sleeping cabin was far less cluttered than it had been, with the puppets, their stage, and the video equipment safely packed away and secure from the high-gravity stresses of battle. Only one puppet remained and gazed down at them from atop Severin's wardrobe.

Lady Starkey put on her undress uniform, and Severin helped her into her tunic, holding her hair out of the way as she buttoned her collar. When he pulled on his own clothes, he didn't bother with anything more formal then the worn blue jumpsuit he usually wore aboard *Expedition*, at least when he wasn't playing host at formal dinners.

"I have a present for you," he said. He reached atop his

wardrobe and picked up the Alois puppet, which he presented to her. "He's to keep watch over you, to keep you safe," he said.

She laughed and took the puppet, then kissed its ridiculous face. "I'll have him with me in Command," she said. She ran fingers through her hair. "Do I look all right?"

"You look brilliant," Severin said. He reached to embrace her, but she restrained him while she used her sleeve display to summon her shuttle crew from the galley, where they'd been enjoying the hospitality of *Expedition*'s crew. Then she let Severin take her in his arms, and she kissed him fiercely.

"After we win the battle?" she said.

"We'll write our own rules," he said. "You, me, and Alois."

He walked her to the airlock and delighted her shuttle crew by kissing her good-bye in public. Before bed he dealt with reports, messages, and other documents that had piled up while he was with Lady Starkey, and then was readying himself for sleep when he received a photo from her.

The photo showed the Alois puppet in the mesh bag attached to the side of Lady Starkey's Command chair. Its orange-yarn hair and large, absurd nose overhung the bag's elastic opening, and its mouth hung open in a broad grin.

Alois is making himself at home, Severin read.

Don't forget to kiss him good night, Severin sent and turned out the light.

SULA SPENT THE night before the battle in her cabin, tucked in bed with a cup of honey-sweetened tea and surrounded by the sound of derivoo. Some found the traditions that surrounded the performance too artificial and the subject matter too melodramatic, but Sula thought that missed the point. A derivoo singer, standing alone onstage in her traditional flounced skirts, sang of her confrontation with fate and displayed scornful resolution in the face of tragedy or defeat. She might have been deserted by a husband, she might have lost a child, she might have murdered a lover in a fit of jealousy— but she stood unbroken at the end and cried aloud her anguish and her defiance.

Derivoo was a human art form, and at its best spoke of what it meant to be human, to be tossed and battered by fate, to be torn by raw emotion and raw desire, to survive and still to somehow cry aloud, not a protest, not a complaint, but a scornful acceptance of death and destiny. *Do your worst!* the derivoo cried, and a listener had no doubt that the worst would be done.

Some people recoiled from the savagery of the subject matter, but these were people who couldn't face the truth of their own illusions and terror. Derivoo was *true*, a faithful record of what it was to be human, to live a typhoon-tossed life that was only a prelude to death.

The gentle scent of tea floated on the air while the music blasted a storm of emotion and tragedy into Sula's ears. For the first time she found herself wondering what derivoo song could be made of her life.

There was certainly enough material. One lover killed in the storming of Zanshaa High City; one lover deserting her for promotion, patronage, and the daughter of a high-ranking

Peer; and another lover, long thought dead, now reappeared and trying to extort money from her. *The Loves of Earthgirl*, she thought. Less a song than a whole opera.

But no, she thought, the most juicy material was something else entirely. Caro Sula lying dead of an overdose in her flat in Maranic Town, while her friend Earthgirl stepped into her place, into the privileged world of a high-status Peer, and to a guaranteed place at the Cheng Ho Academy followed by a commission in the Fleet. At the end of the song, she thought, she'd be standing defiantly over the body, holding aloft the pistol-shaped medical injector.

Ridiculous, she thought. Her life would never make a song.

And there would be enough tragedy tomorrow. Sula waited for the derivoo to finish her song and then turned off the music and tried to sleep.

She dreamed about Caro Sula. For years she had dreaded the possibility that Caro would return to her nightmares, and now here she was, sweet and smiling, dressed in colorful summer silks and a sequined jacket, just like the clothes she'd worn in Maranic Town years ago.

"Come on, Earthgirl," she said. "I've got to meet a friend!"

Sula didn't want to go—she knew that horror would follow—but the dream compelled her to walk after Caro through the boutiques of the Arches, where Caro had spent so much time and money that last summer of her life. Caro's platform shoes clattered on the tiles as she led Sula into a little bistro—the balding man behind the zinc counter looked familiar, though Sula couldn't remember his name—and then Caro led Sula into an alcove and dropped into the lap of

Gareth Martinez, who had been waiting on a lacy wrought-iron chair. He seemed pleased to find Caro sitting across his thighs. Caro put an arm around his shoulders and kissed him fiercely on the cheek. Her green eyes glittered.

"I think he's gorgeous, don't you?" she said. She laughed and kicked out her feet, showing far too much leg. Martinez put one big hand on her smooth thigh.

"Sit down, Earthgirl," Caro said. "We're going to be here a while." She signed to the balding man. "Bring a lemonade," she commanded.

Sula sat on another wrought-iron chair and watched as Caro and Martinez kissed. Their kisses were greedy and ferocious, and Martinez's hand slipped up Caro's skirt. Sula crossed her legs in discomfort and shifted her weight on the chair. Caro tore herself away from Martinez's kiss and looked at Sula.

"Poor Earthgirl." She sighed. "There's no man for Earthgirl. What's wrong?" She turned back to Martinez. "What's wrong with Earthgirl?" she said again and kissed him.

Now they were in Caro's bedroom, on the rose-colored satin sheets Sula remembered. Sula sat on a corner of the bed, her legs still crossed. A lemonade had appeared in Sula's hand, the glass dewed with condensation, the tips of her fingertips cold. Caro and Martinez were tearing off each other's clothes. Lemonade tingled on Sula's tongue.

Half naked, Caro and Martinez caressed each other. Sula felt heavy and useless and glutted with arousal. Caro feasted on Martinez's throat, her kisses marching down his chest. She looked up at Sula again, and sadness touched her features.

"It's sad that you can't play with us," she said. "But I know what will make you feel better." She got on her hands and knees and crawled across the satin sheets toward Sula.

"Don't forget this," Martinez said and handed Caro a med injector. Caro gave a mischievous smile, dialed in the dosage, and crawled to Sula.

"Want some?" Caro said. She pressed the injector to Sula's neck. "Want some, best sister?"

She pressed the trigger, and the hiss was swallowed by Sula's wakening scream.

IT WAS USELESS to lie to Terza, Martinez knew, pointless to try to ease her anxieties by painting an overoptimistic picture. She had access to all the official reports. She knew the odds.

In his video letter he expressed as much confidence as he could get away with. "We've gamed it thoroughly," he said, "and we'll win. Our ships are as ready as they'll ever be, and Tork seems not to have learned any new tricks. So whatever else may happen, you and Chai-chai should be safe. I have no intention of risking myself needlessly, but—" He restrained the impulse to shrug. "Well," he said, "it *is* war. But please believe that I will do my level best to come back to you."

He took a breath. "I'm going to send a separate message to you intended for Yaling. I don't know if you can get it to her—on a message missile, I suppose—but I don't want her to see it until she's old enough to understand. I'll record it separately and send it along soon. In the meantime—" He looked at the camera with an expression he hoped could be read as sincere. "I'll see you in a very little while."

He'd made notes for his message to Yaling, but on reading they all seemed foolish, so he improvised.

"Hello, Yaling," he said. "This is your father. I feel a little awkward recording this, because I don't know when or if you'll see it, or whether, when you view this, you'll have any memories of me at all." He breathed in. "I'm about to lead hundreds of warships in a battle against superior numbers, so there exists the bare possibility that you may never see me again—in person, I mean, not a recording." He blinked. That *was awkward*, he thought, and he considered looking at his notes again, but decided against it.

"I'm doing this partly because there's no one else, and partly because I want to stop the violence that was started by Lady Tu-hon, Lord Tork, and the Gruum government in Zanshaa. That violence has been directed mostly against Terrans, and I'm fighting for the future of our species. If we're beaten, you'll have a very limited future ahead of you, and if we win—well—" He waved a hand. "You'll have everything you deserve."

He paused to gather his whirling thoughts. "So please don't ever think that your mother and I have abandoned you on some fool's errand. I know I've been gone for months, but I'm here for your future, and I'm thinking about you all the time, and I have your picture in front of me every day."

He looked at his desk, where the images of his family bordered the display, and then looked up again. "I love you, Mei-mei, and you've never left my thoughts. If we never meet again—well—" He waved off the possibility with a flap of his hand. "Try not to forget me," he said, "and I know I won't forget you."

He ended the video with a move of his hand near the sensor, and then he slumped in his seat and wished he had a shot of Laredo whisky. Facing those feelings was *hard*, and he knew he shouldn't be dwelling on thoughts of death in the hours before a battle.

Yet those thoughts, he supposed, were inevitable.

He considered the whisky again, then decided against it.

Better a clear head, he decided, when facing odds of nearly two to one.

CHAPTER 15

"General quarters. Now general quarters. This is no drill."

The announcement had been repeating every minute for some time. Martinez thought the ship's crew had probably got the message by now.

"Communications test," Martinez said. "Can everyone hear me?"

Banerjee, Santana, Ricci, and Sula all checked in. "Right then," Martinez said. "Everyone fire up."

He reached for the med injector in its pocket and dialed in his dose. There was a hiss close to his ear as he shot the pharmaceutical stew into his neck. Other hisses echoed off the walls of the flag officer's station. Martinez saw that Sula hadn't used her injector, and that her attention remained fixed on her displays.

"Lady Sula?" he said. "You haven't taken your meds."

"I use patches," Sula said and twisted her neck to show a patch in place.

"Nonii," Martinez said and then looked at her—haggard,

her pale skin blotchy, her lower eyelids a line of red. "Are you all right, Lady Sula?"

"Didn't sleep well," she said. "But I'll be fine once things start."

"Nonii," Martinez said again. It wasn't as if he was going to send her to the sick bay. He needed her here even if she were dying of pneumonia.

He reached above his head and drew down his displays to the locked position. He studied the picture while he shifted his shoulders within his suit, trying to find a comfortable position on his couch. He knew he'd be here for hours, he might as well relax while he could.

He thought about putting on his helmet and decided he'd rather not be stuck inside it just yet. He'd be breathing sweat and stale air soon enough.

"Main display, go virtual," he said, and the bland box of the flag officer's station faded while space blossomed in his mind, the long line of Tork's fleet strung out across the darkness, their antimatter torches still pointed at him as they continued their deceleration. They'd pulled hard gees for two days to avoid over-shooting, but now they were coming on more easily, a closing speed that would bring them into action in about an hour. Tork's crews would have been punished by those gee forces during the deceleration, as well as being abruptly jolted into terror by missile ambushes and thrown about during evasive maneuvers.

That might have made them angry. They might well be spoiling for revenge, Martinez thought, but that would require energy they might no longer possess.

You know *what's going to happen*, Sula had told them. They'd gotten a good idea of what she meant in the time since, and even now they might be staring at the Fourth Fleet as a songbird might stare at a prowling snake.

He hoped so, anyway.

The Fourth Fleet was decelerating as well, though at a mere .75 gravity, to allow Tork to overtake them. Even though both fleets were flying at a speed of around 0.17 *c* from Martinez's point of view it looked as if Tork were advancing on a stationary target.

The Second Battle of Shulduc, like the first, would be fought in an empty quarter of the system. The system's gas giants were elsewhere in their orbits, and no asteroids or comets had made an appearance. Martinez might have preferred a more crowded combat zone to the emptiness, as that might have provided a greater opportunity for doing something clever, but he'd have to accept this empty space whether he liked it or not.

Square in the middle of the enemy formation was Battleship Squadron One, directly opposite *Perfection of the Praxis*, which Martinez had placed as a decoy in the middle of the Fourth Fleet. He assumed that Tork would be unable to resist attacking the presumed flagship with his own, especially as his own battleships outnumbered *Perfection* three to one.

Perfection of the Praxis and the two heavy cruiser squadrons supporting her—Division One of the Restoration Fleet—was under the command of Squadron Commander Conyngham, an officer Martinez had met only recently. Conyngham had spent the last war as a prisoner of the Naxids, captured on the first day of the rebellion, and his career had been permanently sidetracked. Despite uninspiring jobs and lack of advancement, he'd stayed in the service, and had helped Michi take the Fourth Fleet on the first day of the rebellion. He was a tall, elegant man with deep brown skin that contrasted with his white hair and goatee, and he had accepted his role with resignation.

"As I understand my role," he'd told Martinez when they'd met, "if I get killed, I'll have done my job."

"You don't have to get killed," Martinez said. "You'll be the butterfly dancing just outside the range of the kitten's claws."

Conyngham laughed. "Perhaps you can advise me about the best way to get the largest, most ungainly butterfly in history to *dance*."

"Tork's battleships won't be dancing any better than yours."

Conyngham remained skeptical. "But he'll have three dancing elephants to my one."

"We'll *all* be outnumbered," Martinez said. "Just try to think of it as a target-rich environment."

Still, Conyngham seemed resigned to making a target of himself, and Martinez hoped he transmitted this obliging attitude to his crews. If Conyngham mismanaged his force, the whole center of the Restoration line could collapse.

Martinez watched as the Righteous Fleet continued its advance. Its line was longer than that of the Fourth Fleet, and it threatened to overlap the defenders—"Doubling" was the worst possible outcome, when the enemy wrapped the line and it was caught between two fires. Martinez issued orders to the van and rear divisions to stretch the line. The van consisted of Jeremy Foote's division of three light squadrons, and the rear a two-squadron division under Chandra Prasad. The line didn't have to be stretched as far as Martinez had expected, because of the four squadrons that Tork was keeping out of his line.

So far, so expected. These were all maneuvers that Tork could have predicted. The preliminary to the battle was developing just as the Supreme Commander might have wished, the Restoration forces using tactics right out of Tork's playbook and setting itself up to be crushed by superior numbers.

Martinez scarcely had to give any orders at all. The Fourth Fleet had been drilling this battle every day for the last month, and everyone knew what to do. His directives would only be necessary once battle was joined and the situation teetered on the edge of chaos.

He exited the virtual display, and the uninspiring sight of the flag officer's station rose to his senses. He spun his acceleration cage around to face Ricci.

"Lieutenant Ricci," he said, "you might as well bring our solar missiles into the fight. Keep them in the sun on the approach, and make sure they have the latest information as to the location of the enemy. We don't want them hitting our ships by mistake."

"Yes, my lord."

The "solar missiles" were those Martinez had hidden near the system's sun. They would keep the sun behind them on the approach in hopes that the Righteous Fleet wouldn't detect their burning antimatter torches.

Because of the length of time it would take the signal to reach them, and the even longer time it would take for them to reach the site of the battle, it would still be hours before they arrived.

Martinez spun his cage again and observed Santana and Banerjee, both facing the wall displays. They were conversing in low voices, and he was reassured to hear no edge of alarm or panic in their speech. He spun toward Sula and found her lying motionless on her couch, eyes closed, her head tilted toward him, the med patch clear on her neck. He realized she had fallen asleep.

Well, he thought, *why not? A relaxed attitude to battle was probably a good thing.*

And no drooling, he observed.

There wasn't any point in waking her now. There was nothing for her to do until the action started.

He went back into the virtual display, performed some calculations with the computer, then consulted the chronometer. He waited another eleven minutes before giving his next order.

"Martinez to all ships. Commence turnabout maneuver at 10:08 hours precisely."

Which gave everyone a few minutes to get ready. Acknowledgments flashed onto his display. He reached for his helmet.

"Might as well armor up," he said and remembered the bolt that had almost fractured his skull his first time in the flag officer's station. He put the helmet on and heard the hiss of circulating air. The scent of antiseptic and suit seals stung the back of his throat.

Thirteen seconds before the scheduled maneuver, the alarm rang for zero gee. Martinez couldn't help but look toward Sula and saw her shift slightly in her sleep. When the engines cut out and gravity vanished, she floated free in her harness and made a kind of glottal noise as her eyes flashed open. She scanned her boards in surprise, then relaxed as she discovered that the battle had progressed as planned.

Martinez felt a shimmer in his inner ear as *Los Angeles* pitched end over end, then stabilized with the engines facing the enemy. Another alarm rang for high gravities, and Martinez braced himself for what came next.

The engines fired, and the bars of Martinez's acceleration cage sang as six gravities punched him back into the couch. He dived into the virtual realm again and saw the Righteous Fleet receding as the Fourth Fleet sped away.

What he hoped Tork would see was his enemies running away, and this was confirmed when the Righteous Fleet cut its deceleration, pitched over, and fired engines in pursuit.

Martinez intended more than simply goading Tork into chasing him, because not all the Righteous Fleet's crews could stand six gees' acceleration.

The Lai-own species were flightless birds, and they had retained the hollow bones of their ancestors. It was dangerous for them to accelerate at more than around two and a half gravities, and Martinez was hoping to compromise the enemy order by forcing the Lai-own squadrons to fall out of the pursuit.

But in the meantime he, and everyone under his command, had to endure six gravities. His vac suit's inner liner closed on his arms and legs to force blood to his brain. He grunted with every breath, and every time he inhaled it was like being punched in the abdomen. His vision, even that projected directly into his visual cortex, began to narrow.

Through his narrowing vision he kept his attention fixed firmly on the enemy, and he saw gaps opening in the enemy line as Lai-own squadrons fell behind. *Success!* He would have exulted if all his energies weren't directed toward keeping his lungs working.

Tork would have done much better to have kept his fleet together and accelerated at a slower rate. After all, the Restoration Fleet had to fight somewhere between here and Harzapid, and Tork would catch it sooner or later.

Martinez kept up the acceleration for another fifteen minutes, seeing the Lai-own squadrons—twelve of them, nearly a hundred ships—dropping farther and farther behind. By now the four reserve squadrons behind the line had passed them.

"Martinez to all ships," he finally ordered. "Fire screening barrage on my mark. Twenty, nineteen..."

The long countdown was to give the Fourth Fleet's weaponers and officers time to react. By the end of the countdown, Martinez was panting for breath and sweat was prickling on his forehead. Miniwaves pulsed from his couch, keeping his blood from pooling under high gravity.

Four hundred missiles leaped from their tubes, were carried into space by chemical boosters, then reoriented, fired their antimatter torches, and raced into the gap between the fleets.

"Stand by for turnabout," Martinez gasped.

The four hundred missiles detonated, produced a storm of neutrons, gamma rays, and short-lived pions, while their tungsten jackets created blazing, expanding fireballs, all of which created an opaque radio wall between the Fourth Fleet and Tork's sensors.

"All ships commence turnabout," Martinez said. The zero-gee warning sounded, and Martinez took a grateful breath of free air as the engines cut. *Los Angeles* again pitched end over end, its nose now pointed toward the enemy.

"Fire decoys. Launch pinnaces. Assume First Combat Formation, and accelerate at two gees."

Tork was about to get a surprise.

He would be straining his senses, and his sensors, to find out what was going on behind the screen that the Fourth Fleet had just laid down. And what he would finally see, emerging from the screen, was the entire enemy force flying through the radio hash and bearing down to engage.

And the Fourth Fleet would have grown to *twice its previous size*.

To this point Martinez hadn't bothered to fire decoys because Tork knew exactly how many ships he had, and because if he had used decoys, the fleets were in sight of each other long enough that Tork would have been able to work out which were decoy and which warships. But now, with an engagement coming on in just a few minutes, Tork and his staff didn't have the time to make that calculation. All they would see were over five hundred ships aimed like bullets between their eyes. And though they would *know* that half those ships were harmless, they wouldn't know which half, and the very sight of all those drive signatures emerging through the fog might shock them into making mistakes.

The Fourth Fleet made some adjustments to its order while under cover, shifting into what Martinez had called the First Combat Formation. Kung's division and Martinez's Division Two both dropped their rate of acceleration to let the rest of the fleet surge ahead, reordering to fill the gaps with warships and decoys. The mobile reserves had detached themselves from the line and soon halted their advance entirely. Martinez felt himself floating in his harness as the engines cut.

Los Angeles approached the cloud, its sensors straining to seek out the Righteous Fleet on the other side. Then the cruiser flashed through the expanding, cooling fireballs, and the enemy was revealed.

Tork had figured that something was up behind the antimatter screen, and while waiting for the situation to resolve, the Righteous Fleet had cut its engines to observe, all except for the Lai-own ships still scurrying to catch up. When they saw the Fourth Fleet emerge from the murk, they pitched over their ships and began a deceleration to give themselves a chance to reorder their line before the battle started. Their attempts to plug the gaps were slow and almost random.

In organizing his enormous fleet, Martinez realized, Tork hadn't done anything like the Fourth Fleet's creation of the division. He was issuing orders to his squadrons one by one, which meant that most of his ships would be stuck in formation exactly where Tork had put them at the beginning. His vast force of over four hundred ships was just too unwieldy to maneuver properly.

"All ships but the reserve," Martinez said, "engage at will. You are free to starburst at any time."

He watched as the Fourth Fleet approached the disorganized enemy, as missiles raced out from both sides to be blasted by point-defense weapons or by countermissiles. The battlespace became murky with radio haze. One by one, the Fourth Fleet divisions starburst into the bobbing, weaving formations of the Martinez Method, designed so that the ships wouldn't be so close together that a single volley could wipe them out, while defensive fire could be concentrated at maximum efficiency. These were the tactics that Tork had officially rejected as breaking with the perfect legacy of the ancestors, and his squadrons remained frozen in the comparatively rigid formations that had been standard in the Fleet for millennia.

Brave *lost*. Words marking the Fourth Fleet's first casualty formed in a corner of Martinez's display, the event duly reported by *Brave*'s squadron leader.

The only element of the Fourth Fleet that hadn't engaged was the center—*Perfection of the Praxis* and its two supporting cruiser squadrons had hung back as if they were afraid of engaging Battleship Squadron One and its enormous firepower. That fear, Martinez felt, was perfectly justified, for each of the Praxis-class ships carried eighty-four missile launchers.

Martinez hoped to tempt Tork into an unwise pursuit of Conyngham's Division One—and if not that, to at least keep the enemy battleships pinned in place, unengaged but unable to advance. Even without engaging, Conyngham had sent his squadrons into the weaving, stochastic-seeming patterns of the Method, as if to taunt Tork with his lack of orthodoxy. Tork hardly hesitated at all—Battleship Squadron One, along with its supports, moved to engage, preceded by a wave of a thousand missiles.

Conyngham's ships drew away while engaged in a frantic defensive dance, antiproton beams flashing out, a surge of countermissiles racing from launchers to knock down the enemy strike. Martinez saw one of Conyngham's cruisers erupt in a hellish antimatter storm and winced.

Thrasher lost.

Able lost.

Judge Jeffreys *disabled, drifting.*

An intense general action had begun along the length of the line. Martinez could see brilliant expanding fireballs as ships were blasted into ionizing radiation. With fireballs and radiant hash clouding the displays, he couldn't see every detonation, but he could read data from the radiation detectors that spiked as ships exploded behind the obscuring clouds. His anxiety rose as he realized he couldn't always see which ships had blown up, or which side they belonged to. The battle was too big for him to control, or even to see properly.

The lagging Lai-own squadrons finally rejoined the Righteous Fleet, but there was no place for them in the battle array—their places had been taken, somewhat haphazardly, by other ships. Some of the Lai-own squadrons hung back, firing missiles around their replacements, and others merged with the squadrons already present, creating a tangle of uncoordinated targets and—Martinez imagined—massive command-and-control issues.

Conyngham's command was invisible behind hundreds of radiation blooms. Missiles detonated up and down the line, a constant rippling brightness. There must have been thousands of missiles racing to their destruction at any one time. Despite their awkward deployment, the addition of nearly a hundred ships to the enemy line was beginning to take its toll on the Restoration squadrons.

Bombardment of Kurthag *lost.*

Standard *depressurized.*

Judge Jeffreys *lost.*

Storm Fury *lost.*

The messages of loss and annihilation were coming too fast for Martinez to keep up.

"Lord Fleetcom." Sula's voice came low in his ear. "Now or never." This only confirmed Martinez's own instinct.

"Lieutenant Ricci," Martinez said. "How long before the solar missiles arrive?"

"Forty minutes, Lord Fleetcom."

Crisis *lost.*

Loyalty *lost.*

The moment decisive, Martinez thought.

"Flag to Lord Fleetcom Kung," Martinez said. "You should consider yourself free to engage the enemy. Flag to Division Two: assume Double Hammer Formation. Accelerate at one gravity on a bearing of—" He called up the compass function into his virtual display. "Two-nine-one degrees absolute. Evolution to begin at—" A glance at the chronometer.

"11:41." Which would give everyone nearly twenty seconds to prepare, which should be enough, considering they'd been waiting for this order for the better part of an hour.

Right on schedule the fifteen ships of Division Two fired engines, and the two squadrons began a slow spiral around each other. Martrinez was pressed back into his couch, and he felt the ship's eddies in his viscera. The battle began to move closer.

Imperious *lost.*

Javelin *severely damaged, depressurized.*

Martinez had observed, as far back as the Second Battle of Magaria, that Tork had made insufficient use of the third dimension. He intended to take advantage of that.

While each squadron in the Righteous Fleet was organized in a rigid flat spheroid around its flagship, the squadrons themselves were stretched out head-to-tail in a long line. With Tork's battleships in pursuit of Conyngham, that line now resembled a shallow V, its point consisting of Battleship Squadron One under their Supreme Commander. That line was under strain, particularly at the points at which it bent to accommodate Tork's advance.

Martinez intended Division Two to enter the fight at one of those points of strain, and to utilize the third dimension to reinforce a friendly squadron already engaged. The two squadrons of the Double Hammer would engage north and south of the already-engaged squadron, envelop the enemy, and destroy him, after which the Double Hammer would find more enemy to fight.

He couldn't have superiority in numbers. But he could

achieve local superiority in crucial parts of the battlespace, and this he intended to do.

Judge Solomon *lost.*

Obedience *drifting, will not respond to signals.*

Eager *lost.*

"Lord Fleetcom," Sula said. "May I suggest altering course to two-seven-seven absolute?" Irregular scarlet lines slashed through Martinez's virtual display, hand-drawn by Sula from her own display. "There's some disorganization in the enemy forces there. I think they're more vulnerable to us."

Martinez studied the enemy line and agreed. "Flag to Division Two," he said. "Alter course to two-seven-seven absolute."

He felt the nudge as the ship altered course. The two squadrons had gained sufficient separation from each other, so Martinez ordered them into the Method's starburst formation, and soon his inner ear was teased by minor course changes as *Los Angeles* shifted its position within the fluid formation.

Supreme *lost.*

"Lady Sula," he said. "Keep a lookout for the enemy reserve squadrons. If they start moving, I need to know."

"Yes, Lord Fleetcom."

He was hoping with Division Two to create a decisive intervention. If the enemy committed their reserves at the right time, they could reverse that intervention, or make a decisive intervention of their own.

"Lord Fleetcom," Sula said. "Kung's division is moving."

The Restoration had now committed all reserves. There

was nothing left. If the enemy reserves committed to the attack, Martinez had nothing with which to counter them.

Kong Fuzi lost.

Cyrus lost.

"Flag to Division Two," Martinez said. "Each ship to fire two missiles as part of a covering barrage."

His heart lifted as his displays showed the missiles streaking toward the enemy, looping to hit from north and south. There was a kind of freedom in making a commitment that couldn't be retracted, that would lead to life or death, victory or defeat.

Rapid lost.

Submission lost.

Martinez's mouth was dry. He took a sip of water from the tube inside his helmet.

"What division are we reinforcing?" he asked.

"Mustafa's, Lord Fleetcom," Sula answered.

"He seems to be doing fairly well."

Mustafa seemed to have exploited some disorganization on the part of the enemy, possibly a trio of squadrons that hadn't meshed well, or that were receiving contradictory orders, or were simply overstrained in their effort to keep the bending line together. Mustafa's ships were in the whirling dance of the Martinez Method, riding the chaotic hull of a dynamic system, and they were pummeling the enemy with volley after volley. Though the radio haze made it difficult to be sure of the numbers, it seemed the enemy had lost perhaps half their number, and Mustafa something like a third.

Mustafa was killing the enemy faster than they could kill

him, but if the killing kept up at this same rate, the Restoration would run out of ships before Tork did.

Defiant *lost*.

Tumult *lost*.

Obedience *lost*.

"All ships commence fire," Martinez ordered, and the bright sparks that were missiles leaped from their tubes, reoriented, ignited, and raced for an enemy that was suddenly not only outnumbered, but effectively surrounded. The two enemy squadrons reacted differently—one maintained its rigid formation to present a defensive wall against the enemy, while the other starburst, each ship following its own track away from the others so as not to clump together and present such a grand target.

Both decisions were bad ones. The starburst ships, each without support, were hunted down one by one by darting missiles, and the other squadron held out for a while until their defense was overwhelmed, and they were all destroyed at once. The Restoration ships found themselves encircling nothing but expanding fireballs and flying debris.

Unity *lost*.

Security *drifting*.

Judge Kybiq *lost*.

The next moves in the fight stacked up in Martinez's mind, a neat list. "Flag to Squadron Leader Mustafa," he said. "Regroup your forces and double the enemy to your rear. Flag to Division Two: engage the enemy toward their van. Squadron Twenty, alter course to three-four-four absolute by zero-zero-one absolute and advance at one and a half gees. Squadron to re-form starburst on flag. Squadron Eleven is to operate independently and at discretion."

Asking ginger-haired Carmody to operate at his own discretion might be taking a bit of a chance—he was of the charge-and-be-damned school—but Martinez had decided it was useless to keep close control of his units in a conflict this vast. Either he trusted his officers or he didn't.

Acknowledgments flashed in a corner of the screen. The zero-gee alarm sounded and Martinez felt a shimmer in his inner ear as *Los Angeles* reoriented on its new course. Then the alarm came for acceleration, and Martinez dropped back into his couch and viewed the conflict ahead of him.

Adept *lost.*

Arrestor *lost.*

Suddenly the radiation counters leaped—a titanic spike in neutrons and gamma rays that jumped off the scale in the most literal way. A cold hand closed on Martinez's throat as he stared at the counter. Ships had been wiped out—a *lot* of ships—and all at the same moment. But whose?

He remembered to breathe and inhaled recycled air that reeked of sweat and spent adrenaline. Then a possible answer came to him.

"Lieutenant Ricci," he said, "did the solar missiles just arrive?"

"Yes, my lord. They struck the enemy rear."

I hope, Martinez thought. Because by that point the missiles were traveling so fast they might have had a hard time distinguishing friend from foe in the brief seconds before impact.

He'd hidden four hundred missiles near the sun. How many of them had actually hit the enemy?

"Keep monitoring and tell me what's actually happened there," Martinez said.

"I'm checking the feeds from the pinnaces," Ricci said. "I'm feeling good about this, because I kept the missiles updated with the tactical situation up till the last minute."

"Very good," Martinez said.

Cosmos *lost.*

"Lord Fleetcom," said Sula, "Kung's division has enveloped the enemy line. I think they've wiped out a squadron or maybe two."

"Very good," Martinez said again—a ritual response, for all that it was, in fact, very good.

Martinez and Kung had broken the enemy's line in two places, which meant that what had been one large sprawling battle had now become at least five smaller ones. Division Two would be rolling up the enemy all the way to the van, and achieving local superiority all the way unless the enemy could find some way to react. Mustafa's division, meanwhile, would be attacking toward the enemy center, and likewise would be enjoying numerical superiority with each encounter, gathering strength as he moved and liberated one Restoration unit after another. Kung, meanwhile, would be battling his way toward the enemy rear, while liberating other units to fight their way centerward.

In every one of these fights, the Restoration would have local superiority. And if they chewed up enough of the enemy, they would have every other kind of superiority as well.

The only sub-battle where the Fourth Fleet hadn't achieved superiority was the fight in the center, with Tork's battleships fighting Conyngham's division. That part of the battlespace was so filled with eye-searing fireballs and sensor-baffling radiation that Martinez couldn't tell what was happening, but at least all the fireballs meant Conyngham had ships left in the fight.

Protector *lost*.

Devastation *lost*.

Absolute *lost*.

Absolute was Fulvia Kazakov's ship. She'd been Martinez's premiere on *Illustrious* and absolutely steady in the horrific situation following the murder of Lord Gomberg Fletcher.

Damn.

Red lines scrawled themselves across Martinez's display. "I'd recommend this course on the attack," Sula said.

"Give me the bearing."

"Three-three-eight absolute by sixty-five absolute."

Martinez gave the order to Squadron Eleven, and no sooner had the *Los Angeles* swooped onto its new course than Lieutenant Ricci's voice rose elated in his headphones.

"The solar missiles took out six enemy ships, Lord Fleetcom! Six at once!"

Of four hundred missiles, only six had hit an enemy. But that, it seemed, was fairly standard.

More importantly, this action freed Chandra Prasad commanding the rear division of the Restoration fleet. She'd be able to work her way toward the center, doubling the enemy all the way, while Kung was fighting his way toward her.

Autocrat *lost.*

Eradicator *lost.*

Division Two had already engaged the enemy squadron ahead of them. The target's numbers were severely depleted, as were those of the Restoration squadron opposed to it, and the enemy ships vanished in a wave of fire before they were able to organize a response. The next enemy squadron put up more of a fight, but it was in a hopeless situation and died nearly as quickly. Martinez sent the Restoration division liberated from the fight to reinforce Mustafa.

Fortune *lost.*

Hull breach on Forward. *Drifting.*

There were about ten enemy squadrons between Division Two and the van. The next saw Division Two coming and left its position in the line to come abreast of the squadron next ahead. The united squadrons put up a stubborn defense, but they were surrounded and outnumbered two to one, and in the end were obliterated. Their chief contribution to Tork's cause was to delay Martinez's advance, and to give warning to the squadrons ahead of them. The next squadron ahead abandoned its position for a pell-mell retreat at heavy acceleration.

Sula's voice came into Martinez's headset. "Pursue, Lord Fleetcom?"

Martinez fully intended to chase them down. He ordered Division Two and all other available ships into the pursuit. As the gravities built, and the Torminel wrestlers gathered to squat on his chest, he heard Sula's gasping voice on his headphones.

"Enemy reserve's moving!"

Martinez's heart gave a lurch. A look at his display showed that two of Tork's four reserve squadrons had lit their antimatter torches and were arrowing for the fight. But calculation showed they weren't heading for Division Two, but for the area where Kung had made his breakthrough.

Martinez fought against gravity to fill his lungs, then spoke in a series of grunts. "Flag to Fleetcom Kung. Two enemy reserve squadrons are heading for you."

All he could do was warn, and with the message being transmitted through confusion and sensor-baffling radiation, he couldn't be sure the message would be received.

The other two reserve squadrons remained in place, drifting on the edge of the battlespace. Martinez wondered if Tork had forbidden them to engage without his personal order.

Dart *lost.*

Victor *lost.*

Shi Huangdi *lost.*

Martinez watched with a feeling akin to wonder as the entire enemy van, eight entire squadrons, came apart. As if the fleeing squadron were a signal, other units were now pulling out of the fight, albeit in somewhat better order.

"Flag to all van ships! Pursue! Engage the enemy closely!" The battlespace ahead blazed with increased fury.

Challenger *lost.*

Explorer *lost.*

Perigee *lost.*

As soon as he'd given the order for close pursuit, Martinez found himself almost regretting the order and thought he might simply let the fleeing enemy run. Once the enemy were clear of the battlespace, he could turn his own ships around and drive for Tork to finish off the Supreme Commander and with him, his cause.

But some of his own units were already closely engaged, and it would be difficult to extricate them from the enemy without running risks. While Martinez was considering this, Lord Jeremy Foote, commanding the van division, made the decision impossible. He let the enemy withdraw to a safe distance and then began a furious acceleration that must have left half his crews unconscious. Once he had pulled ahead of the fleeing enemy, Foote altered course so as to block the enemy's retreat.

It was a bravura high-gee maneuver that demonstrated Foote's yachtsman's instincts, and it was decisive. Martinez couldn't let the enemy escape unless he was willing to let them overwhelm Foote, and though he wouldn't have mourned Foote's death overmuch, he would very much mourn the loss of a division of ships.

Not that he wasn't losing them anyway.

Thunderbolt *lost.*

Constellation *lost.*

Judge Di *lost. Command of division assumed by Senior Captain Hao.*

Martinez took a breath. *Judge Di* was Kung's flagship. The Fourth Fleet had just lost its third in command.

There was nothing Martinez could do about it except to wish Captain Hao well.

"Lord Fleetcom." Sula's voice. "Suggested lines for attack."

The fleeing ships had been trying to sort themselves into

some kind of order, and Martinez saw that Sula's suggested maneuvers would act to wedge the enemy units apart. "Approved," he said. "Send the bearings to the signals board."

Viper *lost.*

Brazen *lost.*

Division Two, leading miscellaneous units that had been left free when the enemy retreated, plunged into the confused tangle of enemy ships. Though the enemy ships were all around, the Righteous Fleet's response was uncoordinated. Some units tried to run, some tried to fight, some just tried to defend themselves and hoped for the best. Foote's division was hidden behind a wall of expanding fireballs. Thousands of missiles seemed to be racing in all possible directions. Antimatter bloomed closer and closer, and *Los Angeles* entered an opaque wall of overlapping fireballs. The battlespace faded from Martinez perceptions, and he felt frustration throbbing in his veins.

"Recommended course, Fleetcom." Sula's calm voice was accompanied by the usual red slashes on his display. He saw at once that the recommended course would take Division Two out of the zone where the enemy might be expected to fire and allow it to launch a surprise barrage once it emerged from the fireball screen.

"Approved. Send the bearings to signals."

More missiles detonated in the vicinity. Hull temperature was rising. Martinez thought he scented smoke in his vac suit and told himself that it was his imagination.

"Flag to Division Two," he said. "Each ship to fire three missiles on bearing zero-two-zero by zero-seven-zero relative."

Radiation spiked high on the detectors. Ships lost nearby, but Martinez couldn't tell whose ships they were.

The missiles were already well on their way when Division Two raced from the fireball cloud.

They were thirteen ships now. Three were missing.

Shock drove the breath from Martinez's lungs. In all his commands, he'd lost only one ship in battle, and now he'd lost three from his immediate command in just a few moments, as well as dozens—maybe hundreds—from all the units of the Fourth Fleet.

"Recommended course, Fleetcom," said Sula.

The enemy squadron targeted by the missiles was dissolving, bursting apart like shrapnel, the ships going through furious evasive maneuvers as Division Two's missiles pursued them. Martinez ordered more missiles to chase them down before he considered Sula's plots.

"Approved. Bearings to signals."

Miniwaves hummed along the broad muscles of his back. Martinez checked the display for the two squadrons the Righteous Fleet still had in reserve and found them still in place, hovering at a distance from the battle. Why were they still there? If they wanted to make a decisive intervention, now was the time—they could intervene in Martinez's fight, they could reinforce the other reserves in fighting Kung's intrusion, or they could reinforce Tork. They were doing nothing at all, and that made Martinez more uneasy than if he saw them moving to engage.

Victorious *lost.*

Striker *tumbling, not responding to signals.*

Guardian *lost. Squadron command assumed by Captain Shang.*

Guardian. That was Carmody's ship, commanding Division Two's Heavy Squadron Eleven. Martinez's mouth was dry. The enemy's shots were coming close.

The fleeing enemy squadron died in hellfire, but not before Division Two was closely engaged elsewhere. Sula's tactical recommendations shifted the battle's center of gravity from one place to another, always driving one group of ships outside of supporting distance from another, or prompting them into an unwise countermove, or opposing and neutralizing an enemy tactic. Martinez was sometimes able to overleap Sula's ideas and ordered the shift that would follow the shift that Sula hadn't yet offered him. It was as if his mind was traveling in time.

The collaboration was effortless. They shouldered enemy units out of the way, only to shift course and hammer the enemy that the move had just unmasked. They isolated enemy squadrons and pounded them from all directions. It was as if the two fleets were engaged in a whirling dance of fire, but Martinez and Sula were in the center of the dance, revolving in a close embrace, compelling the other dancers to adopt their rhythm, their steps.

Enemy ships blazed and died. The remainder were surrounded, Foote's division on one side and Martinez's force on the other. They were packed into a defensive ball, the target of a thousand missiles.

"Message from one of the enemy captains, my lord," said Santana.

"Signals, let's see it."

The image appeared of a Daimong staring at the camera with his black, expressionless eyes. He was wearing a vac suit with the faceplate up, and his features were frozen in an expression of metaphysical anguish. "This is Senior Captain Kinlarc of the *Universal* to the commander of the Fourth Fleet. We surrender!" His voice was like the sound of metal clashing with metal. "Stop shooting at us! *We surrender!*"

Martinez stared in Kinlarc in surprise, then responded. "Martinez of the Fourth Fleet to Captain Kinlarc. Who exactly is surrendering? *Universal*? All of you? Some? Respond please."

But there was no response, because before an answer could come, waves of missiles broke through the enemy defenses. The enemy survivors were all overwhelmed at once, and Kinlarc and *Universal* and its crew were turned to raging subatomic particles all at the same instant as two thousand of their comrades.

The sub-battle wasn't quite finished, because enemy missiles had to be tracked and blown up, and then Division Two, Foote's division, and the remnants of other Restoration divisions were drifting through cooling fireballs, and Martinez knew that even though the Second Battle of Shulduc wasn't over, he'd just won it.

"Flag to all ships near the van," he said. "All divisions to form on their flagships. Orient to course one-four-one absolute and accelerate at three gravities on my order." He finished the order with a bout of coughing and took a drink of water to soothe his dry throat.

A few ships failed to reply entirely. A number signaled

Unable to comply, and Martinez told them to concentrate on repairs, and to rejoin when they could. Once the mobile ships abandoned them, they could be easily picked off by the enemy reserve, but the reserve remained hovering on the edge of the battlespace, and showed no sign of moving.

Legion *lost.*

Renown *lost.*

Apogee *lost.*

Restoration ships capable of movement and maneuver formed into their divisions. Martinez found himself in command of just thirty-one ships belonging to divisions that had totaled seventy-two just that morning. Foote's division, with only six ships remaining out of twenty-four, was particularly hard hit, but he had thrown his entire command as a roadblock in the enemy's path and had paid the penalty.

Martinez pushed up his faceplate, but the air in *Los Angeles* was no cooler than the air in his suit. "Thank you all," he said to the crew assembled in the flag officer's station. "That was brilliant." He looked at Sula. "Now we can finish this."

He saw the emerald flash of Sula's eyes.

"Let's do it," she said.

"Flag to all ships," Martinez said. "Accelerate at three gravities on my mark. Three, two, one, *mark.*"

His cage swung to its deadpoint as the engines lit. *Los Angeles* was heading for the center of the battle, where Tork's battleships and their supports were still engaged with Conyngham's command. Conyngham had been drawing away from the main battle, pulling Tork after him, and by now they were an engagement entirely their own. Enough of Division One had survived to put up a fight, because the drumbeat of explosions was continuous, and the area was so saturated with expanding fireballs and radiation that Martinez couldn't see what was happening, or who had survived.

The rear of the battle was now another separate action, where Chandra Prasad, Kung's division, Mustafa's ships, and associated forces were still engaged.

Lawgiver *lost*.

Whirlwind *lost*.

Wakeful *lost*.

"Flag to Squadron Leader Prasad," Martinez said. "Please report status. Flag to Senior Captain Hao. Please report status."

Chandra's reply arrived a few minutes later. She leaned forward on her couch, and the camera showed mainly her forehead and a few strands of blazing red hair that had escaped her cap. "We're in the final stages of mopping up. We've got less than thirty ships left, but the enemy are down to a dozen or so. Also, we received your message to Hao, and I think Hao's ship was destroyed, but it's all such a tangle that I can't tell. End message."

No reply came from Hao, so it seemed that Chandra was right.

Arbiter *lost*.

Fencer *lost*.

Those were the last friendly ships reported lost from Chandra's fight, because it looked as if the battle for the rear was going entirely her way. Whatever was going on in the battle for the center, the participants were too busy to report anything at all.

It would be another twenty minutes before *Los Angeles* would be able to engage Tork's units. Martinez sent a ciphered message to Division One telling them he was coming, and when he expected to arrive. Slightly to his surprise, he received an answer from Conyngham himself, which meant *Perfection of the Praxis* was still in action. Sweat formed bright beads on Conyngham's forehead, and his eyes were bloodshot.

"The sooner the better, Lord Fleetcom," he said. "End message."

Martinez decided to take Conyngham's message to heart. "Van ships," he ordered. "Increase acceleration to four gravities on my mark. Ten, nine . . ."

Banerjee's voice sounded in Martinez's headphones. "Message from Squadron Leader Prasad, Lord Fleetcom. On the Command channel. It's being deciphered now."

Martinez finished his countdown, and another Torminel wrestler climbed onto his chest as *Los Angeles* accelerated. The message from Chandra Prasad appeared on his displays. Chandra was reclined on her couch, her face strained against acceleration.

"We've dealt with the enemy here, Gare," she said. "We're coming to Conyngham's assistance with the twenty-four ships still capable of action. Do you have any orders for me, or shall we make it up as we go along?"

"Flag to Chandra Prasad," Martinez said to Banerjee. "Use the Command channel. Message follows: *'You go south of the tangle, I'll go north, and our missiles will meet in the middle.'*"

That would be clear enough, he trusted, and would keep the two groups of rescuers from running into each other.

He dropped his faceplate, took a drink of water, and went back into a virtual battlefield. Conyngham's fight was still too confused for him to make much sense out of it, but he could see ships, some as big as the giants of Battleship Squadron One, appear briefly between fireballs.

In the end, Sula had said to Tork, *there will be just you, alone, in your flagship's magnificent ballroom wondering why no one else has come to the dance.*

She was wrong. Plenty of people were coming to the dance, people like Foote and Martinez and Chandra Prasad, and they were bringing all their friends with them.

He wondered what Tork would make of all these party crashers turning up to spoil his brilliant triumph. *Pirates, murderers, and traitors.* He doubted that Tork would ever consider that his ideas or his tactics might be wrong—he would probably think that Martinez had *cheated* somehow.

Which of course was perfectly true. Martinez had cheated every chance he got, while Tork had remained true to his principles and would die for his rectitude.

Good, he thought.

EXPLORER *lost.*

The item was one in a long list of destroyed ships in a corner of one of Severin's displays. He hadn't noticed it when it first appeared, but now he couldn't stop staring at it.

He'd been stunned when he first noticed that two-word message, and after he regained his wits he'd accessed the recordings of the combat and discovered that *Explorer* had been destroyed in the confused action that had followed the counterattack by the enemy's two reserve squadrons. Chandra Prasad, Severin's division commander, had been forced to adjust her ships' bearing and formation in order to receive the enemy attack while continuing the action against the enemy's main line. Severin's squadron was caught between two fires, and he had been fully occupied with keeping track of a hundred threats and organizing some kind of response to them. He could see that he was losing ships, but in the heat of the moment he hadn't kept track of which of his ships were being hit.

Lady Starkey was gone, annihilated, along with her crew, her ship. The Alois puppet he'd given her—"For protection"— had failed.

Severin's lover had been killed, had been transformed into plasma expanding into the void, and he hadn't even noticed when it had happened. Guilt and incredulity stabbed his heart like a brace of knives.

During the action his squadron of eight had been reduced to five, of which only four were capable of further action. They had hit the enemy hard, and they'd won their local sub-battle and destroyed the enemy reserve as well as the rear of their line, and now they had formed around Chandra's flagship and were bearing down on Tork's battleship squadron. It would take at least fifteen minutes to reach Tork and his battleships, and that left Severin a lot of time to watch the corner of one of his displays and stare at those two words.

Explorer *lost.*

Severin felt as if he, too, were a hollow bubble of gas expanding into space, losing cohesion, losing energy, dissipating, leaving behind nothing but a vast and inexorable grief that seemed to fill all the universe.

He thought about Lady Starkey, her laughter, her mobile face. He could feel her moist kiss on his lips, inhale the warm scent of her hair. The memories were so strong that he wanted to offer them as evidence that she was still, somehow, alive.

Reports appeared on his screens and he dealt with them robotically, his conscious mind still overwhelmed by the grief that clutched at his throat and throbbed in his veins. Tork and his battle with Conyngham grew nearer. Chandra sent orders for his squadron's deployment, and he acknowledged and passed the orders on. Shifts in gravity tugged at him, rolled the acceleration cage. The two words, Explorer *lost*, continued to burn in a corner of his display.

He shifted his attention to the vast growing radio blur that hid Tork's squadrons, and another set of emotions began to stir in his heart. Anger, bitterness, hatred, and a growing desire for revenge.

Severin hadn't bothered to hate the enemy till that point—he had been baffled by their stupidity and their greed, but he'd viewed these as problems to be solved, or faults to be satirized, not villainy to be hated.

But now he boiled with fury, and his hands formed claws, as if he could run up to Tork and tear open his throat with his bare hands.

Chandra Prasad's face appeared on one of her displays. "All ships should consider themselves free to engage," she said.

"With pleasure, Lady Squadcom," he replied, and he began to pick his targets.

DIVISION TWO REACHED the turnover point, where they would have to decelerate in order not to overshoot the enemy, and there was half a minute of glorious weightlessness while *Los Angeles* pitched over. Martinez gave a course correction to carry his warships north of the blazing fight, and he remembered to check the enemy's two reserve squadrons, still floating on the fringes of the battlespace. Even if they charged into the fight now, he thought, they couldn't prevent what was about to happen.

The engines roared again, acceleration cages swung, and the gravities built. Martinez could feel the swooping, evading motions of the ship, the miniwaves pulsing on his back to keep his blood from pooling, hear the hiss of the suit's air intake, smell the sour sweat inside his suit. His vision was entirely occupied with the battle.

With Division Two now flying north of the battle, Martinez had a different angle on the action, and he was able to make out Conyngham's division more clearly. *Perfection of the Praxis* fought on, dodging and weaving as much as possible for a ship its size, point-defense weapons lancing out at the hundreds of enemy missiles arrowing right for it. Its escort of sixteen ships had been reduced to nine, all fully engaged, whirling with *Perfection* in the mathematical dance of the Martinez Method. Martinez felt his heart swell with admiration for Conyngham and his courageous, skillful defense.

As Conyngham's division intercepted the Righteous Fleet's missiles, the erupting missiles formed a hot, burning screen between Division One and the enemy. Tork was firing blind into an opaque wall. This didn't matter so much, since he knew approximately where his enemy was, but it meant he had less time to react to missiles incoming from Division One, and as he was continually passing through the fireballs he might also be blind to Martinez's approach.

And to Chandra's. She had started closer to the battle than had Martinez, and she'd arrived south of the fight just ahead of him. Her missiles were already lancing out into the heart of the storm.

"Flag to all van ships," Martinez said. "Open fire on the enemy."

Missiles launched from their tubes, reoriented, and burned for the enemy. Martinez could see Tork's point-defense beams, normally invisible, flaming as they sliced through fireball plasma—and then the flaming lances were *all* he could see of Tork, now completely invisible behind the wall of fireballs that had been Division Two's missiles. Tork's ships were now surrounded by a globe of fire.

A few missiles raced out of the globe and were picked off by the Restoration point-defense, hardly one of the massive salvos the battleship squadron could have launched. Tork seemed to be concentrating on defense for the moment while he worked out his options.

Nevertheless Tork scored the next hit. An enemy missile

dodged all the interlaced defensive fire, and one of Conyngham's escorts erupted in a storm of blazing antimatter. Martinez snarled and ordered more missile fire.

He knew another warship had been destroyed because the radiation meter spiked, for all that the explosion was masked by the blazing screen that hid Tork's forces. More missiles launched, more fireballs blazed between Tork and the Restoration Fleet.

If he were Tork, Martinez thought, he'd use the obscuring fireballs to mask a change of course, then try to break out with his remaining forces, overwhelm Martinez or Chandra, then run for Wormhole One and Zanshaa. He found himself waiting for the move, Tork's huge ships appearing from behind the blazing screen, and he had the order for a response and a course change on the tip of his tongue.

What came instead were three enormous spikes on the radiation meter, each a few seconds apart, each far larger than any previous spike. All of Battleship Squadron One, he realized, had been annihilated as their combined defense suffered catastrophic failure.

Martinez felt his heart lift. There were gasps of surprise from the crew in the flag officer's station, then something like a suppressed cheer.

Martinez remained focused on the battle. Tork was dead, but the fighting wasn't over. The battleships' escorts—some of them, anyway—were still in the action.

"Flag to all enemy ships," he said. "Send in the clear. Message follows: The Supreme Commander is dead. It was Tork who started the war, and there is no longer any point in further combat. We can collaborate on creating the peace. I urge you to surrender."

There was no reply, and half a minute later he saw burning antimatter tails racing out of the fire globe. The remains of Tork's command had starburst, every ship for itself, and were flying from the disaster like fragments of a grenade.

They were, of course, doomed. Single ships couldn't survive the combined fire of the entire Fourth Fleet, and within mere minutes each was scattered like glowing confetti on the solar wind. As momentum carried the Fourth Fleet onward, the great fire globe that marked the death of the Righteous Fleet was left behind, expanding and dispersing to nothing.

Martinez tried to restrain the exultation that sang in his blood. The fight wasn't over. There were still the two enemy reserve squadrons on the fringes of the battlespace, overlooking the action like birds sitting on a wire.

"Flag to all ships," he said. "Well done, everyone, and congratulations on our shared victory. Form on your division leaders. Report to the flag the status of your ship, personnel, and missile reserves, and let the flag know if you need assistance."

"My lord!" Banerjee's voice mingled surprise, wonder, and bubbling joy. "Message from the enemy! It's in the clear!"

Martinez banished the virtual battlespace from his perceptions and watched as a Daimong appeared on one of his screens. He wore a vac suit without a helmet, and his round unblinking eyes stared from a gray face fixed in an expression of openmouthed astonishment. His voice was a musical chime.

"Senior Squadron Leader Rivven to the commander, Fourth Fleet. My colleague Squadron Leader An-dar and I were pleased to hear your request for collaboration in ending the war. We hope, however, not to *surrender*, but rather to *defect*. We are pleased to place ourselves, our ships, and our crews at your disposal. Please consider us your auxiliaries. We shall await your orders. End message."

This time the cheering in the flag officer's station was unrestrained. From Sula there was cynical laughter.

Martinez was trying to work out a response to Rivven's offer. He wrestled his helmet off his head and put it in the mesh bag by the side of his seat. He could feel sweat cooling on his forehead.

Martinez waited for the cheering to end and then told Santana to send his message in the clear.

"Fleet Commander Martinez to Squadron Leaders Rivven and An-dar: Your message is very welcome. I intend to speak in person to you very soon, but in the meantime I must give you some very inconvenient instructions. Please order your ships to fire all their missiles due north of your current position, each missile to explode at a safe distance. Hold your ships in readiness to be boarded by representatives of the Restoration. When we have more leisure, we shall meet and discuss items of mutual interest."

"He held back from the fight until he knew who won," Sula said. "I hope you're not going to trust him."

"I can trust him to follow his own self-interest," Martinez said. "I plan to offer him plenty of reasons to stay on our side."

"Well," Sula conceded, "there's no enemy left to keep us

from getting to Zanshaa, so I'd say that fact will loom large in his decisions."

Martinez called Dalkeith. "Congratulations, Captain. Could you train some cameras on those defecting squadrons? I need someone to count every missile as it's launched."

There was strain in Dalkeith's lisping voice. "I'll do that, Lord Fleetcom. But we have trouble in one of our missile bays. Bad trouble."

"What kind of trouble?" Martinez said. In the Fleet, you never wanted the word *trouble* connected with a part of the ship that held antimatter-powered weapons.

"I don't know," Dalkeith admitted. "I can't seem to get a complete story. They all tell me they're working on it."

"Have you sent anyone down there?"

"Who would I send?" Dalkeith said. "All the experienced weaponers are already in place. My weapons officer here in Command is new to the job."

"Right," Martinez said. "Stand by." He clicked to another channel, then told his comm, "Page Khalid Alikhan." Alikhan had spent thirty years in the Fleet and retired with the rank of master weaponer, and he was almost certainly the most experienced weapons specialist on the ship.

"My lord," Alikhan answered, "now is not the time."

"Can you give me a—?"

"*Not now.* End transmission."

Which left Martinez alone with his imagination, and his imagination was a very good one. One catastrophe after another played out in his mind.

The moment mortifying, he thought, if *Bombardment of*

Los Angeles managed to blow up now, a victim of its own munitions.

He had to restrain himself from jumping off his couch and rushing down to battery one to take command. That wasn't his job—*Los Angeles* wasn't his ship, it was Dalkeith's, and the ship had its full complement of weaponers trained to handle emergencies, all stationed in three Command rooms hardened against radiation. In battle and under high acceleration they would use large robots with powerful hydraulic arms to perform any necessary tasks.

They were trained, Martinez reminded himself, but without any actual experience in dealing with any kind of dangerous situation.

His commander key allowed him use of any camera on the ship, and he asked for the feed from weaponer Command Station One, which commanded battery one. He was relieved to see the weaponers all in their couches, all alive, all participating in an animated conversation. He checked the other two Command stations and found them all undamaged, though with about half the weaponers talking intently and the other half staring fixedly at their screens. He saw Alikhan in Station Two, reclined on his couch, his faceplate closed. He was talking while looking at one of his screens, but Martinez had no audio, and the video feed was of poor quality and told him nothing but that Alikhan was working on the problem.

Martinez decided to go straight to the source and turned to a camera looking out over battery one, receiving only a blank screen accompanied by the words *CAMERA MAL-FUNCTION.* The other camera showed nothing but a green-yellow murk. Was that *smoke?* Martinez wondered. Was *Los Angeles* actually on *fire?*

With the green-yellow cloud providing a background on which Martinez could let his imagination paint whatever disaster seemed most promising, his mind began to gnaw at the problem. He wondered what fire could cause smoke of that peculiar color. He wondered what catastrophe had caused the fire in the first place.

Missile launching systems were a weak point of a warship, and as a consequence they were overbuilt, designed to load and fire their weapons under extreme conditions, even if the ship was accelerating at fifteen gravities and being bathed in hard radiation. But a launcher was still a mechanical device and prone to the sort of malfunctions that could affect mechanical systems. Nor did the origin of the problem have to be mechanical: *Los Angeles* had been plagued with electric faults since its hasty conversion to a Terran ship, and of course there could have been a fault in the missile itself.

"I heard what Dalkeith said, Lord Fleetcom." Sula's voice. "What's going on?"

"I can't tell. Something big. Take a look at the video."

"I don't have access to that feed. I only have the tactical officer's key."

Martinez used his privileges to give her access to the video. Sula looked at the green murk in surprise.

"Ah. Hah," she said.

"Rivven's squadron, and that other one, have begun firing missiles," Banerjee reported.

"Very good," Martinez said. The problem with the defecting squadrons had just been assigned a lower priority.

Martinez called up another screen showing missile consumption and found that while batteries two and three had only 22 and 24 percent of their magazine stocks remaining, battery one had 47 percent. Whatever the problem was, it was preventing the battery from firing.

Martinez turned to Santana. "Flag to Division Two," he said. "Reduce acceleration to point five gee." That would make it easier to get personnel into the missile battery.

The weight on Martinez's chest eased. "Smoke's clearing," Sula said. "Someone's got the fans working."

Martinez turned to the battery one display and saw the murk was thinning. He waited, eyes fixed on his display, and then the last of the yellow-green mist was swept away, and he saw wreckage strewn across the open bay. One of the big six-armed robots was disabled, hanging from a stanchion by one of its remaining arms, and the parts of another robot seemed to have been blasted to bits and now constituted a layer of rubble on the deck. Every surface in the battery looked as if it had been gone over with a sledgehammer.

"We've got to clear that up," Martinez murmured. He imagined what would happen to all that wreckage if *Los Angeles* underwent any sudden, high-gravity maneuvers and realized that this was exactly what had happened, that the debris had been flying through the battery with every shift in course.

He contacted Dalkeith. "There's a considerable amount

of debris in missile battery one," he said. "It's been tearing all over the battery with every course change. We've going to have to send a party down there to secure it all somehow."

"What about the robots?"

"The big ones have been wrecked. I don't know what did it. You'll need to send all our mobile damage-control robots down there, with a work party to tell them what to do."

"Yes, my lord," Dalkeith said. "At once."

"Those squadrons are just *fountaining* missiles," Banerjee reported. "It's like a huge fireworks display." Martinez had lost interest in what Rivven was up to.

He paged Alikhan. "We'll be under reduced gravity for as long as necessary," he said. "Captain Dalkeith is sending a party to battery one to mop up debris there, and I thought you might care to join them."

"That debris includes a live missile, my lord," Alikhan said. "I will go at once."

Martinez felt his mouth go dry. "Fortune attend you," he said.

Live missile. Everyone on the ship should be holding their breath.

One of the two heavy doors leading into battery one jammed, presumably because the mechanism had been hammered by debris, but the other slid open and revealed weaponers in vac suits. These looked at the debris, then drew back to let a robot enter. The robot was box-shaped, featured powerful hydraulic arms, and moved on wheels, which soon buried themselves in the wreckage. The wheels spun hopelessly. Weaponers wrenched the robot free, then stepped into the room to clear as much of the debris out of the robot's way as possible. This involved tossing or sweeping the metallic carnage into piles to create lanes for the robot, which advanced with deliberation into the room.

The scene played out as a pantomime, because Martinez had no audio from the room.

A drizzle of hydraulic fluid fell gently from the broken robot hanging above. Martinez trained the camera until he could see the missile, half buried in wreckage, its red-and-white color scheme blackened by flames. He thought about that missile being hurled around the room and shuddered.

The Fleet had procedures for disposing of a misfired missile, and these involved opening a hatch, after which a cradle would roll out and the missile could be placed in it. The cradle would vanish back into the hatch and travel to a remotely powered workstation where the missile could be taken apart and its antimatter containers removed from the casing, which could then be safely discarded. Any attempt to remove the antimatter containers without the proper authorized hardware would result in a deliberate release of energy sufficient to kill anyone in the vicinity and wreck the tampering device, whatever it was. It could even wreck the *Los Angeles*, especially if the energy release hit the unfired missiles sitting in their tubes.

By now Martinez identified Alikhan standing among the weaponers—even in the shuffling walk adopted in light gee, his upright posture and brisk movements were perfectly recognizable even in a vac suit and helmet. He supervised clearing the rubble from around the missile, then brought up the robot to lift the missile in its arms and carry it to the disposal hatch.

Except that the hatch wouldn't open. Its mechanism had been battered by flying debris, and for a few moments the weaponers stood around the hatch discussing what to do with it. Alarm clattered in Martinez as he saw wrenches and pry bars being brought into the bay, and he was on the verge of sending an order not to start ripping open a critical piece of equipment, but Alikhan very clearly argued against the action, and eventually the pry bars were put aside. Alikhan made a proposal, accompanying it with illustrative arm gestures, and Martinez saw people nodding. The robot reversed and began moving out of the weapons bay, with two crew for escort.

Presumably the intention was for the missile to be taken to another of the weapons bays and disposed through a functioning hatch, but Martinez wasn't sure whether the long form of the missile could be maneuvered through the intervening corridors without getting jammed in a doorway or a corridor. Whoever was operating the robot would have to be very skillful.

The cleanup in the missile bay continued. More robots arrived and began picking up wreckage and dumping it in bins. Torches were deployed to cut up debris too large for the bins, and one accidentally caused a fire in some spilled lubricant until automatic extinguishers tracked the fire and triggered.

Then the broken robot, the one that had been hanging from a stanchion above the work party, lost its hold and began to fall. Maybe the draining hydraulic fluid had weakened its grip.

In half a gravity it fell more slowly than it might have, but the slower fall just gave Martinez more time to appreciate what was going to happen when it hit. *"Look out!"* he called, but he wasn't on a live audio circuit to anyone in the missile bay, and he only startled the others in the flag officer's station.

The robot came crashing down in utter silence, and even though *Los Angeles* was accelerating at only half a gravity, the machine still weighed tons, and Martinez watched as Alikhan and two other weaponers vanished under piles of cascading wreckage. He began unwebbing himself.

"Santana," he said, "tell Dalgleish to send stretcher parties and the ship's doctor to battery one." He unlocked his displays and pushed them above his head, then looked at Sula. "I'm going down there myself before we all blow up. I'm leaving you in charge here, and you have my authority to dispose the Fourth Fleet as needed."

Sula looked at him in surprise. "Yes, Lord Fleetcom."

He felt her eyes following him as he ran for the room's armored door.

CHAPTER 16

The accident had started with the failure of a missile to launch from its tube—the precise causes would be determined later, after an inquest. The chemical rockets that were to carry the missile safely into space had already ignited, and if allowed to burn in the tube would melt parts of the missile and possibly damage the antimatter container.

A switch tripped automatically, and the inner hatch opened, allowing the chemical rockets to burn straight into battery one—alarming and dangerous, but the area affected was hardened, and it wasn't nearly as dangerous as allowing a missile to run hot in the tube. Normal procedure was for a weaponer to use a robot to pull the missile from the tube, then hold it harmless until the chemical rockets exhausted themselves, after which the missile could be disposed and disassembled normally.

The robots resembled titanic sea creatures with a large array of tentacles, all hydraulically powered and strong enough to hold the robot in place against many gravities' acceleration.

There were two such robots in the battery, each controlled by an operator with several years of experience.

The operator of the first robot had run dozens of drills with a dummy missile, but he had never handled one actually belching fire before, and it hadn't occurred to him that he should be careful where to point it. He seized it with two of the robot arms and held it roughly at port arms, with the searing fire directed diagonally across the body of the robot. The blazing rocket exhaust sliced its way through the robot within seconds, hit the main hydraulic reservoir, and flash-boiled the fluid into a yellow-green fog that blinded the robot operators. The robot limbs, their fluid boiled away, failed completely, and the weakened robot came apart at the same moment. Half the robot, along with the missile, fell at three gravities' acceleration into the second robot, smashing it to rubble. After which, violent maneuvering by *Los Angeles* kept redistributing the wreckage at high speed over the battery.

In trying to reach battery one, Martinez found that all the ship's elevators had been locked down once the ship had gone to general quarters, and he needed his commander's card to override the lockdown and bring the elevator to the level of the flag officer's station. He took the elevator eight decks down to battery one and was greeted by the sight of one of the small robots cradling the battered missile, waiting for the elevator doors to open. Martinez ducked around the warhead, pushed past a weaponer standing by the robot, and walked straight to the battery.

Those weaponers still on their feet stood in attitudes of

shock. Dust drifted in the air. Martinez began to give orders, then realized that no one could hear him with their faceplates down. He had to reconfigure his comm so the weaponers could hear him, and by the time he'd succeeded the weaponers had recovered from their own trauma and begun to clear wreckage from the bodies lying under the fallen debris. With some assistance from the damage-control robots, the largest piece of wreckage was shifted, and the three bodies were revealed.

One was clearly dead, his helmet shattered along with his skull, but Alikhan and one other were still alive. Martinez knelt by Alikhan and looked through the cracked faceplate. Alikhan was pale and clammy and clearly in shock. One eye was open to reveal a pupil so dilated that it looked like a dark well leading directly into the brain. There was no response when Martinez tried to speak to him.

The ship's doctor arrived with a pair of assistants, and Martinez gestured her over. "This man is critically injured," he said. "He needs to go to sick bay immediately."

The doctor—with her wide green eyes, dark brown skin, and freckles—looked so young that it was hard to credit she'd even attended medical school, let alone graduated. "If he's badly injured," she said. "We don't want to move him right away. Moving him might kill or cripple him." She looked at Alikhan's feet and frowned. "Can you elevate his feet a little? That may help with the shock." Seething with impatience, Martinez found a piece of rubble and put it under Alikhan's heels. Meanwhile the doctor was using a specialized hand comm to read the vital signs automatically recorded by

Alikhan's suit. Then she paused, her lips moving in silence, and appeared to be reciting some kind of checklist to herself. Martinez wanted to scream at her to hurry. She looked up at him.

"His helmet's broken," the doctor said, "and he's breathing the air in here. How toxic is it?" She shook her head violently. "No. We'll get him out immediately." She gestured at a pair of stretcher-bearers.

Martinez followed the stretcher to the door, then realized the doctor wasn't following. He turned and saw the doctor crouched over the other living victim. He knew it was her job to look after *all* the injured, and he managed to resist the impulse to grab her and haul her to the sick bay. Instead he mutely followed the stretcher to the elevator, then up six decks to the sick bay. The room had a crisp disinfectant smell. Alikhan's helmet was removed by one assistant while another held his head gently, and an inflatable brace was placed around his neck. He was scanned without having to take him off the stretcher or get him out of his suit. The doctor arrived with a second stretcher, and the second victim took Alikhan's place in the scanner. The doctor viewed the scans while her assistants wrestled her out of her vac suit, then she recited more silent checklists to herself, and then stood.

"Let's get him out of the suit," she said.

They feared they would injure Alikhan by wrestling him out of his vac suit, and so some ingenious cutters were deployed to slice away the suit, along with the jumpsuit beneath. A drip was placed in each arm. Fast-healer hormones were injected, and Alikhan was covered by a viridian-green blanket to conserve his body heat. The doctor looked at the scans again and frowned, then turned to Martinez.

"There are broken bones, but bones heal quickly these days," she said. "My assistants will strap him up. There may be some internal bleeding in the abdominal cavity, but the evidence is ambiguous and I don't want to go in unless I have to. What concerns me most is a subdural hemorrhage in his brain, so I've lowered his blood pressure to lessen the bleed, and I'll keep him monitored to see if surgery is warranted."

"I see," Martinez said. His tongue seemed unusually thick, and he had to make an unusual effort to speak around it.

She gave him a curious look. "Is he a particular friend of yours?"

"He's been in my household for fifteen years or more," he said.

She nodded, then turned to Alikhan. "I'd advise his retiring from active duty after this. After this, any high accelerations could be hazardous."

"Yes," he said. "Thank you."

She called up the scans of her other patient. Martinez stood by Alikhan, still pale beneath his blanket. He held out a hand, then hesitated because he didn't know which parts of Alikhan were damaged. He decided to put his hand on Alikhan's arm, which at least had no bruising. Alikhan's skin was still cool.

I am no longer young, my lord, he remembered Alikhan saying. *Some days I think I would do better to remain here on the ring . . .*

Martinez had talked Alikhan onto *Los Angeles*, and all the while wondered if he was killing him.

He had an answer to that question now.

"Well," he said to Alikhan, "you heard the doctor. We'll carry you to Zanshaa for the victory parade, and you'll never have to leave the planet again."

Alikhan remained unconscious, his expression a little disdainful, his chin held high by the neck brace. His curling mustachios had suffered no damage.

"I promise," Martinez said, and he felt the hollowness of his words as he turned to return to his duties.

SULA ASSEMBLED THE reports that came in and discovered that the Fourth Fleet now consisted of seventy-eight ships, of which nineteen were too badly damaged to be able to keep up with the rest. Two she suspected were derelict, because they were tumbling and nothing had been heard from them since the fight. Of the fifty-nine remaining, at least twenty would need a dockyard before being able to fight at full capacity.

Missile reserves averaged 18 percent.

In addition there were the sixteen defectors that hovered on the edge of the action. She supposed they could be counted as part of the Restoration now, at least in theory.

Pinnaces rejoined their ships. Unlike the battles in the Naxid War, most of the pinnaces had survived—a larger percentage than the warships themselves, and homes had to be found for the pilots launched from ships that had been lost.

Sula detached ships to aid the damaged warships, and to get a closer look at the ships tumbling away into the void. Other ships were detached to board and inspect the defectors. Sula pitied those who would have to board the Daimong ships and endure the rotting-flesh stench of the close-packed crew.

Fortunately other races had long experience with Daimong, and ships' pharmacies stocked a variety of drugs that would deaden the sense of smell.

"Message, urgent and personal, from Captain Vijana," said Santana.

"Let's see it then," Sula said.

Vijana's pointed face and burning eyes appeared on one of Sula's displays.

"You survived!" Sula said. "Well done."

"Surely you're not going to accept those monsters' surrender!" he said. "Wipe them out when we've got the chance!"

"We might find their ships useful," Sula pointed out. "This war might not be over."

"Then kick them into space and take over their ships!" Vijana said. "This is all a part of some plan! They'll stab us in the back the first chance they get!"

"You think it's a conspiracy?" Sula said. "A conspiracy that begins with sacrificing over four hundred of their own ships in order to get an inferior force close to us? I can't help but think that's unlikely."

Vijana snarled. "You're not going to trust them, are you?"

"No, I'm not." An idea occurred to her, and she grinned. "No," she said, "I'm going to compromise them so thoroughly that the Zanshaa government won't take them back no matter how hard they beg."

"They're up to something," Vijana warned.

Sula lost patience. "Lord Naaz," she said, "you're really addressing this protest to the wrong person. You should be talking to Fleet Commander Martinez."

"They said he was unavailable."

"He'll be available eventually. Talk to him then, because right now I'm busy." She ended the transmission.

She was finding Vijana more exhausting than battle.

It was then that she remembered that no report had been made to Harzapid. Raw images of the battle would have been broadcast through the wormhole gate, but there would have been little context, and maybe, with all the fireballs and radio blooms, Harzapid couldn't even know which side had won.

It was really Martinez's job to make a report, but he had run off to the weapons bay, and if he was actually involved in saving the ship she didn't want to interrupt him. Sula took a few minutes to compose a message, then turned to Banerjee and Santana.

"Message to Fleet Commander Chen," she said. "Use the Command cipher of the day. Message follows." She took a breath, then looked into the camera. "Lady Fleet Commander, on behalf of Fleet Commander Martinez I am pleased to report a complete victory over the forces of Lord Tork. His entire fleet has been annihilated, with the exception of sixteen ships under Squadron Leaders Rivven and An-dar, which have joined the forces of the Restoration. Our own casualties are severe—a report will be attached—but in a short time we will advance on Zanshaa with something like seventy-four ships, which should be enough to overwhelm the twenty or so that Tork left in the system.

"In the meantime, we need as many replacement missiles as possible. Our stocks are very low, so please send supplies as soon as you manage it."

The message had been sent when she received a communication from Dalkeith.

"Can we stand down from quarters?" she asked. "We can maintain a state of high alert in Command, but I think we can safely send most of our crew to their dinner."

And me to the shower, Sula thought. She was smelling body odor wafting up the open neck of her vac suit and wasn't enjoying it.

But she was stuck here till Martinez returned.

"Secure from general quarters, then," she said. "What's the status of the problem in the weapons bay?"

"The missile was shifted to another battery and disposed of properly. Weaponers are safely disassembling it now, and all that remains is cleanup."

Missile? Sula thought. That certainly explained Martinez's dash to battery one.

"Do you know where Fleet Commander Martinez is right now?" she asked.

"No. He hasn't been in touch with me."

"Thank you. End message."

The first lieutenant's voice barked from speakers to tell the crew they were relieved from quarters. Sula sent a message to the Fourth Fleet permitting them to do the same.

"Page Fleet Commander Martinez," Sula told her comm.

Martinez took a few moments to answer. "Yes, Lady Sula," he said.

He didn't sound like a commander who had just won the largest battle in the history of the empire. He sounded like someone so beaten he was barely able to set one foot in front of another.

"I've been managing the Fourth Fleet as you asked," Sula said. "Shall I make a report?"

"Has anyone started shooting?"

She smiled. "No. Though Vijana is urging me to wipe out the defectors."

"Well, unless he starts, you can secure from quarters and report to me later, in my office."

"Very well."

"End transmission."

Well, Sula thought, that *was interesting*. But she'd received permission to get out of her suit and take a shower, and she intended to take advantage of it.

She unwebbed and stood, bouncing slightly in the low gravity. She put one hand on the acceleration cage and turned to the signals staff. "There's going to be a lot of signals traffic," she said, "and I'm going to have to leave all three of you to deal with it. I'll have someone bring up some food and drink for you. Alert me if any important messages come in, but otherwise put everything in my queue."

"Yes, my lady," said Santana, and Sula made her way out.

In her quarters she found Macnamara and Spence waiting, and she sent Macnamara to her kitchen to make up some
sandwiches and drinks to send to the signalers back in the flag
officer's station, while Spence assisted her in removing her vac
suit. She took a few extra blissful moments in the shower and
then dressed in a clean undress uniform and went to Martinez's office, moving in the hopping shuffle standard in low gee.

She found him behind his desk, paging fitfully through
his messages with a distracted look on his face. Torminel
wrestlers grappled on the walls. Martinez still wore his vac
suit, with the gloves and helmet on his desk. He rose as she
entered and spread his hands, as if in apology.

"Alikhan usually helps me take the suit off," he said.

"Is Alikhan still in the weapons bay?"

Martinez's face was grim. "He was critically injured," he
said. "The doctor is doing her best."

"Ah. Hah. I'm sorry." She raised her hands. "I can help you
with the vac suit."

She helped him wrestle off the top half, revealing the
sweat-soaked jumpsuit underneath. She tried not to recoil at
the sour smell.

"You can manage the bottom half yourself," she said. "And
I'd recommend a shower."

He looked down at himself as if he'd never seen his body
before. "I'll be back in a moment."

He went into his quarters, and while he coped with the
lower part of the vac suit and the sanitary gear, she looked at
her message queue. Some of the damaged ships were request-

ing particular parts or specialists for certain kinds of repair, and she did her best to coordinate a response.

She finished the job and studied for a moment the wrestlers on the wall, comparing the techniques with what she'd learned in the Fleet's close-combat course during the last war.

The difference, she decided, was lethal intent.

Martinez returned from the shower. He too wore undress and trailed a faint odor of lemongrass-scented shampoo. He sat behind his desk and glanced at his displays.

"You should be opening a bottle of champagne," Sula said. "We've just won the greatest victory in the annals of the Fleet."

He looked at his display. "It could also be argued that we suffered the Fleet's second-greatest defeat," he said. "A hundred and seventy-five ships! That's seventy percent lost. And we'll lose more in the next few days, as we find which of the damaged ships have to be written off."

"We've still got enough force to take Zanshaa," Sula said, "and then we're in charge, and the people who started this will pay."

"They'd better," Martinez said. He was grim, a little muscle twitching along his jawline.

Sula looked at Martinez and felt a soft surprise. By now she'd expected him to be all ego, preening and celebrating his own genius, but instead he was somber, near-overwhelmed by the tally of the dead.

"Shall I give you my report?" she asked.

"Certainly."

She gave it, including the fact she'd sent a message to Harzapid, and as she recited facts and statistics from memory her eyes drifted again to the Torminel grapplers, their bodies caught in attitudes of strain and struggle, their eyes blazing with fury and their lips drawn back to reveal snarling teeth. Frozen in enmity, straining through an eternal opposition.

Martinez listened in silence, his eyes fixed on something a hundred paces away.

Sula finished, and there was a moment of silence. "Any questions?" she asked.

His eyes went to her. "No, thank you. That was very thorough—and thank you for sending the report to Lady Michi. I should have done it myself, of course."

She stood. "I'll leave, then, unless you have instructions for me."

He offered a faint smile. "I don't, but next time I forget to do something, I'm sure you'll step into the breach."

Martinez rose and walked around his desk to show her to the door. Her skin prickled with his nearness. Sula waited, hesitant, suddenly aware that for some time she had been *listening* for something, some throb of a violin or a chant of a derivoo, some whisper from a distant world. He paused by her, puzzled perhaps.

"Must I do *everything*?" she murmured and hooked a hand behind Martinez's neck and drew his lips down to hers. He didn't seem surprised at all. His arms went around her, and his kiss was devouring and ferocious.

At last she heard what she had been listening for, the triumphant cry of a derivoo that turned her blood to scorching fire. She thought of the cool surfaces of porcelain, the red sunrise over the Sea of Marmara, warships dying in fire.

There didn't seem to be a lot of point in talking. He half carried her to his sleeping cabin, and there they tore at their clothing, tumbled onto the bed, and coupled in silent fury.

How long has it been? Sula wondered. *How many years?*

Too many. She peaked a second before Martinez did, and from that elation of heart and body she came back to the world slowly. Martinez lay gasping in her arms. She felt a surge of triumph, as if she'd just won a second war.

"I want you to know," she said as she looked into his eyes, "that this time I'm not running away."

He took a moment to absorb this. "Yes," he said. "It's like you said. We'll be in charge, and then we'll make the rules to suit ourselves."

She kissed his jawline, and then her senses widened to take in the room, the dim light, the tangled bedclothes, the pictures of Martinez's family obscuring the Torminel pornography. Her eyes narrowed as she looked at Terza.

If this fails, she thought, *if he wrecks this somehow, I'll enjoy telling Terza all about it.*

Another tide of triumph rose in her, and she could barely restrain herself from laughing aloud.

Martinez raised his head and cocked one eyebrow. "What's so amusing?"

Sula draped an arm across her forehead, cutting off Terza from view. "The whole fleet is waiting for orders," she said, "and here we are, making them wait."

He kissed her shoulder. "They can wait a little longer."

"I think the first thing you should do," she said, "is compose a message of congratulations to the Fourth Fleet. You need to tell them how brave and brilliant they were." She moved her arm from over her eyes and looked at him. "Unless you'd rather I did it."

"No." He sighed. "I'll do it right away. But I hope you'll join me for supper."

"Oh yes," she said. She could see Terza's portrait over his shoulder. "Yes, I will."

CHAPTER 17

"Well," Martinez said. "We've won, but we've lost a lot of friends. You can read all that in the updated report I sent an hour ago."

He looked into the camera and imagined Terza gracefully reclined on a sofa in her brown uniform, her dark eyes focused on the screen, and wondering if her husband had changed somehow, and if so what changed him.

"Tell Chai-chai to send me pictures of trees, or birds, or clouds," he said. "Anything but space and planets and warships." He gave the camera—gave Terza—what he concluded was a helpless look. "I'm too busy to send a longer message," he said. "But I wanted to send you something . . . Just from me to you."

He ended the message and was thankful he no longer had to try to project sincerity to a camera.

Martinez hadn't exaggerated when he said that he was fully occupied, but his mental image of Terza faded slowly. Displays glowed in his desk and on the walls. Tables, facts, statistics, and reports whirled in his mind, alongside the faces and names of those who had been lost. It seemed as if Death had made a point of stalking his friends and subordinates.

No less than four of his officers on the old *Illustrious* had been killed. Fulvia Kazakov, his first lieutenant; his third lieutenant Ahmad Husayn; his sixth officer Juliette Corbigny; and his former signals lieutenant Lady Ida Lee, all promoted to command of their own warships, and now dead along with their crews.

Ismir Falana of his *Courage*, Garcia of the old *Corona*. Garcia had never had any luck, having been captured on the first day of the Naxid War, and then finally achieved command rank only to die in her first engagement.

Carmody had not been a great friend, and was certainly no genius, but he'd been a courageous officer, and Martinez was sorry to lose him. Lady Starkey was gone—Martinez didn't know her well, but she and Nikki Severin had established a reputation as the lovebirds of the Fleet, and Martinez knew that Severin must be crushed.

Ari Abacha, his old friend, had been in command of *Striker*, now severely damaged and tumbling off into the void. Martinez had little hope for his survival, or that of his crew.

Lord Jeremy Foote, perhaps unfortunately, was still among the living.

Martinez had sent the triumphant message to his command that Sula had suggested, and he'd told the Fourth Fleet just how brilliant and courageous they'd been. By the time he was done speaking, he realized he'd meant every word of it.

Martinez swallowed the last of his coffee, bitter and cold. His cook Marivic Mangahas had delivered the coffee herself, since Alikhan was unavailable. His requests for updates on Alikhan's condition had been so frequent that the doctor had finally told him—quite sharply—that if there were any change in Alikhan's status, she'd send him an alert. With that he had to be content.

His sleeve display flashed with a message from Santana. "Captain Abacha wishes to report to you in person."

His heart gave a surprised surge. "Yes," he responded, and Ari Abacha's image appeared on his sleeve. Abacha wore a vac suit with the helmet off, and there was a feverish gleam in his eyes. Martinez transferred the image onto his desk display.

"By the all, Gare," Abacha said. "I've had adventures!"

Abacha didn't look as if his adventures had been particularly trying. His hair had a glossy sheen, his mustache was perfectly groomed, and his chocolate skin was without bruise or blemish. But then he had a hairdresser on his staff, as well as a personal bartender, so perhaps he'd been tidied and relaxed before he sent his message.

"Are you on *Striker*?" Martinez asked.

Abacha continued to grin at him for a while—he was three light-seconds away—and then Abacha's eyes widened. "*Striker*'s lost, Gare," he said. "Depressurized, and a maneuvering thruster jammed full on, so we were pitching end over end. The other thrusters were knocked out and we were out of control and useless, so I ordered everyone who could get to a shuttle to evacuate. Gee forces would have been ferocious fore and aft, and the only crew to get away were in the central part."

"We didn't get a report."

Another six seconds passed before the answer came.

"Communications melted in the blast, my friend!" A hand came into the frame holding a cocktail glass, and Abacha took it. He took a hearty swig, then turned back to the camera. "We had two shuttles and my own personal cutter. One of the shuttles was slag, but I got most of the survivors into one, and when they launched I got on board the cutter with whoever was left." He took another swig. "But we couldn't get the blasted thing to work! We had no navigators, no pilots, no engine techs—they were all on the other shuttle! The shuttle tumbled as badly as *Striker*, and we couldn't correct!"

"Couldn't you call for help?"

Seconds ticked by, and then Abacha sighed. "We couldn't get the signals console to work."

Martinez stared at him. "Ari," he said, "when we were together at the Commandery, you were a *communications specialist*."

Abacha looked offended when the response reached him. "Gare," he said, "I can communicate with signals perfectly well, but that doesn't mean I'm a *mechanic*."

"So where are you now?"

Abacha didn't wait for the question to reach him, but started his story anyway. "The shuttle sent out a distress signal, and *Staunch* picked them up. Then *Staunch* looked for us and found us, so now I'm a guest of Captain Hui. We're going on now toward *Striker*, in hopes we can rescue any crew remaining." He bit his lip. "It's going to be tricky trying to stabilize *Striker*, though."

"Remind the captain how we and Sula rescued Blitsharts," Martinez told him.

When this reached Abacha, he took a few seconds to puzzle his answer. "Harder to do with a couple of big ships," Abacha said, "but we'll manage what we can." He finished his cocktail and held out the glass for a refill.

"Best of luck," Martinez said. "Give my regards to Captain Hui."

"I will, Gare." A bright smile creased his face. "Say, she's quite the looker, isn't she?"

"I suppose she is."

"Let's have drinks soon, hey?"

"Certainly. End message."

The orange end-stamp filled the screen. Martinez shook his head. Apparently Ari Abacha was unchanged by war, battle, and the loss of his ship. All he looked forward to was the next cocktail party, or the next pretty face.

Martinez found himself envying Abacha's simplicity.

There was a knock on his office door, and the next pretty face entered. At the sight of Sula he felt his blood surge, and the breath caught in his throat. He rose, and Sula closed the door behind her, then took off her uniform cap and tossed it casually onto his desk. Slowly, in the half-gravity, it landed on his coffeepot and hung on the spout. Her lips twitched in amusement.

"Forgive me for not saluting," she said and stepped close to kiss him. Her fragrance—lilac-scented soap—spun in his senses. Their arms went around each other. The kiss was like a slow-motion explosion in his head.

Somewhere in the deep recesses of his mind, he was aware of a throb of sadness. He knew that this was going to hurt people, people he cared about; but the person he cared *most* about—the woman he'd wanted from the first second, ten or more years ago—was in his arms, and all other considerations had shattered into fragments at the first touch of her lips.

After a few moments, they both had to come up for air. "I've asked Mangahas to prepare supper for two," he said. "So shall we eat now, or would you rather—"

"I'm starving," Sula said.

They went to the dining room and sat at the narrow end of the wedge-shaped table. Martinez used his sleeve display to tell Santana to contact him with only the most urgent communications and put the rest in his queue. Mangahas bustled out to pour Martinez's wine, and to ask Sula what she wanted to drink. "Can you manage lemonade?" Sula asked.

"Certainly, my lady."

Mangahas bustled out again, and Martinez paused a moment to view the woman seated next to him. Her brilliant green eyes looked at him with a degree of speculation, as if she hadn't quite worked him out yet. For his own part, Martinez felt perfectly transparent.

"We should share Macnamara," Sula said, and the thought was so unexpected that it took Martinez aback. Sula cackled. "Not *that* way," Sula said. "Honestly, you are too easy."

"Apparently I am."

"Until you can replace Alikhan," Sula said, "Macnamara can serve at table, brush your uniforms, disinfect your vac suit, and polish your silver buttons."

"Isn't he doing all that for you?"

"He and Spence are underemployed. I like doing things

myself." She cocked an eyebrow at him. "You've never been without servants, have you?"

"No, I haven't," Martinez said, then corrected himself. "Well, at the Nelson Academy our dormitory complex shared one old retired rigger who kept things clean and picked up after us."

She was amused. "That's pretty much the definition of a servant, you know."

"Yes, well." Martinez cleared his throat. "He wasn't *my* servant, that's my point." He smiled at her. "I *do* know how to hang up clothes, you know. Fold shirts neatly. I've been known to wash a cup now and again."

"Clearly a man of great accomplishment."

He looked at her. "I thought about making the bed," he said, "but I decided to leave it in its current disorder. Maybe I wanted to preserve a recent memory."

Her green eyes sparkled. "Or make new ones."

"Yes," he said. "That, too."

Mangahas entered with Sula's lemonade. "I can bring in the soup, if you're ready," she said.

"Lady Sula is starving," Martinez said.

What Mangahas produced wasn't soup, exactly, but a small bowl of rice congee with crispy chicken and ginger. Sula ate with zest, and Martinez enjoyed watching her unalloyed pleasure in the meal.

He didn't eat more than a few spoonfuls. Desire for the woman next to him seemed to have dulled his other appetites.

The congee was followed by a dish of pickled vegetables, and then by pork. "What is this sauce?" Sula asked.

"Adobo," Martinez said. "We have it on Laredo, but I hardly see it away from home."

"Did you teach Mangahas your family recipe?"

"I don't know any family recipes."

Sula returned her attention to her plate. "Well, it's delicious, wherever she learned it."

Dessert was a custard with candied taswa fruit. Sula spooned into it with eyes glittering. Martinez finished his second glass of wine and thanked Mangahas.

Mangahas left the decanter of wine, refreshed Sula's lemonade, and carried the dirty dishes away. Martinez decided he needed no more wine and put the stopper in the decanter.

His greatest victory. The shocking loss of friends and colleagues. Alikhan fallen. Sula in his arms. And all in just a few hours.

Sula looked at him. "Tell me about Laredo," she said.

He considered the request. "It's a whole world. Rather a large subject."

"Tell me about your bit of it, then."

So he did. His ambitious father finding new ways to make new fortunes. His dreamy, romantic mother who named her children from characters out of novels. The shaded country house on the Rio Hondo with its verandas and the stable of Lord Martinez's antique automobiles. The imposing town house on a tree-lined square. The lake house. The ocean house. The big sailing yacht, the smaller motorboat. His older brother, his three younger sisters.

"Was Roland always so . . ." Sula hesitated. "So *Roland*?"

"Pretty much. He was so far above me that I was always surprised when he paid me any attention, let alone a compliment."

"And your sisters?"

"They were a pack of chattering little girls when I left Laredo, and when I met them in Zanshaa, they were formidable young women. It was quite a surprise."

"And they outnumbered you."

"That was intimidating." He glanced at her "And your childhood? You were on Zanshaa?" And immediately Martinez kicked himself, because he knew her childhood had ended when her parents were executed, flayed alive for defrauding the government.

"Sorry," he said. "I wasn't thinking."

"That's all right," Sula said. "I don't remember much about that time."

For good reason, he thought, and then his sleeve display chimed. It was Santana, and since Santana had been told not to disturb him unless the message was urgent, Martinez was obliged to accept it. He told Santana to put the signal through, and his sleeve display lit with the image of Captain Hui, Ari Abacha's host.

"Lord Fleetcom," she said, "I've caught up to *Striker*, and I regret to report that no rescue seems possible. The ship is not only pitching, it's yawing and rolling as well. I'm surprised it's still in one piece. I can't grapple to *Striker* without matching her motion, and pitching like that would make most of my ship uninhabitable, and the odds are high that there would be a collision and my own ship would suffer damage." Hui looked into the camera and visibly steeled herself. "I'd like to request permission to destroy *Striker* with a missile."

"Does Captain Abacha concur?"

After the six-second delay, Hui responded. "He doesn't want to have a part in destroying his ship. But he hasn't objected."

Martinez couldn't blame him. He wouldn't have wanted to give the order destroying any of his earlier commands, either.

"Can we see some video of *Striker*?" Sula asked, looking over Martinez's shoulder.

"That was Lady Sula," Martinez explained. "Can you send us video of the *Striker*?"

Hui hesitated. "Ye-es. Stand by." She switched channels and began giving instructions to someone off-camera.

There was a lengthy pause in which Martinez shifted the image to one of the wall displays, and then the image shifted to the darkness of space, with *Striker* whirling like a pinwheel against a background of stars. "Oh no," Sula murmured.

Damage was plain to see, with parts of the ship torn or melted and open to space. The energies that had blasted through the ship would have annihilated anyone they encountered, but theoretically people in hardened bunkers, like the weaponers' shelters, might have survived, as Abacha had survived in Command. Martinez and Sula studied *Striker*'s whirling image for a quarter of an hour, then tried to mate salt and pepper shakers in hopes of imagining ways of getting the two cruisers grappled in order to moderate its uncontrolled motion and search the ship for survivors.

"No," Sula concluded finally. "It can't be done." *Striker* could prove fatal to *Staunch*, the collision so damaging that Hui's ship would be sent to a dockyard for repairs or even destroyed.

"Agreed," Martinez said. "Captain Hui?"

After an interval, Hui appeared onscreen. "Yes, Lord Fleetcom?"

"We concur," Martinez said. "You can't do anything for *Striker*. You have permission to destroy *Striker*, and then return to your squadron."

Six seconds later, they watched as Hui's face registered a mixture of sadness and resolution. "Yes, Lord Fleetcom," she said. "At once."

The orange end-stamp filled the screen. Martinez sighed, turned off the wall screen, and turned to Sula. "Well," he said. "We're now down to seventy-seven ships."

She put her arm around his shoulders, something she hadn't been able to do with Hui and assorted signals personnel watching. "I'm not very good at offering comfort to people," she said, and put her head on his shoulder.

"You're doing just fine."

Her green eyes turned up to him. "My own comfort comes from—I don't know—things that happen to be beautiful."

"You have your porcelain collection," he said.

"Yes."

"And Marivic Mangahas's cooking."

She laughed. "Yes."

"I have very little beauty around me," he said, "only pictures of Torminels wrestling."

"You should have brought something with you."

He looked at her. "I have something beautiful now."

She dropped her eyes. "But I'm still rubbish at comforting people."

He put his arms around her. "You just need to try a little harder."

They kissed for a long moment. Their earlier encounter had been fast and urgent, the collision of two desperate and hungry people; but this kiss seemed almost reflective, perhaps profound. It was like the difference between street food and a wine tasting.

After a pleasing few moments, Martinez suggested they retire to his sleeping cabin.

"I hear it has an untidy bed," Sula said.

"It does," he said.

"We can make it even more untidy."

"I hope we will," Martinez answered.

They did. Locked in a complicated embrace, looking into the subdued green fire of her half-closed eyes, he wondered where their lost ten years had gone.

Here, he thought. *They're right here.*

CHAPTER 18

Alikhan hadn't regained consciousness, but his color was better, and he seemed to lie comfortably under his viridian Fleet-issued blanket. His eyes were slitted very slightly open, as if he were silently supervising the medical bay, but his eyes were motionless behind the lids. A neck brace still held his chin high, and over his hair he wore a net of detectors that gave a picture of the interior of his skull.

The brain bleed had been controlled. Broken bones were strapped or splinted. Lacerations had been glued back together. Save for the uncomfortable fact that he hadn't awakened, Alikhan was healing.

His appearance seemed wrong, but that was because when the attendants had washed his face, the wax he used to curl his mustachios had washed out, and the mustachios now lay flat against his cheeks.

Martinez touched the cool skin of his shoulder. "Well," he said, "you won't be seeing Zanshaa for a while. We've decided it's better not to subject you to the high gees and maneuvers necessary to get to Zanshaa, so we'll be transferring you to one of the ships heading for Harzapid. They'll be burning at one gee or less for the entire journey, and you'll be in a hospital sooner than if you stay with *Los Angeles*."

Martinez waited for a few seconds, half expecting Alikhan to respond, but the silence was broken only by the shuffling of one of the ward's attendants as he passed by Alikhan's station.

"I'll be supervising your transfer to make sure they won't drop you," Martinez added, "and—"

He fell silent as an alarm began to chatter. He looked wildly at the displays behind Alikhan's bed and saw cursors drawing jagged pictures on their screens. He had no idea what that meant but terror touched his nerves.

The attendant who had just passed bounded back on the run as more alarms began to sing. The attendant took one look at the displays and said, "You should leave, my lord. It's about to get very busy in here."

Martinez backed away reluctantly, and the doctor knocked against his shoulder as she ran to Alikhan's side. Other aides arrived, and Martinez shifted to a far corner of the medical bay, where he stood next to a cart filled with cleaning supplies that tinged the air with the scent of disinfectant.

There was frantic activity around Alikhan involving the deployment of more remote detectors, a cart of surgical equipment being rolled to his side, and an oxygen mask that, when placed over his face, automatically sent tubes crawling down his trachea. Alikhan's chest began to rise and fall to a rhythm not his own. The doctor reacted swiftly to each development without having to run checklists in her head. Electrodes were applied to the chest, and the doctor called out commands to increase the voltage.

The activity lasted only a few minutes. Martinez could tell from the slump of the doctor's shoulders that the brief battle was over. The alarm still wailed up and down his nerves, blocking the sadness he knew would come as his adrenaline ebbed.

The aides began to disassemble Alikhan's station, retrieving the equipment and breaking it down. The doctor walked slowly to Martinez. He saw no sympathy in her eyes, but something closer to frustration and anger.

"I'm sorry, Lord Fleetcom," she said. "It was an intraparenchymal bleed—in the brain stem. The bleed wrecked the vagus nerve, which regulates breathing and blood circulation. There was nothing anyone could have done. For all intents and purposes, he was dead by the time I reached him. I could have kept him on the respirator, but the heart had already stopped and there was no point."

"Thank you, Doctor," Martinez said. He looked over her shoulder at Alikhan, motionless and unnaturally pale on his bed.

"I'll send you an official report and a copy of the death certificate," she said. "I'll append video of the bleed as seen by the sensors."

"I don't think I'd care to view it," Martinez said.

"I'm staff, I'm not in your chain of command," the doctor said. "I have my own superiors who want every casualty documented."

"Well," said Martinez. "Do what you must."

THREE HOURS LATER came the double funeral, Alikhan and the other weaponer who had died in the same accident. The bodies would be shot out an airlock and burned to atoms by the cruiser's fiery tail. Both had been placed in viridian-green body bags. Martinez had found Alikhan's medals in a box in his sleeping cabin and made sure the box was placed in the bag. He felt he heard Alikhan's voice. *Some days I think I would do better to remain here on the ring . . .*

Yes, Martinez thought. *Absolutely.*

The other weaponer who died in the battle was a volunteer. Martinez hadn't talked him on board the warship, like he'd strong-armed Alikhan aboard *Los Angeles* against Alikhan's better judgment.

The airlock atrium was small and held only a few people, officers and a delegation of senior petty officers with mustachios brandished like weapons. Video cameras broadcast the ceremony for any of the crew who wished to watch. Martinez stood at attention next to Sula. Dalkeith, in charge of the ceremony as ship's captain, read the funeral service in her child's voice, ending with the words, *"Life is brief, but the Praxis is eternal. Let us all take comfort and security in the wisdom that all that is important is known."*

Never had Martinez taken less comfort in that phrase.

Dalkeith turned to the petty officer standing by the airlock. "Proceed, Miss Srisuk."

Lights blinked above the airlock as its air was evacuated, then a hum as the outer door opened. Srisuk touched a code into her hand comm, then turned to Dalkeith and braced.

"The airlock is empty, Lady Captain."

Dalkeith gave a signal and the ship's speakers began to intone the melancholy opening chords of Seekrin's "Elegy."

"The service is complete," Dalkeith said. "The funeral party is dismissed."

People braced, then began to drift away. Martinez thanked Dalkeith, then looked at the crowd congregating around the elevator and decided to take the stairs. He turned to Sula. "Join me in a climb?"

"Why not?"

The helical staircase, one of two that connected the engine control rooms aft to the docking probe station at the bow, was narrow and steep here, not the grand wood-paneled and brass-railed magnificence it became on the officers' decks. Martinez's legs worked the stairs mechanically, plodding upward. Sula followed.

"I'm sorry about Alikhan," she said. "I didn't know him well, but he seemed a fine gentleman."

"He was."

"At least he died trying to help the ship. I don't think he would have liked one of those homes for retired petty officers."

"I don't suppose he would," Martinez said. "But he wouldn't have ever had to go to such a place—I would have gone on employing him at home."

Martinez found himself breathless as he wound upward. His exercise routine emphasized muscle building to counter high gravities, and at home he'd add a cardiovascular component. But on the ship he'd mostly been fighting real gravities, and aerobics were difficult to manage in the confined quarters and with his schedule.

He decided to start taking the stairs whenever possible, just to get his wind back.

"I'd feel better," Martinez said, "if I weren't hosting a dinner party later today."

"We'll feel better once it's over, that's certain."

The dinner was a social necessity. Around Martinez's wedge-shaped table would be all the surviving division and squadron commanders, including the defectors Rivven and An-dar. It would be the first chance Martinez had to gauge their attitude toward the Restoration, and to gauge as well his other commanders' attitude toward the defectors. He could only hope that Vijana wouldn't be openly hostile.

They came to a landing, and the scent of lemon polish told Martinez he'd arrived in the glossy paneled quarters of the officers. A broader set of stairs opened in front of him. Martinez checked his sleeve display.

"Apparently I have over a hundred messages to deal with," he said.

"You can route some of them to me," Sula said. "You need a secretary now more than a tactical officer."

"If you're willing." He headed for the broad, brass-railed stairs, then looked over his shoulder at her. "Thank you."

"I'll see you at dinner," she said. "And again, I'm sorry about Alikhan."

"Me, too." *At least*, he thought, *Alikhan had no family*, and so Martinez would be spared the agony of writing condolence messages to his wife and children.

He would have to write enough of them in the days to come.

SEVERIN GAVE A dinner to remember the dead. His squadron of eight ships had lost three, along with all their crews. He set places at dinner for the three lost captains, with a candle and a photo next to their plates.

He couldn't bear to look at a picture of Lady Starkey for the length of a dinner, and so instead of using a photo, he wound a Lorkin puppet around the candlestick.

Puppetry is pain, he thought.

At the beginning of the meal he offered a toast to the dead, which his captains solemnly echoed. With the exception of the one woman who didn't drink, the others had seconds or thirds on their cocktails, then began gulping wine. They were more uneasy than Severin under the gaze of the dead and were bolting their alcoholic anesthesia as fast as they decently could.

Severin led his captains into a discussion of how they thought the empire would change after the war and found they hadn't spared a great deal of time considering the problem. If anything, they expected the postwar period would be just like the prewar period, with a stable government under Lord Saïd, and nothing else changed except for the execution of certain members of the Gruum government.

"But if nothing changes," Severin said, "how do we keep something like this war from happening again? We've had two wars in ten years; what's to stop a third from breaking out?"

There were few answers. "Maybe we need the Shaa again," one captain said. "I mean, not the Shaa, obviously—but someone in that role."

"The Naxids tried to make themselves into the Shaa," another pointed out. "We didn't follow *them*."

"Who has the authority to become the Shaa?" Severin asked. "If a group declared themselves the next Great Masters, who would respect that? Who would obey them?"

The first captain spread her hands. "I can't say."

"I can," said another. He was perhaps a little more drunk than the others. "If the new Shaa are *us*—that is, the Fleet." He hesitated, remembering his host. "And the Exploration Service, too, if you like."

"So we should run things from now on?"

"We have the missiles." The officer spoke defiantly.

"The Shaa didn't have the missiles," said another officer. "People obeyed them anyway."

"They had the missiles at the *start*. They used them on Lorkin and so on."

The dinner reached no conclusions, but then Severin hadn't really expected it to. The stability of the empire was a problem that had so far found no solution.

The lack of a solution didn't deter Severin. He was very good at solving problems.

What he was beginning to realize was that his officers were wrong. More of the same wasn't going to work. What the empire needed was *complete change*. The Peers were going to have to step aside, or be pushed to the side, and another power was going to have to take over.

Who that might be, Severin didn't know. But he planned to be a part of it.

LADY KORIDUN'S BLUE eyes shone as they gazed from the video screen. She wore the formal purple robes of a planetary governor, with their gold-and-scarlet brocade, and her gray-and-sable fur was glossy. Behind her was a window showing Harzapid's night sky, with the arc of the planet's ring shining against the darkness.

"Congratulations on your sublime victory, Lady Sula," she said. "One of the Fleet officers here showed me the recordings and explained how you'd won, and I was delighted when I recognized your tactics. Catching the enemy between two fires—you did that on the *Striver*, of course. So I'm sure that was your contribution as tactical officer."

The mobile reserves had been Martinez's idea, but Sula decided there was no point in disillusioning Lady Koridun on the point. Koridun's hero worship was refreshingly simple, and good for Sula's morale besides. She raised her glass of Citrine Fling and silently toasted her friend and supporter.

Lady Koridun's eyes ticked toward something out of the frame, and then back in. A nervous habit, Sula supposed.

"I want to talk to you about your friend Hector Braga," Koridun said. "He's been using your name to raise investments for his development company, and Ming Lin has been telling everyone that he's not being truthful. This, ah—*disagreement*—has reached Lord Mehrang, who has asked the authorities for an investigation to find out if he's being defrauded." Lady Koridun plucked at something on her desk. "I thought I should ask you for clarification before I proceed. Are you in business somehow with Mr. Braga? Do you have any information that could be of use in the investigation?

Please reply as soon as possible, and in the meantime—congratulations again for your victory at Shulduc."

Sula sipped at her drink, carbonation tingling against her nose, and considered. She replied to Lady Koridun and labeled the message personal and private.

"I am not in business with Hector Braga," she said, "and I haven't invested in his business. I don't know what's going on exactly, but I know that Mr. Braga is a friend of Roland Martinez, so perhaps we ought to be cautious." She tried to give an impression of someone who's just had a very bright idea.

"Is there some way you can quietly get Mr. Braga out of the way?" she asked. "Not charge him with a crime, and not subject him to any kind of interrogation, but hold him in custody long enough for the controversy to die down? That might satisfy *most* of the parties involved. We really all have much more important things to do than deal with this, don't you think?"

There, Sula thought. Keep Lamey on ice for a while, until the Fourth Fleet stood over Zanshaa, and nothing Lamey could say or do would matter. After which he could retire to Spannan with Lord Mehrang's money and live quietly ever after.

SQUADRON LEADER RIVVEN was short for a Daimong, below Martinez's height. His immobile gray face was frozen in an attitude of pale indignation.

"Twelve years ago I won two thousand zeniths on the yacht races at Felarus," he said in a melodic tenor. "I was celebrating my luck with my friends at the Cosmos Club, and Tork was at the next table. He told us that we were being too noisy and ordered us—*ordered* us!—to be silent until he had finished his supper." His vocal apparatus made a disgusted buzzing sound. "That was Tork! He knew nothing but how to step on people's joy."

As a reason for defecting with his entire squadron this seemed absurd, but Sula supposed she should be grateful that such a trivial slight could produce such profound consequences.

"And his order to board all Terran ships!" Rivven continued. "What madness!" He turned to Martinez. "And all because you got such an ovation at the anniversary celebration for the Battle of Magaria! Tork was burning with jealousy! I'm sure that was the cause of all this!"

Martinez seemed uncomfortable. "I'm not sure whether to consider myself flattered," he said.

"Flattered? No." Rivven made a gesture of finality with one flat hand. "You should be *honored*. Tork hated only those with real talent." He turned his round black eyes to Sula. "The way you flayed him in that broadcast, Lady Sula! You satirized his vanity—and he had no answer, because it was true! You predicted that Tork's fleet would be whittled away ship by ship, and that's exactly what happened!" He raised his drink to his immobile lips and thumbed the spout to pour a dollop of mig brandy into his mouth. "I assure you that there were a great many officers who wished themselves back in Zanshaa, or who talked among themselves of defection. But they hadn't the courage to do it, and they died along with Tork's cause."

Rivven's monologue had been going on for the length of the dinner. He drank mig brandy and related anecdotes demonstrating his own superior judgment and character, while his colleague An-dar spoke little and nibbled intoxicating thu-thu pastilles.

Chairs and tableware suitable for Daimong and Lai-own had been brought from storage. The officers' chefs had collaborated on the dinner: Sula's cook prepared the little packets of delicacies suitable for a Daimong's mouth-parts, while Mangahas and the wardroom chef put together the rest, including the thu-thu pastilles and sauces suitable for the Lai-own palate.

Impeccably groomed, Lord Jeremy Foote sat at the far end of the wedge-shaped table, speaking little and maintaining an attitude of easy superiority. Chandra Prasad sat with arms folded, one foot tapping the floor with impatience as she endured Rivven's self-important monologue. Alana Haz seemed almost carefree, happy to have survived, as did Ranssu Kangas, who had been promoted to acting squadron commander on the death of his senior. Conyngham's hair seemed whiter, and his face more lined, than before his epic fight with Battleship Squadron One.

Opposite Haz, Nikki Severin sat in glowering silence while anger simmered behind his eyes. At least he seemed not to be directing that anger at anyone in the room, but—now that Tork was dead—at the enemy in general. Sula thought that there would be no more puppet shows for some time—Severin's sense of humor seemed to have died with Lady Starkey.

Naaz Vijana, on the other hand, did not bother to hide

his hatred of the non-Terrans, but glared at them openly, as if daring them to practice their treachery here. Fortunately he'd been placed at the far side of the table, next to Jeremy Foote.

A jolly little meal, Sula thought. Anger, impatience, superiority, hatred, suspicion, and deep mourning, all in an overcrowded room. She figured that Martinez should keep the intoxicants in circulation and hope for the best.

She poured herself more tea and added cane sugar syrup.

By now it was clear that the numbers of the Fourth Fleet would stabilize at seventy-seven warships. Two ships thought derelict had turned out to be salvageable and were now on route to Harzapid for refit, along with sixteen more ships that had been badly damaged. Spare crew were being shifted to the remaining fifty-nine warships, which were continuing their half-gravity deceleration until repairs were completed, after which they would accelerate to Zarafan, Zanshaa, and the end of the war.

The Shaa had made their empire by force, Sula thought. She and the Fourth Fleet would do the same. By now it seemed inevitable that they would stand in the sky above the capital and dictate to the Convocation—they would send certain people to prison, to interrogation, to execution; and they would put their own allies in charge of the imperial bureaucracy and the security services. Most of these people would be Terran, at least at first, but the other species would soon regain their former status as they proved their loyalty to the new regime.

But once the Fleet began dictating the new arrangements, how could they stop? Sula didn't see it. *What's wrong with being military dictators?* she'd asked Roland. He wanted to attempt a return to something like normality, but Sula didn't understand how that could be accomplished.

Once they employed the threat of force—of *annihilation*—how could that threat ever be removed?

"I wonder, Squadcom Rivven," Martinez was saying. "When did Tork last communicate with Zanshaa?"

Sula refocused her attention. Someone other than Rivven was speaking.

"Tork sent a missile from Toley," Rivven said. "I suppose it announced that your command was offering battle, but that the battle would be in Shulduc or somewhere beyond. For myself, I wonder if he was candid about our losses to that point."

"I doubt it," said An-dar. "He would never have sent a message to report anything less than a triumph." He clacked his peg teeth in emphasis.

"You have the ciphers he would have used, yes?" Martinez said. "I'm wondering if we can send a misleading message to Zanshaa."

Rivven's voice turned to a purr. "Reporting a victory that never happened?"

"Report of a victory might increase the persecution of our friends," Martinez said. "I was thinking of something . . . more *ambiguous*."

Sula saw Martinez's point at once. "A qualified victory," she said. "Something that forced the Restoration to retreat, but that failed to wipe us out."

"Yes," Martinez said. "And heavy casualties in Tork's command. Defections, perhaps. Tork's determination to continue an unwise pursuit."

"Make it clear Tork might be running into a trap," Sula said. "We might want people in the government to start wondering if Tork might lose," Sula said. "We want them to start quietly making plans concerning what to do in the event of a Restoration victory."

From Rivven came a dulcet chime of approval. "Excellent!" he said. "I think I know just what's needed."

THE DAIMONG VOCAL apparatus was infinitely flexible, and Rivven was able to give an imitation of Tork so perfect that only a careful electronic investigation could discover it was a fabrication—and Sula couldn't imagine why anyone would order that investigation.

The script had largely been written over the supper table, with wine flowing and the officers' sadness and mourning transformed into hilarity. The more absurd ideas had been rejected—there would be no attacks by a Lorkin fleet—and the end result was a plausible rant in which Tork admitted to a hundred and five prebattle losses due to "treachery and surprise attacks," and then a further hundred thirty in a battle in Shulduc, this counting three squadrons that had defected to the Restoration during the course of the battle. As these squadrons had been commanded by Lai-own and Torminel, Tork ordered that the Investigative Service, along with the Intelligence Section, begin an investigation of all Lai-own and Torminel officers, their friends, and their families to discover if they had pro-Restoration sympathies.

"After all, why should only Terrans be abused?" Chandra Prasad pointed out. "Let other species be persecuted for a change."

According to the report of the pseudo-Tork, the results of the battle were a victory for Tork. Losses for the Restoration were "vast," but "a disturbing number have escaped through the wormhole leading to Harzapid." Tork would reorganize his fleet and pursue, but in the meantime would send fifty-nine badly damaged ships to Zanshaa for repairs under the command of Squadron Leader Rivven. Tork trusted that victory would buoy the morale of the Righteous Fleet, which had suffered from constant bombardment of propaganda insisting that the Zanshaa government was corrupt, untrustworthy, and using the Fleet to hide its own misdeeds.

The report was deliberately vague on the number of Restoration ships killed, which Sula hoped would make Zanshaa uneasy. And if they added up Tork's admitted losses, and included the fifty-nine ships needing repair, they would discover that Tork had lost more than half of the Righteous Fleet in pursuit of his inconclusive victory, and was now plunging onward, with a fleet low in morale and threatened by defection, in pursuit of an unspecified number of escaping enemy.

Sula figured this was exactly the sort of thing that might cause the elite of Zanshaa to reconsider their political choices.

The supper broke up when Martinez and Sula took Rivven off to Martinez's office to record the message without the background clatter of silverware and clinking glasses.

"I'll listen to it again tomorrow morning," Martinez said, "and if I can't think of any way to improve it, I'll send it to Zanshaa."

Pleasure burbled in Rivven's tones. "I think this was an inspired idea, Lord Fleetcom."

"And an inspired performance."

Martinez and Sula escorted their guests to their shuttles and sent them on their way, then summoned the personnel elevator for the ride to the officers' decks. Martinez gave her a look.

"Would you care to join me for coffee?"

Sula smiled, then shook her head. "I'm too tired," she said. "Listening to Rivven was exhausting."

"It was, wasn't it?"

The elevator door whirred open, and Martinez brandished his commander's key at the detector in order to gain access to the officers' levels. The doors whirred shut.

"Besides," Sula said, "there's a picture of Terza on the wall of your sleeping cabin. I prefer not to make love while your wife watches."

Martinez blanched. "I, ah—I'll take care of that."

"Thank you."

Sula kissed Martinez's cheek as she left the elevator, then went to her own cabin pleased with herself.

Every so often, she thought, she should remind Martinez who was really in charge. That this time she was using him, not the other way around.

The next time Sula visited Martinez's sleeping cabin, the portrait of Terza was nowhere to be seen and had been replaced by drawings made by Gareth the Younger. Sula supposed that under the circumstances she couldn't object.

THE MESSAGE MISSILE from the pseudo-Tork was sent on to Zanshaa. The Fourth Fleet gradually increased its acceleration to a full gravity. The ships, even with their hasty repairs, managed the acceleration without inflicting further damage on themselves. Gravities were increased to one and a half for certain hours, though there were always a few hours of reduced gravity for the fleet commander and his tactical officer to use as they pleased.

The damaged ships bound for Harzapid accelerated in the opposite direction and soon vanished through Shulduc Wormhole Two, though not before Martinez plundered them for experienced officers, noncommissioned officers, and enlisted. Graduates of the Harzapid training schools would make up their numbers while they were under repair.

Unless they were making repairs, Martinez gave the crew as much liberty as he could. The crouchbacks' lives were relaxed, without the drills and exercises that had occupied so much of their time. They'd proved themselves in combat, and they had earned a small indulgence.

Though not where conduct was concerned. Captains reported an uptick in disciplinary problems. After months confined aboard ships, and following a battle of annihilation, the crew felt they were entitled to some misbehavior, and so drunkenness and fights and what the service referred to as "insolence" was on the rise. Martinez privately urged lenience.

After all, he was up to some bad behavior himself.

Michi Chen's congratulations arrived eight days after the battle, the amount of time Sula's signal took to reach Harzapid and the reply to work its way back through the chain of relay stations. "The victory was brilliantly executed," she said. "But then I never expected anything less."

At Michi's words Martinez felt the tug of vanity lifting his chin and filling his chest. He was alone in his office, and suddenly he wanted Sula with him, to share the triumph that had begun to blaze in his heart. He sent a copy of the message to her, with a note that said, "This is something that belongs to the two of us."

Then he released Michi's message to the Fourth Fleet.

"With your permission, Lord Fleetcom." Gavin Macnamara, Sula's servant, appeared white-gloved in the door of Martinez's office, bearing his midday meal on a tray.

"Of course," he said.

The meal was a chicken stewed in tomato sauce, something that could be made easily out of cans. With all the visiting back and forth within the Fourth Fleet Martinez was finding himself at the center of too many elaborate meals, so he was trying to eat simply when he was alone.

Macnamara placed his plate, goblet, and carafe of water on Martinez's desk, efficiently though without Alikhan's careful precision. Glancing up, Martinez thought he detected a degree of disapproval in Macnamara's expression.

"I think Macnamara knows about us," he told Sula when she arrived, a few minutes later.

"I'm sure the whole ship knows," Sula said. "Maybe the whole Fourth Fleet by now."

He didn't think he cared to think about that, even though he knew that keeping a relationship secret on a warship was like trying to hide a Hunhao sedan in a wardrobe.

Sula flipped her uniform cap toward his desk and managed to drop it neatly on his water carafe. She was glowing, her emerald eyes alight. Martinez hoped that he was the cause of that glow, but he suspected Michi's message had more to do with it. He rose, took her in his arms, and kissed her.

"I don't think Macnamara approves," he said.

"He thinks you're going to leave me and break my heart," she said. She looked at him at close range, her warm forehead pressed to his, her eyes searching his. "You're not, are you?"

"Not a chance," he said and kissed her again.

A DAY LATER another message arrived from Michi, and as Martinez watched it he felt the glow of victory fade. He called for Sula to join him.

This time she didn't throw off her cap, but walked in with a grave expression. "What's wrong?"

"Take a seat and watch this."

He put the video on a wall screen. Michi appeared, her face somber. "Gareth, I'm about to give you some instructions, and I imagine you won't like them." She paused after that ominous beginning, then took a breath.

"The political leadership has decided that the Fourth Fleet should stop at Zarafan," she said. "As you've won such a crushing victory over Tork, they're hoping that the situation can be resolved politically, without Terran ships appearing over the capital and forcing a peace at gunpoint." Her shoulders moved as if she had begun to shrug, then thought better of it. "If the political effort fails, you'll be ten days from Zanshaa, and with full magazines and rested crews."

She took a breath. "Roland is already heading toward you in an Exploration Service shuttle, accelerating as fast as he can. Your task, after you secure Zarafan, will be to put him in contact with the political leadership in Zanshaa, then stand by for whatever happens afterward. You'll be going to Zanshaa, one way or another. Written orders will follow, but I thought I'd better warn you ahead of time." Her look softened. "You've done brilliantly, Gareth, you and Lady Sula, but maybe it's time the military took a step back and let the politicians do what they do."

The orange end-stamp filled the screen. Sula let out a long exhalation, and Martinez realized she'd been holding her breath for some time.

"Are they *crazy*?" she asked.

"I think they might be." He shook his head. "My only consolation is the thought of Roland spending weeks under heavy gravities."

"Even if he were squashed flat as a platter, that wouldn't be consolation enough." Sula turned to look at him across the corner of his desk. "Perhaps we could simply ignore the order," she said. "We know the local situation and they don't."

Martinez felt his mind spin. "Split the Restoration?" he said.

Sula offered a wry smile. "Months ago I asked what was wrong with our becoming military dictators. Roland and the others didn't have an answer, but after a while I thought that maybe Roland's problem with the military being in charge is that Roland isn't in the military."

"The military doesn't know that much about running an empire," Martinez said.

Sula shrugged. "Could we be worse?"

Martinez considered this. "I think we could. Because we'd be in violation of the Praxis, which means that few people would be behind us. They'd do what we ordered so long as we were pointing a gun at them, and the second we weren't, they'd bash us on the head." He looked at Sula. "Isn't this what the Naxids tried? And what was your response to *them*?"

Her lips twitched in amusement at Martinez neatly turning her argument. "I was helped to no end by the Naxids themselves," she said, "who made a lot of mistakes that you and I wouldn't make."

"Well," Martinez said. "There's a lot of time between now and the time we'll have to start decelerating for Zarafan. We can try to change minds back on Harzapid."

"I'll send my protests in," Sula said. "You can send yours. No doubt they'll be filed wherever such protests go."

He sighed. "I've been on this ship for seven months now, the rest of Division Two has been on weeks longer, and Foote longer still. The Fleet isn't like the Exploration Service—our ships weren't designed for crews to live in transit for more than a few months. Maybe we all need a rest at Zarafan."

"We could rest at Zanshaa. It's only ten days farther on."

Suddenly Martinez felt enormously weary, as if merely the mention of all the time he'd spent on *Los Angeles* had been enough to remind himself that he was exhausted. "I'll send my protest," Martinez said. "And you can send yours."

She rose from her chair and straightened her tunic. "I'll do that." She looked down at him. "I hope I'll see you later, when we're both in a better mood."

"I'll do my best to cheer myself up," he said. "And if I can't, you can do it for me."

Sula gave him a skeptical look. "What makes you think *I'll* be more cheerful?"

"Because telling people that they're wrong always cheers you up."

She considered this. "True enough," she said. "I hope you'll be cheerful when it's *your* turn."

He waved a hand. "I'll be looking forward."

After the door closed behind her, Martinez stared for a long moment at the Torminel wrestlers on his wall, then called up the signals display on his desk and told it to record. He could send a protest to Michi—and he would—but he knew she'd send him a bland, political reply. The only person he might trust to tell him what was going on was Terza.

Since the battle he'd continued his daily messages to her, though he felt uneasy about it, as if he were somehow cheating on Sula with his wife. He told Terza about his daily business, about the conduct of affairs in the Fleet, news about people they knew. He'd told her about Alikhan's death, and how he felt unmoored without Alikhan's years of experience to rely on. He'd praised Gareth Junior's artworks and sent a photo of the drawings on the walls of his sleeping cabin.

But this signal would be important, and he began the complicated business of negotiating the tangle of his thoughts and asking the necessary questions.

THE FOURTH FLEET, still decelerating, passed through Shulduc's Wormhole Two toward Harzapid. A few days later, their deceleration finally ended and turned into acceleration, and they passed through the wormhole again on their way to Zarafan.

From the point of view of the crews, nothing changed. They stood the same watches, performed the same duties, ate the same meals, and underwent the same accelerations with the same resignation they'd employed all along. Sometimes the monotony drove them to anger or resentment, and then there were disciplinary hearings, but for the most part they were too exhausted to do anything but plod through their jobs.

A few went mad, though not in interesting ways. They just slowed down until they could no longer work, and barely manage to feed themselves. Medical opinion was divided, but most said they'd probably recover quickly once they got off their ships and got a change of scenery.

The Fleet Train began their resupply. Swarms of missiles rained into the Shulduc system, then were taken under Restoration Fleet control, slowed, and added to the ships' armories. The defectors An-dar and Rivven were resupplied last, but they registered no complaints. The Fleet Train transport ships, which had cleared the area of the anticipated battle, re-versed their courses and began the long acceleration in pur-suit of the Fourth Fleet. They wouldn't catch the Fourth Fleet until after it had reached Zarafan, but they'd be welcome whenever they appeared.

Martinez reorganized the Fourth Fleet. Some squadrons were down to a very few ships, and these were broken up and sent to other units as reinforcements. Division commanders now controlled formations the size of squadrons, but they officially retained their positions as division commanders. Squadron commanders like Severin remained squadron commanders, but they commanded formations the same size as one of the new divisions, ten or eleven ships apiece.

The mathematics of the Martinez Method didn't care how many ships are plugged into the formula. It would work for any number.

Michi Chen's reply to Martinez and Sula's protests ar-rived and took many words to say nothing. Neither Martinez nor Sula was surprised.

Terza's response to Martinez told him more. "We were worried about staying within the Praxis," she said. "Dictat-ing a peace from orbit is different from a settlement voted by the Convocation, and the Praxis prefers the latter." Her dark eyes were filled with concern. "Since your victory was so to-tal, we're hoping that the Convocation will vote out Tu-hon's faction and restore Lord Saïd's government."

If they haven't killed him, Martinez thought.

"If not Saïd, then my father," Terza continued, as if she'd read Martinez's mind. "Or someone else; there's a long list."

She sighed. "Michi assured us that there's no force the Zanshaa government can deploy to stop you once you move on them, and they'll know that. We're just hoping that some sanity enters the Convocation once they understand their situation."

I might get a medal or two, Martinez thought, *but it's Roland who will get to play the Savior of the Praxis.*

"YOU USED TO wear Sandama Twilight perfume," Martinez said.

"And you asked what's so special about twilight on Sandama," said Sula.

"I said maybe we'd find out. And maybe we shall."

They were lying together in his sleeping cabin, her head on his shoulder, her arm thrown across his chest. The room was illuminated only by a video screen showing a silent succession of astronomical scenes, and Sula could see Martinez's body outlined by the shimmering reflection of planets and suns.

The bed was quite untidy.

A suspicion crossed her mind, and she raised her head. "Why are you bringing up my old perfume?" she asked. "Do I smell bad or something?" She raised her elbow and took a careful whiff of her armpit.

"Not at all," Martinez said. "You smell of soap and floral shampoo. But if you had Sandama Twilight, I'd splash a little on my pillow, so that I could dream of you when you're not here."

Tendrils of warmth coiled themselves about Sula's heart,

and she rested her cheek again on his shoulder. "I haven't used that perfume in years," she said. "If there's some in ship's stores I'll buy it, but otherwise you'll have to wait till we get to Zanshaa."

There was a moment of silence, and then Sula realized that the silence implied something.

"You were going to correct me and say 'Zarafan,' weren't you?" she said.

"I was."

"It's a mistake."

"I know." Ringed planets shivered in his eyes. "But I'm not going to split the Restoration. We can't afford it."

Sula clenched her teeth. She'd known this was coming, she'd sensed it in his reluctance to talk about whether he would ignore Michi's order and strike directly for the capital.

"I have till 1400 to change your mind," she said. At that hour the Fourth Fleet would have to pitch their ships over to begin the deceleration that would allow them to dock with Zarafan's antimatter-generation ring.

"I've got a plan for taking the ring by surprise," Martinez said. "We should manage the thing without casualties, and the best part is that Rivven and An-dar will be even more compromised, and even less able to switch sides."

"Yes? Then name the second-best part." Sula waited, but Martinez had no answer.

"Roland and his friends are afraid we'll be violating the Praxis if we go to Zanshaa," Sula said. "I don't care, because the Praxis is a dead letter anyway. And if we win, the Praxis is whatever the hell we say it is."

"I have made that argument," Martinez said. "I was over-ruled." A muscle in his cheek twitched. "Politicians want a political solution," he said. "The military wants a military solution."

"We already *have* a military solution," Sula said. She clenched her teeth. The stop at Zarafan was so obviously a mistake that her blood simmered in sheer frustration.

"So we don't win the war, but Roland does," she said. "I think I'll skip his victory parade." She wanted to turn her fingers to claws and gouge Martinez's chest just to shock him out of his passivity.

"Well," she said, "at least your family won't need the Chens anymore. Once Roland takes the throne you build for him, you can shuffle Terza out of your life without any repercussions. Maurice will probably dance a jig."

She saw the hurt spring into his eyes, and for a brief moment felt remorse, and then remorse was submerged beneath a feeling of satisfaction.

Every so often she had to remind him that his life was going to change, and that some of the changes were not subject to negotiation.

THE FOURTH FLEET turned over on time and began their deceleration. Once again combat drills began, to acquaint the new squadrons with each other's ships and captains. The ships all moved with an easy efficiency, as if they were controlled by a single intelligence—veteran captains and crews, blooded and at ease with their work.

Martinez wrote a script for Rivven to record—in his own person, not Tork's—to send to Zarafan.

"I have received revised orders from Supreme Commander Tork," Rivven said. "The damaged ships are to repair at Zarafan in order to be ready to reinforce the Supreme Commander in the event of a catastrophe. I append a list of items required for repairs and resupply, and Supreme Commander Tork requires that Zarafan supply these by the time the damaged ships arrive, in approximately twenty-two days. Any resupply missions are to be halted at Zarafan for use by my force."

Rivven, as usual, acted his part extremely well, but Martinez was not quite ready to let him send the message on one of Rivven's own missiles, so he fired the message missile from *Los Angeles* instead. Over the next twenty-two days Rivven fended off questions first from Zarafan, then from the Fleet Control Board in Zanshaa's Commandery. Those ominous words *in the event of a catastrophe* had set alarms bleating in the corridors of the Fleet administration. Message missiles came pinging in through wormholes, demanding more information. The messages were ignored until the Fourth Fleet entered the Zarafan system, when they were in direct communication with Zanshaa via wormhole relays, and Martinez had Rivven report to Zanshaa that the Supreme Commander had forbidden him to answer any such queries.

Rivven also mentioned that fifty-nine damaged ships would dock on the ring, while his and An-dar's squadrons were to remain orbiting the system in order to "repel enemy counterattacks." This message was relayed to Zanshaa, which demanded to know about the likelihood of any such attacks.

The demand was ignored, because within a few days of the query's reception the Fourth Fleet docked on Zarafan's ring. Zarafan's Fleet dockyard was modest in size—no more than two squadrons had ever been based there—and it couldn't play host to fifty-nine ships, so the extra were berthed in adjacent civilian docks. It was at the Fleet dock that the reception party awaited, Junior Fleet Commander Trie-var and his staff, all splendid in dress uniforms, and all startled witless when armed Terrans came boiling out of the moored ships, led by Martinez strolling with his pistol in its holster, and Sula with her machine pistol aimed between Trie-var's eyes. Martinez demanded the ring's surrender and got it, but parties were already bound for Ring Control, the officers' hostel, and the elevator terminals to make sure that Trie-var's commands were obeyed.

Trie-var and his officers were placed under arrest and put in a hotel under guard. Martinez spoke to them later, told them that Tork's vast fleet had been annihilated, and that a political settlement of the war was imminent. It was hard to judge the reaction of all the officers present, but it seemed to Martinez that Trie-var was relieved.

Resupply proved to be abundant. Kung had plundered Zarafan's dockyard and destroyed what he couldn't carry away, but Tork had ordered production ramped up to serve the needs of the Righteous Fleet, and the Fourth Fleet absorbed those supplies and demanded more.

A message from Roland Martinez was relayed through the wormhole relays to Zanshaa. Roland himself hadn't arrived in the Zarafan system yet, but he made a point of trying to erase the ravages of high gee before his broadcast, and he looked proper and sober in his wine-red convocate's jacket. His hair was glossy, and his buttons shone. He informed the Convocation that Supreme Commander Tork and his entire command had been destroyed, with the exception of the squadrons of Rivven and An-dar, which had changed sides.

The Restoration could take Zanshaa easily, he pointed out, but desired a political settlement that would leave the empire at peace for generations to come. The Restoration desired that the Commandery order all warships to cease hostile action, and for the Convocation to reinstall Lord Saïd as the Lord Senior—and if not Lord Saïd, then some other name agreeable to the Restoration. Some members of the Convocation would be confined and subject to investigation, but no member who had not ordered or voted for the persecution of imperial citizens would be molested. All officers of the Fleet would retain their current rank and seniority.

The Restoration would also like to be put in touch with Lord Saïd, Lord Chen, Lord Ngeni, Lord Oda Yoshitoshi, and Fleet Commander Pezzini as soon as possible.

The message was sent in the clear, so that anyone working the station relays would be able to see it, as well as anyone at Zanshaa who happened to be listening. A message missile followed, repeating the message again and again as it passed through system after system, to Zanshaa and on to Magaria, all broadcasting in the clear so that anyone receiving on the right channel could hear the Restoration's message.

Martinez liked the idea of the missile so well that he sent another missile in the other direction, toward the Martinezes' home planet of Laredo. He followed it with a message to his father, sent by the regular wormhole relay. Anyone in command of one of the relay stations could intercept the message, of course, but he had taken the precaution of using a cipher he'd sent to Laredo with his sister Walpurga.

Why not? If the station commanders agreed that the war was over, they might as well send the message on.

Less than a third of the Fourth Fleet's ships required serious repair, so the intact ships' crews were sent on liberty when they weren't busy topping up their ships' antimatter supplies, aiding their comrades in the damaged ships, or gorging on the fresh food that had been shipped to them from the planet's surface. They were ordered never to travel alone, and to carry sidearms and stun batons, but so far no one seemed inclined to harm them.

Martinez viewed Trie-var's palatial quarters in the Residence of the Lord Commander of the Dockyard, with its hand-painted tiles, paintings that didn't involve Torminel wrestling, and chesz-wood furniture, and shifted out of *Los Angeles* along with his staff. He showed Sula the facilities and invited her to have her choice of the guest suites.

"I hope that when I pick a suite," Sula said, "you'll pay me a welcoming visit."

Martinez spread his hands in a gesture of acceptance. "I would be honored, my lady."

Sula grinned. "You damn well *will* be," she said and set off on her inspection.

Martinez watched her leave, and the hairs prickled on the back of his neck as he realized that she was trailing the scent of Sandama Twilight. He settled into his office chair and swung it around to gaze at the Boulevard of the Praxis, just outside and filled with groups of crouchbacks having their first liberty in months. They were in raptures as they bounded along the boulevard, intent on making the most of their freedom. Even though they were restricted to the dockyard and the immediate neighborhoods established to cater to the needs of the Fleet's crews, they weren't going to let the bounds on their freedom put an end to their enjoyment.

Just watching them, Martinez found himself relaxing into a wordless and undefinable happiness.

Maybe Roland was right, he thought. Maybe the war could end right here, and the happily-ever-after begin.

SULA CHOSE AN office before anything else, with an anteroom large enough for a substantial communications staff. Once she was established behind her desk, and with her computer access assured, she called up the plans of the Residence of the Lord Commander of the Dockyard. She asked for a list of unused sleeping rooms, and to her surprise a U-shaped pattern emerged behind the main building. The area was labeled "Celestial Court," named after a class of cruisers apparently, and was separate from and behind the Residence.

She equipped herself with a key that would open the courtyard's doors and went out in search of the court. Sula followed a covered lane to the building, then saw a series of blue doors opening off a rectangular court filled with lankish trees covered with fragrant red and yellow blossoms. Apparently the apartments were lodging for middling-level visitors, and the Restoration officers in charge of billeting hadn't yet realized they existed.

Sula chose an apartment with two bedrooms, a kitchen, a dining room, and a comfortable front room with armchairs and a settee. The colors were pale gold and an earthy red, there were crown moldings joining the walls and ceiling, and chandeliers of brass and crystal. A rather grand pier glass mirror stood between the front door and the narrow hall window.

It needed only some porcelain on display to make it complete, she thought.

She assigned the apartment to herself, and then put her staff and servants in larger rooms in the Residence. This would give her and Martinez privacy, and put some distance between herself and Macnamara's disapproval.

After arranging for her billeting, Sula took a stroll through the court. The U of the court was closed by a fence of metal pickets topped with elaborate spearlike points, and a gate that required a code to open. Beyond the fence was a lane, and beyond the lane a small park. Sula supposed that anyone determined enough would be able to get over the fence without trouble, and that in any case enemies could fire their weapons between the pickets and blast any unguarded members of the Restoration wandering by. Accordingly, she informed the head of the Military Constabulary that a back door into the Residence had been left unguarded and suggested a couple of constables be posted there. The young lieutenant said it would be done within the hour.

All safe. Sula regarded herself in the pier glass, picked a piece of lint off her sleeve, and marched off in the direction of her office.

CHAPTER 19

"Am I imagining things," Sula asked, "or is your father-in-law soused?"

Martinez narrowed his eyes and took another look at the video. Lord Chen certainly seemed off his stride, uncomfortable in his hooded leather chair, his eyes continually darting off-camera as if seeking the approval of an invisible watcher. Chen had put on weight and his face was puffy, which wasn't surprising if he'd been under house arrest for the last ten months. Alone and separated from his family, even the ones he disliked, might have left him with no company but his wine cellar.

"I am . . . ready," Lord Chen pronounced with deliberation. "I am prepared to do my utmost to help bring about reconciliation and the end of the war." After which he looked offscreen again, as if for approval.

"I can't really tell," Martinez said. "He might be a little too conscious of being watched."

"He's got to know that we know," Sula said.

Because of course Lord Chen was recording this under the supervision of the people who had been holding him as some kind of prisoner. Whatever he said would be with their permission. Everyone knew that.

What the video told the Restoration was that Lord Chen was alive and had not been obviously mistreated. And judging by what he said or did not say, it would also be possible to tell how much information had been given to Chen, or to the local population. Judging by his words, he either didn't know much or was forbidden from saying anything.

"I should also like to send greetings to my family and friends," Chen continued. "Please let them know I am well, and wish them the very best."

The orange end-stamp filled the screen. Sula looked at Martinez. "I still think he was drunk," she said.

"You're probably right," Martinez decided.

He had increased the polarity of the windows to darken the room while they watched the video, and now he gestured at his desk to bring in the full outside light. He had, Sula thought, adapted well to Trie-var's imperial style, the Residence with its grand vista of the Boulevard of the Praxis, the vast desk, and the echoing marble floors. Flowers in tall glossy celadon vases filled the air with sweet aroma. The hand-painted tiles on the wall showed bright alloy abstract designs on a background in which dark blue wave forms alternated with waves of an even darker blue—and the shining alloy echoed the silver buttons on Martinez's tunic, while the deep blues were a dark halo behind him and seemed to make him all the brighter by contrast. From his thronelike chair he could sweep the room with a glance. The disk of the Golden Orb shone at his throat.

Sula thought the room suited the commander of the Fourth Fleet, and the ruler—for all practical purposes—of the Zarafan system.

Martinez inhabited those roles well. Once he had stepped out of *Bombardment of Los Angeles*, away from the claustrophobic quarters of the ship on which he'd lived for months, it was as if he'd given himself permission to expand. He'd strolled toward Trie-var's reception committee with his hands empty of weapons, his presence enlarged by an aura of majesty that seemed to grow as he walked. The armed Terrans pouring out of the ships behind him, swinging wide to surround Trie-var's party, seemed almost secondary, Sula included.

"I'm Fleet Commander Martinez," he'd told Trie-var in a perfectly conversational tone. "Tork's failed. His ships are gone, and the war is over. I'm afraid I'm going to have to ask for your surrender, though I assure you any confinement will be brief."

Sula's heart had nearly burst with admiration.

Since then Martinez had managed to retain a degree of grandeur. The shock of Second Shulduc's losses seemed to have faded, and he was now beginning to congratulate himself for his victory.

Sula made a point of reinforcing this self-expansion. She wanted Martinez in control, and she wanted him ready to lead the charge on Zanshaa, and to defy his family.

A pity that Roland's arrival would soon turn Martinez's role into that of lackey, a role he would share with Sula and everyone else in the Fourth Fleet. Roland would arrive in three days or so: his launch was in the system and was making ferocious deceleration burns on its track to Zarafan.

Sula sat on a straight-backed armchair across a corner of Martinez's desk. She turned her body slightly to make more room for her sidearm—she was going to have to get used, once again, to going everywhere armed. He turned from Lord Chen's video to her. "Fortunately," he said, "our other friends have been a little more . . . present."

The Zanshaa government, which Sula suspected was compliant only to prove they hadn't executed their high-ranking enemies, had so far sent videos of Saïd, Martinez's brother-in-law Oda Yoshitoshi, and Fleet Commander Pezzini. Lord Convocate Oda had cheerfully offered compliments to the forces of the Restoration. Pezzini had been in a bad temper and had denounced things generally—but then that was characteristic of his behavior at all times and places. Lord Saïd, the former Lord Senior, had spoken in thoughtful, well-formed, complex sentences that seemed so artificial that Sula wondered if he were somehow transmitting a message in cipher—though she'd been over a transcript thoroughly and was unable to find any hidden meaning. Saïd had spoken of the difficulties in assembling a quorum of the Convocation, which was not normally in session at this season—and this was crucial, because if the Zanshaa government was to be toppled according to the forms of the Praxis, it would have to be by vote of the Convocation.

Sula had the impression that, behind his maze of words, Saïd knew of the destruction of Tork's fleet, but thought it unwise to speak this knowledge out loud.

"If Lady Gruum and the others delay the assembly of the Convocation," Sula said, "we'll have no choice but to go to Zanshaa after all."

"They only need the Convocation to elect a *new* government," Martinez pointed out. "The *old* government can simply resign. And if I were Gruum, I'd be negotiating terms for the resignation with Saïd right now."

"If her allies will let her. Tu-hon is a murderous fanatic, and if I were Gruum I'd be afraid of her."

"All the more reason to make sure Tu-hon has no power."

Sula laughed. "She has the *Fleet*."

"The Fleet's power is nothing compared to ours."

"True. But what Tu-hon has is enough to dominate Zanshaa until we arrive. And also—" She made a gesture that encompassed all space from horizon to horizon. "In the last war the government—*our* government—fled Zanshaa. When the Naxids took Zanshaa, it became an anchor around their necks. How do we know the government isn't fleeing right now?"

"The Naxids took the capital and thought the war was over," Martinez said. "We won't make that mistake."

"Won't we?"

"Nonii." Martinez spoke firmly.

"Roland won't decide to pause at the capital and continue negotiations from the high ground?" she said.

Imperturbably, Martinez raised an eyebrow. "I will dissuade him." He was getting very good, Sula decided, at being a proconsul.

"I'll look forward to that," she said.

"In the meantime," Martinez said, "we have some decisions to make about our new recruits."

Terrans had been swarming onto the ring with the intention of volunteering for service to the Restoration. Forty percent of these were veterans, or crouchbacks on active duty who had been sent to the planet on leave or who were active in noncritical duty. The rest were young, enthusiastic, and untrained. Martinez and Sula had been trying to screen them for talents they might begin to use right away—accounting, logistics, transport—and move them into critical positions from which non-Terrans, for safety's sake, had been furloughed. Even though none of the local non-Terrans had threatened to evolve into a local version of Colonel Dai-por, Sula still thought it better to keep non-Terrans away from antimatter, weaponry, crucial ship systems, and the food supply.

But even these duties absorbed only a certain number of the new Terran recruits. The rest were zealous, eager, and bored, a dangerous combination. Drunken fights, vandalism, attacks on other species, and general mischief were becoming common in the areas adjacent to the dockyard, sometimes even in the docks themselves, and were diverting the Military Constabulary from more important duties. Something had to be done to get the situation in hand.

Sula had decided to shift some of the superannuated officers and petty officers, those too old or injured to ship out on a warship, and put them in charge of training. The large transport ships, including the big immigration ships stalled at Zarafan by the war, would be designated as training schools. She called up the plan on her hand comm and explained the plan to Martinez.

"I have only one question," Martinez said. "No . . . two really. First, is this the best use of our veterans? And second, wouldn't it be a better use of our resources to send the untrained recruits home?"

Sula shrugged. "We're going to need to rebuild the Fleet after all its losses. This will give the Fourth Fleet a head start, and a reserve of trained personnel we can use to occupy Zanshaa's ring."

He smiled, and she felt a warm pleasure blossom beneath her sternum. "Case made," he said. "I'll leave you to implement it."

Sula nodded, picked up her hand comm, and rose. "Anything else?"

"I have supper with the squadron commanders tonight," Martinez said. "After which—" He waved a hand. "I'll be drunk."

"I can handle drunks," Sula said.

"I thought you could," he said and gave her a little wave as she left the office.

She greeted Lalita Banerjee at her desk in the outer office, then took the stairs down to her own office on the first floor. One of the Military Constabulary, marked by his red belt and armband, braced and brought his rifle to the salute. She passed into her own office and sent for tea.

She'd been longing for tea that hadn't been sitting in a ship's pantry for nine months, then Shawna Spence had visited a shop near the dockyard and found fresh first cuttings from estates on the planet below. Spence had bought the shop's entire supply, and now Sula savored the bright, coppery taste of the tea every day.

A modern Guraware tea set had been found in storage, and Spence brought the pot in on a tray, along with a cup and saucer, and a pitcher of cane syrup. Sula thanked her, prepared the tea, and inhaled the fragrance before taking a sip. A warm sense of contentment began to shimmer in her senses. She couldn't remember the last time she'd been this relaxed.

She had plenty of work, but the work wasn't desperate or urgent, and if she didn't complete it on time, she wouldn't kill her friends or allies through negligence. She had survived the largest battle in imperial history and done her part to win it. Her remaining enemies would scatter like dust motes before a broom.

All of which was excellent reason for her buoyant state of mind, though she couldn't hide from herself the knowledge that the real cause of her benign mood was Martinez.

She had been deliriously happy with Martinez once, nearly ten years ago, a period that had lasted two nights and part of a third before he'd suggested getting married, and she'd been delighted until he mentioned the Peers' Gene Bank, where she would be required to make a donation of her DNA. Which, she knew, would expose her as an imposter. When she hesitated, Martinez had demanded an explanation, and then she'd taken an angry, fatal misstep and blown the relationship to bits.

She'd regretted her blunder within hours and showed up

at Martinez's door to beg his forgiveness, only to be told that he'd just become engaged to Terza Chen. This revelation had sent her into such a dark, despairing spiral that she'd volunteered for a stay-behind unit in Zanshaa, as close to a ticket to suicide as she could find. Instead of getting herself killed, she'd captured the High City and become queen of Zanshaa, at least until one of Tork's appointees replaced her.

Sula sipped her tea from Guraware soft-paste porcelain and compared that time to this. She had now been with Martinez for two months, not two nights, long enough that spending their free hours together had begun to seem normal, maybe even routine. His evolution into the grand figure she'd seen in his office had been partly her doing. The Gene Bank was no longer an issue—after the High City victory, she'd commandeered the bank long enough to replace all Sula DNA with her own.

Viewing her own situation, she had finally decided that she was happy. Happiness was a sufficiently unfamiliar emotion that it prompted a degree of suspicion, and she found herself probing her own mental state in a way that was alien to her. Finally she'd decided simply to accept happiness in the same way that she accepted the aroma of her tea, as something that infused her life and being.

Nothing stood in her way but Terza and the family's relationship with the Chens. Martinez seemed to accept as inevitable the cutting of his ties with Terza and the Chen family. He cared about his children, one of whom would become Lord or Lady Chen after Terza, but he seemed resigned to having to make arrangements about their future.

As for Sula, she wasn't looking forward to being a stepmother, but she supposed she could put up with his brats if she had to. She would much rather Terza kept them.

Carefully, not spilling a drop, Sula refilled her teacup. She added cane syrup, then raised the cup to her lips and sipped.

Bliss.

THE DINING ROOM in the Residence of the Lord Commander of the Dockyard was far larger than that of *Los Angeles*, and so the division commanders were encouraged each to bring a guest. Most brought their flag captains, premieres, or tactical officers. Severin brought no one. Ranssu Kangas brought his brother. Chandra Prasad brought Vonderheydte. *Interesting*, Martinez thought.

Chandra and Vonderheydte seemed hyperaware of each other as the officers mingled before supper, alert to each other's presence even when they weren't near each other, their relationship as plain as if a smoldering line were drawn between them in the air. Martinez wondered if anyone had observed a similar line drawn between himself and Sula, and he couldn't help but suppose that people had.

In Chandra, he decided, Vonderheydte had almost certainly met his match.

Poor Marietta, he thought.

In the tight-knit group he recognized that released, relaxed state that he felt in himself. They had all survived battle, and each had looked death in the face and triumphed. They had won the war, and now it was up to the politicians to create the peace.

All things seemed permitted now.

The only individual who seemed not to participate in the prevailing cheer was Naaz Vijana. "Rivven and An-dar are free in the system while we're tied to Zarafan's ring," he told Martinez. "They could attack us and hurt us badly."

"We'd have plenty of warning," Martinez said. "Their orbit isn't close to us at all, and our ships are still on alert."

"They could be communicating with Zanshaa through the wormhole," Vijana said.

The crews at the wormhole stations hadn't yet been replaced by Severin's Terrans, so that was possible. "What could they say?" Martinez asked. "Any information they could transmit would just confirm that we've won, and the Zanshaa government's lost."

Nevertheless he decided to emphasize security in his remarks before the dinner. "We should remind ourselves that the war isn't over yet," he said. "Our ships need to remain on constant alert. Terrorists might attack our forces on the ring, as they did in Harzapid. Missiles may be sent through the wormholes in some last-second suicide ploy. There might be enemy squadrons at large that we don't know about." Vijana excepted, his officers stared at him blankly, as if he'd just said something just a little beyond their grasp. He cleared his throat. "In the next few days we'll be running drills based on these possibilities, so prepare your crews." With a degree of relief he reached for his cocktail and raised it. "Enjoy yourselves tonight, friends!" he said.

As Marivic Mangahas's food began to roll out of the kitchen, Martinez felt himself lapse into the same pleasant unconcern with which he looked at everything these days. He'd won the war, the details of the peace were up to Roland, and he was spending nearly every spare moment with the woman who had never completely left his thoughts for the last ten years. His life was tranquil and gratified and absolutely glutted with love. Even he had trouble taking his own alerts and exercises seriously.

When the last course was cleared away and the last toast was drunk, the group mingled again, and people said their good-byes and made their way out, past the guard where they could collect their sidearms and make their way into the street. Martinez poured himself a parting glass of wine and found himself standing next to Vonderheydte, who stood nearby holding a half-empty glass. Martinez held out the decanter. "A refill?"

"Yes. Thank you, Lord Fleetcom."

As he poured he glanced at Vonderheydte and saw exhaustion drawn across his delicate features. Charitably, he decided to attribute this to the war and not to Chandra.

"I hope you and Chandra are happy," he said.

Vonderheydte brightened, and his weariness fell away. "She's wonderful, my lord!" he said. "I'm ecstatic! This time it's the real thing!"

"I'm happy to hear it," Martinez said. "But what's going to become of Marietta? She left her husband and children to be with you."

Defiance flared in Vonderheydte. "I'm fighting for her," he

said. "And her husband. And her children. I'll keep fighting till everybody wins."

Martinez nodded, then hesitated. "She has enough money, does she?"

"Oh yes," Vonderheydte said. "When we planned our escape, we sent everything in her accounts to Harzapid."

"Well then," Martinez said. He felt he really hadn't the moral right to press this any further, not with Sula in his bed and a wife and son in Harzapid.

"Cheers, my lord." Vonderheydte raised his glass. Martinez raised his own.

"Cheers."

A few moments later he encountered Chandra. "I feel as if we should both look across the room at Vonderheydte," he said, "and then I'd say something world-weary and cynical, and we'd both nod. But I'm really not in the mood."

Amusement tugged at her lips. "You're saying that Vonderheydte lacks seasoning, then?" She laughed. "How many times has he been divorced?"

"I'm saying that you're probably too highly seasoned for him." Martinez recalled his own time with Chandra, when they were both junior lieutenants, a mad time of mutual passion, mutual accusation, and mutual betrayal. "Of course he's very happy," Martinez added. "I hope you are as well."

Chandra offered a catlike smile. "I'm not so much happy as *satisfied*."

"Well," Martinez said, "satisfaction suits you."

The last of his guests trickled away. Martinez went to his office and sent Sula a message in text: *I'm drunk.*

The response almost immediately. *Shower. Shave. Put on fresh clothes. Then come. You can sober up later.*

He was happy to obey.

SHOWERED AND GROOMED, he was just putting on a clean tunic when his sleeve comm chimed with a message just arrived. *From Lord Martinez, Rio Hondo, Laredo.*

Sent through the regular communication relays. Apparently their crews had all decided that the Restoration was going to win the war, or maybe that their job was to deliver messages no matter who was sending them. Martinez used his own key to decipher the dispatch.

One of the advantages, Martinez thought, of belonging to a family where nearly everyone shared a certain body type and cast of features is that you knew what you were going to look like when you were older. Lord Martinez resembled most of his children in his olive skin, mesomorphic upper body, long arms, and strong jaw. His hair was a halo of white above his dark jacket and white linen, and the lines in his face seemed less accidents of gravity than the imposition of character. Martinez could see that he'd finally adopted the white kilt, which he'd probably been entitled to for a decade or two.

"Hello," said Lord Martinez. "I take it that I'm addressing my son Gareth." He paused, as if to give any other observers a chance to stop watching, then continued. "I want to say that Yaling, Girasole, and the rest of the family are well, and that I hope you'll pass on this information to Terza, Roland, and anyone else who might be interested. Yaling will be sending her own message separately, but for right now I'd like to confine this message to matters pertaining to the war."

Lord Martinez shifted in his chair and glanced off-camera, presumably at his notes. "First of all, we've been sending out shuttles with Terran crews to replace non-Terrans in the wormhole relay stations. We've extended three systems out from Laredo and will go farther if we can." His expression turned grave. "If the Zanshaa government should win the war, or if we see an enemy fleet coming this way, our crews will destabilize one of the wormholes connecting us to the rest of the empire, the wormhole will evaporate, and we'll be cut off—but we'll be beyond the reach of our enemies. I trust that things will go well with you, but if they do not, there is a refuge here in Laredo if you can reach it."

A cold smile touched Lord Martinez's lips. "We are also building warships. Six Celestial-class light cruisers, the same pattern we built in the last war. Five of them are nearly ready for launch and shakedown, but while we can find crews of merchants who can take the ships from one place to another, we can't properly crew them. We have no military academies, only a handful of Terran Fleet personnel, and no instructors or training facilities. And though we can generate plenty of antimatter, we have no current ability to make missiles. So if there is any way to send trained crews in our direction, please do so. Along with ships full of missiles, if you have them."

The cold smile grew warmer. "Other than that, I'm pleased to report that things are very peaceful here on Laredo, and the economy is doing well once the banks were able to rid themselves of the high reserves required by the Imperial Bank in Zanshaa. The settlements on Chee and Parkhurst are expanding nicely, and last night we had the first frost of the year. More in our second transmission."

The orange end-stamp filled the screen. Martinez took a few moments to mull on the message and to bask in the first contact with his father in many months, then forwarded the message to Sula, Terza, and Roland. The second message had arrived, and he deciphered it.

This time it was the entire family saying hello: his father; his mother; his sister Walpurga; his daughter, Yaling; and Roland's daughter, Girasole. He recognized the paneled rooms, rustic furniture, and fur rugs of the Martinez country house at Rio Hondo. The contents of the video were trivial and wonderful at the same time, greetings and blather about the family that wrapped Martinez in a soft, warm comfort of nostalgia.

He couldn't keep his eyes off Yaling. It had been nearly a year since he'd seen her, and here she was taller and bright-eyed, with longer hair. She was restless in her grandmother's lap and squirmed a little. She was far more articulate than he remembered her, with an improved vocabulary, and she held something made of wire and wooden spools in her hand, which Martinez eventually recognized as a puzzle. Her hands were slim now, whereas he remembered them chubby.

He felt a cool hand of sadness close around his throat. Yaling was six now, and that meant that there was a sixth of her young life that he had lost forever.

He'd missed nearly as much time with Gareth the

Younger, but then he'd had a video from Chai-chai nearly every day, and so his son's change hadn't been so shocking.

When the video ended he watched it again, and then he forwarded the video to Terza and Roland. He finished buttoning his tunic and made his way to Sula's door.

Sula was reclined on the sofa, wearing a blouse that buttoned up to her right shoulder and loose trousers with a drawstring waist. Sandama Twilight floated on the air, and her sidearm in its holster rested on a cushion nearby, just in case some enemy kicked in the door and came in shooting. Martinez showed her the video from Lord Martinez.

"Why is your father wearing a skirt?" she asked.

"It's a kilt," Martinez said. "A kilt made of white deerhide."

"I see," she said. "So why is your father wearing a deerhide kilt?"

He sat beside her on the sofa. "It's a thing some of the men on Laredo do. When they feel they've reached the age of wisdom, they put on a kilt."

"So if I'm on Laredo, and I have a question, I go to a man in a kilt?"

He shrugged. "It seems to work as well as anything."

"Do women wear kilts?"

Martinez smiled. "Women don't need to advertise their wisdom."

She laughed. "Good answer!" Then she shrugged. "That system can't help but be better than the Convocation."

"You'd know better than I." He looked at her. "You're already working out how to get those crew to Laredo, aren't you?"

"The problem is occupying a certain percentage of my brain cells, yes."

He leaned closer to her. Sandama Twilight swirled in his senses. "I was hoping you could focus your brain cells on me for the next several hours."

She held out her arms. "You're at liberty to try to engage my attention."

"So now I'm competing with a problem in logistics?"

"I have every confidence that you'll succeed."

He put his arms around her and kissed her, and he felt a twinge of vanity at the thought that he seemed to have focused her attention admirably.

MARTINEZ STOOD WITH Sula at the airlock door, waiting for airlock operators to signal that the docking tube had been pressurized and that Roland Martinez could leave the shuttle that had brought him from Harzapid. A pair of armed guards stood casually nearby, just in case the shuttle proved to be full of armed terrorists or something. Martinez supposed he could have sent the constables away, but they were part of the only reception committee Roland would get, and so he let them remain as a bulwark to Roland's dignity.

There was no room for the shuttle at the Fleet dockyard, so Roland was landing in a civilian yard that had been requisitioned by the Fourth Fleet. The place was relentlessly functional and smelled of stale air and machine lubricant. It was painted in dull, rather grimy colors, and the occasional bright banners plastered with slogans—*Work Harmoniously! Strive for Increased Efficiency! Carelessness Leads to Accidents!*— seemed out of place. The Fleet yard, covered with murals showing Fleet personnel striving for peace under the Praxis, was a hall of wonders by comparison.

There was a lot of bustle. The ships of the Fleet Train, with supplies from Harzapid, had finally caught up to the warships of the Fourth Fleet. There were now more supplies than the Fourth Fleet could consume, with only a few exceptions. The Shankaracharya sensor suites, in Fleet Train holds for months, were now being installed in the warships, and there weren't enough of them. More had been shipped up from the planet below, and now at least half the Fourth Fleet would be equipped with the new sensors.

The airlock lights flashed, and one of the civilian airlock operators turned to Martinez, gave a wave, and trudged away, followed by her partner. Martinez, used to salutes, felt a little bit disrespected.

Roland, when he appeared, showed little sign of the bruising gravities he'd undergone on his trip from Harzapid. He wore his wine-red convocate's jacket, his hair shone, and his big jaw was pushed forward as if it were the prow of a ship breasting the waves. He carried a case in one hand. Behind him walked Hector Braga, the fixer Sula called Lamey, whose brightness of dress was a contrast to his haggard appearance. He slouched as he walked, and his face looked raw, as if someone had repeatedly punched him. High gravities clearly hadn't done him any favors, but his blue eyes were bright and alert and suspicious.

Roland looked around, as if he were expecting a larger reception committee, but if he were dismayed by the small welcoming party and the bleak surroundings, he took it in stride. He approached Martinez and Sula, waited for a salute, didn't get one, and then spoke.

"Does my quarters have a good communications system?" he asked. "I'm going to need to send a lot of messages."

"We've put you in a very nice hotel near the Fleet dockyard," Martinez said. "We're assigning you a communications tech, and you'll have a secure line to Fleet Administration and our ciphering facilities."

Roland gave him a skeptical look. "I suppose you'll be listening in on my messages to Zanshaa."

"Of course," Martinez said. "I'll also be giving you all sorts of unsolicited advice."

"Well," Roland shrugged. "I guess I'm used to *that*." He turned to Sula and offered his case. "Michi told me to bring this to you. I'm told it's important."

Sula offered a skeptical look and took the case. She opened it, and Martinez saw the gold reflected in her eyes and took a breath because he knew what the case contained. When she reached into the case and drew out the gold baton, Martinez braced to attention with a click of his heels. Roland, less prompt, drew to attention as well.

Hector Braga just blinked.

"Ah. Hah," Sula said.

The baton was gold, with a transparent spherical head that contained liquids in different shades of gold that swirled in layers like clouds on a gas giant. Sula held the empire's highest decoration up to the light and watched the glittering liquid eddy within its globe. Then she returned the baton to its case.

"As you were," she said.

Martinez relaxed. "We're going to have to coordinate when we'll be carrying our Orbs," he said, "otherwise we'll spend our days saluting each other and failing to accomplish anything."

"I'll send you a memo," Sula said.

Roland turned to Sula. "Since my brother intends to offer me advice," he said, "I suppose you'll have tips for me as well."

"Yes," Sula said. "Beginning with this nonsense of how difficult it's going to be to recall the Convocation. If they can't get a quorum with just the convocates loitering around the cocktail bars of the High City, I'd be amazed."

"Oh, I agree with you," Roland said. "They're trying to delay in hopes something's going to save them. But that something will never arrive, and in the meantime we can work out a settlement that will encourage the majority of the Convocation to throw the guilty to the executioners in order to save their own skins."

Sula gave him a skeptical look. "Just because *we* can't figure out what *something* will save our enemies doesn't mean *they* won't figure it out if we keep giving them time."

"Whatever it is they come up with," Roland said, "I have utter confidence that you and Gareth will leave it scattered wreckage and ash floating in the empty space between planets."

Martinez wished he had as much confidence as Roland. That morning had been the first new exercise of the Fourth

Fleet, with each ship wired into a virtual environment. The scenario envisioned the enemy sending the two squadrons known to be at Zanshaa into the Zarafan system at near-relativistic speeds in hopes of annihilating everything before them.

The scenario had been devised by Chandra Prasad, who in the last war had specialized in creating scenarios of annihilation.

Sula had commanded the Fourth Fleet while Martinez had remained above the action, watching on a link as alarms flashed from one ship to another, as virtual warships decoupled from the virtual ring in an attempt to maneuver, their point-defense beams flashing out at the oncoming wave of enemy missiles . . . Even though Martinez was participating as an umpire, the horror of the defenders' situation had clutched unbidden at his nerves as he watched the scenario play out.

The end result was the Zarafan ring blown to bits, with most of it raining down on the planet below to shroud it for years in a cloud of debris. Half the Fourth Fleet was destroyed, along with the entire attacking force. The scenario showed that it was past time, Martinez thought, for the Fourth Fleet, along with its commander, to wake from the pleasant collective dream of victory and remember that the war was far from over.

It was also time for more of the Fleet to launch from Zarafan's ring and get into space where they could maneuver. He would send away squadrons as soon as repairs were completed on their ships, and there were a number of squadrons that could go immediately. He would put them on notice later that day.

Los Angeles would be one of the last to depart, because the extensive damage to missile battery one was taking a great deal of time to repair. Which was gratifying in its way, because it would allow him to continue his idyll with Sula.

Roland's aides and servants began to emerge from the airlock, carrying baggage. Martinez directed them to a waiting vehicle, then took Roland to his car. Roland looked over his shoulder at Sula.

"You aren't joining us, Lady Sula?"

Sula nodded toward the shuttle. "I'll be meeting your passenger," she said.

"All right then. Congratulations on your decoration."

Sula waved a hand. "I'll look forward to you saluting me again."

They really *were* going to have to develop some kind of protocol for carrying the Orb in each other's presence.

Martinez swung himself into the glossy madder-red Hunhao limousine. "Violet Harmony Hotel," he told the driver.

Roland seated himself opposite Martinez. "The hotel has an auspicious name, don't you think?"

Martinez was unwilling to commit himself. "We'll see," he said.

"WE'RE GOING TO have to talk," Lamey said. He had hung back as Martinez and Roland headed for their car, and would have to go to the hotel in the other van, along with the servants and the baggage.

"What about?" Sula said. "Something new, I hope."

Lamey's blue eyes narrowed. "You know what we need to talk about."

Sula had recovered from the shock of seeing him. She had assumed he was in Lady Koridun's custody back on Harzapid, but apparently he'd eluded her. She tapped a message into her hand comm. "Who appointed me your savior?" she asked.

"We can save each other."

She blinked at him. "I don't even know what that means," she said. Her hand comm chimed. She looked at the display, then back at Lamey. "Sorry," she said. "I have an appointment."

She left him glaring and walked toward the airlock. She followed the boarding tube into the launch that had brought Roland from Harzapid. The air was sour here—the filters hadn't been cleaned lately, and fresh air from the ring hadn't yet been pumped into the ship.

Lord Nishkad waited in the ship's lounge, his worn graying scales blending into the neutral background of his seat. His black-on-red eyes were dull—he shouldn't have undergone heavy gravities at his age.

"Lady Sula," said Nishkad. "Congratulations on your decoration."

"Thank you, Lord Squadcom," Sula said. "I hope the journey wasn't too exhausting."

"It was, of course," said Nishkad, "but that's all right. We have a lot to accomplish."

DROWSING, SULA SMELLED the coffee that Martinez was making in the kitchen and realized with some surprise that it had been months since a nightmare had torn her awake. Not since before Second Shulduc, and she would imagine that the horrific losses of that battle would have brought on the nightmares, not quelled them.

But then that was when she'd begun with Martinez.

Apparently Martinez kept nightmares away. Sula hadn't been aware that this was within his power.

She surrendered the pillow she'd been hugging, rolled onto her back, and opened her eyes. The room came slowly into focus, the murky corners, the shadow pattern of the cove molding, the overhead lamp with its LEDs in baroque balloon glass. She raised her hands and scrubbed her face to bring feeling to her skin, then caught a whiff of her own armpit and decided to take a shower.

Afterward, damp hair in a towel, teeth brushed, Sula put on a dressing gown and walked into the dining room, where Martinez was answering correspondence and drinking coffee. He looked up at her.

"How many times each day do you shower?" he asked.

"Not enough," she said, and grinned. "Though I will share my shower on request."

"I made you breakfast," he said and gestured toward the teapot and a tray of pastry.

"Thank you," she said.

"Since you pointed out that I've always had servants and might be lacking in basic skills," Martinez said, "I've learned to make coffee and tea."

"For the first," Sula said, "you pour beans into the hopper and press a button. And for the second—well, we'll see."

She sat on his left and poured tea into a delicate Vigo hard-paste cup. She lowered her head to the cup and gave a delicate sniff. "Well," she said, "it *smells* like tea."

"Probably tastes like it, too."

"Let's not jump to conclusions."

She held the pot of cane syrup over the cup and began the long, slow, delicious pour. She glanced at the messages on the wall display. "Anything new?" she asked.

"Conyngham's reported Division One as complete and ready for action," Martinez said. "But then we were expecting that."

"That leaves only Division Two."

"Which has essentially completed repairs, though there's still some paint to slap on and brass to polish," Martinez said. "That'll be done in a couple days."

"And then?"

He took a deliberate sip of his coffee, then looked at her. "We go to Zanshaa," he said. "It's been delayed too long."

Sula had only been urging that course of action for the last eighteen days, since Roland's arrival.

"What changed?" she asked.

"The last dispatch from Zanshaa, where they said it was impossible to summon the Convocation for three days on either side of the Equinox Festival because the convocates were visiting their districts. Their government is so clearly stalling that I've decided it's time to send them an ultimatum."

"An ultimatum in the form of warships."

"Absolutely."

She poured the last golden drop of syrup, then stirred her tea. "If I weren't so thirsty," she said, "I'd kiss you."

"You can kiss me later."

"After you've shaved," she decided. She sipped from her cup and was modestly surprised that it tasted like tea.

Experimentally, Martinez rubbed the bristle along his jawline. "No time for a shave," he said. "I'm about to see Roland to tell him we're shipping out for Zanshaa."

She raised an eyebrow. "Would you like me to come with you? You might need a one-two punch."

"If punch one fails," Martinez said, "I'll release your punch two. But I don't want Roland to feel outnumbered."

"Oh?" Sula said. "You mean the way *we've* felt since the beginning of the war?"

"Yes. That." He bent to kiss her cheek, which was thankfully left unscratched by his bristle, and left, buttoning his tunic.

"Fortune attend you," Sula said and reached for a piece of pastry.

Her mind buzzed with questions of procurement and logistics. Lord Nishkad had quietly put out the word that Naxids with military experience were welcome to join the forces of the Restoration. The response had been such that she thought she would have enough Naxids to crew every single vessel on Zarafan's ring and send it off to Harzapid—or perhaps to Laredo, to provide crew for Lord Martinez's new cruisers. Or both. And she could pack the ships with recruits, trainers, and supplies.

Sula hadn't told Martinez or his brother what she intended. She decided that she would present them with a fait accompli, just as she'd done at Harzapid when Michi was on medical leave.

Do the thing well, she thought, and you wouldn't even have to ask permission.

MARTINEZ HAD EXPECTED Roland to put up more resistance, but even Roland was seeing the point of the Fourth Fleet taking action. "We can pressure the Convocation to meet," he said.

"We can pressure them to do more than that," Martinez said.

"Please not," said Roland. "I'd like them to be able to claim that getting rid of Tu-hon and her claque is *their* idea."

"If it was their idea," said Martinez, "they'd have done it a long time ago."

Roland was in his room at the Violet Harmony Hotel, standing in shirt and stockinged feet on thick carpet the color of smoke. Light shone through beige window blinds, and an unfinished breakfast sat on his polished table. Martinez stood before him in his undress uniform, with the disk of the Golden Orb around his throat.

"We've taken over the relay station at Wormhole One, both the one here and on the other side," Martinez said. "They won't see we're on the way until we're out of the system, and then it will be six days before we appear in Zanshaa's system." He grinned. "If they have any ideas of unseating Tu-hon, they'd better move quickly before we get there."

Roland pushed his fingers back through his dark hair. "I

hope this—Well, never mind." He walked to the tray. "Want some coffee?"

"I'll pass. I've got about a thousand orders to issue by the end of the day."

"I imagine you do." Roland filled his cup from a silver pot. Steam rose, along with the scent of coffee. Roland frowned in the direction of his cup, then looked at Martinez.

"I've been hearing stories about you," he said. "You and Lady Sula."

"I think," said Martinez, "those stories aren't your business."

"Depends." Roland sipped his coffee. "Depends on how badly you plan on blowing up your life."

Martinez felt his hackles rise. "Not blowing up," he said. "More of a controlled demolition."

Roland looked thoughtful. "Lord Chen would be of limited use to us in the future," he said. "But when Terza inherits, she's going to be formidable."

"You can talk to her after the war," Martinez said. "My marrying Terza was your idea, anyway."

Roland seemed on the verge of saying something, then apparently decided not to. "I'll do my best," he said finally.

"I'll see you in Zanshaa," Martinez said and made his way out.

He really *did* have a thousand orders to give. He sent Conyngham and Division One orders to depart the ring at the earliest possible moment and head toward Wormhole One and Zanshaa. To Division Two, he gave positive orders to leave within two days. To the rest of the Fourth Fleet, which was distributed in discrete packets between Zarafan and Wormhole One, he gave orders for them to form into a single unit and prepare for heavy acceleration. He ordered the large cargo craft and the big immigration ships to prepare to move on to Laredo, but he delayed giving orders to the new recruits to embark until he could better calculate where the recruits were needed, and how best to make use of the small number of veterans suitable for use as training officers.

When he finally looked up from his work it was late afternoon. The remains of his lunch sat on his desk next to a cold pot of coffee, but he couldn't remember eating the lunch, or what it had tasted like. He rose from his chair, stretched, and decided that his workday was over.

Martinez went to his lodging, showered, shaved, and splashed on aftershave. He donned clean clothes. His heart felt lighter by the minute, and he imagined himself and Sula on *Los Angeles*, soaring in orbit above Zanshaa.

He glanced out the window and saw the florist's shop in front of his residence, and his heart lightened again. He left the residence, nodded to the two armed guards on the gate, and crossed the Boulevard of the Praxis to the florist, where he was greeted by the Cree proprietor. Zarafan's ring had no seasons as such, and it was autumn in Zanshaa, but Martinez decided that he wanted to live in springtime and bought a vast bouquet of white and purple lu-doi blossoms. He returned to the residence, took the covered passageway to the courtyard behind the residence, and turned toward Sula's apartment.

The gentle scent of the lu-doi floated through his senses and merged in his thoughts with Sula's Sandama Twilight scent. Things were back on track, he thought. And once they got to Zanshaa, everything would change.

"WELL, EARTHGIRL," SAID Lamey as he prowled through Sula's door, "at last I found out where you live."

Sula, sitting in an armchair working on a book of mathematical puzzles, put her book and pencil on a table and squared the book so its lines were parallel with those of the table.

The air was scented with the dinner, sitting under covered dishes on the table, that Sula's cook had delivered. Two portions, one bottle of wine, one bottle of Citrine Fling.

"Lamey," she said, "what do you want now?"

He was the peacock again, blazing in gold and burnt orange, lace gouting from his sleeves and throat. He no longer looked like the hunched, beaten figure who'd lurched off the shuttle, but a thinner version of himself—restless, calculating, with a smoldering energy. His blue eyes were chips of ice.

"You've been avoiding me," he said. In a few strides he crossed half the distance between them, sending alarm sizzling along Sula's nerves. She stood to face him before she found him looming over her chair.

"Do you have anything new to say?" Sula said. "I'm not in real estate sales, I really can't help you with your development project."

"But you can introduce me—"

"I don't *know* anyone here!" Sula said. "Go to Roland—he knows everybody."

Lamey gave a sigh, and his shoulders slumped a bit. "He won't talk to me anymore. He insists his money's all tied up on Rol-mar."

Sula suppressed a laugh. "When none of your friends want to talk to you, maybe you should reconsider your message."

He glared. "My *message* is just fine!"

"Or maybe it's just *you*, Lamey," Sula said. "Nobody knows who you are, exactly. When the Chee Company started its planetary development, they got Lord Mukerji to be the face of the company. People *knew* him, they were comfortable with him." She waved a hand. "Surely you can find some well-connected aristocrat who lost his money in the crash and could use a job talking people out of their cash."

"I *did*. I had Lord Mehrang. The problem is that he's a complete shit and nobody likes him." His eyes narrowed. "Besides, why should I find a new Peer," he said, "when I've got *you*?"

This time she couldn't stop a laugh from bubbling past her throat. "You want me heading your *sales department*? For all's sake, Lamey, I've never won awards for popularity. I can't talk people into *anything*, that's why I have to do everything for myself—"

"I'm betting you can talk Gareth Martinez into a lot," Lamey said.

Cold anger filled her. "He doesn't have the kind of money you need," she said.

"Maybe. Maybe not." Lamey grinned. "Everyone says the

two of you are very close these days. But it isn't Gareth I'm interested in, or Roland either, but their father."

She laughed again. "Lord Martinez? I don't know him, but I'm pretty sure he didn't make all his money by turning to his son's friends for investment tips."

He stepped closer to her. Alarm sizzled through her veins. "There's some urgency involved here, Earthgirl," Lamey said. "A friend of mine on Harzapid says Mehrang is sending some of his friends after me. And you know what his friends did, right? On Esley?"

"Wiped out an intelligent species," Sula said. But Yormaks and Lamey seemed in widely different categories, and she felt skepticism where Lamey's threat of extinction was concerned. "So now he's sending those people after you?"

"He's sending people to get his money back. And what'll happen to me when I can't give it?" He snarled. "Nobody told me that Peers behaved like linkboys, right? Especially now it's war, and nobody knows up from down or right from left."

"I think you know how to stay alive."

A grin twitched at a corner of Lamey's mouth. "Yes, I surely do. I'm going to get a big investor on my fishing line, and that investor's going to be Lord Martinez."

"I don't know him, and—"

He took a long step toward Sula and sank his fist into her solar plexus. The air went out of her in a rush, and she bent over. Tears came to her eyes as an impotent rage stormed in her head. She'd been through the Fleet Combat Course, and the White Ghost had lived with danger for months, but all of that had proved useless against Lamey's unexpected attack, and now here she was as helpless as she'd been when she was a sixteen-year-old schoolgirl, and Lamey the soft-spoken gangster in charge of a pack of linkboys.

"I think you should listen for a change, Earthgirl," Lamey said. "I said *listen*. So here's what's going to happen."

Sula coughed as she tried to drag air into her lungs. The terror of asphyxiation rose, and she fought it down.

"See," Lamey said, "I could tell people about Spannan, and your real name, and how you stepped into a dead girl's place. But—as you pointed out—you're valuable to people here, and they might not believe me or they might be able to protect you." He laughed. "I made you a convocate, Earthgirl! I was the one who gave you all the power you think you have! But that doesn't mean you can stand up to me!" He laughed again. "But no, I thought about it, and I know who would be interested in hearing what I have to say."

He reached out, touched her jaw, and brought her head up so that he could look at her. Her skin crawled at his touch. "See, I'm not going to talk to anybody *here*. All your friends are here, and so is your boyfriend. But I can message Terza Chen, because I think she'll be very interested in my information." His breath warmed her cheek. "You think Terza won't fight you? And when Terza calls her husband to heel, what happens to Earthgirl's dreams then? So you'd better do the best sales job you've ever done in your life when Gareth comes, and get him on your side when the two of you lean on the old man for funds. Because . . ."

Sula's sidearm cleared the holster, and she pressed the pistol to Lamey's chest and fired twice. Somewhere glass shattered. Lamey's eyes widened, and he tried to take a step, but his legs failed him and he fell to the ground. His blue eyes looked at her for a long, startled moment, and then they faded.

Sula let the pistol hang like a lead weight at the end of her arm, and then she coughed and reached with her free hand to the side table for her tea. Porcelain clattered, and half the tea spilled before she got it to her lips, and then she had to cough again and sprayed tea on Lamey's gold-and-orange suit. Her stomach queased. She put a protective hand to her midsection and forced herself to straighten.

There was a knock on the door, and Martinez came jauntily in with a vast bouquet of flowers. He stopped dead in the entryway, his eyes shifting from Sula to Lamey lying pale on the carpet, and then back to Sula again.

Angry rebukes pursued one another through Sula's head. She had been fooling herself. She thought she'd been in charge of her own fate, and Martinez's as well. She thought she could forget that Lamey would want repayment for his favors. She'd thought she'd maintained a supremacy over Martinez and had been guiding their relationship to where she wanted it.

Until Lamey had threatened Martinez. And then she laid Lamey out at Martinez's feet, like a cat dropping a dead bird at the feet of her master.

She watched as the lu-doi blossoms fell from Martinez's nerveless hand and tumbled to the floor. She straightened and folded her arms.

"So," she said, "are you going to help me hide the body?"

CHAPTER 20

Martinez went through the cleanup like a sleepwalker. Hector Braga's body was rolled up in the carpet he lay on, and the carpet was secured with strapping tape. A thin, small puddle of blood remained on the tile floor. The bullets had passed through Braga's torso, then hit a pier glass in the entry hall and shattered it. The pistol rounds were caseless, so there were no casings to match to Sula's weapon; but all firearms were test-fired at the factory, and a record of striations kept on file in case there was ever a need to find a weapon used in committing a crime. Martinez found the two flattened bullets embedded in the mirror's backing, and he plucked them out and handed them to Sula without a word.

The smell of propellant stung the back of his throat. Seared forever in his mind was the image of Sula standing, arms folded, over Braga's body, her pale face frozen, her eyes disdainful, the smoke practically rising from the barrel of the pistol. *Are you going to help me hide the body?*

Yes, he would. And then he would arrange never to see her again.

A person who knew his way around an antimatter-generation ring wouldn't have any trouble finding a place to hide a body, but getting it out of Celestial Court was more problematical. Carrying Braga out through the Lord Commander's Residence was impossible, and the barred gate behind the court was in plain sight of anyone traveling the lane, or in the small park beyond. Yet that seemed the only exit.

"Can you check a van out of the motor pool?" Sula asked.

"Why don't you do it?" Martinez said. He saw no point in having his name on any incriminating records.

"Because I've got an idea of how to move Lamey to the gate."

"Right then." He activated his sleeve display, then looked at the carpet. "Has he got anything that will identify him?"

Sula gave a wordless snarl. They unrolled the carpet, confiscated Braga's hand comm, identification, and his rings, and then rolled him up again. Martinez left for the motor pool feeling as if he were staggering under five gravities.

Walking away from the Celestial Court, Martinez sensed a ponderous oppression lift, as if gravity had faded to a single gee, and he felt as if he were breathing in the wind of liberation. He thought about walking away, locking himself in his quarters, and leaving Sula to deal with the body herself.

He had no idea why she'd killed Hector Braga. He knew the two of them had a past when they were both young on Spannan, but he'd never imagined anything that could lead to Braga lying dead at Sula's feet.

She hadn't even offered him an explanation. It was as if the necessity of an explanation had never even occurred to her. She'd just folded her arms, the pistol still in her hand, and asked if he'd help her cover up a crime.

He needed to get rid of the body. If he didn't, it might turn up again in a way that could hurt him.

At the motor pool he checked out a viridian-green Sun Ray van, and the great weight descended on him again.

After his brief hour of freedom, Martinez turned into the lane. He drove over the curb and parked with the side door close to the barred gate, and the two Military Constabulary guards on duty advanced warily as they cradled their rifles. Martinez left the van and they braced.

"I've got to sneak a dignitary out the back of the Residence," he told them. "Could you go to either end of the lane and make sure no one's paying attention?"

His voice sounded false, as if he were speaking the most obvious lie in the world, but the two constables opened the gate and trotted to their respective corners. Martinez rolled up the side door of the van and walked into the court.

Sula appeared with a motorized cart, the kind the Residence used to move furniture and luggage. Braga rolled in his carpet on the cart, surrounded by camouflage in the form of luggage, a lamp, and a dining room chair.

"Where'd you find the cart?" he asked in surprise.

"I *looked* for it," Sula said, in a tone that froze any more questions in advance.

Martinez glanced left and right at the constables and saw they were looking out for observers, so Martinez climbed into the van, seized the rolled carpet, and yanked while Sula shoved. He'd grabbed the feet without realizing it, and through the carpet he heard Braga's head thumping on the sill as he came inside. The dining room chair wobbled and fell over. Martinez lay for a moment breathing hard, a stretch of the carpet a weight in his lap, and then he shoved the carpet away and rolled down the van door. Sula retrieved the chair and motored the cart back into the court, then returned, closed the gate, and jumped through the van's passenger door. Martinez set a course deeper into the dockyard. Neither of them spoke as the van moved on its silent electric motors.

A sensation of moist, cloying, palpable dread filled the van. Martinez's heart slowed, speeded, slowed again. He felt sweat gathering under his collar.

He dismissed throwing Braga out an airlock. Anything released from the ring would be at escape velocity and would float slowly away from the planet and into space. An object as large as a body would be spotted on radar, and some very advanced telescopes would be trained on it to discover what it was before a shuttle was sent out to retrieve it.

In the end the rolled carpet was hidden in a disused refrigerator. The walk-in refrigerator had been on the heavy cruiser *Judge Kasapa*, had been damaged at Second Shulduc, and had been replaced. The discarded unit was in a warehouse filled with scrapped hardware, all of it so useless that the Fleet wasn't even bothering to guard it. At some point in the indefinite future the scrap would be sold to the highest bidder, and the body would either be discovered or it wouldn't. Martinez hoped that it would have decayed to the point where identification would be impossible, but in any case Martinez, Sula, and the Fourth Fleet would be long gone, and running the empire. A magistrate would need a lot of convincing evidence before he set about any kind of investigation.

Sula and Martinez didn't speak until he drew up before the back gate of the Celestial Court. "Buy a new carpet," Martinez said. "Replace that mirror. Wash the floor in something that will destroy DNA."

"What destroys DNA?" Sula's voice was hoarse and dull and showed no interest in the answer.

"I have no idea," Martinez said, "but I'm sure you know how to do research."

She left the Sun Ray and Martinez returned it to the motor pool. Back in the Residence, he went to his bedroom and stared at his bed for a long moment, then realized he'd never be able to sleep. He called to Mangahas for coffee and sandwiches, and he stayed up late writing orders. He told Dalkeith that he and his staff would be shifting back into the *Los Angeles* tomorrow, and then he sent notices to his staff to that effect.

Sula's pale, disdainful face seemed to stare at him from every dark corner of the room. The scent of propellant still hung in his nostrils. He realized he could never be in the same ship with Sula again and thought about how to replace her. His squadron and division commanders had all earned their places and might view the post of tactical officer as a demotion. He decided instead to invite Paivo Kangas. Though his brother, Ranssu, commanded a squadron, Paivo was a lieutenant-captain in command of a frigate, and the post of tactical officer could be regarded as a step up.

Martinez realized that Macnamara would remain with Sula, and that he'd need a new orderly. He wanted someone as wired into the culture of the enlisted crew as Alikhan had been, and so he searched through records for highly rated, retired petty officers who had returned to the colors and come up with a number of plausible candidates. He offered them the opportunity to audition for the job, and then went to his room and carefully packed his belongings after laying out clean linen and a uniform for the next day.

He didn't know what to do with Sula, other than make sure he was never alone with her again. Then he remembered her plans for using the transport ships as bases for training and decided to put her in charge of that. Accordingly, he drafted orders for the transports to organize as Division Nine of the Fourth Fleet, Lady Sula commanding. He drafted the order to Sula, then decided not to send it until morning, after he'd had a chance to think.

He got a bottle of brandy from the buttery, drank two stiff shots, and went to his bed. His head had barely touched the pillow before he realized he'd scented it with Sandama Twilight, and he leaped from his bed as if his nerves had been jolted by an electric shock. He threw the pillow in a closet and found a new one, but adrenaline kept him from sleeping for a long time, and then his sleep filled with dark, uneasy, doubtful dreams.

SULA SCRUBBED THE tiles with a conventional cleaner that she found in a cupboard. It might not destroy DNA, but at least no one would find a pool of blood on her floor.

A more complete cleanup would have to wait until morning, along with the new carpet and the new mirror.

She might as well follow Martinez's orders, she thought. Her own ideas seemed to be worthless.

For the moment she felt numb, but she was aware that the numbness would soon crumble like a dam made of spun sugar and release a flood of horror, reproach, and black despair. *Why didn't I tell him?* she thought. She searched her mind for some kind of justification she could have offered.

I did it for you. Unlike, it must be said, her other murders.

Right. *I did it for you.* That would completely have worked. Martinez would have come back to her in a second.

The floor was as clean as she could make it, and the room reeked of disinfectant. She put it and the cleaning materials away, then returned to the living area. Her motions felt strange to her, as if she were just learning to walk, feeling the floor beneath her feet with every step.

She stopped in the dining area and stared without comprehension at the dinner plates beneath their covers, the bottle of wine in its ice-filled cradle. Cooking scents threatened to turn her stomach. She pushed the nearest dish away, and it rang on the crystal goblet intended for Martinez.

Sula looked at the goblet, and then at the wine nearby. Droplets of condensation shone on the bottle like gemstones.

A powerful need for the alcohol struck her, and for a moment she stared at the bottle without breathing. Then she reached for it and poured.

How much worse can it get? she thought, and drank.

MARTINEZ WOKE IN the morning to the sound of an alarm from his sleeve display. Martinez jumped from the bed without quite realizing where he was, then shrugged into his uniform tunic and cued the display.

"This is Senior Squadron Commander Foote, Lord Fleetcom." This early in the morning, Foote's superior-sounding High City drawl managed to sound even more annoying than usual. "I'm the duty officer on the communications desk, and we've received a transmission from Zanshaa that I think you should see."

"Have they surrendered?" Martinez asked.

"No, my lord. The opposite, if anything."

Martinez dressed quickly and walked downstairs to the Residence's communications room, a lushly appointed expanse filled with scalloped, gilded desks, chairs with sinuous curves, and video displays in ornate frames. Foote awaited him, his uniform immaculate, his face set in an expression of studied unconcern. His cowlick waved like a blond flag on the side of his head.

"What's happened?" Martinez asked.

"It's a news item," Foote said. "It wasn't addressed to us, but they must have known we'd see it."

Foote triggered the recording, and Martinez saw a news reader offering her report in her sonorous Daimong voice. "The Commandery led the people in rejoicing at the appearance in the Zanshaa system of a hundred and sixty-six ships of the Third Fleet, under the authority of Fleet Commander Lord Pa Do-faq, victor of the Battle of Hone-bar in the War of the Naxid Rebellion."

Martinez felt a stir of annoyance at this claim, since he'd always viewed *himself* as the victor of the Battle of Hone-bar, for all that Do-faq had been the senior officer commanding.

The news item continued with a telescopic view of a new, bright constellation composed of the deceleration torches of the Third Fleet heading for Zanshaa, and then cut to a clip of Do-faq. "I am pleased to be able to contribute my forces to those arrayed against disorder and rebellion," he said. "I am further pleased to announce that a further forty ships, once held hostage by the deceased traitor Nguyen, will be on their way to Zanshaa as soon as their conversion from Terran crews is complete."

Do-faq looked older than Martinez remembered him and had lost the youthful dark feathery hair on the sides of his head. The added maturity made him look even more like a stern, successful commander, ready to set the empire to rights.

The news reader went on to recapitulate how Nguyen had held the Third Fleet at Felarus by threat of force, but that Do-faq had secretly mobilized specialist teams and killed the Terran rebels before they could fire their weapons. Nguyen and his officers and crews had met their just end, and Do-faq had been accelerating for Zanshaa for the last two months, the journey kept secret until their triumphant arrival.

"Do-faq," Martinez muttered. "Damn." Do-faq was far from a hidebound conservative like Tork. He had been an early supporter of the Martinez Method and had drilled his own squadron in its intricacies on the return trip from Hone-bar. He was a good commander, and Martinez couldn't count on his being as predictable as Tork had been. In any fight, Do-faq would be using Martinez's own tactics against him.

"If we count Rivven and An-dar," Foote said, "we have seventy-five ships. We're very close to Zanshaa here. Do-faq could arrive here in a matter of days with more than twice our numbers."

"And there are the sixteen ships Tork left at Zanshaa," Martinez said. "That gives Zanshaa's complete numbers at a hundred and eighty-two."

Roland will never let me hear the end of it, Martinez thought. If Roland hadn't insisted on stopping the Fourth Fleet at Zarafan, they'd be at Zanshaa now, being turned to ash by Do-faq's cruisers.

Tactics and countertactics were already playing themselves out in Martinez's mind. Missiles flashed, lasers crackled, and only one possible result presented itself.

"There's no way we can fight them," he muttered. "Not a damn hope. We're going to have to retreat to Harzapid and hope that Wei Jian's Second Fleet defectors finally turn up, and that we can use the nineteen ships under repair. That would give us . . ." He paused in calculation.

"A hundred and fifty-seven," Foote said promptly.

"Making victory at least possible."

Foote gave him an inquiring look. "We're assuming the news item is true," he said. "But what if it's disinformation aimed at getting us to make a precipitate retreat?"

"I want our best analysts looking at that recording for any hint that it's faked," Martinez said. "But right now, we have to assume that the enemy are doubling down on their chance of victory."

And that means we have to double down as well, Martinez thought. He called for a flask of coffee to be delivered to his office and ran up the steps while composing orders in his mind.

And as he ran, he thought about how he was going to have to fight the rest of the war without his finest weapon. Because no one had ever made a better team than he and Sula, and now he wanted never to see her again.

Walter Jon Williams is a *New York Times* bestselling author who has been nominated repeatedly for every major sci-fi award, including Hugo and Nebula Awards nominations for his novel *City on Fire*. His most recent books are *The Accidental War, Conventions of War, The Sundering, The Praxis, This Is Not a Game,* and *Quillifer*. He lives near Albuquerque, New Mexico, with his wife, Kathleen Hedges.